MW00465792

just this once

just this once

escape to new zealand book one

ROSALIND JAMES

Text copyright © 2012 Rosalind James

ISBN-13: 0988761904
ISBN-10: 9780988761902

author's note

The Blues and the All Blacks are actual rugby teams. I have attempted to depict the illustrious history of the All Blacks in an accurate manner. Sadly, however, the characters in this book exist only in my own mind, and are not intended to resemble or represent any actual individuals, living or dead.

table of contents

new zealand map

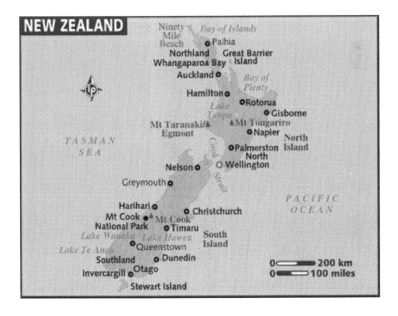

A New Zealand glossary appears at the back of this book.

prologue

♡

"Wow. Welcome to New Zealand."

Hannah said the words aloud. There was nobody around to hear her, after all. Despite the chill lingering in the morning air, she stood where she was for a few seconds more. The turquoise sea beckoned, its border of golden sand strewn with pale scallop shells left behind by the receding tide. It was exactly where she'd longed to be, these past weeks. And it was everything she'd hoped.

She dropped her towel and sandals and stepped into the cool water. Aiming towards the point at the far end of the bay, she delighted in her steady progress. Her mind settled down into the familiar rhythm, focused only on her strokes and her breath as the minutes went by.

Looking up at last to check her position, she felt a twinge of alarm. Had she not been swimming straight? The point was in the wrong place, wasn't it? She treaded water, turned in a circle. Realized with shock that she'd come much farther than she'd expected. What had felt like her own fast pace had in fact been a powerful current in the outgoing tide. One that was doing its best now to pull her out to sea.

No need to panic, she told herself firmly. All right, she was in some kind of rip tide. Now that she had stopped swimming, she could feel its strength. But she knew what to do, didn't she? She had to swim across it, that was all. This happened to people all the time. She would aim for a course parallel to the shore rather than trying to force her way directly back against the current's full power. Once she escaped the band of rip, she could turn back toward shore again. Back to safety.

She changed directions deliberately, swam strongly and steadily, working on maintaining her parallel course. Her progress, though, seemed discouragingly slow. The rip was wider than she had anticipated. It might even have shifted, a nervous little voice whispered in the back of her mind. She had heard that could happen.

She forced that treacherous voice back with an effort. She couldn't do anything about it now, other than what she was already doing. Keep swimming parallel, she told herself fiercely. She could swim for an hour without stopping, she knew. That meant she could swim even longer if she had to. Eventually, she would get out of this. Willing herself to stay calm, counting her strokes, she made it to one hundred, then two hundred.

And felt the change as she was caught by another, stronger rip. She had swum straight into it, and was once again being pulled out inexorably with the current.

The first stirrings of real panic shortened her breath. She forced the fear back, focused on breathing with her strokes, and began to count again. One hundred strokes, she told herself. Count. Breathe. But as she counted off sixty, then seventy, she could feel herself tiring, and knew she was losing the battle.

Where were the people? She hadn't seen a soul when she entered the water. Nobody knew where she was, and there was nobody to see her struggling. Nobody to help her. Nobody to save her.

How could this be happening?

All she had wanted was a vacation.

chapter one

♡

" I need a vacation."

Hannah Montgomery blew out a frustrated breath on the words. She was running late. And she hated to be late, hated feeling rushed and flustered. The meeting started in half an hour, and she had planned to get there early so she could review her notes beforehand.

She was ready, though. She had spent the entire previous evening preparing her materials, after all. She took one last quick look in the mirror. Professional and neat, check. Dark gray slacks, fitted blouse, heavy hair subdued in its usual neat, braided coil. She looked fine. She *was* fine.

Grabbing her laptop case and double-checking that she had all the files she needed, she headed for the car. The fifteen-minute drive across Berkeley to her office would settle her down and help her focus on the day ahead. She wasn't going to be late, just not early. It was going to be all right.

But her usual tools—the classical music on the car stereo, yoga breaths, her morning run, even her pep talk—weren't doing the trick this time. Instead, she kept thinking back to the phone conversation with her sister that had delayed her. And worrying.

If worrying were an Olympic sport, she thought ruefully, she'd have at least one gold medal, for sure. But there was

Kristen, rushing into "love" with another guy, who had cheated on her and broken her heart. Again.

Well, she'd calmed Kristen down, and that would have to do for now. She'd call tomorrow and see if she could help her sister make a plan.

Shaking it off and putting thoughts of Kristen firmly into their designated compartment in her mind, Hannah took a few more of those yoga breaths. Pulling to a stop in front of the large building that housed TriStyle Woman's offices, she gave herself a final once-over in the car mirror and headed toward the conference room for The Ordeal.

Beth met her at the door. "I beat you today," her second-in-command teased. "First time that's ever happened. Usually Miss Prepared here is fifteen minutes early for these things, putting the rest of us to shame."

"Kristen called," Hannah sighed. "Another breakup."

Beth squeezed her arm in sympathy. "Well, you know there's nothing like The Ordeal to give you plenty of time away from your problems."

"I know. I went for a run this morning, just to pep myself up and put myself in a positive frame of mind."

"Then I'll be watching you, boss. I expect to see some of that post-endorphin serenity."

Hannah laughed and moved to set up her place at the conference table. By the time she had her laptop, notes, and materials arranged just as she liked them, the room was beginning to fill. And The Ordeal had begun.

She couldn't remember who had first named it The Ordeal. Probably Emery. The irrepressible Product Director had a wicked sense of humor that kept them all looking at the funny side of TriStyle Woman's office politics—and their boss, Felix Meister.

And speak of the devil, here was Felix now, his horns practically showing. The Ordeal was his favorite time of the season.

Emery claimed that he enjoyed it because he knew how much they all hated it, but Beth pointed out that Felix would have had to understand his staff's feelings for that to be true.

Ominously, he was carrying a stack of catalogs. Hannah groaned inwardly. She knew what this meant. Another suggestion that they copy another company's product line. Reminding herself of those endorphins, she waited to see what it was this time.

Felix didn't disappoint. Two long hours into the all-day product meeting, he launched into his latest brainwave.

"I was reviewing some other sportswear catalogs, and I noticed they have a much larger swimsuit line than we do. Take a look at these, and tell me what you think," he began, pulling out catalogs and projecting one website after another displaying slinky, sexy string bikinis and high-fashion suits.

"I also looked at the fashion magazines," he continued, passing around a selection of magazines with pages marked. "With, as you can see, the same results. If anything, even more emphasis on color and trim. And, obviously, smaller, sexier suits."

Finally, he produced the coup de grace—last summer's TriStyle Woman catalog.

"Compare the suits you've just seen to the ones we carry," he pronounced triumphantly. "Most of our suits are one-pieces, and the two-pieces are so utilitarian. And we don't have any bikinis at all. I did some research, and found that bikinis are the most popular swimsuit style among women eighteen to thirty-four. I'm sure I don't need to remind you all that our average customer age is twenty-eight. Lots of women buy a new swimsuit every year, and the average woman has three swimsuits. Three! So why," he wound up for the big finish, "aren't we doing more in this market? Why is our swimsuit section so small and so boring? We can change that, and we should. I'm thinking we double our swimsuit line for summer, and make it much sexier. Double space in the catalog, double space in the stores. Really make a splash, if you'll excuse the pun." He chuckled with satisfaction and sleeked back his thinning black hair, looking around expectantly.

Emery was, as always, the first to speak into the stunned silence. "Could it be," he drawled, "that we don't carry tiny bikinis because we're a...*fitness* company? Do you think the models in the *Sports Illustrated* swimsuit edition swam up to the beach in those suits? Is that why they're all wet and sandy?"

The two assistants sitting at the end of the table giggled, and Felix flushed angrily.

Here we go, Hannah thought. She stepped into the breach. "I think what Emery is trying to say," she began as she flashed a quick warning glance at the Product Director, "is that the swimsuits you see in those catalogs are certainly popular and attractive. But they're not what our customer is coming to our stores or catalog to find. The reason our swimsuits all look so athletic is that you can't do a serious swim in a string bikini or a bandeau top. We know that our customer doesn't necessarily do triathlons. But she thinks she might train for one soon. And she's buying our products for her workouts, as you know."

She adopted her best serious, diplomatic tone, while trying not to sound patronizing. "But you have made me realize that we may be too conservative with the cuts and colors we're choosing. Emery and Beth, maybe you could do a broader search and see what styles and brands we might add to give more pop to our swimsuit line. I think Felix makes a good point. No reason our customer can't look good while she works out, right? And maybe she wants more than one suit, one for her serious workouts, and another for when she goes on vacation, with a little racier cut. Felix, could you leave us those magazines for reference when you leave today?"

Felix looked mollified, Beth and Emery made a note, and Hannah gave herself a mental thumbs-up. Another crisis averted. And how many more to go?

Lunch, as always, was sandwiches brought into the room, offering no chance for a real break. By five-thirty, Hannah had a pounding headache behind one temple and was more than ready for the meeting to end. Several more interactions had required handling with tact, but she thought she had been fairly successful. Now, though, she just wanted to go home.

When Felix suggested she walk him out to his car, she knew she would have one more chance to bring her diplomacy skills out for an airing that day.

He didn't waste any time. "I'm getting pretty tired of Emery's attitude," he complained as they left the building. "Does he know who signs the checks? I've been thinking of replacing him anyway. He's awfully expensive. I'm sure we could find a young person just out of school who'd be glad to grow into the job, at a fraction of his salary. With the job market the way it is, there are lots of hungry people out there."

Hannah reminded herself that it was Felix's ego talking. Probably. She stood for a few seconds before responding, slowing him down and forcing him to focus on her.

"Of course," she answered slowly, "you'll do what you think is best for the company. And that's your prerogative. But I should point out that Emery is the best I've seen. You know our sales are up thirty-four percent since he joined the company two years ago. I don't think that's a coincidence, do you? Do you have any problem with the job he does? And you know," she continued, after Felix had reluctantly admitted Emery's talent, "our team works really well. I'd hate to disrupt that. I'm not sure we could be as effective with someone else in that slot. And most of all," she finished, blue eyes wide and sincere and looking straight at Felix, "I'm concerned that not everyone would stay if Emery left. Getting rid of him, if it were perceived as a move to save money by hiring someone cheap and not as good, would be a signal that I don't think you'd want to send."

"Oh, I'd never do that," Felix blustered. "Of course, if you feel that way about it...But you'd better talk to him. He can't get away with being so disrespectful."

"You're right, of course. And I will definitely bring it up with him. But," she offered cheerfully, "I thought on the whole, the meeting went very well, didn't you? I'm excited about the new lines."

With relief, she saw that he was willing to let her shift the conversation, and she soon had him in his low-slung sports car and on his way. Giving herself a mental shake, she turned around and headed back into the building.

I need a glass of wine, she thought. *A big glass of wine. And a bubble bath.*

♡

Back in the building, Emery was whacking his head theatrically on the "Stress Relief Device: Bang Head Here" sign on the wall of the office Hannah shared with Beth. The sign got a workout every time Felix came in.

"Bikinis!" he moaned. "Hannah, you fool, why haven't you realized the potential of... the Brazilian Thong in the fitness market? *Fio dental,* the dental floss bikini! How did I miss that it was triathlon gear?"

"Yes," Hannah said severely, "but you were bad, Emery. You know you were. OK, I'll admit, I had a hard time not laughing. But it isn't actually a bad idea, once we water it down a bit. And you shouldn't set him off like that. Can't you be just a little more tactful? Could you wait two seconds instead of the words coming into your head and right out of your mouth? You're going to push him too far one of these days. And I might not be able to save you."

"I can't help it," Emery complained. "You know as well as I do, the guy's an idiot. I swear, I'm self-medicating before the next Ordeal."

"I don't like them any more than you do," Beth put in. "But we *are* lucky he's not here every day. At least he knows that we know how to do our jobs, and he lets us do them, more or less."

"You're right," Hannah sighed as she sank into her chair, kicked off her shoes, and wiggled her toes. "We aren't going to get this kind of experience anyplace else. Put in the years, grow the company, move up. That's our plan."

chapter two

♡

An hour later, relaxing at last in that bubble bath, Hannah reluctantly admitted that it was getting harder to keep the plan in mind. It had all seemed so straightforward seven long years ago, when she had been an eager new college graduate with ambition and energy to burn. These past few months, though, she had begun to question her goals. It wasn't just the stress, the twelve-hour days, and the trouble she'd been having in getting to sleep. It was the tiny tic at the corner of her eye that flickered all day to remind her that she wasn't as firmly in control as she thought.

She needed a vacation, that was all. And she was going to get one. She began to make plans in her head, and to feel more cheerful.

"New Zealand." She said the words out loud. Three weeks in New Zealand.

When she'd told her friends about the trip, they'd been surprised, even a little shocked.

"By yourself?" her best friend Susannah had asked when Hannah had first mentioned it during their weekly phone call. "Will that be any fun for you?"

"I can see that it wouldn't be fun for *you*," Hannah had responded, "but you know, not all of us are blissfully married to

Dream Boy. And actually," she said more seriously, "I think the going-alone part might be what I'm looking forward to most. I probably seem selfish, but everything's been pulling at me lately. I have a good job, great friends, a wonderful family. But...I don't know. I think I need some time by myself. Some space to see what I want, without any demands or any schedule, even a friend with me. Can you see what I mean?"

"Well," Susannah answered dryly, "I can certainly see why you want to escape your wonderful family for a while. You know it's true," she insisted as Hannah made a sound of protest. "You're the only twenty-something I know with teenagers."

"You know I don't have teenagers," Hannah objected. "And they might still be searching, but they're good kids."

"Kids? You're only three years older than Kristen, you know. And yes, I think it's great that you're doing something for yourself for once. Anyway, being in New Zealand in summer sure sounds more appealing than staying here and watching it rain."

"I think New Zealand could be rainy too, in November. But it'll be exotic, Southern Hemisphere rain. A whole different proposition. Anyway, I haven't had a day off since Christmas, so three weeks sounds great. And the beach sounds even better— even in the rain. Felix was pretty upset when I told him how long I'd be gone, but I'm afraid if I don't get away, he might not have me here at all. I suspect he could see that."

"It's good for him," Susannah answered roundly. "He takes advantage of you. Let him be without you for a few weeks and see how much you do. And who knows? You might meet somebody cute. A vacation romance. Wouldn't that be great?"

"Right," Hannah scoffed. You've known me for, what, ten years now? How likely is that? You know I'm no good at casual. And I might just remind you that I've been in a dry spell that's lasted, oh, quite a while now."

"I know, honey," Susannah said, serious now. "But it isn't good for you to shut yourself away like that. You should at least be dating more. And don't tell me you don't meet anyone," she overrode Hannah's objection. "Because I know you do. You're so pretty, I know guys are interested. It's good to be picky, but do you think you give them enough of a chance?"

"It's the hair thing, that's all," Hannah answered glumly. "Sometimes I think I should cut it off. Ugh, dating. Too hard."

"OK, first, it's not just the hair. I don't think you ever even look at yourself. And second, getting involved with someone isn't supposed to make your life harder. It's supposed to make it easier. If you ever got something back from your family instead of having to step up all the time, you'd know that."

"Well, whatever the case, nobody can say I haven't got something back from you. The best thing Berkeley ever did for me was give you to me as a roommate. But I'll have to take your word about the benefits of romance for now, and enjoy my vacation by myself."

And now she was only ten days away from that three-week vacation. She couldn't wait.

♡

The following evening, Hannah was reminding herself of her vacation again. This was becoming a habit. She was on the phone once more with Kristen, commiserating over Loser No. 9.

"You'll be proud of me," Kristen was saying. "I did go in to work both days like you said, even though I wanted to take time off. Although you know, Becky at my store took two days off last year when her cat died. So I think losing my boyfriend would entitle me to a sick day. Breakups are the worst thing for your mental health. You'd know that if you dated more."

Ouch. Hannah knew that her little sister's occasional digs came from her insecurity, and reminded herself that she understood and loved Kristen—and that she wouldn't want to trade places, despite her own less-than-exciting love life.

"Is Becky still working there, then?" she asked innocently.

"Well, no," Kristen admitted. "She got fired, because she took too many days off. But I *told* you, Hannah, that was for her *cat*. Not a *breakup.*"

"Anyway," Hannah told her firmly, "I *am* proud of you for going in to work. You've showed them that you're reliable. You know how important that is. And you sound like you're doing much better today."

"I am doing better, I guess. But I still don't understand it. Why did Todd do that to me? I mean, he slept with my *friend.* At least I thought she was my friend. I guess she wasn't. And then he didn't even act sorry when I found out. He said he'd wanted to break up anyway. And now I have to go look for a new apartment, and everything. I can't keep sleeping on Trish's couch much longer."

"Just think, though," Hannah coaxed. "Now you have the chance to start over, find a new place and fix it up, use all that taste of yours. But do you think that maybe Todd just wasn't man enough, not ready to be a grownup? That was a lousy thing to do, and if I were there, I'd sure be tempted to tell him what I think of him. But maybe you guys went a little fast. Maybe you didn't know him as well as you thought you did."

"I know. You're right. I went too fast. I *always* go too fast, don't I? But I was sure, this time. He was so cute, and he told me I was beautiful and took me out all the time, remember?"

"No thanks to him for that. Since you're the most beautiful woman any of those losers is ever likely to see. And a whole lot better person than they deserve. Sweetie, maybe it'd be good to wait a while before you date somebody else. Maybe this is a chance to take a break. Because don't you think this is a pattern? Before Todd, didn't Steve do something very similar? And then Alex…"

"I know, I know," sighed Kristen. "You don't have to remind me, I'm a screwup with men. I just can't seem to find the right guy. And I know, you're going to tell me now to concentrate on my career. But I don't *want* to be you, Hannah. I want someone to love, who'll love me back. I don't want to be all competent and powerful like you, and alone."

Ouch again. "I'm not exactly a forty-five-year-old virgin, Kristen," Hannah reprimanded her sister, unable to repress a flash of hurt and annoyance. "I do date. And there's nothing wrong with being able to take care of yourself. You're doing great at the store. I'm so proud of you. You're not a screwup. But our childhood messed us up. Me as well as you and Matt. It's up to us to fix it, and we can do that if we try hard enough. Speaking of which, did you ever call that therapist?"

"No. But maybe I should now, huh?"

"I think it'd be a good idea. You don't have to go lie on a couch for two years, you know. Just go talk to her a few times, see if it helps. Then you can decide if you want to go any more. Because I won't be around to talk to for a while. And anyway, I'm sure I tell you all the wrong things sometimes. Will you try it, just so I feel better while I'm gone?"

"OK," Kristen said with another sigh. "I promise, I'll call her tomorrow. But it's going to be weird, having you gone so long. I'll miss you. And I know you think I'm selfish and don't appreciate you, but it's not true. Matt and I both know how much you've done for us. And that we make you crazy when we mess up. But Hannah," she burst out, "don't you ever get tired of being so responsible all the time? Don't you ever want to be impulsive, and buy shoes you can't afford just because they're so pretty, and drink too much, and go to bed with Mr. Right Now, and call in sick to work just once, when you're not? It's like you aren't even normal, sometimes."

"Gee, you make it sound so attractive," Hannah laughed. "No, I have to say that I don't get tired of being responsible. I like knowing I have things under control. I don't feel comfortable if I'm out on the edge. I guess we're different, that's all."

But after she had exchanged good-nights with Kristen and hung up, Hannah thought about what her sister had said. Wasn't she just a little tired of always being in control? No, not exactly that, she decided. What she had told Kristen was true. She had certainly never seen the attraction of getting drunk. But maybe she needed to broaden her horizons, take some risks.

Maybe she'd take surfing lessons on vacation, she thought, then laughed at herself. Learning a new skill probably wasn't what Kristen had had in mind.

The next week was a blur of activity as Hannah labored to get everything in order so she could leave the office for three weeks. She knew it would be worth the effort, but she was feeling drained as she sat with Beth and Emery on her last day, making final plans.

"So we've gone through the product and catalog schedule. Do you have everything you need for the Friday meetings with Felix, Beth?"

"You've left us so many notes, I think we're prepared for everything short of nuclear war," Beth assured her. "Emery and I can handle things. Nothing momentous is going on right now. I'll take care of the web sale and coordinate with the stores, we'll work on the new product line and the catalog, and when you come back, we'll be on schedule, you'll see."

Hannah smiled at her in gratitude. "I know I can leave it to you guys. You're the best."

"What did Felix say when you told him you wouldn't even have a cell phone on your trip?" Emery asked eagerly. "Did his face go all purple again? I love it when it does that."

"Well, I don't think he was thrilled. But I told him I needed a real break in order to come back refreshed and ready to put in my best effort over the Christmas season, and that distracted him. I will find a way to check my emails from time to time, though. If anything does come up that you need my help on, you know you can ask."

"You just enjoy your vacation," Beth told her firmly. "You deserve it. You've covered for the two of us often enough. We're prepared. We can handle things. You need to have faith in us."

"You're right," Hannah answered, chagrined. "I do trust you—both of you. Old habits die hard, I guess. Thank you for pointing that out."

"Oh no," Emery groaned. "Are we going to have to hug now? Would you get out of here and go on vacation already? We've got it. Get out."

"I was going to work on those sales projections," Hannah protested. "They want them tomorrow, so I thought I'd knock them out before I left tonight. My plane doesn't leave till tomorrow afternoon."

"Give that to me," Beth ordered. "I can do them, and turn them in on time too. Didn't we just *talk* about this? Here you go, backsliding already. You go home and get packed. Have an early night and relax. You don't want to rush onto the plane all stressed. That's no way to start a trip. Who knows, maybe you can even go shopping tomorrow for some cute vacation clothes."

Hannah laughed. "Recall if you will that I work at a clothing company. And that my sister works at the best department store in the Bay Area. I'm almost embarrassed to tell you how much I've treated myself."

"Which means, what," Emery asked caustically, "you bought yourself a new swimsuit and a pair of sandals? You know you need to expand that wardrobe, girl."

"No, Joan Rivers, I went out and bought all kinds of actual, real new clothes, so quit being so snippy. And before you ask, no, they aren't earth tones, black, white, gray or, heaven forbid, navy blue. Pretty, girly clothes. So there."

"I'm certainly glad to hear it," he responded. "I keep telling you, you've got to stop fighting your looks. You look like Rapunzel. OK. So go with that. The Wicked Queen called, and she wants her wardrobe back."

"Emery," Hannah sighed. "You know that if I dressed in the colors you like—OK, the colors I like, too—nobody would take me seriously. Rapunzel doesn't get many jobs in the corporate sector. Whereas the Wicked Queen..."

"Yes, Cruella de Vil has the big car and the flourishing fur business. I just hate to see you damping it down so much. When you get back, show me what you bought, OK? Better yet, take me shopping with you next time. I've been wanting to get my hands on you for a long time. I'll catch you in a weak post-vacation moment when your defenses are down, and look out, world. I promise, I'll keep you professional. But I do think you could expand your horizons a little now. You're not a beginner. You don't have to wear black to be taken seriously anymore."

"You're my guru, Emery. And I've been listening to you, don't worry. I did think about your suggestions when I picked my vacation wardrobe. I figure, New Zealand is a brand new country where I can be Rapunzel for three whole weeks if I want to. And I won't have to impress a soul with my cold-hearted professionalism. Doesn't that sound great? And now," Hannah said, handing over the sales projection file to Beth, "If you'll really take care of this for me, I'm going to take your advice and get my beautiful storybook self out of here."

TriStyle Woman had become her real home in these past seven years, she realized with gratitude as she drove home, light with relief and anticipation. She had poured her own blood, sweat, and tears—sometimes literal tears, she admitted—into the fledgling company, but it had been worth it.

But now it was time to think about other things. She parked her trusty Civic outside her small apartment building, and hurried into her much-loved, tiny one-bedroom with its view of sky and trees, and its half-packed suitcase.

Full of Rapunzel clothes, she thought happily. *For the new me.*

chapter three

♡

She didn't feel much like a new version of herself, let alone a princess, two days later. The twelve-hour overnight flight from San Francisco had left her physically and mentally rumpled. Being squashed into a middle seat in the 747's central aisle, smack in the middle of the Economy section, was no recipe for a restful night. The crying baby in the row ahead hadn't helped either. Even in her exhausted state, though, her heart lifted when the plane touched down and the flight attendant announced, "Haere mai—Welcome to Aotearoa New Zealand!"

Hannah looked eagerly out the bus window as she rode into the city, through green hills and past neat, tidy houses. Of course, she'd known it would be summer here. But it still came as a shock to take off in the gray drizzle, and arrive to look over an expansive, sparkling harbor full of boats, under a blue sky with just a few puffy white clouds, the sun shining in the brilliantly clear air.

To her disappointment, Auckland didn't seem very exotic. After all, though, her only real impressions of New Zealand were from watching *The Lord of the Rings,* and she couldn't really expect it all to look like Lothlorien. Or Mordor, thank goodness. It didn't even look very foreign, except for the Maori place names. How in the world did you pronounce Papatoetoe?

She'd been told, though, that in order to see the real New Zealand, she had to get out of the sprawling city in which almost a third of the country's four million people lived. The following morning saw her taking her courage in both hands and picking up her rental car.

She only had to drive a few hours, she told herself bracingly. People learned to drive on the left every day. Surely she could do it as well. But by the time she had capped off her day by navigating the narrow, winding roads of the Coromandel Peninsula, she was shaking with exhaustion and more than ready to pull into her modest motel accommodation.

"You just sit there for a while. I've had enough," she told the little car with a sigh as she stepped out of it. She wouldn't drive anywhere again until the following afternoon. Meanwhile, she'd take a coastal walk, explore the shoreline of the tiny town, and take herself out to dinner. And look forward to her first ocean swim the next day.

♡

Finding herself wide-awake again at six after another early, jet-lagged night, she decided that there was no time like the present. Pulling on her purple and red racing tank and sliding a pair of sandals onto her feet, she grabbed her goggles, cap, and towel, made her way down the hill to the beach, and stepped into the water.

And found herself caught in a rip that defied all her efforts to swim across it to safety, the powerful outgoing current carrying her inexorably away from shore and out to sea.

Stupid, she thought despairingly as she struggled against the rip. Stupid to venture out so far just because the sea looked calm, without checking tides and currents. No use thinking about that now, though. She had to keep going. Strong and slow. Eighty strokes. Ninety. Getting more tired now. One hundred and seventy strokes. One-eighty. She had been out in the water too long.

Too tired. Keep swimming parallel. Sooner or later, she had to get out of this.

The world became focused on effort. Stroke. Breathe. Stroke. Breathe. Parallel to the shore. Stay parallel. Stroke. Breathe. It finally crossed her mind that she might not make it. She struggled to push the thought aside. She was strong, she reminded herself. She could do this. She just had to keep going. Swim. Stroke. Breathe.

She never knew how much longer it had been, but she could feel that her strength was almost gone despite all her efforts. Dimly, she heard a voice from behind her.

"All right there?"

She turned her head and saw him—a man in a kayak, looking down with concern.

"I think...I'm stuck," she gasped. "Can you help me?"

He held out the paddle to her. "Grab hold."

She did, and felt her hand shaking. It took all her strength to hold on, but she knew she wasn't letting go. Not now. She felt herself moving towards him as he pulled her to the side of the boat with the paddle. One arm came out, grasped the back of her suit, and hauled her up against the kayak.

"Hold the side," he ordered. "I'll take you to shore. You'll be all right now. I've got you."

She was vaguely aware that it was awkward for him to paddle with her holding on next to him, but he managed somehow, moving quickly and expertly towards the beach. Even when the boat neared the shore, she still gripped the side for dear life.

He aimed the kayak squarely at the beach, paddled hard, then coasted as the boat glided swiftly up to the shore, its bow grating on the sand. He jumped out fast, tossing his paddle up onto the beach. Grabbing hold under her shoulder with one hand, he hauled her easily onto her feet, braced her against him. She would have fallen if he hadn't been holding her, she realized. Her legs were trembling—and the rest of her wasn't much better.

He swore softly, then sat her down higher up the sand and turned to his boat, pulling it out of reach of the lapping waves. She dropped her head to her knees, utterly spent.

He reached into the boat, grabbed a water bottle, and held it out to her. "Drink."

She drained it, then gripped the empty bottle just for something to hold. The adrenaline that had flooded her body during her efforts was leaving her now. Feeling sick and weak, she pulled off her goggles and cap with shaking hands. Her heavy braid fell down her back, chilling her more, and she hugged her arms around her body for warmth and support. She could see her rescuer clearly now as he ran to a nearby pickup parked on the beach, grabbed a towel, and returned in seconds with it. Pulling her up, he wrapped it around her, then gently set her down again.

"Rest a bit. You're all right now." He squatted to rub her dry with the towel, massaging warmth back into her cold, shocked limbs, watching her all the while. She was barely aware of his attentions as she sat huddled, head bowed.

At last, seeming satisfied that she was recovering, he pulled the boat up toward his truck, took gear out of it—fishing gear, she realized dully—and threw it in the back, together with his paddle. Then quickly hoisted the boat onto a rack and strapped it down.

Once he had everything stowed, he returned to where she sat on the sand and crouched down next to her again. She tried to smile, to thank him.

"I'm sorry," she said through teeth that still insisted on chattering. "I'm all right now. Please, you can go."

He stared at her, eyes intent on her face. "Nah. You're not all right. Not yet. Come on."

Again he helped her stand, holding her as they walked the short distance to his truck. He opened her door and gently settled her into the passenger seat, then drove off the beach via a ramp and up to the road. He had put the heater on, she realized. He must be roasting. The shakes were stronger now as she realized how close she had come to drowning. She felt an alarming urge to cry, and her breath came ragged as she fought it.

Her rescuer pulled to a stop at a seaside café, left the motor running and the heater on, and said again, "Wait."

Helplessly, she did as she was told. She didn't think she could have gone anywhere if she had tried.

He was back in a few minutes, holding out a tall cup. "Drink this."

She put two hands around the cup and sipped cautiously. As she drank the hot, sweet tea, she felt the heat swirling down inside her, warming her. He hadn't asked her any questions, she realized, or talked to her beyond those few commands. Just sat next to her, watching as she gradually stopped shaking so hard, warmed by the heater and by the hot liquid inside her.

He seemed to be breathing more easily himself now, and she became aware of how he must have felt as he saw her struggling and pulled her to shore. Another wave of embarrassment overcame her at the thought. As soon as her teeth were no longer chattering and she trusted herself to speak, she said, as calmly as she could manage, "I'm sorry. I guess I wrecked your fishing trip. I'm OK now, though. I can go. Thanks for everything." Awkwardly, she pulled the towel out from under her and held it out to him.

He smiled. "I've never met a girl who wanted to get away from me so badly. Let's go back and get your clothes. You can change out of those wet togs, and we'll get some food into you."

"I just walked down from the place I'm staying," she explained. "It's only my towel and sandals back on the beach. I'm OK now, really. You've done so much already."

"You need to eat something hot," he insisted. "We'll pick up your gear, and I'll drive you wherever it is you're staying. You can take a shower and change, and I'll take you out for breakfast. You have to let me wait for you," he insisted as she hesitated. "It's the least you can do, after ruining my fishing trip and all. You can't leave me wondering if you're all right, now that I've done my Good Samaritan act."

As he retrieved her belongings and drove the few blocks to her motel, Hannah realized that part of the reason she had wanted to leave was embarrassment at her own stupidity. She wanted to hide away, like a dog crawling under the porch to lick its wounds. But the other part, she admitted to herself, was him. She had hardly noticed what he looked like as he pulled her to shore and helped revive her. But now, in the close confines of the truck, she found him overwhelming.

Dressed in a T-shirt and shorts, he was a big man. A very big man. Without the regular features of a model, but with a strong jaw and cheekbones, his dark hair cropped close to his head, his was a face to be reckoned with. In fact, he was the kind of man she'd normally shy away from. Too rough-looking, and definitely too big. But he had been nothing but kind to her. Besides, she still felt shaky, and his solid strength and competence gave her comfort.

"I'll wait," he told her again when he had parked outside the motel. "Take your time."

Fifteen minutes later, after a hot shower, some scented body lotion, and a rough towel-dry of her long, thick hair, Hannah was looking in the mirror, thankful that she had had her fair brows and lashes tinted before leaving on vacation, so she didn't look completely washed out. It was ridiculous to primp for him. This wasn't a date. He was making sure she was all right, that was all. But she still pulled on her favorite new sundress, a deep primrose yellow printed with tiny purple and blue flowers, in a halter style that made her feel like Marilyn Monroe, if slightly less curvaceous.

Shrugging mentally at her own vanity, she muttered, "Might as well look my best, since he's already seen me looking my worst. Even things out a little." She combed conditioner into her hair and pulled it back into a loose braid to dry, then teased tendrils out around her face and slicked on her favorite pink lip gloss. Slipped on her new narrow sandals, with the beads on their thin leather straps and the low French heels.

"OK," she told herself as she looked in the mirror. "That's as good as it's going to get. Let's go."

He was leaning against the truck with his arms folded across his chest, staring out to sea, as she approached. Hearing the tap of her heels in the sandals, he turned, looking momentarily startled. Score one for the yellow sundress, she told herself with a flush of satisfaction.

"Here I am," she announced. "A bit less of the drowned rat, I hope. Thanks for waiting."

"Not any kind of a rat at all, I'd say," he decided as he opened the truck door for her.

Two points, she thought, realizing at the same time that she shouldn't get into his truck again. She'd really had no choice before, and nobody could fault his manners, but she didn't know him, after all. She asked, as casually as she could manage, "Would you mind if we walked? It's only a few blocks. And I think it would be good for me to walk off the shakes a bit more."

She had surprised him again, she saw. But after a moment, he answered, "I can see I'll have to get a mate to vouch for me. I'm pretty well known around here, actually. But of course we can walk."

"I haven't thanked you properly for saving me," she told him as they made their way down the steep hill. "I was lucky you were out there so early, and that you saw me and came to my rescue. I do realize what a debt I owe you."

"No worries. I was there, and we were lucky. There's a bad rip on that beach. Loads of drownings over the years, though you wouldn't know it to look at it. Best to swim between the flags where the lifesavers are, or on a beach you know is safe, in En Zed. I'm guessing you haven't been here long. Are you Canadian?"

"No, American. I haven't introduced myself, I realize. I'm Hannah Montgomery. And yes, you can bet I've learned my lesson. I'll be a lot more careful in the future, believe me. The sea looked so calm and beautiful, I couldn't resist. It never occurred to me that I could have a problem. I've swum in the Bay, back home. But not in the ocean."

"Drew Callahan." He glanced down at her as he spoke, then added after a beat, "American. I would've guessed Canadian. You have a soft accent. Where are you from, in the States? Someplace near water, I've sussed that out."

"The San Francisco area now, but I grew up in a more rural part of California. I suppose I don't have a big-city accent. And you're right, I'm here on vacation, and this is only my fourth day. Obviously, I have a lot to learn."

"Not so much," he shrugged. "You've had one of those experiences you'll remember, I reckon. And it gave me the chance to meet you, so there's the upside."

Startled, she looked across at him. He quirked an eyebrow at her, and she burst out laughing. "Maybe it was all a desperate ploy on my part, have you thought of that? Women are probably flinging themselves in your path all the time to get rescued."

He smiled at that. "Well, never so dramatically. But we're here now." He guided her into the little café with his hand on the small of her back. She felt its warmth and knew she liked it. A big hand, a big man. But his solidity, instead of feeling threatening, felt comforting. Maybe it was the accent, she thought confusedly.

They were almost the only customers this early in the morning. The girl at the counter took their orders, and Drew guided her again to a little table in a backyard garden.

"You know," she told him, "I don't think I've been to a café yet where the counter staff had New Zealand accents."

"Kiwis don't stay home, that's why. The young people just want to get out, see the world. And there's not enough good work here. We lose a lot of younger people to Aussie. Australia," he explained at her questioning look. "Have to import our tourist workers. Makes for a disappointing authentic experience for the Yanks, expecting to hear all those Kiwi accents and getting Romanian instead."

"Do a lot of people leave here, then?" she asked in surprise. "It's so beautiful, though. I've only been here a few days, but I can't imagine leaving if I were lucky enough to live here. Did you leave and come back?"

"Nah. I like living here, and I travel heaps. More than enough. Never wanted to move overseas, even though most of my mates did."

"What do you do that you travel, if you don't mind my asking?" He didn't look like a businessman—at least not like the businessmen she knew. But maybe they grew them bigger over here.

And he was certainly that. Even relaxed, his arms were massive and muscular, his chest broad. His thighs seemed almost as big around as her waist, and she had realized while walking next to him that he must be six foot three. *Hope he doesn't have to travel Economy,* she thought, remembering her cramped flight. She smiled, imagining him in the middle seat.

"What's funny?" he asked. When she explained her mental image, he laughed aloud. "Too right, I'd be cramped. Luckily, I don't have to fly economy much. I'm a rugby player, so I have some games overseas as well as here in En Zed. Get to see the world, you could say."

"Oh. That explains how you look," she said without thinking, then blushed when he smiled again. "I don't know much

27

about rugby," she hurried on, "though I've seen some American football back home. My father was a big fan."

"Not too different in some ways. Less padding."

She looked more closely at his face and saw that he did look a bit battered. His nose, she thought, had probably been broken and reset, and she saw a scar on his chin and another coming down near an eyebrow. She had to admit that they only added to the appeal of his rugged features. A little flustered, she was glad when their coffees came, followed shortly by their breakfasts. He had insisted on ordering eggs and toast for her, and had a mountain of food on his own plate.

She asked, appalled, "Is that *breakfast?*"

"The Big Brekkie, we call it. Eggs, sausage, bacon, hash browns, toast, fried tomatoes, mushrooms. But this is my light breakfast, because I'm not in serious training. During the season, I'd be having a steak as well."

She shuddered. "Well, I can see that you'd need it, since you have an athletic job. But that isn't advertised as 'Rugby Players' Breakfast,' right? It's just a regular menu option. Does everyone eat like that?"

"Nah, it's just that we're a nation of farmers. Farmers and Maori. Lots of big fellas with hearty appetites."

"I'm surprised everyone doesn't weigh three hundred pounds. I've only been here a few days, but you sure have a lot of tasty food. I've never seen so many cafes. It's like the whole country is a giant cruise ship. And you know what they say about cruise ships," she continued solemnly.

"What's that?"

"People gain a pound for every day they're on the cruise. I can see I'm going to have to step up my workouts, or I'll be waddling back home."

"No danger of that, I'd say." He smiled at her appreciatively.

He had excellent table manners, she was glad to see. She still remembered the date she'd been on where the man had held his fork in his fist. How could you not learn how to hold a fork? she had wondered at the time. Drew wasn't hard to watch anyway. Maybe she would even have forgiven him the fork thing.

"Well," she told him at last, "I'd better get back, and let you get on with your fishing or whatever."

He didn't rise immediately. "You'll need to rest today. When you have that much adrenaline in your body, it hits you like a hammer after a bit. But would you like to come out on the water with me tomorrow? I reckon I'm your lifesaver now. Need to keep an eye on you in case you get swimming out into any more rips."

"I'd love that," she answered in surprise.

"I'll pick you up at nine, then. And this time, I hope you'll ride in the ute with me. It's going to be a slow trip to the marina if you have to run alongside."

She laughed. "I think I can risk it. You don't seem too bad, so far."

"My mum will be glad to hear it. She hates it when I attack women." "You don't have a mobile, do you?" he asked once they had arrived back at the motel again. "A phone," he explained at her questioning look.

"Oh! No. You could reach me through the motel office, though, I suppose, if your plans change. Or if you decide I'm too big a risk."

"No chance of that. But good to know. I'll see you tomorrow, then. Go have a rest now." He reached for her, kissed her gently on the cheek, then strolled easily back to his truck.

She opened her door, but couldn't resist turning and watching him walk away. It was a pleasure. He didn't swagger, exactly. But he walked like he owned the ground he was covering. Arms wide and swinging, body relaxed and upright, big strides. She sighed. He looked good.

Inside her room again, she sat on the edge of the bed and pressed her hands to her cheeks. She had never met a man who affected her this way. Not even close. What was it? He was nothing like the men she usually dated. They had muscles too, some of those men. But they were gym-built muscles. Drew looked like his muscles were there for a purpose.

For bringing other men to the ground, she reminded herself. She might not know much about rugby, but she knew it was brutal. He hadn't seemed brutal, though. He'd been kind, and considerate, and not much louder or any more...boisterous than she was herself. Weren't rugby players supposed to be hard-drinking types, breaking up the bar every night?

She shook her head. She was too tired to think about it anymore. In fact, she suddenly felt too tired even to sit up. She'd lie down for a minute and take a rest. She was on vacation, after all.

♡

When she woke, it took her a moment to remember where she was, before the events of the morning came flooding back. To her astonishment, it was three o'clock, and she'd been asleep for four hours. She thought about her plan for the day, her hike, and realized she had to write it off the list for now. She'd lie on the beach and read a book instead.

She looked up an hour later from her shady spot under the trees, envying the bronzed girls lying out in the sun. They looked lovely, their bikinis showing acres of tanned, firm skin. But a tan wasn't healthy, she reminded herself firmly. Anyway, she was fair-skinned, and that was all there was to it.

Would Drew be expecting one of those carefree girls? She wished suddenly that she could be a bit more like Kristen. Her vivacious sister was perfectly equipped to handle a day on a boat with a sexy rugby player. Whereas Hannah...well, she'd never been a party girl.

But he had asked her, she told herself. Because he liked her. And she had said yes, because she liked him. Maybe she wasn't his usual type. Well, he wasn't her usual type either. And it was a simple outing on a boat. She'd just have to go with it.

She sighed. Going with it had never been her strong suit.

chapter four

♡

Hannah woke during the night to the sound of rain on the roof of the little motel. Maybe it was just as well. She had come on this trip to be alone, after all. Not to have a fling with a stranger, no matter how attractive he was. And Drew unnerved her. She felt far from her usual controlled self with him. Maybe it was better if this—whatever it was—ended here. Her treacherous heart, though, refused to go along with that sensible plan, and felt only disappointment at the thought of not seeing him again.

Her cool logic wasn't necessary, it turned out, as the storm passed and the following day dawned clear. By nine, she was ready—had been ready for some time, if the painful truth were known, wearing her suit under a sarong-style skirt printed in tropical colors, gauzy blouse, and wide straw hat to protect her fair skin from the sun.

She was amused to think that Felix's Bikini Meeting had indeed brought results, at least from her. Afterwards, she had gone to Kristen's store and had let her sister help her select a second, more attractive suit to take with her in addition to the strictly utilitarian one she normally wore. It was still designed to get wet, rather than for lying provocatively on the beach, but the one-piece's warm color ("It's not orange," Kristen had told her, when Hannah resisted. "It's tangerine. *Big* difference."), high-cut legs, and thin, crisscrossed straps accentuated her curvy, athletic figure and were definitely made to appeal, rather than to resist chlorine.

"It'll fade in three months," she had objected to Kristen as her sister rolled her eyes.

"You're only on vacation for three *weeks,* Hannah," Kristen had told her firmly. "This is the one. Buy it."

Hannah had succumbed, although she had privately wondered when she would ever wear such an impractical suit. Now she was grateful to her fashion-conscious sister. She might not be in Kristen's class, but she looked good.

When she heard Drew's knock, she picked up her straw bag and opened the door to him. Maybe he wouldn't look as good to her today, she thought half-hopefully. No such luck, though. If anything, he seemed bigger and more solid than ever, in long swim trunks and a close-fitting T-shirt made of some quick-dry material, his hair covered by a baseball cap.

He looked down at her with an appreciative light in his gray eyes and smiled a welcome. "I'm glad to see you're ready. I half expected to cool my heels while you finished your makeup."

She laughed. "I'm afraid that takes me all of two minutes. I read these articles about all the steps you're supposed to take, and how to get them down to twenty minutes. But I can't be bothered, I suppose."

"Well, I reckon that means you don't mind getting wet. Which is a good thing. I brought snorkeling gear and was hoping to coax you into the water again. Something about getting back up on the horse."

"I'm surprised you trust me in the water after yesterday. I thought you might decide to beg off and take somebody less prone to drowning instead."

"Nah, as long as I'm there to save you, no worries. I do a pretty good line in rescues. And you're even getting into a closed vehicle with me today." He held the truck door for her. "My mum will be so pleased."

"Your fatal charm won me over," she sighed. "What can I say. But did you say we're going snorkeling? I'm embarrassed to say I've never been. I'd love to try it, though. Is it hard to do?"

"Dead easy," he answered confidently. "Don't worry, I'll show you."

It was a short trip down to the marina, where Drew took her through the locked gate to the pier. She asked him curiously, "Do you have your own boat here, or do you rent one?"

"It's mine, not a hire. Can't use it all the time, of course, but like all Kiwis, I love being out on the water. Got to have our boats. I come out here every chance I get."

The boat was a sleek motor launch, not overly large, but even to Hannah's inexpert eye, clearly top of the line. Drew helped her aboard and set about stowing their gear and getting the boat ready to launch. He obviously knew what he was doing, and she settled herself in the seat next to his captain's chair, watching his preparations with interest.

"Even though I've lived in the San Francisco area for ten years now, I don't know much about boats, I'm afraid," she confessed. "I love to swim, but that's about all the water knowledge I have. So I don't know anything about hauling lines in or making anything fast. If you need my help, though, just tell me what to do, and I'll do my best."

"Don't need a mate for a boat like this," he assured her. "Nothing for you to do. We'll be off straight away."

Within minutes, they were indeed out on the ocean. Hannah marveled again at the clear water, the beauty of the beaches and rugged cliffs they passed, and felt herself relaxing in the sunshine. Drew pointed her to a thermos of coffee, and they were both quiet as they enjoyed the clear morning, the feel of the wind, and watching the boat cut through the water, raising a wake behind them. Drew seemed to handle the boat with confidence but without aggression or bravado, enjoying the day rather than trying to dominate the water or impress her with a show of speed.

He stopped not far from shore, near a headland at the end of a deserted beach, and dropped the anchor.

"Snorkeling time," he told her. "This area is all a marine reserve. Heaps of fish to see. I brought you a wetsuit as well. You'll be more comfortable and be able to stay out longer."

She looked at the rubbery blue garment doubtfully as he pulled it from the duffel. "Are you sure it'll fit me?"

"Give me credit. I'm used to sizing up my teammates, you know." He grinned at her wickedly, and she found herself blushing once again.

"Go below and get changed, if you like," he offered.

Even though she could have stepped out of her clothes and into the wetsuit on the deck, she was grateful for his consideration. Somehow, she felt shy about doing something as intimate as taking off her clothes in front of him. She told herself it was silly. After all, she'd met him—if you could call it a meeting—in her swimsuit. But still, she took advantage of his offer and headed down the stairs into the small but well-appointed cabin to remove her clothes and pull on the wetsuit.

She arrived topside again to find him outfitted in his own wetsuit, pulling out masks and snorkels. "You look like a very pretty dolphin," he said approvingly. "Let me show you how this works. You just have to remember, if you're tempted to dive down, to let go of the snorkel and hold your breath," he told her as he finished the demonstration. "But where we're going, it's shallow enough that we can stay on the surface."

Dropping down the boat's ladder into the sea, he showed her the direction they would be going, put his face into the water, and began to swim. She copied him, and realized with wonder that she had entered a new world.

The sea floor below them was full of marine life. Seaweed that resembled thick bushes, and another type like fronded, long-leafed plants, waved in the current. She was excited when she saw her first fish, a beautiful electric blue, and then amazed when she found herself swimming over a two-foot long silver animal that seemed totally unconcerned with her presence. She lifted her head from time to time to make sure she was still following Drew, and he too stopped and looked back often for her.

He was leading her toward the headland, she saw. As they approached, she realized why. Cut into the side was a large, triangular opening with large rocks surrounding it. A sea cave, she marveled.

Drew stopped, treading water, as they neared the entrance. Pulled out his snorkel and told her, "It's a tunnel, through to another bay that's only accessible this way. We'll have to swim around the rocks, and the waves will push at you. You'll need to ride with them. Let them help you rather than fighting them. Are you OK to do this? I'll stay behind you, make sure you're all right."

"Sure," she answered.

In truth, she was a little nervous. The tunnel was long and dark, and she could already feel the waves being pulled into it, and herself rising and falling with them. But she would be with Drew, and he clearly knew what he was doing. He could be under no illusions as to her skill in reading the water, after all. She gave herself a mental shake and put her snorkel back in, ready to try.

As she entered the cave, the waves did take her. Remembering what he had said, she stroked with their push and aimed to guide her progress between the rocks, reaching out with her hands and pulling herself through in places. It grew darker as she continued in, and she felt the unease from the day before return. She reminded herself that Drew was behind her, watching out for her, and focused on the triangle of light ahead of her at the tunnel's end.

She kept moving doggedly between the jagged rocks, and found herself after a few minutes coming out the other side at last. She raised her head and saw she had swum out of the tunnel into a narrow bay, the beach and water empty of any other people. Nothing but the sea ahead, the beach behind and a headland on either side. And Drew next to her, his head up as well, checking her progress.

"How'd you go?" he asked. "Any problems?"

"No. It was a little exciting, but I did what you said, and I was fine."

He nodded and put his head back under, beginning to swim slowly. Following his example, she discovered even more marine life than on the other side. A school of brightly colored fish darted by, making patterns in formation like swallows in the air. Large sea stars dotted the ocean floor, some in the traditional star shape, others with slender, elongated arms, in different sizes and shades of pink, purple, and orange.

Drew touched her hand suddenly, and she turned. She looked where he pointed, and blinked in surprise at a large ray, hovering just over the sea floor, that darted suddenly away, its thin tail flicking behind it, as their shadows fell across it.

As they swam on, she found herself over another of those huge silver fish she had noticed on the other side, and decided to try to follow it. She was delighted to find that she was able to keep up, and was being taken on a Fish Tour of the bay. The big animal didn't seem bothered by her presence above it. Its meandering course took her past others of its kind, though it didn't seem to be interested in them, and to areas with colorful smaller fish and more of the darting schools.

She had been happily swimming with her fishy friend for about fifteen minutes when she suddenly found herself almost face to face with a huge jellyfish. Startled, she looked around to see several more suspended in the water ahead of her and to either

37

side. Her heart pounded as she looked at their beautiful, translucent bodies, with their streamers hanging down several feet below. She didn't know what kind they were, but she certainly didn't want to find out the hard way. She turned as neatly as she could, pulling her arms in toward her body to avoid touching the translucent shapes all around her, and fairly levitated across the bay toward Drew. His head came out of the water as she approached at speed.

When she told him what she had seen, he answered calmly, "Yeh, we can get those. We're all right in the wetsuits, just faces and hands, but best not to swim into them and get your hands stung. We may be ready to swim back anyway."

She agreed. The encounter with the jellies had shaken her a little. The trip back through the tunnel was less frightening this time, now that she knew what she was doing. She enjoyed the leisurely swim back, the feeling that she was part of the sea rather than just swimming over it. It was like a garden, she thought. A garden under the sea.

Back on the boat again, Drew handed her a large towel and took one for himself as they compared notes over the fish they had seen. The big fish she had followed was a snapper, she found. "Tasty," he commented. "You should try it." They pulled off their wetsuits together, and she realized in surprise that she no longer felt shy. Something about exploring the ocean together, sharing the experience, as well as the physical exertion, had relaxed her.

When she was free of the heavy wetsuit and was blotting her long braid of excess water, she looked up to find him watching her with considerable interest.

"I like that costume," he told her. "Much better."

"My sister will be glad you approve. She made me buy this suit. She even told me it wasn't orange, though I still have my doubts. She says it's tangerine."

"I'm not too good on the fruit colors, but I'd say whatever it is, it works. Tell your sister cheers for me."

He looked pretty good himself in a swimsuit, she thought privately. Without the T-shirt, his broad chest was nothing short of spectacular. She had always preferred slim men, and now she wondered what she had been thinking. Surely nothing could attract her more than the power latent in all that muscle.

She had wondered at first, seeing the boat, if he had expected sex to be part of the outing. She knew that athletes had more than their share of opportunities, and guessed that few women could resist his attraction—and that they hadn't made much effort to. But although he was clearly interested, she wasn't feeling pressured. In fact, other than taking her hand to help her into the boat or directing her attention to something in the water, he hadn't touched her at all.

Which was maybe just a *little* disappointing. She was certainly enjoying looking at him, and watching him move through the water and climb in and out of the boat had been a pure pleasure. She wouldn't mind, she admitted. Not at all.

No holiday flings, she reminded herself sternly, but the warning didn't carry quite the same conviction as usual.

Drew caught her looking, smiled back at her. She looked away quickly, reached into her bag for a wide comb, and set about unfastening her braid. She felt his eyes on her as she settled into a seat at the side of the boat, spread her hair out around her, and began to pull the comb through the long, heavy mass, beginning at the bottom and working her way to the top.

"I reckon I've seen a mermaid now," he said slowly. "I've never seen anyone with that kind of hair. Or so much of it."

She smiled ruefully as she continued at her task. "I know, and I ask myself every day why I keep it. I work out a fair amount, and just washing and drying it takes me an hour. I keep thinking

I should cut it off and be done with it, but I've had it this way for so long, it'd feel like losing a part of me."

"That would be a crime," he said seriously. "I've met a lot of blondes. But I don't think I've ever known anyone with hair exactly that color. It's so blonde, it's almost white."

"My friend Emery calls it Rapunzel hair. You know, Rapunzel, let down your hair? When I was little, I always wanted sleek black hair, like Snow White. Or shiny golden hair, like my sister's. I guess we always want what we don't have."

She pulled her curtain of hair around to the front and set to work with the towel and comb again, blotting and untangling. The fine strands began to curl as they dried, becoming tendrils around her face and waving in spirals down her back.

Finished, she fastened it again in a loose braid that reached well below her waist. When he protested, she laughed. "You wouldn't thank me if you had a yard of hair whipping around your face while you tried to drive your boat. Believe me, it can really get in the way." He'd have taken that chance, Drew decided. The sight of all that hair had done something to him. Aloud, he just said, "Pity. It's quite a show, best I've seen in a while, watching you in your togs with your hair around you."

And, he thought, the only thing better would be watching her *without* her togs, with her hair around her. And him. He forced the image from his mind as he saw her blushing faintly again. She blushed more than any woman he knew. Of course, most of the women he'd known had long since passed the stage of blushing. Over anything.

That was what was so intriguing about her. That reserve, combined with the adventurous spirit that had brought her here on her own. Her willingness to try something new even after her near-disastrous experience of the day before. Her delight in something as simple as snorkeling. He wanted to see more of her. A lot more. In both senses of the word.

He'd need to go slowly, though. She wasn't some rugby groupie. Or even like the models and media types he dated these days. He was getting pretty tired of predatory women, now that he thought about it. It had been a long time since he'd really pursued anyone. A long time since he'd had to. It looked like he'd be doing the asking this time, though. Suited him fine.

She seemed surprisingly unconcerned with her looks, too, even though they were having a fair effect on him. She'd fixed her hair just now without so much as looking at a mirror. She hadn't checked out her appearance the day before, either, not stealing those little glances into shop windows or the café's mirrors as most women would have.

On a hunch, he asked, "You have a sister, eh. Is she as pretty as you?"

"Oh no. She's gorgeous," Hannah answered immediately. "That's the first thing anyone would say. She's the beauty of the family. But she's a sweetheart, too. She's insecure, though you might not know it."

"Why's that?"

"Being so beautiful is hard. You feel like people, especially men, only value you for your looks. You can start to think that you have nothing else to offer. It's hard to find someone who wants to get beyond that. I suppose it's like being a rich man. You want someone who wants you for more than what they can get out of you. But how do you know why they want to be with you?"

More true than you realize, he thought. "So you're the ugly one in the family, are you?" he asked with a grin.

She laughed. "No, I know I'm not ugly. But I'm not in my sister's league. You'd know that if you saw her. I'm not jealous of her, though. My mother wasn't too good about it. Because she was beautiful too, she thought that was the most important thing there was for a woman. She commented on it all the time.

It isn't good for children to be praised for something they had no hand in creating. I was luckier. I got attention for doing well in school and being responsible. Which at least was something I did myself."

It was the most personal speech he'd heard her make. Clearly, this was something she'd spent a lot of time thinking about. "Where do your parents live?" he asked.

"Oh, they've both passed away now," she answered matter-of-factly. "It's just my sister, my younger brother, and me. That's my family. What about you? I know you have your mother, unless you made her up," she told him sternly.

"I'm sorry," he said. "About your parents. Mine are both very much alive. They live in Te Kuiti, a few hours south of Auckland. Farming country. That's where I grew up. I have a younger brother too, but he's in Wellington, the capital. He's a doctor, works in the emergency room. Pillar of the community."

"Hmmm," she teased. "He's a pillar of the community, and you're a lightweight playboy, right? Somehow I don't think so. Even if you *are* a rugby player. You strike me as a pretty responsible guy."

"I do my bit," he admitted. "But I'm not saving any lives."

"May I remind you," she pointed out, "that you saved mine yesterday? So I don't think you can say that anymore. You're going to have to accept being a hero yourself."

He winced a bit at that, and was grateful when she saw it and hastened to change the subject.

"I hope you brought something to eat in that bag," she told him. "Seeing the size of the breakfast you had yesterday, I'm guessing the answer is yes. I'm thinking all that in *The Lord of the Rings* about breakfast and second breakfast, not to mention afternoon tea, was a New Zealand addition."

"Luckily, you happen to be correct," he answered, pulling a small cooler from one of the boat's compartments. "On both counts, I reckon." He poured more coffee for them both, and offered her a small pie. At her questioning look, he laughed. "Yet another Kiwi invention, I'm afraid, designed to put the kilos on. Bacon and egg pie."

"Bacon and egg *pie?*" she responded faintly. "So bacon and eggs aren't enough, are they? You have to cook them in dough, too? I've heard of bacon doughnuts. I thought *that* was bad."

"Try it," he urged. "And you'll be converted. It's a religious experience, bacon and egg pie."

"It is," she exclaimed in surprise after her first bite of eggs, onions, and slices of meaty New Zealand bacon baked in flaky pastry. "Though this is definitely another pound added to the cruise ship total."

They ate apples and tiny, seedless tangerines with their pies, chatting easily now about his family and her brother and sister. He laughed at her stories about her brother Matt's peripatetic lifestyle, working just enough to save the money to travel, and then jumping off to yet another destination, where he lived on his wits, as often as not.

"I think his ambition is to visit every single country," she told him. "And he doesn't exactly do it in style. I found out later that he ran out of money in Spain, and spent the evenings playing poker in order to eat the next day. He won, too," she said a little proudly. "Good to know his education wasn't wasted. His college degree is in math. I'll admit, I'm looking forward to seeing him use it for something besides poker, instead of working as a bell-man and valet parker in hotels. But he says the tips are good and he's doing what he wants. And it's his life, I know."

Drew looked at her quizzically. "You sound almost like a mother when you talk about your brother and sister. Why is that?"

"Wow. You're good. You got that pretty fast, didn't you? I'm sorry, am I over-sharing? You don't really want to hear all this, I'm sure."

"Yeh, I do," he insisted. "I'm intrigued. You're young, you're pretty, but you don't seem like the other pretty young women I meet. And I'm wondering why."

"Well, thanks for that. I think. I guess it's because my father died when I was twelve. And my mother…didn't handle it well. Oh, she didn't drink, or abuse us, or anything like that. She just…gave up. She wasn't really equipped to handle life on her own. So she kind of checked out, and we had to do it ourselves, I suppose. Raise ourselves. Which makes you grow up faster. But we managed," she finished brightly, "so this story has a happy ending."

"I'm guessing," he said slowly, "that what you mean is, *you* managed. Raised your brother and sister. And took care of your mother too, I reckon."

"As much as I could," she admitted. "But I'm not complaining. I was lucky. I was able to do it, most of it, anyway, and everyone turned out more or less OK. Except my mother. She wasn't…I couldn't really do too much about that. But I found out at a young age that I could do a lot, even if things seemed hard. I hire a fair number of young people, and I can tell you, a lot of them don't seem to know that. They don't get that they can put their minds to a problem and solve it, that they can shape their futures. They get carried along by the tide, like somebody else is in charge of their life. I know I'm in charge of my life. So I'm lucky," she said again.

Privately, Drew thought that she had been anything but lucky. But he admired her determinedly positive attitude and her obvious work ethic.

He turned the conversation himself, then, and they chatted more lightly as they packed up the remains of their lunch and prepared to depart. She disappeared into the cabin to put on her coverup for the ride home, and though he was disappointed at the loss of the picture she made in that orange costume—tangerine, he reminded himself with a grin—he liked the look of her in any-thing. Or in nothing, he thought again. Especially in nothing.

"I have a commitment in Auckland tomorrow," he told her when he had docked at the marina and they were back in the ute again. "But I'll be here the next day. Can I take you to dinner?"

"Sure. I'll be here four more days, and I'd like that."

He frowned. "Where are you off to next?"

"Rotorua. Not sure I'm pronouncing it right. That seems to be someplace I need to visit. Where they have the geothermal area. But I wanted a week here first. My beach vacation."

"Yeh," he smiled. "I know Rotorua a bit. I'll pick you up at seven-thirty, then, day after tomorrow."

"What should I wear?"

"Noplace too posh on the Coromandel. What you had on yesterday was good."

"Good to know. I'll look forward to it. And thank you for today. I loved it. That was one of the best adventures I've ever had."

"Led an exciting life, have you?" he asked dryly.

"Not so much," she admitted. "Making up for it a bit now, I guess. Almost drowning yesterday, and going for my first snorkel today."

"Glad to help with your adventures," he assured her as he pulled up to her motel.

By the time he came around to help her out of the tall vehi-cle, she had already opened the door and hopped down.

"You're disappointing my mum again," he sighed. "Here I was, ready to show you my manners, and you didn't give me the chance."

"Tell your mother I'm very impressed, so far. And thanks again," she said as she turned at her motel door.

And that's as far as you're getting today, boy, he told himself. Never mind, he had a fair bit of determination. And every inten-tion of using it.

"I'll see you day after tomorrow, then." He took her by the shoulders and kissed her gently, his mouth moving over hers, keeping it soft. And felt the zing of the contact straight down to his groin. Oh, yes. There was chemistry there, no worries.

He stepped back and saw her smiling up at him, pulled her closer, and kissed her again with a bit more heat, giving into temptation and letting his tongue briefly touch the deep bow of her upper lip. He'd been staring at that bow all day, and he was only human, after all. He let her go at last, and watched as she unlocked her door and stepped inside.

Four more days. Good as gold.

chapter five

♡

Despite two perfectly enjoyable days on her own, Hannah found to her annoyance that she was looking forward with eager anticipation to her date, and taking far more care than usual in getting ready. Choosing the dress was simple enough—the only other one she had brought with her. She thought ruefully that after tonight, Drew would have seen pretty much her entire wardrobe.

Well, this would be their second date. No, third, if you counted the charity breakfast after he had rescued her. And given her recent track record, the third time was likely to be not the charm, but the end. Because no matter how tempted she was, she wasn't going to bed with someone she had met three days ago. If he were like most men she'd known, buying her two meals (and a bacon-and-egg pie, she reminded herself) would be about as far as he'd be willing to go without a return on his investment.

This was why she didn't date more. Oh, well. At least she'd get to look at him for another evening. She'd have bought *him* dinner for that.

Right on time, she heard the knock on the door, and opened it to find him looking just as good as she remembered, in gray slacks and a black polo shirt that did nothing to hide his biceps. She sighed with pleasure. *Works for me,* she thought happily.

When he leaned in for a kiss hello, she couldn't resist putting her hands on his forearms to feel those muscles for herself. They felt even better than they looked, warm and solid, with all kinds of interesting dips and bulges. Before she could stop them, her hands were sliding up his arms for the pleasure of touching the swell of his biceps.

Good arms, she thought hazily. *Very good arms.*

She gave herself a mental shake and pulled back. Well, *that* was classy. Jumping him as soon as he opened the door.

No holiday flings. But the sensible voice was getting fainter all the time.

♡

The drive to the restaurant was quick—which was probably a good thing, Drew admitted to himself. Her legs looked too good in that short dress, and the view as she'd hopped up into the tall vehicle hadn't been bad either. After that kiss, the last thing he needed, if he were going to spend a civilized evening wooing her over dinner, was to spend a long drive looking at her legs.

She had worn her hair down, he saw with pleasure, pulled away from her face in some sort of complicated braid and then curling down her back, and it looked even better tonight. He'd had to juggle his appointments to fit them into a single day, but he hadn't wanted to wait to see her again. And now that he *had* seen her, and touched her, he was glad he'd made the effort.

She'd been bang on time, too. No waiting about. For such an attractive woman, she was surprisingly open and easy to be with. He began to think he would enjoy the evening even if it didn't end the way he hoped. No question, he wanted to see her naked tonight. But looking at her wasn't bad anyway, even with her clothes on.

"I hope you fancy fish tonight," he said as they pulled up outside a charming restaurant set in a garden of ferns and flowering plants. "I forgot to ask."

"I love it," she assured him. "I don't go out to dinner that much anyway, except the occasional hotel restaurant at some trade show, so this is a real treat."

He was laughing as he came around the truck to help her down, holding her hand as she swung out. "You are the most surprising girl. You aren't supposed to tell me that. Didn't your mother teach you anything?"

He sobered, remembering that her mother probably *hadn't* taught her anything about dating. "Sorry," he amended. "But I've never had a woman tell me she doesn't get out much. Reckon they'd like you to think they're in high demand."

"Oh." She offered a rueful smile and a shrug. "I work too much. At least that's what my friends tell me."

As they entered the restaurant, Drew nodded to the smiling young woman who hurried to greet them, welcoming him by name. Several other staff members and a number of customers turned to watch them as their hostess led the way to a corner table, and a waiter pulled out a mobile phone to snap a quick picture.

When they were seated, Hannah leaned forward and told him quietly, "That guy just took your picture."

"I mentioned I was a rugby player, eh. Part of the job. Some people know my face. And these days, people see anything, they take a photo."

She gave him a searching look. "That's so true," she said at last. "I went for a long hike today by the ocean. I couldn't believe how many pictures people take. Whenever I came across some-one at a spot where there was a good view, they'd just, boom, take a picture or two and move on. Instead of looking, I mean."

They were interrupted by two young men bearing napkins and pens, asking for autographs. Drew signed good-naturedly, but turned away with a firm "Cheers," leaving them with no choice but to return to their seats.

"It's a scenic country," he continued, as if the interruption had never occurred. "Everyone wants to post their photos and show their friends back home."

To his relief, she clearly sensed his desire to ignore the attention he had attracted. "But how exciting is it, really, to look at somebody's pictures?" she asked. "That's what I was wondering. How interesting is it to see somebody in front of a fern tree? And then in front of an ocean view? And then in front of a rock?"

He smiled. "Reckon they don't think they've been on holiday if they don't have the photos to prove it. But I'm more like you. I'd rather just look. People talk too much too, don't they?"

"Yes!" she agreed. "Exactly! They pull up in their car, walk onto the beach, talk to each other about it, take pictures, and then drive away! What's the point of coming to New Zealand if you aren't going to walk, or swim, or kayak, or *something?*"

"On behalf of my country," he said solemnly, "I have to be grateful for every tourist who comes here, however they want to enjoy themselves. Maybe," he teased, "they've heard it's easy to drown here."

"You aren't supposed to keep reminding me," she told him loftily. "I've moved beyond that. I asked about safe swimming beaches and am now fully informed. In fact, I went for a swim this morning at one of them."

"You need to be careful, still," he warned. "Especially swimming alone."

"Duly noted. I swam parallel to shore, and stayed close. Believe me, I've learned my lesson. I can't always count on a handsome prince to rescue me. I'm trying my best not to be a damsel in distress anymore."

At his suggestion, she ordered the snapper, which came fileted and pan-fried, crispy and delicious. She exclaimed, and he nodded.

"Heaps of snapper in Waitemata Harbour, too, in Auckland. You can stand right on a dock or a bridge and catch them in summer."

"Is the water clean enough, then, that there are so many fish right there by the city?"

"Not perfect yet, but yeh, not too bad. Nothing like pulling a big snapper out of the water and filleting it for your tea. That's what the North Island is supposed to be, you know."

"What? Your tea?" she asked, confused.

He laughed. "Nah. A fish, hauled from the sea by Maūi. He used blood from his nose for bait, and a bit of his grandmother's jawbone for a hook." He chuckled again at her expression. "His brothers mutilated the fish after he caught it. That's why the surface is rough and the shape is so flattened. When you look at a map, you can see it. Lake Taupo is the eye. The Maori name for the North Island is Te Ika a Maūi, the fish of Maūi."

"That's quite a legend. How did you know that?"

"Everyone knows that. The South Island is Te Waka a Maūi—the canoe of Maūi. And Stewart Island, at the bottom of the country, is Te Punga a Maūi—the fishhook of Maūi. Have a look at the map, and you'll see it."

"You pronounce the names so easily," she wondered. "And some of them seem quite long and complex. Do you learn these things in school?"

"It's a bicultural society. A fair few Kiwis have some Maori blood. Loads of intermarriage over the years. And the Maori language, the songs, the legends—they're part of our heritage, even for Pakeha—for Europeans, like me. If you'd ever watched any New Zealand sport, you'd know that we sing our anthem in Maori first, then English. And don't tell me you've never heard of the haka."

"No idea. What is it?"

"You'll see, when you go to Rotorua. It's a chant, a challenge. A bit hard to explain. One of En Zed's most famous exports, along with kiwifruit and wool."

"And rugby," she reminded him.

"That too," he agreed. "We like to think so, anyway."

"I had no idea," she repeated. "I'd like to learn more about it, though."

"Well, Rotorua's the place for that." But he frowned as he spoke. "When do you leave?"

"On Tuesday. Three days from now."

"Not much time. Are you busy tomorrow?"

"I hadn't decided yet. I'm trying to take a break from planning too much on this trip. I do a lot of that. Planning."

"Why don't you let me take you tramping, then? Since I know you won't snap photos all day, or natter about the views."

"You mean hiking? Are you sure? Isn't this supposed to be your fishing vacation?"

"I'm sure. I can fish any day. Not many beautiful women want to go tramping with me, though."

"Then yes, I'd love to go. I like to walk more than anything, in beautiful places," she confided. "Except maybe swimming. And walking is much safer, isn't it?"

"Long as you don't fall off the track. Reckon I'd better be there, just in case."

♡

After dinner, Drew suggested a walk on the beach, and Hannah gladly accepted. Her tension returned, though, as they left the restaurant—getting his picture taken again in the process, she noticed. She was ridiculously attracted to him, but reminded herself how awkward she would feel afterwards, sleeping with someone she had just met. She had tried it once during her college years, and still winced at the result. The guy hadn't called again, and when she'd seen him later on campus, she'd wanted to hide. After that, she had become even more guarded. She just didn't seem to have the casual sex gene.

If Drew wanted to take her to dinner, it would have to be for the pleasure of her company, she told herself firmly. And if he didn't want to see her again because of that—well, who knew if he'd want to see her again if she *did* sleep with him? She wasn't sure she'd be much good at it anyway, after this long.

She pushed the thought from her head and focused on the sights and sounds of the ocean at night as they walked down wooden steps onto the long beach stretching to either side beneath the restaurant. She shivered a little in the breeze, and Drew turned to her.

"Too cold?"

"No, I brought a sweater," she told him as she pulled it out of her bag.

He took the cardigan and held it for her to pull on, then took her hand as they continued to walk. The heavy, rhythmic swish of the waves approaching the shore, the steady pace, his warm hand around hers began to relax her, and she sighed with enjoyment.

She smiled. "It's like a personals ad, do you realize?"

"Pardon?"

"You know. I love a glass of wine and moonlit walks on the beach."

He laughed. "We aim to please." He turned and pulled her in to him, put his hands on either side of her face, then just stood and looked at her, her eyes raised to his.

"I love your mouth," he told her. "This little bow on your top lip." He traced the shape of that protruding bow lightly with his tongue. "Been wanting to do this all night."

His mouth closed over hers, gently at first. She sighed and moved further into his arms. He smiled down at her, then kissed her again, his hands cradling her head, his mouth moving over hers as her arms crept up to hold his shoulders. He felt her slide her hands down his back, and reached out to pull her closer.

He'd been waiting to do this all evening. Watching her mouth as she talked and ate, looking at her smooth, untanned skin and her slender hands. Wanting to feel that skin under his hands, his mouth. Wanting to feel her hands on him. He ran his own hands down her sides to her waist, held her there. And kept kissing her, until he had to have more. He pulled back, looked around for the bench he remembered, pulled her into his lap.

"I'm too heavy," she protested. "You don't want me here."

He settled her more comfortably, his hands on her hips. "Oh, I want you here. I couldn't want you here much more. Can't you tell?"

She was blushing again, he knew, even if he couldn't see her in the dark. "It's all right," he reassured her. "Let me hold you."

Hannah felt herself melting against him as he kissed her again, pulling her hair back from her neck to run his hand down her back. She shivered as his lips moved to trace the line of her jaw, down to kiss the sensitive spot under her earlobe, then further down her neck, felt a rush of sensation as his hand slid down to cup her knee, then ran slowly up her thigh.

His thumb reached around to stroke her inner thigh, and she squirmed a little against him as a moan escaped her. The hand on her leg held her, thumb stroking, while his other hand moved to find her breast, and he took her mouth again in a deep kiss. She gasped into his mouth, his hands burning her where they touched her, her body straining towards him.

"You feel so good," he muttered at last. "Let's get out of here, eh."

She came back to herself, pulled the ragged remnants of her self-control around her. "I can't. It's too soon for me. I can't do this, not now."

She pulled away to slide down next to him on the bench, hugging her arms around herself in distress. "I'm sorry. I'm not good at this casual thing."

He leaned his head back, took a deep breath. "Right. I'll take you home, then, shall I?"

She nodded miserably. She wasn't sure if she was being smart, or making a big mistake.

"Oi." He put his hand under her chin to turn her face to his. "It's all right. Your choice. Wouldn't have been mine," he grinned ruefully, "but we can't always get what we want, can we." He reached for her, kissed her gently. "Come on, let's get you home. Before my good intentions desert me."

She laughed a little shakily. "Before mine do, more like." She let him pull her to her feet and walked with him, her hand in his, back to the truck.

He helped her up, then swung around into his own seat for the short drive back to the motel.

"It's OK if you don't want to take me tomorrow," she ventured. "I'm guessing here that women don't say no to you very often."

"Probably good for me. But why wouldn't I want to take you tramping tomorrow? I'll admit, I'd rather take you back to my bach tonight—my house. But I'm patient. I'll let you get to know me a bit better, see if you can resist my charm."

"I can barely resist it tonight," she admitted. "Just…just let me be sure, OK?"

"I can do that," he agreed.

But he reckoned he was allowed to kiss her a few dozen times more, give her something to think about overnight.

chapter six

♡

It was hours before Hannah slept that night. Her dreams were erotic, full of images that embarrassed her to remember when she woke. She admitted to herself that her body was pulling her in one direction, while her sensible brain gave exactly contrary advice.

It was a good thing they were going on a hike today, she thought as she pulled on shorts, boots, and a collared shirt to protect her skin from the intense Southern Hemisphere sun. She wanted more time with Drew before she made any moves she might regret.

Well, to be honest, she simply wanted more time with him. Maybe he was only looking for another notch in his bedpost before moving on, but at least she'd get a better idea of whether it would be worth it. She was moving on too, she reminded herself, the day after tomorrow. And felt a pang at the thought.

Nothing sexual about hiking, anyway, she thought with a mixture of relief and regret. Today should give her a chance to get to know Drew in a less charged situation. If she weren't looking at his bare chest all day, it would be a lot easier to make a rational decision she could live with afterwards.

But when she opened the door to his knock, she was forced to amend her opinion. He stood smiling at her, filling the doorframe.

Arms, chest, thighs, check, she sighed as she looked up at him. Why couldn't he have just a little bit of a pot belly?

"Morning. Glad to see you're ready to go. Bang on time, like always," he said, giving her a kiss that did nothing for her good intentions. Especially as she couldn't resist sliding her hands up his upper arms to his shoulders for the pure pleasure of holding onto them again. Which made him shift his weight, put his hands on her waist to pull her in closer, and kiss her just a little bit more.

"Sure you want to do this walk?" he said at last, with a devilish grin. "I'm feeling a bit tired. Maybe we could think of something else to do instead."

She laughed. "You said you were taking me on this thing. I think I'd better hold you to it. And I don't believe you're a bit tired."

"I don't know. Didn't sleep so well last night. Something missing. How did you sleep?"

She turned red, cursed her fair skin yet again. "Not so well myself. Let's go on this hike, OK?"

♡

"I meant to ask you," she said once they were on their way. "The morning paper had some stories about rugby games. I'm confused. I thought the season was over. Why are there still professional rugby games going on?"

"That's Sevens, not Union." Seeing her bewilderment, he went on to explain. "Different version of the sport."

"So there are two different kinds of professional rugby, and they're both played in New Zealand? That seems like a lot of rugby, especially for such a small country. Do people watch both?"

He laughed. "I haven't even mentioned League, have I. Never mind. Can't have too much rugby. Not in En Zed. It's our national sport. Maybe our national religion. They play both League and Union in Aussie, too, though. Of course, we think we play the real rugby—Union. League players will tell you their version is better, faster. They'll try to tell you it's tougher, too. But we may have a wee bit to say about that."

"I guess I'll have to watch some games and judge for myself," she decided. "I have a feeling, though, that it's all going to seem tough to me. It's about tackling, right? And being in that big ball of people, pushing on each other?"

"Yeh," he responded, hugely amused. "You could say it's about tackling. The 'big ball' is the scrum—the way we restart play. Each team tries to move the other backward, while the team in possession tosses the ball in. It's a bit of a physical contest. There are heaps of rules about the scrum, but that's as much as you'll want to know. Are you keen on sport?"

"Not exactly. I told you I used to watch football with my father sometimes. But I never knew much about it. I watched because he liked to, and I liked to be with him. But I felt sorry for the losers. They always looked so sad."

"You're right about that. Nobody likes to lose. That's what makes you bust a gut, though, to keep it from happening. And not to let your mates down, of course."

"I suppose it's not that different from anything else," she mused. "Just more straightforward. There are lots of times when I don't feel like making the extra effort at work. I guess I go ahead because I don't want to fall down on the job. Or to let people down. If I don't do it, somebody else will just have to pick up the slack."

He nodded. "Not so different."

"Of course," she added, "nobody's trying to beat me up. There is that. I think I'd give up pretty fast if someone came flying out of the copy room and tackled me while I was trying to finish my budget."

"Could be. We'll hope you're not put to the test. Tell me about what you do, then."

"I'm not sure that's much more interesting than the rules of the scrum. But I work for a women's fitness company. We sell workout clothing—running, swimming, bicycling. Plus general workout gear, and casual clothes for active women. Everything I'm wearing today came from our stock."

"Seems like a good fit for you. You're quite keen, I've seen that. Like I said, I've never taken a woman tramping before. And here we are," he announced as they pulled into the almost-deserted parking area near a marked trailhead. "The Pinnacles. It's quite a walk. We don't have to do the last bit, if you'd rather not."

"Sounds ominous. I'll see how it goes. If I'm too slow for you, you can always go on ahead of me and wait."

He smiled and helped her out of the truck. "That *would* be heaps of fun, but I already did my training this morning. Reckon I'll stick with you."

As they started up the wooded track, lush with ferns and palms, Hannah thought about what he had said. "But you picked me up at eight today. What kind of workout did you do before that? Didn't you say you were on vacation?"

"Can't afford to get soft. Doesn't matter what time of year it is, have to keep fit. Nothing too much, though. Just running, this morning."

"I can see there's a real danger of your getting soft," she said dryly. "You'd better work on that."

Walking behind him on the narrow track, she couldn't see anything wrong with his condition. Nothing at all, she decided, eyeing his impossibly broad shoulders and powerful thighs appreciatively.

"Enjoying the view?" he asked, as he waited for her to come up next to him.

She gave a start and blushed. "Yes! It's beautiful. Thanks."

He looked at her curiously, and slowly smiled. "Good. Let's keep on, then."

♡

Good to know, he told himself. She was worth the wait, he was beginning to be sure of it. And unless he missed his guess, the wait was going to be over soon. Which was a good thing. Anticipation was one thing, and he was enjoying it—to a point. But he was more than ready to move on.

She looked so bloody cute in her hiking shorts and boots, with a cap perched on her blonde head. He enjoyed talking to her, too. Being with her. She was interested in everything, full of enjoyment for every new experience. He liked her honesty and her teasing sense of humor. But most of all, he liked her body. And he wanted to see it all. In all sorts of ways. For a long, long time.

"Tell me more about what you do," he said, after they had negotiated a narrow swing bridge and were headed up the track again, the river running beside them, vines twining among trees above the moss-covered banks. "At that fitness company of yours. Besides wear their clothes so well."

"I'm the Sales and Marketing Director. Which means I do a little of everything, I suppose, except the Operations side. The warehouse, Customer Service, accounting, things like that. And I'm not in charge of the actual product selection. I work on that in collaboration with our Product Director. There's always something new to learn, something different to do. That's what I like about it."

"Aren't you too young, though," he asked, taken aback, "to have a job like that?"

"I'm lucky to work for someone who's always willing to give me more responsibility. My boss isn't very hands-on. We like that, though. We have a great team, lots of talented people. It's not like I have to know how to do every job best, or have all the good ideas. All I have to do is recognize other people's strengths and help them work together so the best ideas get out there."

Nothing easy about that, he knew. That was always the challenge, and not everyone was up to it. "How's the company doing, then?"

"Really well, actually. We've been growing every year, both in sales and staff. I like knowing I'm helping women be active. No trophies, I'm afraid, or anyone to cheer for us, but I love getting letters from women, and choosing pictures of real women wearing our clothes for the catalog. Women who are doing all sorts of amazing things. They inspire me."

"Sounds like you have a bit of pressure on you, though. Good for you to get away, I reckon. What made you come on this trip alone? I'm surprised you didn't bring someone with you. That you aren't with someone, as pretty as you are."

"I could say the same thing. Not that you're exactly pretty. But why are *you* here alone? There isn't somebody back home, is there?" she asked in sudden alarm. "You aren't married, or in a relationship with somebody?"

"Hang on." He held up both hands in protest. "How did this get to be about me? Nah, I'm not married. Not living with anyone. Not with anyone. Single and available. What about you? Bit of a holiday away from your partner?"

He laughed at her shocked expression. "Never mind. I may not know you very well yet, but I can tell you're not the type."

"Let's hope not. No, nobody at home waiting for me. And as for a friend to come with me—a *female* friend, I could have worked that out, I suppose. But I wanted to come here by myself. I've never had much time alone, to do what I wanted to do. I haven't had any adventures at all, really. It's so nice," she smiled happily, "and I'm only a week into it. No schedules, no plans. Bliss."

"And now you've almost drowned, and snorkeled through a sea cave," he agreed. "Up here, we're going to have another adventure, if you're ready."

She looked in the direction he pointed. The path wound steeply up a rock-strewn slope to where, far above, jagged rocks thrust against the sky.

"This is where you tell me if you want to turn around," he said seriously. "You can see why they call it The Pinnacles."

"Is it safe?" she asked doubtfully.

"All steps, and ladders, and handholds," he reassured her. "More of a physical challenge. Stamina. I'll watch you, no worries. Somebody counted, I heard, and found there are more than Five hundred steps. What do you think?"

"Five hundred steps. How can I resist? Although now I'm going to feel I have to count them all."

♡

They set off on the steep ascent. The wind was stronger up here, threatening to take the cap from Hannah's head and blowing her shirt against her body. And he was right, there were a lot of steps. A whole lot of them. After the fourth or fifth long flight, she found herself slowing down to maintain her stamina for the long trek.

"Why don't you walk ahead of me?" Drew suggested. "I'll match your pace. Take your time."

After a few more flights, though, she stopped and told him, "I think you should go ahead."

"Why?" he objected. "You're doing fine."

"Because," she said in exasperation. "I don't want you walking up all those steps behind me, looking at my rear end. I know it's big, OK? I don't want you getting that view, and thinking how I should be working on that."

He burst out laughing and pulled her to him. "Sweetheart," he said, still grinning, "who says it's big?"

"It's been mentioned," she answered stiffly. "I'm not one of those skinny girls. I know that. Nobody's going to ask me to model on the catwalk. But I'm strong." She glared at him. "And this is what I have."

"And I love it. Whoever told you your bum was too big was mad. Your bum," he said seriously, running his hands down her back and then, slowly, onto the offending body part, "is perfect. Absolutely perfect," he murmured as he bent to kiss her.

She wrapped her arms around him and returned the kiss, rising up onto her toes on the open track. As his mouth moved over hers, her hands went of their own volition around the back of his neck, pulling his head down to hers, rubbing over the corded muscle at the side of his neck, and then sliding down over his broad back. Her hands settled on either side of his spine, where her fingers felt the ridge of muscle rising strongly on either side.

In response, he kissed her again, harder and more hungrily, his hands moving up and down her lower back, then moving lower, pulling her closer.

Voices from above brought him back to himself. *Good choice of a spot, mate,* he told himself disgustedly. Here they were, hours from the trailhead, and all he could think about was making love to her.

He lifted his mouth from hers with regret. "Someone's coming," he told her gently as he set her away from him.

She blinked up at him, a little dazed. "Oh!" She came back to herself with a visible effort. "All right." She pulled her shirt down around her where it had pulled up over her belly, and gave herself a little shake. "Phew. So." She grinned at him. "Not too big after all, huh?"

He laughed back at her as they stood aside to let another couple pass on their way down the stairs.

"Whoever decided that women should have a flat bum?" he wondered aloud once the coast was clear. "No man, I'll tell you that. We like something to hold onto back there," he teased. "I'll have to study it more to be sure, but based on a quick check, yours is just right. Round. Fit. But if you'll walk in front of me a bit longer, I'll let you know if it's as good as I think it is."

"What an offer," she complained. "I'm all self-conscious now." And in fact, as she set off up the steps again, she *was* self-conscious, feeling his eyes on her. Knowing he liked what he saw sent a tingle through her.

She felt as though he were still touching her as they continued to climb. They didn't talk now, just walked steadily up. Steps, then more steps, until a long ladder bolted directly into the vertical wall loomed in front of her. She swallowed as she looked up, to a series of ladders amidst the rock above.

"I've got you," he said behind her, reaching to pull her against him. "But if you want to turn around and go back down, we can do that instead. In fact, that may not be a bad idea. I'm beginning to think this whole tramp was a mistake anyway. Take us too long to get back from here."

She turned in his arms and looked at him. "I want to go to the top, though. I want to stand right out on the edge with you."

His eyes kindled as he looked back at her. "Reckon we'd better get on, then. Because I want to be on the edge with you, too."

She turned back to the ladder, a surge of power coursing through her. She wanted this, and she was going to take it. But first, she was getting to the top of this thing. She was going to look out over the world from the top, and know she had climbed there.

On and on, up and up. The ladders gave way to single metal rungs bolted into the rock, and scrambles up the steep slope. Drew was there behind her, a steadying hand and an encouraging word, as he negotiated the difficult path with ease. Her breath came harder as the track grew more vertical, but she focused on pushing up. On not looking down, as she pulled up from rung to rung over a sheer face.

She pulled herself at last up a final ledge, around a final corner, and suddenly found the concrete viewing platform in front of her, as far as they could climb. A wall of rock on one side, a simple metal guardrail on the other, with just enough room for a few people. And all around her, sweeping views of rugged hills, jagged rocks, and far away, the sea.

She had done it. She had never loved heights, but she had climbed all the way up here, and now she was at the top. She stood, proud and happy, embracing the fierce wind that blew harder up here, on the exposed heights. She wanted to feel more of that. She wanted to be wild, fierce as the wind. She pulled off her hat, yanked out the band holding her braid, and shook out her hair. And laughed, exultant, as the mass of fine strands rose around her, whipping in the wind.

She turned to Drew. "Isn't it great?" she exulted. "I did it!"

His gray eyes burned into hers as he began to smile. "Yes, you did. You did. And you're beautiful."

She came to him, wrapped her arms around him, pulled him down for a kiss. "Then show me," she urged him. "I can't be smart any more. I'm done."

She didn't need to tell him twice. His arms tightened around her, and he brought his mouth down on hers in a fierce kiss that started out hot, and quickly ignited. He pulled her off her feet, and her legs wrapped around him. He held her there with one powerful arm while the other pulled her hair back so he could reach her neck.

He kissed her there, licked her, pulled her head back gently by the fistful of hair he held to reach the hollow of her throat, and moved on to graze the delicate skin where her neck met her collarbone. His arm beneath her pulled her more strongly against him as he turned her, pressing her against the cliff behind them. The rock was hard against her back as he pushed into her, his hand moving behind her head to cushion her skull. His mouth moved back to hers, feverish now, desperate to taste all of her.

She gasped at the feeling of his mouth, his body, against hers. Reached under his T-shirt, hungry to feel his skin at last against her eager hands. Up from his waist, over the ridges of his back, the skin smooth over the shifting bands of muscle beneath.

Around to his sides then. But it wasn't enough. She wanted more of him. She wanted to be able to see him, and taste him.

He pulled back at last, breathing hard, holding her to him. "We have to get out of here," he groaned. "We can't do this here. Someone else could come up at any time. And I'm not going to have you the first time against the wall. We have to get out of here," he repeated. He set her down gently as her legs trembled beneath her, steadied her against him. "When you finally decide, you don't muck about, do you?" He sounded a little shaky himself as he pulled her hair back from around her face and smoothed her clothes into place. "How fast can you walk, downhill?"

"Fast," she assured him, reluctantly taking her hands off him. "So fast."

"Let's go, then," he urged, as she pulled her hair back into a haphazard ponytail and tied it with her bandana, taming it with difficulty as the wind continued to whip around them. Taking her by the hand, he pulled her toward the start of the trail.

They must have set a record for the return journey, Hannah thought. She wasn't aware of being tired or of the distance. She just wanted to get to the bottom again. To be with him at last. To go someplace where they could shut the door and she could see all of him. Could have all of him. She shivered as she raced along with him, holding hands where the path was wide enough.

You bloody fool, Drew was cursing himself. Whose idea was it to take a woman on an hours-long tramp to the top of a mountain? A woman he couldn't wait to get his hands on? He couldn't have gone any further with her without losing control of himself. And they had met other people throughout the afternoon. No matter how much he wanted her, he wasn't going to risk exposing her like that. But he couldn't wait much longer.

When they finally made it back to the truck, they looked at each other, her chest rising and falling with her panting breath. He pulled her into him and kissed her, more gently this time.

"I want to take you somewhere. I need to take you some-where," he amended. "Take off your boots and get in the ute." He pulled off his own boots and socks as she did the same.

"Why am I taking off my boots?" she asked as he started the truck and headed downhill. "Getting naked bit by bit?"

"That's the idea. You can take all your clothes off now, if you like. But I thought you could start with the boots. Save me some time."

He was driving as quickly as he dared on the twisting gravel road, taking the curves with practiced skill. "We'll stop at a motel," he told her. "Are you good with this?"

She nodded, turned in her seat so she could look at him, one leg tucked under her. "I'm sure. But...I'm all sweaty. Shouldn't I go home first and take a shower?"

He laughed. "Oh, we can take a shower. Later. Good idea. Water. And soap. But you're having me, sweat and all, first."

The words sent another thrill through her. She watched him as he drove, as he pulled into the little town at the base of the mountain at last, and into the drive of a tidy motel.

"Wait in the ute," he ordered. "Don't get out."

He was back within a few minutes with a key, ready to move the truck again.

"Why wasn't I supposed to get out?" she asked, puzzled.

He looked at her, frowning. "You don't want people to see you with me, checking into a motel in the middle of the after-noon. Nobody needs to see that photo."

She was still mystified. Who would there be to take their picture? But she couldn't bring herself to give much attention to the issue, as he was pulling up to one of the simple units, leaping out, and coming around to pull her down with him and through the front door.

chapter seven

♡

Drew slammed the motel door shut behind the two of them, pulling her into his arms even as he did, the key dropping unnoticed to the floor. He pulled the bandana from her hair and threaded his hands through, around her face, kissing her again, walking her backwards until her thighs hit the bed and she sat down suddenly, jolted by the sudden change.

He followed her down onto the big bed, pulling her with him so they both lay sprawled across the duvet. His hands were everywhere, unbuttoning, pulling her blouse from around her and lifting her to take it from her body and drop it over the side of the bed. Then his hand was on the button of her khaki shorts, and he was pulling them over her hips and throwing them where they joined her blouse, disregarded on the rug where they fell.

He pulled back then, looked at her as she lay beneath him, dressed only in bra and panties, her hair streaming around her, behind her, her eyes huge and focused only on him, her lips parted, her breath coming fast now.

Slow down, mate, he told himself. *Slow down and make it good for her.*

But she was pulling at him, reaching to wrench his shirt from his body and run her hands over his chest, his arms, his back, and his resolve was gone, replaced by need alone. She wasn't naked yet, and he needed her to be. He reached for the fastening of her bra, looked at the pink and white of her, had to touch her. To taste her.

He moved down to taste the salt of her breasts against him, pulling one nipple into his mouth as she cried out with pleasure. He licked, bit, sucked, and felt her moving against him, heard her cries as she held his head against her. His hands went lower, wrenched off the panties, and then he was holding her, cupping her against his big hand and feeling the warmth of her against him.

Needing to see all of her, he pulled back and looked. And stared. Her body was all white, rose, gold, the brown of his hand against her where her legs met, against the white of her flat stomach, her hips, her thighs. He moved his hand again, heard her gasp, felt his own heartbeat quicken in response to her movements as she bucked against him.

He needed to see more of her. He moved down her body, gently moving her legs apart and looking at that most secret part of her as she lay beneath him, clutching at him, moving her hands over his shoulders and back. He dropped down, just to touch her, to kiss her, there where she was so open and vulnerable.

Hannah felt as if she were in an electric field. A lightning storm. The feelings were too much, too intense. She wanted him so much, she was about to dissolve. His mouth on her was shockingly warm, electrically hot, taking her spiraling up, up, out of control. Sensation filled her, and she grabbed him by the hair, holding him against her, needing more of him.

Just as she felt she was about to lose control, to go over the top, she knew she needed more. She needed everything. She tugged at his shoulders, pulled him up to her.

"Take these off. Please. I need to see you too." She yanked at his belt and shorts, clumsy in her haste. He helped her, pulling shorts and underwear off in one swift toss, so he was finally hers to hold.

There was a lot there to hold, she realized. She touched him, held him, stroked where he was hard against her. Then reached around to hold him from behind, pull him onto her, frantic to feel him with her, inside her.

"Wait," he gasped. "Condom. Shit." He dove from the bed and turned out the pockets of his shorts, frantically searching. After what seemed like forever, he was back with her, pulling her up with him toward the head of the bed.

"Please. Now." She opened to him, pulled him to her, and urged him to go where he needed to be.

He held back, one last bit of self-control, not wanting to go too fast, to hurt her. He eased inside as she stretched to receive him, gasping and opening her eyes wide as he filled her.

"That feels...so *good*," she moaned as he began to move inside her. "Oh, Drew. Oh, no."

He didn't answer. He couldn't, as he found himself, at last, inside her where he had wanted to be for so long. And slowed his pace. It felt too good to rush, now. He had to feel the silk of her, pull back to look at her beneath him, head back, eyes closed, her mouth just open, sighing. Her hips against him, moving, drawing him into her.

He kept up the slow rock, but felt his control slip as her response became more abandoned, her breath coming out in little cries at each slow thrust. And found himself moving faster, harder, needing more of her.

He raised himself on one elbow as he continued to move, put his hand over her white breast, ran it over the nipple, pinched it between his fingers. Heard her cry out at the added sensation, her head thrashing to the side against the pillow, and lost another vestige of his control. She was so beautiful, so abandoned, he needed more.

"Turn over," he gasped as he flipped her, pulling her by the waist to her knees.

"I need to do this," he groaned, half-apologetically, half-triumphantly, looking at her beneath him, her elbows supporting herself, her wonderful, round bottom rising to meet him as he slid into her once more. He reached one hand around from behind and held her there, his fingers moving over her strongly as he pushed into her from behind, even harder, almost out of control now.

She writhed under him, gasping, rearing back to meet him, stroke for stroke. As his hand continued to move over her, she began to pant, squirming back against him, asking for more, and even more. He felt her strong interior muscles contract around him as she released, spasming against him, around him, the intensity of her orgasm forcing her to cry out, pushing back, over and over, the waves strong and hard.

He couldn't help it. His excitement was so strong, her body beneath him so delicious, her surrender to her pleasure so absolute. He held her even more tightly to him, pulled her roughly up on all fours. Bent his head to the side of her neck, and held her there with his teeth as he exploded into her. Bit down as the spasms took him, out of himself into a place where only sensation existed. The world narrowed into just this, the feeling of emptying himself into her, taking all of her.

He came back to himself at last, collapsed on top of her, pulled her to him and held her. She was breathing hard, almost sobbing, her hair wrapped around her, over her, between them. He rolled to his back, turned her to lie against him, brought his other arm around to hold her more tightly. Lowered his face to the top of her head and kissed her there.

"Did I hurt you?" he asked at last. "I didn't mean to do that. Are you all right?"

She laughed shakily. "If I were any more all right, I'd have burnt up, I think. That was so intense. I can't...I can't handle it."

"Are you hurt?" he pressed. "I was too rough."

"No," she protested. "You were perfect. It was so good. You didn't hurt me. You're just…a lot for me."

"You made me lose control." He smoothed her hair back from her face ran his hand down her body, down the smooth skin of her side, over her hip. "You were so beautiful."

He frowned as the hair fell back and he saw the red mark on the side of her neck where he had held her, bitten her in his excitement. "I've left a mark, though. Sorry."

She looked back at him, eyes trusting. "You didn't hurt me," she said again.

He kissed her gently there, soothing the mark he had made, then fell back against the pillow again, holding her against him, her head under his chin, her hand on his chest.

"When I was growing up," he said slowly, against her hair, "The neighbors had a stud farm, and my brother and I would sometimes see a stallion covering a mare. Can't tell you what that did to us, impressionable boys in the country. And once, when I was fourteen or fifteen, there was a palomino mare that was brought to the stallion. Beautiful pale coat, that white mane and tail. Did something to me, seeing that bay stallion over that palomino mare. Watching him hold her there with his teeth, her backing into him, urging him on. Reckon I've been looking for that ever since. And now here you are. My fifteen-year-old's fantasy. And even better. If I'd known it would be like that, I would've been an even randier young bloke than I was."

"Mmmm," she murmured, still basking in the afterglow, content to be held so close against him, her hand on his chest, stroking him. "Good to know I'm your horse fantasy. Guess that's why my round butt doesn't bother you."

He laughed and swatted her lightly there. It felt so good, he ran his hand over it again. "Must be it," he agreed. "All of you works for me, though, I reckon. Not just the horse bits."

They finally did get their shower, and he had been right. Soap and water, the tiny motel shower forcing them to stand close together, to help each other soap up and rinse off, her heavy hair streaming down her body to her hips under the spray. Clean again, they made love after belatedly pulling back the duvet on the big bed. Slowly, taking their time now, kissing, stroking, letting the heat build until it overcame them again.

Afterwards, they slept, waking as the evening was closing around them, the room fading in the dusk. He held her against him as she woke, disoriented at first.

"How're you going?" he smiled at her as she floated into full consciousness.

"Hungry," she admitted. "You must be starved."

He laughed. "I am, it's true. And I don't want to spend the night in this bed. I've been trying all this time to get you back to my bach with me. Reckon this may be the night I get lucky. I have some steaks there too. If I take you by your motel to pick up your things, think I could talk you into fixing a salad for us while I put them on the barbie? And then staying with me tonight?"

"I think I could be persuaded to do that," she said. "I don't think I'm done looking at you, anyway. I have some catching up to do."

"We can do some more catching up," he promised. "After we get outside of a couple steaks. I can tell I'm going to need my strength."

chapter eight

♡

Waking alone in Drew's huge bed the next morning, Hannah had to admit that this was an improvement in every way over her tiny motel room.

What must it be like, she wondered, to wake up every morning to a view like this? Surely it would be hard to start the day in a bad mood. The room was simply furnished, its natural wood and white walls understated, with the focus on the scene beyond. Sliding doors opened onto a large deck that continued around the other side of the beach house—the bach, she corrected herself. She could lie in bed and look out over the sea and sky. Those doors were open now. Listening to the birds singing outside, she felt as if her body were singing a happy little song right along with them. Her blood seemed to hum and tingle in her veins.

When Drew came into the bedroom, she sat up, pulling the sheet around her.

"Not necessary." He smiled down at her. "I like the way you're dressed now. Brought you a cup of tea." He sat down on the bed to hand it to her.

She was touched by his thoughtfulness. "I need this. A little sore today." She smiled ruefully. "Not just from the hike, either."

"Maybe this won't sound good to you, then. I need to meet some of the boys at the gym in Whitianga this morning. I wondered if you'd like to come along. They have a yoga class there, I know. Thought you might like that. But could be you've had enough exercise and would rather stay here and sleep a bit."

"No," she responded instantly. "A yoga class sounds perfect. Stretch these muscles. Can I buy just a single class, though?"

"No need for that. I'll bring you in as a guest. No worries."

"You don't have to do that," she objected. "I'm happy to take myself to a yoga class."

He sighed. "And I'm happy to take you. As my guest. Better get up, if you're coming with me."

♡

The class, she decided a couple hours later, had been the perfect solution for her sore muscles. Quieting her mind hadn't hurt either, she admitted. The day before had been so exciting—and the night too, she remembered with a blush. She felt more relaxed now, her mind clearer, as she finished showering and changing.

She saw Drew as soon as she left the locker room, part of a group in the lobby at the other side of the large gym. It would have been hard to miss the five big men, chatting and laughing. She hesitated, a little shy about approaching.

Seeing her, Drew broke away from the group to meet her halfway. She was intercepted in her progress across the gym floor, though, by a young man in a pair of startlingly short gym shorts who had been working out with a friend on the nearby machines.

"Morning," he smiled, showing too many white teeth as he came up to her, forcing her to stop. "Saw you coming out of yoga class. Good on ya. Getting flexible, eh," he added suggestively.

Well, that was smooth. "Good morning," she said politely, and made to step around him and continue on her way.

He sidestepped, blocking her way again as Drew approached behind him. "You have gorgeous hair," was his next original gambit. "Couldn't help but notice. Know where it would look even better?" He leaned in and continued softly, "On my pillow."

"Excuse me," she said frostily, and moved again to bypass him.

She needn't have bothered. Drew had his hand on the other man's shoulder. Casanova turned in surprise to meet a pair of icy gray eyes that bored into his own.

"The lady's not interested," Drew growled. "Take a hike."

The young man's eyes widened in shocked recognition, and Hannah could have sworn he actually backpedaled like a cartoon character. "Right," he stammered. "Sorry, mate."

Drew turned back to her, his eyes still angry. "Sorry. Should have seen you sooner, kept that bastard from annoying you."

"Thanks for rescuing me again. But I was doing fine. I know how to handle that by now. It's amazing," she went on conversationally, "how many men think that's some kind of knockout line I wouldn't have heard before. What do they think I'm going to say? 'Oh, you're so right. Let's have sex right now.'"

He laughed and reached out to take her gym bag. "No chance of that from you, anyway. Come on, then. I want to introduce you to my mates."

His friends were even bigger up close, she found. "Let me guess," she offered after shaking hands with the four tall men. "You're rugby players too."

"You've penetrated our amazing disguise, eh," answered Kevin, an engaging redhead.

She laughed. "Not too hard." She looked around the group. "There's just something about you."

As she turned to look at the man to her right, Drew saw that the bruise on her neck was clearly visible, and mentally winced. He saw Kevin's eyes fall to it as well, suddenly speculative. He put his hand protectively around the back of her neck and shot Kevin a glare that had the other man looking quickly away again, his face wiped clean of expression.

At the touch, Hannah turned to him. She stopped, puzzled, at the look on his face. Then hurried on to cover the awkward moment. "But you still get together and work out, even in the offseason?"

"That's the Skip," said Finn, a powerfully built man some years older than Kevin. "Doesn't let us bunk off, does he."

All the men laughed at that as Drew answered good-humoredly, "Too right. Need to keep you lazy buggers up to the mark. Have to go give Hannah her lunch now, though. See you boys here day after tomorrow, then. Same time."

"I like your friends," Hannah told him as he piloted the truck out of the club's parking lot. "They look so fierce, some of them. And they're huge. A little intimidating. But they're nice, I think."

"Not so nice when you meet them on the paddock. But we try to be civilized the rest of the time, specially with the ladies."

"Why do they call you Skip?" she wondered. "Is it a nickname?"

He laughed. "Not exactly. It's just that I'm the captain. The Skipper," he explained, when she still looked mystified.

"Oh, I get it. Like the skipper of a ship. But you didn't tell me you were the captain," she objected.

"What should I have said, then? 'Hello,'" he mocked in a deep voice. "'I'm Drew Callahan. I'm a rugby player, and you should know that I'm also the captain. Why don't you come home with me? Your hair would look bloody good on my pillow.'"

She smiled. "You're a little too smooth for that. Thank goodness."

"Mind if we stop by your motel again, before I take you to lunch?" he asked. "Pick up another shirt?"

"Why? What's wrong with this one? Did I spill something?" She looked down anxiously.

"I meant a shirt with a collar. If you don't have one, I'll buy you one. To cover that mark," he explained, as she still looked confused.

Her hand flew to the back of her neck. "This? It's just a bruise. Nobody would notice it."

"Kevin noticed it."

"Oh." The light dawned. "That's why you were glaring at him like that." She laughed. "The poor man. But he wouldn't have known how it got there. Would he?" she faltered.

"He isn't thinking about it now, if he knows what's good for him," Drew answered a little grimly. "But you'll make me happier if you cover it up. I promise, it'll be the last time. Don't know what I was thinking. Yes, I do," he corrected himself. "I'm not sorry for what I was thinking. But I'm sorry I marked you like that."

"Is it nasty of me to say that I didn't mind it? I don't want anybody to hurt me, or anything," she hurried on. "But when you held me like that, and…and bit me, it was…really exciting," she finished tentatively. "It made me a little crazy, in fact. Maybe just don't bite so hard, next time?"

He swore. "You're going to kill me," he groaned. "Here we are in this bloody ute again, twenty kilometers from anywhere. I have to stop taking you places."

♡

In the end, he took her straight back to the bach. She wouldn't need the shirt anyway, he reasoned. Not if she stayed there with him.

"This sandwich is huge," she protested, when he brought her the toasted chicken and vegetable monstrosity out on the deck. Their lunch had been delayed a bit, but he was making up for it now. "I'm not playing any rugby games anytime soon. I have to stop eating like this."

"I'll finish what you don't," he assured her. "Besides, seems to me you've been getting a bit of exercise yourself, these past few days. Need to keep your strength up."

"Mmmm…Making up for lost time," she answered, around her sandwich.

"Lost time?" he asked, raising an eyebrow.

"It's been a while, that's all. Wait, forget I said that," she added hastily. "You keep telling me I'm supposed to stop sharing these things that make me sound like a loser."

He laughed. "I like it. Good to know what you really think. No games. But just how long has it been? You don't seem out of practice to me."

She flushed. "Well, thanks. I think that's you, though. Seems to me you do most of the work. All I have to do is enjoy it."

"Works for me. I like an appreciative audience. Not to mention someone who follows orders, eh." He grinned again at her shocked expression. "But you're just trying to distract me now. Let's hear the sad story."

She answered reluctantly. "Well...maybe three..." She cleared her throat. "Three years?"

"Three *years?*" he answered, stunned. "Not that I'm complaining," he hastened to assure her. "I'm glad to know you've saved all that for me. But why is that? From what I saw this morning, you must have heaps of men asking you out."

"Yes, and that's about the quality of them. Sure, I go out. Some. I just got disillusioned with all of it. I'm not good at casual sex. It doesn't work for me. Whatever you might think," she added defensively.

"You're not sending out any 'come and get it' signals, no worries."

"My friend Susannah says I'm too guarded. That I don't give anyone a chance. But I can't hop into bed with someone just for fun. Too embarrassing the next day, you know?"

He was too smart to answer that one. "Not every man wants to hook up and move on, though."

"I don't know. Sometimes it seems like that's all they're looking for. That three-date thing."

"What three-date thing?"

"You know. Three dates and you're out? They figure if it hasn't happened by then, there's no return on their investment, and they don't call again. Once that happened to me enough, I suppose I stopped giving them much of a chance. It started to seem so sordid. Like we're all expendable. Interchangeable. They just want to get some, and if it takes too long, they'll get it from somebody else."

"So that's how I did it," he teased. "Didn't pike out, eh."

"OK, I'll admit," she smiled, "I wanted to get some too, in your case. I tried. I told myself I'd regret it, and that I didn't know you well enough, and that we lived too far apart for anything to come of it. But it didn't work. I was pretty sure, actually, that first day on the boat. The rest of it was just me arguing with myself."

"Could have fooled me. I wasn't sure I was getting anywhere at all."

"Well, you were scary," she said seriously.

"Scary? How?" he protested. "I tried bloody hard to be a gentleman. And it wasn't easy."

"You were wonderful. But you're so different from the kind of men I usually meet. Lawyers. Sales reps. You're just so...so big," she said lamely. "Overwhelming. And I was really attracted to you. That was scary, for me. But what can I say. You overcame my scruples. So here I am, being slutty on my vacation. Just what I said I wouldn't do."

He smiled. "You know bugger all about being slutty. But I'll try my best to help you learn."

"Well, you know," she frowned down at her sandwich, "I have to go to Rotorua tomorrow. So if you'll take me back to my motel after lunch, I need to pack." She looked up at him with an effort.

"But you don't want to do that," he protested. "Do you? I sure as hell don't want you to leave now."

"Are you sure about that?" she pressed. "You're on a fishing vacation. You said so. You don't have to be a gentleman now,

Drew. I went into this with my eyes open. I knew I only had a few days, and I decided I wanted to be with you anyway. But there's no obligation."

"Do you think, by now, I don't know how to give someone the push?" he asked, exasperated. "I'm sure I shouldn't say it, but I've had some practice. If I'd wanted to be rid of you, I could have done it. Given you a kiss and had an appointment back in Auckland. Dead easy. Did that occur to you?"

He saw he had upset her, reached for her hand. "I want you to stay with me. I'll even promise to take you to Rotorua before the end of your holiday. But I'd like you to spend the rest of your time with me."

She hadn't realized how much her imminent departure had been weighing on her. She had desperately wanted to extend her stay. But how embarrassing it would have been to hang around here, and know he was wishing her gone. Or to have him leave to get away from her. She flushed, imagining it, then smiled at him in relief.

"I'd love to stay longer. But you have to promise me you'll go fishing, and do the other things you came here for. I'm not going to get in the way. I have my own things to do too," she insisted. "Reading, and swimming—*safe* swimming. What if I want to look at art galleries? You aren't going to want to do that. I'll keep my motel, too. That way, if we need a break, or you have something to do, I can stay there."

"What sorts of things am I supposed to have to do?" he asked, frowning at her. "Bring somebody else back here, do you mean? Have wild parties with strippers? Nah. If you're staying with me, I want you with me. We only have, what? A fortnight?"

"Twelve days," she admitted unhappily.

"Right, then. Twelve days. Let's spend them together. This is good, Hannah. Let's enjoy it."

chapter nine

♡

He was as good as his word. Over the next few days, they explored the entire Coromandel, hiking, kayaking, and snorkeling. At Hannah's insistence, Drew spent time fishing as well. They bought groceries in the tiny shop to supplement the fish he brought home, and picked up produce at the farm stands dotted around the countryside.

The first time he pulled off the road to stop where a wooden box was nailed to poles at the side of the road, she was confused.

"What's this?" she asked as he came around to open her door.

"Thought you'd like some tangerines. Lemons too, for the fish."

"But there's nobody here," she pointed out as they walked toward the little stand.

He laughed. "There's a box, see?"

She looked inside. Sure enough, bags of tangerines, lemons, and avocadoes were piled inside the roughly made stand, with cardboard signs indicating prices. A small metal cash box, chained to the post, awaited their dollar coins.

"Don't people just take things?" she asked. "Or jimmy the box open?"

"Never heard of that. Just a few coins, isn't it." He deposited them as he spoke, and handed her a tangerine from the bag. "Try one."

"This would never work, anyplace else," she told him, popping one of the sweet sections into her mouth.

"That's why I live here," he agreed. "Because it does work."

♡

"Want to drive down to Rotorua today?" he asked her a few days later. "I borrowed a bach from a mate. We can do a bit more traveling too, after that."

"Yes!" she exclaimed. "That sounds great. But, Drew, why do you call it a bach, anyway? It's a vacation house, right?"

"Bach—a bachelor's house. Made out of anything they could cobble together, in the old days. Bits of old tin, old doors. Every Kiwi wants a bach, where they can get out of the city. Mostly on the beach, but also places like Rotorua and Taupo, where there are lakes. For fishing," he amplified.

"How did I guess? Not so much made of tin and old doors now, though, I notice."

"We try to do a bit better these days," he admitted.

"What do I do about my car, though? We won't be coming back here, right?"

"No worries. I've already arranged for it to be collected. I'll drop you back at the airport for your flight."

"You sure make everything easy for me."

"That's the idea, eh."

♡

Hannah smelled Rotorua before she saw it, the stench of sulphur coming strongly through the closed truck windows. "Phew." She covered her nose. "How do people live here?"

"You get used to it," Drew assured her. "Wait till tomorrow. You'll be surprised. You'll barely notice it."

As they drove through town, the ground literally seemed to be steaming.

"Where's it all coming from?" she marveled.

"The whole place is built over a geothermal area. Vents all over the shop in Rotorua. Back gardens," he pointed out. "Golf courses. You have to be careful where you build, here."

When he suggested that he take her to the museum, though, she protested. "You don't want to do that, though. There can't be anything that's new to you. Why don't you go fishing or something, and let me tour the museum by myself?"

"Because the point of this trip is for me to show you New Zealand," he said as patiently as he could. "Which I can't very well do if I'm out on the water, and you're here by yourself."

She was enthralled by the exhibits of Maori artifacts and history in the excellent museum, converted from a Victorian-era bath house and spa. She found herself moved and saddened by the film about the famous Maori Battalion, the most decorated Allied unit in World War II, and with some of the heaviest losses.

"It's so sad," she told Drew, when they were looking at the war memorial outside the museum. "Some of these families lost two or three sons. You can tell by the names."

"It is. It's a warrior culture, though. Nobody fiercer than the Maori. I'll show you more tonight, when I take you to the Maori concert. You'll see why they make such good rugby players. It's more than just their size and strength. Bit of a challenge for Pakeha like me to match them."

That evening, he parked in a lot surrounded by paths in the native bush, with a building in the distance. He spoke briefly into a cell phone, then waited until they were met by a smiling man who shook hands and touched his forehead and nose to Drew's in the traditional greeting, then led them around the side of a building to an outdoor stage, where Hannah could see a group of people filing in.

"Are we late?" she asked Drew softly as they approached the group.

"Nah, just skipping a bit of the preliminaries," he told her as they were seated in the front row in the dark.

The man bent down and spoke to Drew again, shrugging when Drew shook his head. Finally, he shook Drew's hand again and smiled at Hannah. "Enjoy the show," he told her. "We'll make it special, eh."

Hannah looked at Drew, still confused, then turned back to the stage as the show began. She forgot about the encounter as the talented performers enacted the traditional greeting ceremony, from the opening karanga of welcome, to the fierce challenge by a young warrior, finally ending in a speech from the village's chief. A demonstration of weapons practice with clubs, sticks, and spears had her marveling at the group's skills and prowess, while the powerful harmonies and haunting melodies of the songs performed by both men and women moved her almost to tears.

"The songs are so beautiful," she whispered to Drew during the applause.

"Thought you'd enjoy it. Wait till this last bit, though."

The village's chief was talking about the haka, and Hannah remembered Drew telling her about the chant. She was unprepared for the ferocity and power of the demonstration. Although she knew it was a performance, and they did this every night, she found herself shrinking back into her seat from the shouting, stamping, gesticulating warriors. For some reason, they seemed to be directing their entire performance toward herself and Drew, and she found herself wishing that they weren't quite so close.

The show ended, and the audience headed back toward the tent, where, Drew explained, they would have dinner. Drew stood as the group of performers hopped down from the stage and came towards him. Hannah stood up too, uncertain and confused.

One by one, the men and women greeted them. Hannah was charmed to find herself receiving both handshake and the gentle face-touching hongi in welcome.

"Awesome show," Drew congratulated them. "Cheers for that."

"Shame we couldn't get you on to do the *Ka Mate* with us, though," a young man named Rodney, who seemed to be the spokesperson for the group, said regretfully. "Teddy said he asked you."

"I wanted to see your haka. Wanted Hannah to see it too. Bloody fierce. I'm going to remember that."

Drew turned to Hannah to explain. "Every tribe has their own traditional haka. They're not all the same. And this is a good one, eh."

"It is," Hannah told the group with genuine admiration. "I have to admit, you scared me."

Rodney laughed. "Then you haven't seen Drew here in action. He's a warrior. Puts the fear of God into the other team, I reckon." The rest of the group smiled and agreed.

"We'll be off, let you have your tea," Drew said, shaking hands once more all around. "Thanks again."

"Cheers, mate," Rodney acknowledged.

"What was all that about?" Hannah wondered after they were escorted back through the darkened path to the truck, by a young woman this time. "Why didn't we go to the whole thing?"

"Because that's the best part. Except the hangi—the meal they roast in the pit. Every footballer loves a good hangi. But this way I can take you home while you're still stirred up from all that," he grinned.

"Nice to be able to arrange it that way, then," she commented dryly.

"I don't usually do things like that," he agreed. "But they didn't mind."

"No, that was pretty obvious. I'm not sure I understood all that about the haka, though. They wanted you to do a different one with them?"

"Yeh," he shrugged. "The one we do before test matches. But this is their show. It wasn't about me."

"I can see what you mean by the ferocity, though," she mused as he drove them back to the luxurious lakeside home he had borrowed for their stay. "If they play rugby like that, I mean."

He smiled. "Yeh. They play just like that."

♡

"Ready to see Mount Doom?" Drew asked the next day. "We can walk through a geothermal area on the way. Think you'd like that. And then go on to Lake Taupo."

"Mount Doom? I know what you mean. *The Lord of the Rings,* right? Does the area look like that, around Lake Taupo?"

"It really *is* that. One of the locations for the films. There's a track, the Tongariro Crossing, outside Taupo, through a volcanic field. That area was Mordor. Mt. Ngauruhoe—one of our most famous volcanoes—that was Mount Doom. Bet you'll recognize it when you see it. Course, the Maori thought it was something special long before that. It all makes a long tramp, but a pretty good one. What do you think?"

"I'd like that," she agreed instantly.

She wasn't so sure as she shivered in the predawn cold two mornings later, standing outside another beautiful bach overlooking the immense lake.

"It's awfully early," she complained. "It'll still be dark, won't it?"

"It'll take a bit to drive there," he explained. "And we'll want to start at first light. This is the most popular track in New Zealand. Hundreds of people a day do it in the summer. We want to get out ahead of them."

"Because you don't like to be in a crowd," she guessed.

He laughed. "Too right. The only time Kiwis have to queue is at Christmas, in the post office. And we complain about that. The advantage of living in a country where the sheep and cows outnumber the people," he said complacently as he settled her into the truck to begin the drive.

Once they started up the track in the early dawn, with just a few other intrepid souls making an early start, Hannah was glad he'd pushed her.

"It's so beautiful," she said wonderingly, looking at the creek beside the well-formed track, heather-covered ground rolling away and up toward the huge, threatening-looking mountain looming above them. "It reminds me of pictures I've seen of the Scottish Highlands. I thought you said this was Mordor."

"Just wait," he promised. "You still have almost 20K to go, remember. It'll change, no worries."

As they climbed steadily for the next two hours, she began to see what he meant. The landscape became starker, the plant life finally reduced to a few hardy grasses. More mountains were revealed, among them the iconic volcano, its reddish crater clearly showing.

"Mt. Ngauruhoe," Drew explained. "Looks threatening, doesn't it?"

"It does. It's not going to erupt, is it?" she asked nervously.

"Could happen. The last eruption in this area was just months ago. But before it does, you'll see more smoke and steam. No worries today. She'll be right."

Hannah had thought she was in good shape, but she found the long uphill climb a challenge.

"It's annoying," she told Drew as they pushed through an especially steep section, on their way to the track's summit amidst the craters.

"What is?" he asked, turning to give her his hand.

"Your basic lack of condition," she grumbled. "Couldn't you at least pretend to be breathing heavily?"

He smiled. "How hard is your job, most days?"

"Not that hard, now that I know what I'm doing. Why?"

"This is conditioning. Part of my job. Reckon you're doing better at this than I would at those sales projections. I've never been with a woman who'd do this with me."

"Really?" She was pleased.

"Really," he assured her. "But I have a surprise for you at the end. Make it all worthwhile."

Two hours later, they came out the other end at last. Hannah was weary and footsore, but Drew seemed, to her irritation, as if he could have turned around and run the whole thing again. They were met by a young man who shuttled them back to their starting point.

"How do you arrange these things?" she wondered as Drew opened the door to his truck for her again.

"What?"

"The shuttle guy. Things like that. How did he know when to be there?"

Drew looked a bit embarrassed. "Gave him a window, that's all. I had a fair idea of how long it would take us."

"It's going to be hard to go back to my regular old life, after all this luxury," she sighed. "I'm not used to this."

"Then we'd better make sure you enjoy it. Get your money's worth out of your holiday."

"I think I've already got that," she smiled at him.

"Glad to hear it. And here's the next surprise," he announced, pulling off onto a side street as they passed through a tiny town on their way back to their lakeside bach.

"I'm not sure I can walk any more," she said doubtfully. "And I'm pretty sweaty."

"Then you'll like this even more." He pulled a duffel from the back of the truck and walked with her into a modest building set amongst native plantings and a river. More steam rose from the ground all around the area.

"It's a bath house," she exclaimed. "So there's a spa, or something."

"Built on the local iwi's—the tribe's—medicinal hot pools. They own it, and run it. I'll show you."

After negotiating with the Maori woman at the front desk, Drew walked with Hannah through a gate, and they were outdoors again, on a concrete sidewalk with a wooden building on either side.

"Go take a shower," he instructed, showing her the changing room and handing her a large towel from the bag. "And I'll meet you out here again."

"I don't have a suit, though," she protested.

"Just wrap up in the towel," he insisted.

"Drew," she told him as she came out of the changing room to find him waiting, barechested and wrapped in his own towel. "Much as I'd enjoy seeing you, I can't get naked in a pool full of people."

He laughed. "No worries. I know that by now." He held out the key, then turned toward one of the wooden doors along the sidewalk.

"Private," he explained as he opened the door.

The simple concrete-floored area was partially open to the sky, but was otherwise an enclosed room. A wooden bench ran along the length of the back wall, but the bulk of the space was taken up by a huge, rectangular bath of steaming water.

"This isn't a spa," Hannah exclaimed. "It's a pool. I could swim in this."

"Awesome, eh," he grinned. "Most tourists never know about this. Best thing about doing the Tongariro Crossing. Especially with you," he added, tugging her towel off and leading her down the steps into the pool.

She sighed, stretching out in the hot, mineral-laden water, feeling it soaking into her aching muscles. "You're right. This is a treat. How long do we get in here?"

"I paid for thirty minutes. And I told her to give us more time, if we needed it. We can stay in here as long as we like. Until you're cooked through."

That wasn't all he had in mind, she discovered. Relaxed in the bone-melting heat of the water, she found his hands wandering over her body, underneath the water.

"Mmmmm," she hummed, leaning her head back against the edge. "That feels really good."

"What does?" he asked, his hands sliding over her breasts.

"Everything," she admitted, her breath catching. He petted and stroked her until she felt liquid inside and outside, then gently guided her onto him. She buried her head in the side of his neck and let him move her as he pleased. She had never felt so warm, so boneless.

Slowly, slowly, the heat built. Each time Drew pulled her into him, her temperature seemed to rise. She lost the ability to move herself, became pliable in his hands as he moved her over him. Her entire being seemed to center on her warm core, where he touched her. It grew and built until, finally, she shattered over him, the strong contractions seeming to wring the last of the strength from her body. In answer, he emptied into her with a long groan of pleasure.

Afterwards, she curled against him, the water lapping around them.

"Hannah," he smiled against her hair. "Don't go to sleep, now."

"Hmmm?" she murmured, lifting her head at last. "Oh," she sighed. "Is it time to get out?"

"I reckon," he answered solemnly. "Or they're going to find us in here, melted."

She smiled languidly. "I'm not sure how you do that."

"Do what?" he asked, stroking her face and kissing her gently.

"Make me feel so good." She leaned back and looked into his face.

"It's hard work. But I think I'm up to the challenge."

"I think you are," she sighed blissfully.

She was embarrassed watching him pay for two more fifteen-minute sessions, after they had at last showered and changed into the clean clothes he had brought.

"Did you enjoy it, then?" the motherly woman asked them.

"Very much," Drew answered with a smile.

"She could tell what we were doing," Hannah whispered as they left.

"Reckon she could. And reckon we aren't the first ones to do it," he answered cheerfully. "But I like to think nobody enjoyed it more."

chapter ten

♡

"You know, I think I've made up those whole three years by now," Hannah told him the next morning as they lay in bed, looking out over the view of lake and mountains. "And we still have five more days. I guess that's a down payment on the next year or so."

She felt a pang even as she said it. She had deliberately avoided thinking about the time they had left. Now, she forced herself to look at the situation squarely. She was going to leave.

That's why this was a bad idea, she thought again. Oh well. She had done it now. She would just have to compartmentalize, that was all. Enjoy it while it lasted, and move on. That's what other people did, after all. She knew she wouldn't have given this up, now that she knew how good it was, no matter how she might feel later.

Drew held her to him more closely. "Why don't you stay longer? There are so many more places I could show you. Things we could do," he grinned. "*Interesting* things. But seriously. We can change your ticket, give you another week or two. Go to the South Island for a bit."

Her heart leapt, but she knew it was impossible. "I have to get back," she said firmly, to herself as much as him. "I've never taken this much time as it is. It's a busy season, and I'm needed at my job. Besides, I saved all my vacation time for the year to take this trip. I don't have as much as a day left."

"You only get three weeks, then?" he asked in surprise.

"I'm lucky to have that," she protested. "I only started to get three weeks after five years with the company. Most people just get two weeks. Why, how much vacation time do people get here?"

"Four weeks minimum, plus public holidays, of course. Two weeks," he said, stunned. "That's shocking. Don't see how you do it."

"Well, we don't all have to recover from rugby seasons, so it isn't that bad. I'm used to it, I suppose. But that's why this trip has been so wonderful. One of the reasons," she amended. "I've never had this much time off in my life, not since I was old enough to work, at least. And meeting you made it even better. I wish I didn't have to leave. But I have to get back to my life. And you have to get back to yours, I know."

"I do take trips to the States, though," he objected. "The planes fly both ways these days. The end of your holiday doesn't have to mean that we never see each other again."

She looked at him in surprise. "Would you want to do that?"

"Think you're selling yourself short. Yeh, I want to keep seeing you. Maybe you haven't noticed, but I like spending time with you. I've got bugger all fishing done while you've been here. My mates will tell you that if I'm not fishing on my holidays, something's up."

"I'm right up there competing with the fish, am I? I'm flattered. But I'd love to see you again after I go back. If it works out."

But she wouldn't get her hopes up, she thought privately. It was obvious that Drew had plenty of chances to meet women. Once she was across the Pacific again, she doubted that the relationship, if that was what they had, would be sustainable. The distance was just too great. It was hard enough for couples to maintain something that involved driving more than a few hours, she knew. And they'd only had a couple weeks together to build on.

She'd enjoy this now, she told herself, and be happily surprised if she saw him again. Not that there would be much difference in her social life, she admitted. Even less, now. Nobody else was going to look very good, after him.

♡

Time passed far too quickly. Before she knew it, it seemed, they were driving south to Auckland again, toward the plane that would take her home. Drew had taken her to the quiet, nearly deserted beaches of the Far North during their final days together, where they had stayed in yet another house he had borrowed from a friend. He had joked that he simply wanted to get her into the tangerine suit again.

"Can't keep you naked all the time," he had told her. "You keep insisting on getting out of bed. But those togs are the next best thing."

They had spent a blissful few days swimming, kayaking, and snorkeling in the warm waters. No wetsuit needed, she thought now with a smile. Which had suited her just fine, too. Familiarity with Drew's body hadn't bred any contempt. None at all.

On their last day, he had hired a guide to take them on a private tour to swim with the dolphins. One of the most wondrous experiences of her life. And one of the most bittersweet. Watching the playful mammals swim around her, leaping and frolicking, seeming to smile at her with their intelligent eyes, had brought her pure joy. They had seemed so curious, coming close, it seemed, just to check the two of them out, to play with them. She would never forget the feeling, she knew.

The fact that Drew had arranged the trip, that he was willing to go to so much effort to please her, had been wonderful too. But knowing she had to leave the next day, that this was their last time together...the realization had kept catching up with her unexpectedly, bringing waves of sadness that threatened to overwhelm her. In fact, she admitted, she was feeling fairly miserable right now, watching him next to her, knowing she was about to leave.

You had a fantastic vacation, she scolded herself. *You met the man of any woman's dreams, and had a wonderful time with him. You got more than your money's worth.* Back to reality now, that was all. And, she reminded herself, she would see her brother and sister again, and her friends. And get back to her job, see what was happening, pick up the reins again.

But somehow, the prospect wasn't as attractive as it should have been. She had thought she'd be champing at the bit to get back to her job after the unprecedentedly long break. She realized now that, after the first day or two, she had barely thought about the office. She had told Emery and Beth that they could email her, she realized with a shocked start. Yet she hadn't gone online since her second day. Not once. She sighed guiltily. She hoped there hadn't been a crisis.

If there had, they could handle it, she reminded herself now. But what if Kristen had had a problem? Or Matt? She had been so selfish, she thought in dismay, her heart beating harder as she envisioned her siblings needing her, not being able to reach her.

Drew glanced over at her as he drove. "You're quiet. Everything all right?"

She sighed again. "I was just realizing how selfish I've been," she said wretchedly. "I've never even checked my email. I don't know how my brother and sister are doing. If they've needed me, and not been able to get hold of me. Not to mention work. I said I would check in, and then I never did. How could I have done that? Just walked away from all my responsibilities?"

He raised an eyebrow at her. "Don't think you did that," he commented mildly. "You went on holiday, that's all. Everyone needs a holiday. Reckon you needed it more than most. That's what you're supposed to do. Put everything out of your head, think about something else for a change. Keeps you fit, eh. Nobody can focus all the time."

"I think you're being too easy on me. But thanks. There isn't too much I could have done from here anyway, I guess."

"And I think you're being too hard on yourself. Do your sister and brother check in with you, then, when they're on holiday?"

"No," she admitted. "And I worry about them when they're away. Especially Matt. I always feel better when I hear from him again, once he's home. I never thought about it that way. But that's different. They're used to counting on me, to my being there for them. It isn't the same thing."

"They're grown, though, aren't they," he said gently. "It may be better for them to solve their own problems. Hard to grow up if you can count on someone else pulling you out of the fire every time."

"You sound just like Susannah. She says the same thing. That I baby them, and they count on me too much to rescue them. That I'm keeping them from growing up."

"She may have something there," he responded seriously. "Think about it. Maybe this holiday was a good start for you. I know it was good for me," he said with a grin.

"You know it was good for me," she laughed. "You made it good for me. Many times. But you know that I really am grateful to you for everything. It was the best time," she added more seriously. "Thank you for that."

"Well, it was an effort," he sighed. "But it's every Kiwi's duty to see that the tourists have a good experience, want to come back."

She swatted him on the arm. "You'd be busy, if you showed every tourist that kind of good time. I know you're good, but even for you, that might be too much."

"You're right. Reckon it's better if I focus on you. Quality over quantity."

"That works for me," she answered firmly. "Just hold that thought."

When they reached the airport at last, she suggested that he drop her at the curb of the international terminal. "I'll be fine," she insisted. "It'll be so much easier."

He smiled a little and piloted the truck firmly into the short-term parking lot. "You always walk the lady to her door," he assured her solemnly. "Or her security checkpoint. Besides, you need me to carry your luggage."

"It has wheels," she protested. "That's the idea, you know? And besides, if you go in there, you know you'll be harassed."

"Harassed? How?"

"You know. People will come up to you and bother you. Why not just drop me here and avoid all that?"

"I'm used to it. Don't worry about me. Besides, that's what the hat and sunnies are for," he added, pulling them on. "Anonymous, see?"

She laughed. "You're about as anonymous as an elephant in the living room, but all right. Since you're here, muscle boy, you can haul my luggage for me. Keep me from straining myself."

And give me that much longer to regret saying goodbye to you, she thought privately. She wasn't sure if that was worse, or better. Now that the time was here, she wanted to get it over with, even as she longed to postpone the moment when she would have to leave him.

He stood patiently with her through the long line at Economy check-in, even though, sure enough, the cap and sunglasses weren't enough to keep a few passengers from recognizing and approaching him. At last they were at the front of the line, and she was being handed her boarding pass.

Drew excused himself, asking her to wait a moment while he checked on a ticket. She saw him at the empty Business Class check-in, chatting with the agent there. Must be nice, she sighed. Never mind. At least she had an aisle seat this time, which would be a big improvement. She'd had three weeks of luxury. That was enough.

Saying goodbye to him, though, was just as bad as she had feared.

"I'll ring you," he promised, giving her one final kiss. "Make sure you made it back all right."

She wouldn't let herself count on it, but smiled bravely. "I had a wonderful time. Thank you. See you, then."

She moved quickly through the entrance to Passport Control, not wanting to prolong the goodbye or embarrass herself. She felt uncomfortably close to tears, and the last thing she wanted to do was to cry in front of him. That would embarrass him too, she knew. Better to keep it light.

She reached her gate at last, and sat down numbly. Still an hour and a half until her flight. She missed him already. This wasn't leaving after a wonderful vacation. This was just…leaving. And it hurt.

It was time to return to reality, she reminded herself once again. If she had stayed longer, as he'd asked—even if that had been possible, which it wasn't—she would just have become more attached, and this would be harder. No, it was best that she was leaving now. It would hurt, but within a few days, she'd be back in her usual routine. And this would be just another vacation memory.

Wrapped in her thoughts, she was startled to hear herself paged by the gate agent. Now what? She hoped there was no problem with her ticket. Now that she had begun to leave, she just wanted to get it over with. She made her way to the counter with trepidation.

"I need to make a change to your seating. You've been upgraded to Business Premier," the agent explained as she took Hannah's boarding pass and exchanged it for another.

"You're welcome to relax before the flight in the Koru Lounge," she added, offering directions. "I think you'll find it more comfortable."

Hannah stared at her. "There must be some mistake," she faltered. "I only paid for an Economy ticket. I have some miles, but not enough for that kind of upgrade. Maybe you'd better double-check."

"No mistake," the woman insisted. "Those are the instructions I've received." She looked around Hannah to the next person in line, and Hannah stepped back, confused.

Drew, she realized. He had done this. When he was talking to the Business Class agent, he had been arranging for an upgrade.

She frowned. She had no idea what it might be, but the price was surely horrendous, especially arranged at the last minute. He shouldn't have done it. She needed to get used to being back in her normal life again. And that certainly didn't include this kind of luxury. But there didn't seem to be much she could do about it now. She would just have to bring it up with him later, when she talked to him. *If* she talked to him, she corrected herself. With a mental shrug, she took the gate agent's advice and went to find the lounge.

After a shower and massage to relax her before the long flight, she was sure she had already had Drew's money's worth for the experience. And as she sat in her leather armchair in the nose of the plane, a glass of champagne in her hand and a copy of *Vogue* on the table in front of her, she was once again grateful for his thoughtfulness.

She felt the prick of tears again as her chest tightened. It was a good sendoff, but it was still an ending. And she couldn't feel resigned to the end of her time with him, no matter how much she had tried to remind herself that it was temporary. The unaccustomed sumptuousness softened the blow, but she still looked out the plane's window and ached to be out there with him. To be sitting on the deck above the ocean, watching him grill fish filets for their supper and planning the next day's adventure. Instead, she was going back to winter. To rain. To being alone.

But this was a vacation thing for him, too. He had a whole life here, just as she did back home. And she wasn't part of that life. The thought didn't exactly help her mood, but it did enable her to get a grip on herself. She would just have to enjoy this experience too. Save the sadness for when she got home, and this last piece of her vacation was over. Then she would get busy again, and set about the business of forgetting him.

With that resolution, she picked up the new in-flight magazine as the huge airliner began to taxi, deciding to see what she could expect from this trip. Leafing through to find the entertainment section, her hands stopped as she stared at a full-page photo. There was Drew, smiling and confident, looking right back at her.

She almost dropped the magazine in surprise. Then, with a sinking feeling, she read the headline.

Leadership Challenges
Drew Callahan on Motivation, Morale, and Building a Winning Team

All right, she told herself. He had said he was the team's captain, and rugby was a big deal in this country. So they had interviewed him. She had seen how often he was recognized. This wasn't such a surprise. She began to read, curious to see what he had had to say.

All Blacks Captain Drew Callahan is no stranger to team-building exercises. Unlike the rest of us, though, the challenges don't come in the form of ropes courses or late nights at the office. Instead, the iconic leader has spent the past five years helping to mould his team into the highest-ranked rugby squad in the world. He knows he's been successful when his men literally put their bodies on the line for their mates. What does it take to bring out that level of performance? We spent an afternoon with Callahan to find out.

Hannah devoured it all, her bewilderment growing. Drew had said he played for Auckland. But this was another team altogether. She had heard of the All Blacks, of course. Nobody could visit the country without becoming aware of the national rugby team. All Black merchandise was on prominent display in every shopping area, along with countless references in newspapers and advertising. Still, she was mystified by the relationship. How could he be the captain of *both* teams? Yet he had been for years, according to the article.

She let the magazine fall to the table in front of her as puzzle pieces began clicking into place. His hesitation on first introducing himself. Recognition wherever he went. The beautiful vacation homes he had borrowed for their stays around the country, and his preference for staying there instead of in hotels. It was all so obvious now, she wondered how she had missed it.

He must have thought she was an idiot. Not recognizing him in the first place, or catching on to his position. Maybe he even thought she had stalked him, she realized with horror. Oh, no. Had he thought she *was* throwing herself in his path, pretending to drown? She had joked about that, she remembered, and shriveled with embarrassment at the possibility.

She looked up from the article as the attractive brunette flight attendant approached her seat with the champagne bottle again.

"Can I get you another drink, Ms. Montgomery? Or would you like something else?" The woman smiled as her eyes fell to the open magazine. "I heard that Drew Callahan arranged your trip today. He was just working with the airline a few weeks ago, filming an advert. My colleague was there. She says he's lovely."

She paused expectantly, and Hannah summoned a smile. "Yes, he's a very nice man," she answered briefly. She understood the reason for the curiosity, but wasn't about to oblige it and erode Drew's privacy that much more.

The other woman got the message. "Let me know if there's anything I can do for you. I'm Fiona. Ring anytime if I can be of help."

She moved away, leaving Hannah with her uncomfortable thoughts. How would it feel, she wondered, to be discussed like this by strangers? She had never had any illusions about the glamour of celebrity, but had never had this kind of glimpse into their lives either. She couldn't imagine being on display all the time, being public property. What a life that would be. She shuddered. She'd hate it.

chapter eleven

♡

Hannah had to admit that, no matter how heavy her heart, sleeping in a fold-out bed complete with sheets, pillow, and duvet made her second crossing of the Pacific a lot more comfortable than the first. She might not be as happy as she had been on the trip out, but she had certainly arrived better rested at her destination, she thought as she waited for her bag and endured the long line at U.S. Customs in San Francisco.

When she emerged through the big doors into the entry hall, she was relieved to find Kristen there waiting for her. You never knew with Kristen. She could have forgotten the day, overslept... she would always be so sorry, but that didn't mean much when you were standing and waiting. Here she was now, though, all smiles, rushing up to greet Hannah with a hug.

"I've missed you!" Kristen exclaimed. "I'm so glad you're home!"

As Hannah returned the fierce hug, some of her regret left her. How could she not be thrilled to come back to Kristen?

"I'm glad to be here with you too, sweetie." She gave her sister a kiss. "It's wonderful to see you."

She noticed Fiona approaching in a group of flight attendants. "Goodbye, Ms. Montgomery," the brunette called. "I hope to see you again soon."

"Wow," Kristen breathed. "They really are friendly, aren't they?"

"They sure are," Hannah agreed solemnly. She had already decided that she wouldn't share *every* aspect of her trip with her sister. Too many questions, too hard to be lighthearted about her adventure. She would call Susannah, she decided. She knew her friend would listen and understand.

She sent Kristen home after her sister had dropped her off at the apartment. "I need to take a shower, get unpacked today," she explained. "You go enjoy your Sunday. Thanks for picking me up. Let me know when you can come for dinner this week, OK? Then I can hear how everything's been going for you while I've been gone."

Once she had taken the much-needed shower, though, Hannah didn't immediately start unpacking. Instead, shaking her head at her lack of willpower, she turned on her phone and computer and Googled Drew.

And sat back, stunned, as the search engine returned over half a million results.

She reached for her phone, hardly taking her eyes from the images and links on her screen, and speed-dialed Susannah. When her friend answered, Hannah cut short her effusive welcome.

"Are you at your computer?" she demanded.

"I can be," Susannah answered with surprise. "OK, now I am. What?"

"Google Drew Callahan All Blacks," Hannah instructed, and spelled the name.

"Wow, lots of results," Susannah said. "So, did you meet this guy while you were there? Who is he? What's the All Blacks?"

"He's the captain of the All Blacks. The New Zealand national rugby team," Hannah explained. "They're the ones who play teams from other countries. It's a big deal."

"OK, so why am I looking at this?" Susannah pressed.

"Because," Hannah sighed. "I didn't meet him, Susannah. I *slept* with him."

"You?" Susannah gasped. "What do you mean, you slept with him? You had a one-night stand with an athlete? Oh my God, Hannah. I can see why," she went on hastily. "I mean, it's OK if you did. As long as you were safe. But what happened?"

Hannah groaned. "I didn't have a one-night stand with him. And I didn't mean to sleep with him at all. You know how I am. But you're right. He's even better in person than those pictures. And he was great. I met him, and we went out, and I...well, I ended up spending my whole vacation with him," she finished in a rush. "And I had *no idea* who he was, Susannah. He must have thought I was an idiot."

"Why would he think you're an idiot?" Susannah asked reasonably. "I had no idea who he was. I doubt any American woman would know. Why, did he seem upset that you didn't know who he was?"

"No," Hannah admitted. "He liked it, I think. He gets bothered so much for autographs, people taking his picture and all that, I suppose it was nice for him to know that I wasn't trying to meet him, or impressed by his job. But still, I feel so stupid now."

After that, Hannah naturally had to fill her friend in on the whole story. Well, maybe not the *whole* story. Some things were nobody's business, not even Susannah's. She hadn't realized, though, how much she needed to talk over what had happened, to make sense of her conflicting emotions.

"The thing is, I've never felt like this about anyone," she tried to explain. "I don't think it was just the vacation, or New Zealand. It was all so good, right from the beginning. We had such a good time together. But, Susannah," she said desperately, "I know it was a mistake anyway, now. Here I am back here, and he's there, and that's it. It's not like I met somebody nice I can keep seeing. That's probably best anyway, because I'm sure I'd just get my heart broken. He's way out of my league. I know

I have to say, that was a great time on my vacation, a great few weeks. Now I'm here, back to my life, let's go."

"Whoa. How did you start out by saying, I've begun a wonderful relationship with a great guy, and end up with, he'd have dumped me anyway, so thank goodness it's over now?"

"Come on," Hannah said impatiently. "First, he's a professional athlete. He probably makes some ridiculous amount of money—in fact, I'm sure he does, based on what I saw. And look at him. I'm sure he has his pick of women to date. I certainly saw enough of them approaching him, even when he was with me. And second, he's six thousand miles away, did you notice?"

"Fine," Susannah retorted. "So what did he say about that? Was this the end of it, then? I had a nice time, see you around?"

"No," Hannah admitted. "He said he'd come and see me here. But he was probably just being nice, don't you think?"

"I think you don't want to give him a chance. If he said he wanted to come see you, why not see if he meant it before you assume he didn't? OK, the guy's attractive, he's well off, he's famous—at least there he is. But it sure sounds to me from what you said that he was as bowled over by you as you were by him. Give him a chance," Susannah urged again. "There are good guys out there, you know. You're a pretty good judge of character. If you liked him that much, there must be something there."

"Maybe I just liked his body, though," Hannah said gloomily.

"Well, that isn't so bad either," Susannah laughed. "Nothing wrong with that."

Hannah felt better after hanging up. Even if Susannah weren't right, at least there was somebody she could talk things over with now. She wasn't one to ask for a lot of advice, but in this case, she admitted, she was out of her depth.

At any rate, what she needed to do now, she told herself bracingly, was to unpack and take a walk. She'd feel better, more grounded after a trip to the grocery store to restock. Not to mention a few cups of tea.

She was in the middle of ironing and putting away her somewhat crumpled clothes when her phone beeped with a text. Thinking it must be Kristen, she picked it up, her heart leaping when she saw Drew's name across the screen.

Back OK? Miss you.

She texted, *Yes thanks.* Typed *Miss you too,* then deleted it and pressed *Send.*

Seconds later, she jumped when her phone rang. She answered, and heard, "Hi. The flight was all right then?"

"Hi," she replied, her smile huge. It was so good to hear his voice. "You shouldn't have got me that upgrade, though. You didn't have to do that. It must have been so expensive."

"I probably shouldn't tell you this. Should probably let you think I spent all that. But I'm on an Air New Zealand plane half the weeks in the year. Reckon they've made their dollar out of me. I've done a bit of advertising for them, too. They're a big sponsor. Didn't charge me much at all. I'm just glad you were comfortable."

"Yes," she took the opportunity to say. "I noticed you'd done a bit of advertising. When I opened the in-flight magazine and saw your face looking at me, it just about gave me a heart attack. But I feel like an idiot, Drew. Why didn't you tell me you were captain of the All Blacks?"

"Didn't seem necessary, did it. I wasn't being 'captain of the All Blacks' when I was with you. Just a bloke on his holidays."

"Some bloke," she muttered. "You weren't laughing at me? Shouldn't I have known?"

"Nah. I promise I wasn't laughing at you. I'm laughing at you now, a bit," he admitted. "Does that count? Why should you know? I'm not such an arrogant bugger that I think women all over the world have my poster over their bed. I'm not bloody Prince William."

"Close enough in New Zealand, I'll bet," she said shrewdly.

He laughed. "Not even here. Believe me, there are heaps of good-looking fellas on the squad for the girls to drool over. I'm not even on the list. Sorry to disappoint you."

She privately suspected that wasn't true, but it was obviously a subject he didn't want to discuss. "Where are you now?" she asked instead.

"Went back to the Coromandel. Back to the fishing."

"Well, I'm glad you're getting the chance to do that now, anyway. I know how much you enjoy it."

"I'd rather have you here with me," he said seriously. "Fishing or not."

"I wish I were there too," she admitted. "I was glad to see my sister again, but it was hard to leave."

They talked a while longer, and when she hung up, she was at least a little convinced that this was more than a fling for him, too.

♡

It didn't take long for her vacation to seem like a dim memory. Walking through the office door the next day, Hannah felt her role settling back around her like a well-worn sweater, as welcomes were called out and employees stopped by to ask about her vacation and update her on work issues.

A few questions about her trip were enough to satisfy most, confirming her belief that nobody was really very interested in anyone else's vacation. Or their vacation photos, she thought with amusement, remembering her conversation with Drew. She knew Emery would have been more than interested in *some* of the details, but she had no intention of sharing. Instead, she carefully edited the company she had kept out of her brief accounts of the trip.

Soon enough, though, it was back to business as usual. True to their word, Beth and Emery had handled things well during her absence, though they were happy to have her back. Felix, of course, was overjoyed. He kept her on the phone for an hour that first day, going over plans for the next few weeks. What with that, and making it through the pile of material on her desk and in her email inbox, she was more than glad when the long day was over.

By the end of the week, she felt caught up and back in control, if a bit exhausted. Had her days always been this long? By the time she had worked eleven hours or more, got in some exercise, and fed herself, she was falling asleep over a book. No wonder she had no social life, she realized. She didn't have time for one.

She did manage to leave work early on Thursday, though, to have Matt and Kristen over for dinner. It hadn't been easy to find an evening when both were free. No question, they did have the social lives she lacked.

Hannah hadn't seen Matt in almost two months, and she realized how much she had missed her happy-go-lucky brother. It was reassuringly comfortable sitting with the two of them at her kitchen table, as they had so many times before.

"So did you do any adventure sports in New Zealand?" Matt asked her as they finished their meal. "Did you try surfing at all? Bet you didn't even think about kite surfing. I'd love to do that."

"No," Hannah admitted. "I did a lot of ocean swimming, though, even snorkeling. Kayaking, too. And I hiked a lot. It was the most beautiful place I've ever been. Just getting the chance to see it was such a treat."

"You could have done all that here, though," he said, disappointed. "What about Zorbing?"

"I'm embarrassed to say that I don't even know what that is," she told him.

"You know. You have to have seen it," he argued. "You get into a big plastic ball, and they roll you down the hill."

"Nope, sorry. I didn't realize I was missing the chance to roll down a hill in a giant plastic ball."

"I've seen that! That looks really fun," Kristen put in. "It's too bad you didn't try it."

"What about bungy jumping?" Matt went on. "They invented it in New Zealand, you know. And you have to have noticed places where you could do that. I've heard there are lots of opportunities to bungy jump over there."

"I did notice that," Hannah agreed, smiling. "But I must admit, I never felt the slightest desire to try it. Jumping off some tower and falling to the ground, trusting I won't hit it and die— not my idea of a good time. I don't find it very entertaining to be terrified, I guess. It sounds to me like you'd better take your own trip to New Zealand. You can fill me in on everything I missed."

"I'm thinking about it," Matt answered cheerfully. "I'm saving again now. I got some great tips last week, and Christmas is always good. Maybe next year, after Christmas. I should have enough money saved up by then to take two or three months off and travel. I was thinking about going to Australia and New Zealand, maybe some of the Pacific Islands too."

"That sounds like lots of fun," Hannah said. "And the right time of year to go. So you're planning to keep working at the hotel for another year?"

"Yep. That's the plan. And before you ask," Matt cut her off, "no, I have no plans to get a job 'in my field,' or go to graduate school. I want to do this right now."

"I know you do, sweetie," Hannah said a little sadly. "When you get to that point, though, you know I'll help you any way I can."

"You've helped me enough, don't you think?" Matt asked reasonably. "Me and Kristen both. You helped pay my way through college. How many sisters can say that? And I'm grateful. But I need to make my own decisions now."

Hannah got up and moved around the table to hug him. "I've always been glad to help you out, Mattie. And I'm so proud of you. Of both of you. We didn't have much example of that growing up—supporting ourselves, being independent. You're both doing so well. I'll try to back off now, I promise."

Kristen had been sitting quietly, listening. Now she spoke, more thoughtfully than usual. "Matt and I did have an example, though. I mean, there you were, working so hard all the time. You still do. And maybe we should be there for you more, Hannah. It's always been you helping us. But you know, you never call us when you have a problem."

"That's because I'm lucky. I don't have many problems," Hannah replied cheerfully. "I have a pretty good life, you know. Too busy, but I have you two, and I have great friends."

"Speaking of friends," Matt said, getting up and putting his dishes into the dishwasher, "I'm supposed to meet some guys. Sorry to eat and run."

"That's OK," Hannah said, stifling her disappointment. "It was great to see you. Especially since I missed Thanksgiving this year. We'll make up for it at Christmas, though."

Kristen left fairly soon, too. Which was good, as Hannah had another early day on Friday. And lots more to catch up on over the weekend.

Lying in bed that evening, she thought back to what Matt and Kristen had said. She was glad Matt wanted to be independent, though it gave her heart a wrench to think that he didn't need her anymore. But he was right, she admitted. She had been looking out for her brother and sister for so long, it was hard to recognize that they were adults now. Hard not to give them advice or think she knew what was best for them.

Kristen was going to be a tougher nut than Matt in that regard, she knew. Or was she herself the problem? Didn't some part of her take satisfaction in being so important to her sister, in Kristen's reliance on her advice, her guidance? Drew—and Susannah too, she reminded herself—were right. She needed to let Kristen grow up. At least get out of her way.

chapter twelve

♡

Hannah wasn't used to feeling lonely. She spent so much of her day talking to people that she usually enjoyed coming home and having a chance to wind down and relax by herself. Since her return, though, something had changed. Instead of feeling like a haven, her apartment just seemed empty. She found herself spending even more time outdoors, using her lunch hour to run or swim and working late into the evening. She hated to admit how much she looked forward to Drew's calls, even as she schooled herself not to expect them.

But when he called to tell her he was coming to the U.S. in a week, she stopped trying to convince herself that she didn't miss him, and wasn't longing to see him again.

"That's great you're able to get over here," she said. "It's a long way to come, though."

"I have a meeting in LA with an ad exec anyway, for an endorsement deal," he told her smoothly. Who would have been more than happy to come to New Zealand, Drew knew. The man had jumped at the chance to have Drew visit, however, and had quickly taken the opportunity to line up a photo shoot at the same time. He sensed, though, that Hannah would feel less pressured if she thought he weren't making a special trip to see her.

He didn't understand her reluctance to admit that they might have something special. His own feelings weren't very complicated. He missed her, he wanted to see her, and he needed to find out how it would be when they were together again.

"Can you take a day off, so we have a bit of time?" he asked now. "Friday would be good."

"You know I already took all my vacation. But…you know, I hardly ever miss a day. And Heaven knows I put in enough hours. I'll tell Felix I need a day. I want to spend time with you."

"Good, because I'd like to take you someplace special. Do you want to decide where, or do you want me to surprise you?"

"Surprise me," she said without hesitation. "That sounds great."

Felix was just as unhappy as Hannah had expected when she told him she needed another day off. "I gave you three weeks," he complained. "That's a lot, you know. Why do you need this day again?"

"I appreciate the three weeks. And now I have some personal business, so I need to take a day. I realize I haven't quite accrued it yet, but I do need to take this day in advance of the accrual. You know I haven't taken a sick day all year, Felix."

"You're not going on an interview, are you?" he asked, alarmed.

"No. I'm not going on an interview. I have some personal business," she repeated. "I'll make sure we're covered, and I'll be back on Monday, I promise."

"All right, then. But you know I count on you to be there. Don't make this a habit."

One day wasn't a habit, she thought irritably. But she wasn't going to worry about it. She could barely admit how much she was looking forward to Drew's visit.

On Wednesday, he called again from Los Angeles.

"How's it going down there?" she asked.

"Bit dull," he admitted. "Shooting an advert. Standing around, having my hair fixed. Taking a drink from a bottle, then being told how to take a drink differently. They want me back tomorrow because I shaved today, and now they want stubble. Mad."

"It's rough, having to be so manly," she commiserated. "I guess they don't want to see your tender side."

"Saving that for you," he promised. "That's why I rang, actually. Can you be at the Oakland airport tomorrow evening at six?"

"Sure I can," she answered, mentally rearranging her day so she could leave earlier. "Will I be picking you up there?"

"Nah, you said to surprise you, so I'm working on that. Just go to the Southwest counter, and they'll get you sorted."

"Drew," she protested. "I didn't mean for you to surprise me this much. At least tell me what to pack."

"Swimming togs. You know the ones I like. Casual. Nothing too warm. And that's all I'm telling you," he cut her off. "It's a surprise, remember?"

"All right," she said dubiously. "I guess I'll see you tomorrow night, then?"

"You'll see me," he promised.

♡

"You're distracted, Hannah," Emery scolded the next day. "What did I just say?"

"I'm sorry. I was thinking about something else, that's all. I'm paying attention now, I promise."

"Are you feeling OK?" the more sensitive Beth asked. "I don't want to pry, but is everything all right? I was just wondering," she said hastily, "because you're taking a day off, and you never do that. You'd tell us if something were wrong, wouldn't you?"

Hannah threw up her hands. "I can see I need to take more time off, if one day causes such a stir. Everything's fine, I promise.

I'll be back on Monday just like always, ready to go. Let's get back to talking about running shorts, OK?"

Parking her car at the Oakland airport that evening, she felt happier than she had since she had returned from her vacation. She wished she hadn't asked Drew to surprise her, though. Now that the time was here, she wanted to see him now.

At the Southwest terminal, the agent handed her a ticket to Los Angeles. Well, that made sense, and at least the flight was short. She hated to admit that she was a bit disappointed. She wasn't a fan of the huge, sprawling city, and was surprised that Drew had chosen to stay there. It didn't seem like his kind of place either. She reminded herself to be appreciative anyway. He didn't know that she didn't care much for nightlife, after all. They'd never spent any time in the city together. She just hoped he wasn't planning to take her to Disneyland.

By the time the plane touched down in LA, though, Hannah didn't care if they were going to Knott's Berry Farm for the weekend. She saw Drew as soon as she stepped through the security area, and her heart, which had been beating hard already, seemed actually to leap in her chest. She didn't realize she had been running until she hit his chest hard. He swept her up against him, laughing.

It felt so good, being held by him again, kissing him, stubble and all. She lifted her hand to his cheek to feel its roughness.

"Sorry," he grinned. "Didn't wait to shave."

"I like it," she assured him. "They were right. It's very manly. Very sexy." She smiled into his eyes.

"Hold that thought," he commanded as he pulled her with him outside the airport, and into a car that pulled up within seconds.

"So where are we going in LA?" she asked.

"You'll see. You wanted to be surprised, remember?" was the only answer she could get from him.

Instead of exiting onto the freeway, however, the car continued around to another terminal. Drew pulled her out, together with her bag and his own, and hustled her into a much quieter building, with several small gates leading out onto the tarmac.

"Private plane," he explained with a grin. "Wait and see."

"I've never been on a private plane before," she said as they boarded. "How exciting."

"Somehow, it doesn't surprise me that you told me that. It's a short hop, though. I won't get to impress you much, I'm afraid."

He was right. In less than half an hour, they were landing. It was hard to tell in the dark, but the area seemed small.

"Where are we?" she asked, bewildered, as the plane taxied to a stop.

"Catalina Island. I asked around, and this seemed to be the best place to go. Didn't have enough time to take you to Hawaii. This was the closest I could get. Not warm enough to swim much, but we can go out on the water, get you out of the rain, anyway."

The next three days were some of the most relaxed Hannah could remember. If anything, they were better than her final days in New Zealand, because she didn't have the dread of leaving hanging over her. Drew had hired a kayaking guide, and they spent a happy Friday touring the inaccessible parts of the island, watching the cormorants diving, once even spotting a bald eagle fishing.

They pulled up on an isolated beach where Drew, with a grin and a flourish, opened his kayak's compartments to reveal a wetsuit and snorkeling gear. "Open yours," he insisted, and there was her gear, to her delight.

"Just like our first date, eh. I didn't get lucky that day. Hoping to pull today, though," he said seriously, pulling the suit on.

She looked around, grateful to see that the guide had moved off to the side of the beach. "I don't know what that means, but

I can guess. So stop embarrassing me. I think you do that on purpose," she scolded him, half-laughing.

"It's true," he admitted. "I like to watch you blush. And it means just what you think. So rattle your dags. The quicker we do this, the quicker we can get back."

For all his teasing, she knew he enjoyed exploring the undersea world as much as she did, pointing out fish and swimming over when she found something exciting. The water was cold, though, and a half hour was enough. They paddled back with the wind, enjoying a quick ride back to the harbor.

Thirty minutes later, she was finding out why their hotel suite had a hot tub on the balcony.

"Being with you is quite an education. All kinds of new experiences," she said, breathless, against his chest as he pulled her on top of him at last in the warm, bubbling water. "Bubbles instead of minerals this time."

"That's me," he agreed huskily, easing her slowly onto him and watching her eyes glaze over as he filled her. "Always coaching, eh."

He liked this angle, he decided, pulling a pink nipple into his mouth, biting gently, feeling her jerk at the sensation. One hand stayed at her breast, while the other went down to stroke her as she rocked against him. She moaned, clutching his shoulders, moving faster now.

"Drew," she gasped at last. "I need you. More."

He stood up, still holding her onto him, and stepped out of the tub. "What do you need? Tell me."

"I need you on top of me," she admitted. "Please."

He lowered her onto the chaise and obliged her. "Like this?" he asked, as he pushed home.

"Yes. Like that. Please," she whimpered again as he drove harder now, faster, again and again. Her arms reached out, fluttering, seeking something to hold onto, needing to hang on.

He saw it, felt her distress. Grabbed her wrists in one strong hand, pulled them above her head. And pushed her over the edge, following her into a mindless, overwhelming orgasm that pulled the breath from his body.

"I've missed that," he said against her hair, after pulling her to lie on his chest, stroking his hand down her back just for the pleasure of feeling her skin again. "You do something to me."

"You do something to me too," she admitted. "I think you like doing something to me, in fact."

"I do," he agreed. "Every day. You push me someplace new, every time."

"I do?" She was pleased, but surprised. "I don't know any tricks or anything, though."

He laughed. "Trust me. You don't need any tricks. Reckon you've got what I need."

♡

That evening, eating fish together again, she smiled, remembering their first dinner. "You know what's nice about this?" she asked him.

"What?" he went along.

"No cell phone cameras. Nobody watching you or interrupting. No girls flicking their hair at you. It must be nicer for you, too, even though you never say anything about it."

"It is," he admitted. "I'm proud to be an All Black. It's an honor. Special, every time you put on the black jersey. But you're right, it's good to get away sometimes."

"Is that the reason for all that attention, then? It's not just being a rugby player?"

"Yeh. You're always recognized a bit anyway. But when you're an All Black, you're more visible. And I've been on the squad for a fair few years now."

"Plus that little detail of being the captain. I suspect that has something to do with it, too."

He shrugged. "Yeh. There were other blokes before me. And there'll be more after me. It's really not about me. It's about being on the team. And it's a short enough time in the spotlight. Rugby matters to Kiwis, that's all. It's different from other places."

"I gathered that. And the All Blacks matter more than anything else, I take it."

"I reckon. Let's talk about something else now, eh."

She laughed. "All right. I'll take pity on you. I guess the only thing worse than having people take your picture is talking about people taking your picture, is that it?"

"Too right," he grinned.

She entertained him instead for the remainder of their dinner with a description of Matt's disappointment at her lack of adventure on her vacation.

"Apparently I was supposed to bungy jump," she told him, to his amusement.

"Maybe if I pushed you off the tower," he teased. "That's the only way we'd get you doing that fall."

"It's terrible to be such a chicken. I admit it. Have you done it?"

"Course I have. What kind of Kiwi do you take me for? Can't say I'm addicted to it, though."

"I'm glad. It seems dangerous."

"Nah. Not compared to some things. Sweet as."

"Sweet as what?" she prompted, when he didn't go on.

He looked surprised. "Didn't you ever hear that, when you were in En Zed?"

"What?" She was still confused.

"Another new experience for you," he smiled. "Sweet as. Kiwispeak. We don't like using too many words. Or wasting time and effort thinking of metaphors. There was a billboard a while back for a new chocolate cornet. An ice cream," he amended. "It just said, 'Choc As.'"

"I get it. Instead of saying, 'This ice cream is really, really chocolaty,' you just say, 'Choc As.'"

"That's it. Dead easy, see? Two words. Gets the point across."

"It would make my copywriting easier, anyway," she mused. "We're always trying to find the fewest number of words to convey the message. Too bad I can't use that."

♡

"I wish we didn't have to leave," she sighed as they packed up on Sunday afternoon. "I don't feel ready to say goodbye to you yet."

"Are you saying goodbye to me? Have a messy apartment, do you, that you don't want me to see? Don't I get to walk you to your door, at least give you a kiss goodnight, after I paid for this expensive weekend, and all? Come to think of it, didn't you tell me that was the rule? If I take you out, I get sex? After three dates, wasn't it?"

She laughed. "Really? You're coming back with me?"

"One more night, unless your husband objects. My ticket's for Monday afternoon, out of San Francisco. Thought I could take you to lunch tomorrow, anyway. You do get to eat lunch, don't you? You're not actually chained to the desk all day?"

"It only feels like it," she admitted. "You're right, I hardly ever go out to lunch. But I'd love that. And I'd especially love for you to come home with me tonight." Just saying the words gave her a thrill. "My little apartment won't know what hit it. It's never seen that kind of excitement before."

"I remember. Something else you shared. I'll try and make it memorable."

"I hope so. Unless I wore you out too much already, this weekend."

"I think I'm fit for one more night. I've been training, remember?"

"I didn't realize that was what you were training for," she teased. "But I'm glad."

chapter thirteen

♡

I t felt a little strange, showing Drew her tiny apartment. Hannah had always loved the compact, orderly space. It was good to know she had chosen everything in it, even if some of the choosing had happened at garage sales. She liked sitting at her desk and being able to look out at the sky and the trees, knowing that this was her own place.

Drew seemed to realize that it was a big step for her. After she had shown him around, which took all of a minute, he told her seriously, "Thanks for sharing your place with me tonight. I wanted to see where you live. Where you work. So when I ring you, I can imagine you here. Know what you're seeing, when you look out the window."

"It feels good to have you here too. I wish you could stay longer, but it's probably just as well, since I can't take any more time off. It's going to be hard enough going to work tomorrow while you're still here."

She was right. Getting up the next morning and kissing him goodbye was a wrench, even knowing that he'd be coming by the office to take her to lunch. Hannah had suggested they meet at a restaurant, but Drew hadn't been put off so easily.

"Why don't you want me to come and see where you work?" he asked her shrewdly. "You're actually a typist, is that it?"

"I don't think there even are such things as typists anymore," she pointed out. "No, it's just that…people talk, you know? I'm fairly private around the office."

"I can see that. You wouldn't want anyone to know you ever had a date. Could ruin your reputation."

"Probably true," she admitted. "But I guess I can risk it."

Even so, when she heard his voice in the outer office that afternoon, she jumped and dropped her stapler with a crash. Beth turned from her desk in surprise that turned to speculation as Drew entered their shared workspace.

It was shallow of her, Hannah knew, but she couldn't resist a flash of pride in his appearance and the way he dominated the space around him. When he walked into a room, it was hard to be unaware of his presence.

She introduced him to Beth and could almost see her colleague's mental gears clicking over as she registered his accent. Hannah made their escape as quickly as possible. Before Emery came in, she thought desperately. The fun would have really started then.

Over lunch, Drew suggested visiting again in January, before he had to report for practice. She agreed, but refused to let herself get too comfortable with the idea.

"It's a long time from now," she told him. "If it doesn't work out, that's OK. No obligation."

"It's only a month away," he corrected. "Can't you count on me even for a month?"

She shrugged. "Things can happen. We're a long way apart. I know that. I'm a realist."

"A pessimist, more like," he answered, nettled. "Do you think you won't want to see me, next month? Should I not bother?"

"No!" she responded, startled. "I'll want to see you. You know I will. But it's not the same."

"No, it's not the same. Because I have some faith in you."

"I'm sorry," she said wretchedly. "But you meet women all the time, and I know they're looking to date you."

"That must mean," he countered, "that if I needed a date, or someone to spend the night with, I wouldn't have to fly ten thousand kilometers to do it. And yet here I am.

"Hannah," he went on seriously, taking her hand, "This is good. Don't write it off until we see how we go."

She pressed his hand in return. "OK," she said, a little shakily. "I want to see you. Please come back next month." It frightened her to admit, to him and to herself, how much she wanted that to happen.

"You can count on it." He released her hand and stood. "Let's get you back to work, then, earn your salary so you can take another day off, next time I'm here."

Back at the office, he asked her for a tour.

"There's not that much to see," Hannah said doubtfully. But she obliged, showing him what she was working on. He took a copy of the latest catalog ("Reading material for the plane ride, eh"), and chatted with Beth, who was clearly agog with curiosity.

Of course, it only took a few minutes for Emery to get wind of Drew's visit and pop in to be introduced as well. Hannah watched Drew closely, dreading his reaction. She didn't care, she told herself fiercely, how much she liked him. If he were rude to Emery, it was going to affect her opinion of him.

She needn't have worried. Drew seemed to find Emery amusing, laughing at his obvious attempts to get more details about their relationship.

"You'll have to ask Hannah about that, I'm afraid," he smiled. "I'm just here for a visit. And I've got to be off now, catch that plane." He picked up his bag where he had stowed it near her desk. "I ordered a taxi, should be here now.

"Thanks for showing me around, introducing me to your mates," he said as Hannah walked him to the waiting cab. "Emery's a bit of a dag, isn't he?"

"What?" she asked, startled. "He's gay, yes. Is that what you mean?"

He laughed. "Caught that, didn't I. Nah, he's a comedian, like. A bit of a dag."

"Oh," she answered, relieved. "I wish you'd speak English. I was worried for a minute you were some kind of homophobe, and I was going to have to hate you. But you're right. Emery's great. He always makes me laugh, no matter how stressed I am. He's really good at his job, too. Felix can't stand him, of course. Not respectful enough."

"I can see that. Reckon you're going to hear from him about me when you get back in there." He pulled her to him for a goodbye kiss. "Wish you were going back with me. It'll be a long flight by myself."

"Hmmm. Judging from what the flight attendant had to say about you on my trip, I'm guessing you could have company if you wanted it."

He winced. "Yeh. Always looking to make me more comfortable, aren't they. I'll ring you when I'm back home. And we'll make plans soon for next month."

"All right." She kissed him again as the driver moved to put his bag in the trunk. "Have a safe trip." And allowed herself to hope that she really would see him again soon.

♡

"Well." Emery perched on the edge of Hannah's desk and looked at her, arms folded, a devilish smile on his pixie face. "Just what have you been up to, young lady?"

Hannah saw that Beth was looking at her with just as much interest, if a bit more discretion. She sank into her desk chair and said weakly, "Well, I did tell you I had a good time in New Zealand, right? It's just…I didn't want to say anything. I didn't want to make too much of it. He's someone I met on my trip."

"So he's a rugby player," Emery said with satisfaction. "Once we knew that, Beth and I had to Google him while you were out there. Good work, girl. I'm impressed. Must have been the wardrobe. I told you the Rapunzel thing would work for you. And it looks like I was right," he congratulated himself.

Hannah laughed. "Only you could turn this into a triumph for you, Emery. You didn't even help me pick my clothes. I don't think you can take credit for this one."

"So he came all this way to visit you, and you didn't even tell us about him. I have to say, I'm disappointed in you. Come on, share some details. What happened?"

"I met him, and we spent time together. Is that so amazing? Other people have holiday flings, right? This was my fling. Except it wasn't, I guess. Oh, dear." Hannah flapped her hands in distress. "I really like him. And I think he might like me too. I'm pretty confused," she admitted with a shaky laugh.

"Soooo…" Emery said, "I don't get it. OK, the guy likes you. A lot. He came all the way over here. And don't tell me he just happened to travel, what? Five thousand miles? He was in your neighborhood and thought he'd drop by? You even took a day off to be with him, my amazing telepathic powers tell me. Oh, the shock. You like him. He likes you. What are we confused about here?"

"He's too much, I think," Hannah said slowly. "It's a little overwhelming, isn't it? Look at me." She opened her arms wide and gave her chair a spin. "I'm OK, I know. I'm all right. I'm not complaining. But I'm not a supermodel, admit it. Any kind of model. He's just…so much. So attractive. So successful. So…big."

"Now we're getting into it," Emery said. "Well, I can certainly understand that. I mean, who wants a rich, successful guy, who's hot as *hell?* With, I might add, an adorable accent? And one who's so…*big?*" He fluttered his eyelashes dramatically and said seriously, "I can see I need to take him off your hands."

Beth laughed and chimed in for the first time. "Somehow, I don't think you'd have too much luck with that one, Emery. I suspect you're not his type."

Turning to Hannah, she said in her usual thoughtful tone, "I think you might be underestimating yourself. I don't go much for the big jock type myself, but I can see he's hot. All that tes- tosterone—I'm sure he does beat them off with a stick. But has it occurred to you that he might like you because you aren't a party girl? He didn't strike me as much of a party boy himself. Pretty serious, I thought. When you're together, what's it like?"

Hannah felt herself blushing again, and for the thousandth time, cursed the Viking ancestor who had bequeathed her her fair skin. Her thin skin, she thought ruefully. "It's good," she offered lamely.

Emery leaned forward. "How good?" he whispered.

Beth slapped his hand. "Stop it, Emery. Quit teasing. You don't have to share too much, Hannah. But what do you talk about? How does it feel to be with him?"

Hannah answered honestly this time. "It's so easy. You know I'm not all that chatty all the time, and he isn't either. But we can talk, and it's fine being quiet with him too. We like doing the same things. Hiking," she said hastily. "The ocean. Being outdoors. I feel like I've known him a long time. But I haven't. And that's the problem."

"But," Beth objected, "given how you feel, and how I saw him looking at you, what are you worrying about?"

"I guess I'm afraid I like him too much," Hannah admitted. "I'm scared to let myself. I kept telling myself while I was out there that this was a short-term thing. Like a shipboard romance, or those women who sleep with the golf pro." She laughed. "Well, not exactly that. I'm not good at casual relationships, I know, but what can I say, I really liked him. So I told myself, it's OK, you can be self-indulgent, just this once. You'll be careful, and no harm done. And the problem now is," she sighed, "that I don't feel casual. That's what's confusing me. And we don't exactly live near each other, do we? It's not like this can go anywhere. Well, shoot," she moaned, standing up and pacing, her arms wrapped around herself. "I'm a mess. I'm scared of getting hurt, that's all," she repeated.

Emery stood up and gave her a hug. "Honey, even I can get hurt. And you know what a tiny, shriveled little heart I have. Sometimes you just have to go with it. Even a Miss Control like you. Some things you can't put in a spreadsheet. Some things don't balance."

Hannah smiled and felt a little better. Talking it over had helped, even though she still felt shaky, and embarrassed at having confided so much. She took a deep breath. "Thanks, guys. I appreciate it. But we'd probably all better get back to work, huh? Otherwise I'm going to be lovelorn, and we're all going to be jobless too."

They laughed and moved away, Emery giving her one last squeeze. But the conversation reverberated in Hannah's head all afternoon. She *was* scared. What kind of future did they have? Wasn't she just setting herself up for more heartbreak down the road?

Don't worry about that now, she scolded herself. Drew had said he was coming back next month. She'd look forward to that.

chapter fourteen

♡

Hannah's job was always busy to the point of being frantic during the holiday season, and this year was no exception. She was reluctant even to spend the time to attend the annual holiday party that TriStyle Woman was co-hosting with the other tenants of the office complex.

"Why do we have to go to this thing again?" she complained to Emery. "I have a lot to do. Couldn't I just stay in the office and work? You could do my part for me."

"You're supposed to distribute the holiday bonus envelopes, remember, Mrs. Scrooge? I intend to be there with my hand out. And you're giving a speech, aren't you? You know my speech would be totally inappropriate."

Hannah had to laugh at that. "You could be right," she conceded. "I'm not sure I should leave that to you, especially after a couple glasses of wine. All right. Not sure it's going to be worth my getting dressed up for, though. At least it's after work, so I didn't have to go home and come back."

"Do you call that dressed up?" Emery asked, brows raised. "All right, you're wearing a dress. Could we have been a bit more festive, though? I keep telling you, navy blue isn't your color. And you know, a little higher heel wouldn't have killed you."

"It's too hard to walk in them, though."

"Who's walking? The party's in the lobby. Let's at least fix your hair. It's a party, not a funeral. Here, let me take it out of that stupid knot."

She did look better, Hannah conceded, after Emery had finished arranging her hair into a softer style. He then insisted on pulling out her purse and intensifying her usually subdued makeup.

"There. Now you look a little less like the Grinch. Come on. Let's go get this party started."

As they walked downstairs, Hannah had to admit that the huge lobby looked beautiful. A decorated tree stood in the corner, and the modern pillars were twined with lights and garlands. A band was already playing as the building's various tenants congregated around the bar.

"No expense spared," Emery grinned as he brought her a glass of wine. "A cash bar, *and* hors d'oeuvres. And the whole thing will be over by eight. Oh well, cheers." He clinked his glass against hers. "I'm off to look for cute boys. See what Santa will bring me."

Hannah watched him go, laughing. She was soon joined by Beth, and a festive spirit did begin to fill the space. With the lights lowered, inhibitions a bit loosened after a glass of wine, and the band playing, it began to feel less like a work function and more like a party.

As soon as everyone had arrived, Hannah gathered the TriStyle Woman staff around her and passed out the envelopes containing their modest holiday bonuses, thanking them all for their hard work during the past year.

"Our success this year is thanks to all of you," she told them sincerely. "I know how much I appreciate everything you bring to the company. You make it a pleasure to come to work every day. And if anybody needs a cab home, remember, it's on the house tonight," she finished, to gratified applause.

Her duty done, she was happy to relax on a barstool at a tall table, idly watching Emery flirt shamelessly with women and men alike. She turned to a touch on her shoulder to find Mark Maxwell, an attorney from the office across the hall, smiling at her.

"Happy Holidays. You're looking very beautiful tonight. Thought you could use a glass of wine," Mark said, holding it out to her. "I brought white. I noticed that's what you were drinking earlier. May I join you?"

"Sure." Hannah smiled cautiously back at him. He was handsome, she had always thought, but a little too aware of it. And *his* muscles had definitely come from the gym.

"I like this combined office party," he confided. "The scenery's a lot better when it includes TriStyle."

"We're an active group," she agreed. "We like to walk the talk."

"It's working for you," he smiled confidently. His eyes did a sweep of her figure, making her glad she hadn't worn anything more revealing.

"It's pretty crowded in here, though," he went on. "How about getting out of here, going for dinner with me someplace quieter? I've wanted to get to know you better anyway."

"I'm sorry, Mark. It's been a long day, and I'm looking forward to getting home. Thank you for the invitation, though," she said politely.

"What about tomorrow night, then?" he pressed. "I think we'd be good together. I'd like to take the chance to find out."

"I'm sorry," she said again. "I'm not interested, I'm afraid."

"You're missing a treat," Mark urged, leaning closer. "I'm nine inches."

She could only stare at him. "I beg your pardon?" she finally asked, in as icy a voice as she could manage.

"All there for you," he promised, reaching for her hand. "I'll make sure you have a good time."

"I'm sure the two of you will be very happy together," Hannah managed at last. "Excuse me."

She found Emery in the corner, chatting animatedly. At her urgent whisper, he broke away.

"What's going on?" he asked.

Torn between distress, outrage, and diversion, she told him.

Emery shrieked with laughter. "He said *that?*" he finally got out. "What an asshole."

"He is, isn't he? What a thing to say." She started laughing herself.

"And what you told him," Emery gasped. "You kill me, Hannah. Bet he can't believe it didn't work."

"Would that *ever* work?" She laughed so hard that tears came to her eyes as she remembered the scene, Mark's outraged look as she had got up and left. "Who would go for that?"

"Who knows. Somebody drunker and less picky than you. Want another glass of wine?"

"No." She shook her head, still grinning. "I think I've had all the entertainment I can stand for one night. I'm going home. See you Monday."

Drew was much less amused, though, when Hannah told him about her flattering invitation on the phone the following night.

"So you see," she finished with a chuckle. "You don't have a lot of competition back here."

"Bastard," was his comment. "I'd like to meet him for a bit. Show him how well that sort of thing goes over with me."

"You don't have to worry. I told Emery. I think his revenge will be even more effective. I suspect Mr. Wonderful has a new nickname by now. I almost feel sorry for him. What I *really* wanted to say," she added mischievously, "was that men who actually have it don't need to talk about it."

Drew wasn't to be diverted. "I hate to think of you there alone, somebody saying that to you. Wish I'd been with you."

"Yes, I think we can safely assume that he wouldn't have said it if you'd been there. And now you know why it had been three years," she pointed out reasonably. "Lots of jerks out there."

"There is that," he conceded. "Can't help but look good in comparison, can I."

"You look good anyway," she assured him. "But in comparison, yes, you blow them out of the water."

♡

"How in the world do people get into the Christmas spirit?" Hannah wondered aloud one late December evening around seven, as she and Beth looked over sales reports and discussed post-holiday discounts. "What kind of decorations do you have at your place, Beth?"

"None," the other woman admitted. "I always mean to put them up, but we're so busy, it just seems like one more chore. And since I live alone..." She shrugged. "It doesn't seem like there's much point. But my parents always have the house decorated," she brightened. "I guess that's when Christmas really starts for me. Even if it's Christmas Eve by the time I get home, once I've gone to midnight Mass, and sung the carols, and eaten my mom's food, I'm ready to enjoy Christmas."

"That's great. You're lucky." Hannah couldn't help feeling a pang of envy.

"I'm sorry, Hannah," Beth said contritely. "That was insensitive of me. What are you going to be doing this year?"

"It's all right," Hannah reassured her. "Nothing to be sorry about. I like hearing about your family. I'm doing the same thing as usual—having Matt and Kristen over for the day. We'll go for a walk, have dinner. The only difference is we have chicken instead of turkey. Pretty hard for three people to eat a turkey, you know. That's all right, though. I like chicken better anyway, don't you?"

Beth didn't answer her directly. "Do you mind my asking, Hannah—don't you have grandparents, or anything? Why has it been just you and your siblings?"

"Not really. My mother's parents were never very involved, and my father's parents have passed away now. That's OK, though. It was all a long time ago. How did we get on this sad subject, anyway?" Hannah asked briskly. "I should let us get back to work so we can get out of here."

Beth dropped the subject, sensitive to Hannah's mood as always. But Hannah impulsively stopped at the tree lot on the way home and bought a tabletop-sized evergreen that would fit into her small apartment and give it the smell of Christmas. She might not have a lot of family, but she did have a sister and brother, and she needed to make the holiday special for them.

She knew, really, why Christmas always seemed like an ordeal. It wasn't just that her family was smaller than most. Her father had died in November, and her sorrow over his passing had cast a pall over the holiday ever since.

She could recall that first year so clearly. They'd had a tree, but their mother hadn't helped to decorate it. It had been up to Hannah to organize her brother and sister in pulling out the boxes of decorations and putting them onto the tree. She'd put on a holiday CD, but it had all so forced, and Matt had cried.

When Hannah had asked her mother about stockings, Tiffany Montgomery had just looked at her. "Aren't you all too old?" she had asked vaguely.

"The little kids aren't. They need stockings, Mom. Mattie especially. He still half-believes that Santa's going to come. He'll be so sad if there are no presents. How about if I do it? I know what you put in. Could you give me some money, and I can buy the things?"

She had continued to do it until she had gone away to college. Little things—crayons and barrettes and stickers, Matchbox cars.

Batteries, pens, candy when they got older. Silly things, but the tradition meant a lot to her, and to them, Hannah knew.

But filling the stockings on Christmas Eve had never felt as joyful as it should have. It just made her remember what it had been like when her father had been alive. How he and her mother had joked and laughed, shooing their three children off to bed "so Santa can come."

She remembered giggling with Kristen in the room they shared, unable to sleep for the excitement, until her father would come down.

"If I hear one more peep out of you, I'm going to tell Santa to skip this house," he would warn. "Go to sleep now, or Christmas can't come."

Once he had gone, Hannah thought sadly, it seemed that Christmas had never really come again. She had tried, but she had been unable to recreate that joy. Her mother would be abstracted, until she cried. Those were the worst times. Hannah would run for the box of tissues, helpless to do more. How she had wished she knew how to comfort her mother, how to make her happy, how to help her enjoy Christmas.

The little kids were easier. She had read them the stories. *The Night Before Christmas. The Polar Express.* She could still remember all the words. She had watched them emptying their stockings on Christmas morning, glad for their excitement. She had helped her mother make dinner. But no, it hadn't been the same.

Why was she so sad? she asked herself. Why remember all this now? Why not think about the good times instead? There were good memories, from before. But somehow, they got mixed up with the sad ones, the contrast making the sad years that much harder to remember.

She sighed now as she set up the little tree. It had almost been easier once their mother had died, she thought guiltily. At least then they hadn't had to pretend. She would have Matt and

Kristen over for the day, they would exchange gifts and have dinner. Sometimes even go to a movie on Christmas Eve.

On impulse, she picked up the phone and called Kristen. "Hi, sweetie. I realized it's already December twenty-first, and we haven't really talked about our plans. I wanted to ask, do you want to go to a movie this year, Christmas Eve? You guys could stay over if you wanted, and we could have breakfast on Christmas. That would be fun, don't you think?"

Kristen paused. "I was meaning to call you," she said slowly. "I'm really sorry, but I got a chance to go skiing over Christmas with some friends. I don't have much time off, you know, but I got three days this year. It's not like we ever do that much anyway, so I thought you wouldn't mind. Have you called Matt? I'll bet he'd like to go to the movies, if you make sure it's an action movie, anyway."

"Oh," Hannah answered blankly. "Oh, well, sure. If you have the chance to go, you should. You're right. That's OK."

"But will you be all right?" Kristen pressed. "I feel kind of bad. I know you always try to make it nice for us."

"No," Hannah answered more firmly. "You go ahead and have a good time. I missed Thanksgiving this year myself, after all. I'm glad you have enough time off to take even a short vacation for once. It'll be good for you. We can call each other on Christmas. You can tell me how the skiing goes."

Hanging up, Hannah felt an absurd urge to cry. Oh, well. She and Matt would have a good time. It would be nice to have some one-on-one time with him. Maybe they could shake things up, do something different. Go for a hike, a bike ride. It might be more fun if they didn't try to be traditional, but used the day for one of the active interests they shared.

The next day at work, though, she had to change her plans again when Matt called.

"Uh, Hannah," he began. "I know you always have us over for dinner on Christmas, but my friend Steve invited me to his house. His parents live on the beach in Santa Barbara. Would you mind too much if I went down there? They have surfboards and kayaks. It sounded great, so I said yes. Will you and Kristen be OK if I don't come this year?"

"Oh." Hannah felt her heart sinking. "Kristen's going skiing, actually. I guess it's a good year for you to do something else too, since she won't be there anyway."

"Shi—shoot," Matt corrected himself. "Do you want me to stay and keep you company? I don't want you to be by yourself on Christmas. I don't have to go, if you need me."

"Don't be silly," she answered automatically. "I can find company, if I get lonely. It'll be kind of nice to have a break to do whatever I want. It's been so busy here, just sleeping in will feel wonderful. I'll be OK, Matt. You go ahead."

But hanging up, she didn't feel OK. She tried to turn back to work, but couldn't concentrate. She got up abruptly and told Beth she'd be back in a few minutes. It was raining—of course it was raining. She was taking a walk anyway, she decided. Buttoning her coat and pulling on a warm hat, she stuffed her hands in her pockets and walked.

You're sad, she told herself. All right, be sad. It *is* sad. She couldn't help feeling a flash of anger at her brother and sister as well. But they were young, they had a few days off, and they wanted to spend those days with friends. That was all right, she told herself firmly. Their family Christmases, after all, weren't exactly joyous celebrations. Hadn't she just been thinking that the other day?

But that was all she had, she thought bleakly. However imperfect, that had been her Christmas. What was she supposed to do now? Roast a chicken and eat it by herself? She laughed, but felt tears pricking at the back of her eyes as she pictured herself dining in solo state at her decorated table. All right, scratch that. She would just have to come up with something fun to do on her own.

She briefly considered calling Susannah. Maybe she could fly to San Diego for the day? Then sighed. No. Susannah and her husband would be visiting his parents, she remembered. Anyway, what man wanted his wife's best friend spending the family holiday with them? She'd have to get through the day on her own.

What she had told Matt was true, she told herself bracingly. She *had* been working too much. She could go to a movie by herself on Christmas Eve, since she had the day off. Any movie she wanted, no matter how sentimental or romantic. Buy something fattening for Christmas breakfast. Sleep in, listen to music, watch *Miracle on 34th Street*. Read a romance novel. Spend the whole morning in her pajamas. It would be nice. It would be fine.

chapter fifteen

♡

Hannah made it through the rest of the day, leaving earlier than usual, at six. The rest of the work would have to wait. She needed an early night. Her emotional afternoon had drained her. She would stop by the gym, crank up her most upbeat playlist, put in some mindless time on the elliptical machine.

By the time she reached her apartment again, armed with takeout Thai vegetables, she still felt tired, but in a better way. She would sleep tonight, she thought. A shower, dinner, and an early bedtime. She'd feel better tomorrow. And then she'd have two days off. No matter that she'd be alone, two days off would be wonderful. She would make them good.

She stopped in the lobby, hesitated over whether to check her mail, and decided to wait until the next day. Maybe she'd have some Christmas cards. Better to open them on December twenty-third, after her last work day. They'd give her a lift for the holidays, something to put on her dresser and look at.

She'd been right, she told herself the next day. Now that she had adjusted to being on her own over the holiday, she found herself looking forward to her time off. It had been the shock, that was all.

Once she and the Operations Manager had sent the staff home at two, she firmly set about enjoying her Christmas. She stopped by the Cheese Board Collective and picked up her Christmas morning treats, then did some last-minute grocery shopping. For a final guilty pleasure, she went by the bookstore and bought herself two new books. She had done her shopping for family and friends weeks ago. This was her own Christmas present. She was going to have a treat, and be lazy, and do just what she liked for two whole days. And she wasn't going to check her work email or answer any calls from Felix. Not until December twenty-sixth.

Juggling her purchases as she entered her apartment lobby, she remembered her mail. Hopefully there would be some cards in there by now.

Opening the box with difficulty, she was pleased to find two red envelopes. And a small package with a New Zealand stamp, straining the hinges of the mailbox.

Suddenly her day looked a whole lot better. She took the steps two at a time to her apartment, forced herself to put all her things down before she sat on the couch and ripped open the packaging. Opened the piece of paper inside to find a brief message in Drew's bold, angular handwriting.

Missing you. Merry Christmas, Drew

Tears filled her eyes as she ran her fingernail underneath the wrapping paper to reveal a small, flat white box. She removed a layer of cotton batting, pulled back layers of tissue, and uncovered two intricately detailed silver hair combs. The finely filigreed design was inlaid with sparkling stones, while a single, larger black stone adorned the middle of each embellished piece. She unfolded the small tag in the box and discovered that the combs were made of sterling silver, inlaid with marcasite and onyx.

She sat for a minute, holding the combs in her hand. Then, unable to wait any longer, stood up and went to her bathroom mirror. Pulled out the pins that held her hair in its coil, then drew each side in turn up and back from her face and carefully inserted the heavy combs. Unlike most hair jewelry, she found with delight, they were substantial enough to hold the mass of her hair. In contrast to the heavy weight of the combs themselves, the delicate style of their embellished tops was perfect for her, the silver and black flashing against the paleness of her hair and adding an ethereal touch. They looked absolutely beautiful, absolutely right. And Drew had thought of this, shopped, and sent them to her.

Fishing her phone from her purse, she punched in his number. It was Christmas Eve there already. He would be with his family, she remembered. Maybe she should have texted instead? Oh well, if he was busy, he wouldn't answer, and she could leave a message.

He picked up, though, after the fourth ring. "Hannah?" He sounded pleased. "You're ringing me early. Are you away for your holiday, then?"

"Yes," she smiled. "If you call being home from the office 'away,' I am. How are you? Are you at your parents' now?"

"Yeh. My mum's feeding me already. She's got a job, eh."

"I imagine she's used to it," Hannah laughed. "You must have been an expensive teenager."

"She'd tell you so. Used to make me do the shopping. Said if I was going to drink that much milk, I could fetch it home from the shops myself."

"I'll bet. But Drew. I just opened my present. Thank you. They're so beautiful. How did you know what to buy? How did you find them?"

"You're pleased, then? They're big enough for you? I had help," he confessed. "I asked my mate Hemi's wife, Reka, to help me shop. She's Maori, so she has as much hair as you do. She said they had to be big and heavy to hold it all."

"She was right," Hannah said happily. "They're perfect. And that's rare. So did she choose the style, too?"

"Nah," Drew said a little proudly. "I found them. But I asked for her opinion," he admitted. "She asked me to describe you, and agreed these would be right. Glad you liked them."

"I didn't send you a present, though," she realized, conscience-stricken. "I wouldn't have known what to get you, but I should have sent you something."

"I keep telling you, I'd rather do things for you. Just glad to find something that pleases you, that's all."

"You found it," she assured him. "Is your brother there now too?"

"Yeh. My mum's fussing about, but she's chuffed to have us both here. My dad had me out mowing the grass earlier."

She laughed. "I can see they know how to keep you in line. I'm sure it's good for you. I'm glad you're able to have the whole family together." As she said it, she couldn't help the lump coming back to her throat.

"What about you?" he asked. "When do your brother and sister come?"

She cleared her throat, tried to sound casual. "They're not, actually. They both had the chance to do something fun this Christmas. Kristen is skiing, and Matt's at the beach, getting the chance to surf, which will make him happy."

"So what are you doing, then?" he asked sharply. "Where are you going to be, Christmas?"

"Oh, I'll be here. Taking it easy. Having a two-day vacation. It's fine, really. I've had so much time off lately, I shouldn't need any more, but I confess, having two days just to be lazy is sounding really good right now. It's been a busy December."

He wasn't to be put off. "Can't you go someplace for Christmas dinner, though? Spend some time with friends?"

"I'm fine," she insisted. "I'll talk to Matt and Kristen on Christmas, and I'll have a good day by myself. It's never that exciting anyway, just the three of us. So I'll go to the movies tomorrow night, and I'll relax on Christmas Day. I'm fine," she said again.

"I wish I'd known," he objected. "Would've brought you down here."

"No, you wouldn't. You know I only have two days off. I'd have to turn right around as soon as I got there and fly home. Besides, you're with your family. I'll be all right. Really. And I'll see you soon anyway."

"Yeh," he answered slowly. "You will. I'll book the flight in a few days, and let you know. You're taking a day off, right? This time, why don't you show me around. I'd like to meet this sister and brother of yours too."

"As long as you don't say anything nasty to them about Christmas," she said searchingly. "I mean it, Drew. I'm good. They have a right to do what they want. They don't owe me anything."

"They owe you a lot, seems to me," he retorted. "But I won't say anything. We'll have dinner, though. And you can take me to all the San Francisco sights. I'll be the tourist this time. We can walk across the Golden Gate Bridge."

"It's a date. It'll be great. It might be raining, though. Be prepared."

"I'm from New Zealand, aren't I. We're prepared for rain. If we didn't go out when it was raining, we'd never go anywhere."

"I forgot about that. All right, then. I'll let you get back to your family. Have a good Christmas."

"I'll ring you on your Christmas," he promised. "Boxing Day here."

"That would be wonderful, but don't worry if you're doing family things and can't manage."

"I'll ring you, Hannah."

♡

She was glad she had Drew's visit to look forward to over the next few weeks. Christmas wasn't exactly bad, but it wasn't exactly good either, she had to admit. The thought that she would be seeing him again so soon, though, made up for a lot.

Thank goodness she had actually accrued the day this time. Felix still made a big show of his magnanimity in granting her the Monday off, which annoyed her. When had he started to think of her as his indentured servant? Did she owe him every minute of every day?

Never mind. She had the time off, and she was spending it with Drew. This time, she told Emery and Beth that he would be visiting, so they would know she'd be unavailable for a few days.

"You can still call me in an emergency, of course," she hastened to add on Thursday afternoon when she reminded them of her plans.

Emery rolled his eyes. "Right," he drawled. "We'll just interrupt that, shall we, to let you know that there's a problem with the sizing of the yoga pants? Yeah, that's happening. When does his flight get in?"

"Tomorrow at noon," Hannah said happily. "But he won't get over here till one or two."

"Are you crazy?" Emery asked. "You're going to meet him at the airport."

"I can't do that. I only have a day off," she protested. "He'll get the key, and I'll see him at home after work. He knows that."

"Hannah." Emery was clearly holding onto his patience with an effort. "Let me explain something to you. This job doesn't matter. It's not going to keep you warm at night. And that man certainly is. I know which one I'd take. Beth and I are here. Go pick him up at the airport tomorrow. Come in for the morning if you have to. But I am personally pushing you out the door at eleven."

Beth chimed in. "Emery's right. There's no reason not to take the time."

"What if Felix calls, though?" Hannah asked.

"We'll tell him you're in a meeting," Emery told her firmly. "And you will be. A long, *long* meeting, unless I miss my guess."

"Emery. Stop," Hannah warned, laughing. "But all right. I will. Thanks. Just cover for me, OK?"

"We shouldn't have to cover for you," Beth pointed out. "It shouldn't be necessary. But we will anyway."

chapter sixteen

♡

When Drew walked through the arrival doors, Hannah couldn't imagine why she hadn't planned this all along. His face broke into a grin as he saw her.

Heedless of the group of flight attendants intent on capturing his attention or the large duffel bag he was carrying, she ran and leapt into his arms. He scooped her up, laughing, and kissed her hard before setting her back down on her feet, keeping his arm around her to hold her close.

"What a surprise to see you here. Wasn't expecting that," he told her.

"That was Emery. He pushed me out the door. Literally," she laughed. "He said..." she colored. "Well, he said I had to meet you."

"What did he say?" Drew pressed. "I think I need to hear this."

"Never mind," she answered hastily. "I don't want to tell you. Anyway, you're here. How was the flight?"

"Not too bad. They could make those beds longer, though."

"That's the disadvantage of being so big," she teased. "They were fine for me."

"There are advantages too," he pointed out. "Take me home and I'll show you."

She had arranged to have her brother and sister over for dinner on Sunday night. When she told him the plan, Drew asked, "Wouldn't you rather go out, so you wouldn't have to cook?"

"I think it'll be more relaxed if it's here. If you don't mind eating something simple."

In fact, she was a bit nervous about the meeting, and hoped the familiar setting would make things more comfortable. When she had called Matt to invite him to dinner to meet a friend who was visiting from New Zealand, he had asked eagerly, "Is she hot?"

"Actually, it's a man," she told him. "Someone I met when I was over there."

"And he's visiting you here?" Matt asked, surprised. "Are you sure he's OK? Maybe I should check him out."

"Don't worry. I know something about him. Nothing shady, I promise you. Thanks for being concerned, though. Anyway, you'll get the chance to see for yourself, won't you, if you come to dinner?"

"I will," he answered, in a serious tone she didn't often hear from him.

If anything, though, Hannah was more worried about Kristen. Well, not Kristen, if she were honest with herself. Even when she had been dating more, she had grown wary of introducing men to her beautiful sister. It seemed that once they saw Kristen, they weren't content with the pale imitation that was Hannah. Watching Drew make a move on her sister would be too painful.

He wouldn't do that, she told herself firmly. His manners were too good, for one thing. And it wouldn't be Kristen's fault, anyway. Her sister couldn't help being beautiful and charming. It was who she was. Hannah would just have to see what happened.

"Drew, this is my brother Matt," she said when her brother appeared at her apartment on Sunday night. "Matt, this is Drew Callahan, my friend from New Zealand."

Drew reached to shake Matt's hand. Matt was clearly taken aback by his size. He wasn't small himself, but Drew dwarfed him, and Hannah could see that it made her brother uncomfortable and a little defensive.

She rushed to fill the breach. "Matt's really interested in adventure sports," she told Drew. "You can tell him about bungy jumping, and Zorbing, and all those things I don't know anything about."

She sighed with relief as Drew engaged her brother in easy conversation, his steadiness seeming to calm Matt's near-hostility.

When Kristen arrived, late as always, Hannah couldn't help stealing a look at Drew. He greeted Kristen politely, but didn't seem overly struck by her looks. At least he hadn't rushed over to monopolize her—and stare down her cleavage. Maybe it would be all right.

When they were all eating Hannah's beef stew and cornbread, she was dismayed to find Matt beginning to question Drew in a way she'd never seen from him before.

"So you met Hannah in New Zealand, huh? How did that happen?"

"I met her on the beach," Drew returned affably. "And we went to breakfast."

Hannah decided not to correct his account. Her siblings didn't need to hear about her embarrassing near-drowning.

"You must have got to know her pretty well, that you're visiting her all this time later," Matt continued.

"Matt," Hannah protested.

Drew put his hand on hers. "It's all right," he assured her. Turning to Matt, he answered, "You're right, we did get to know each other pretty well. And now I'm visiting her, as you say. What else do you want to know?"

"Well, what do you do, for a start?" Matt continued, as Hannah cringed with embarrassment. "How is it that you're traveling over here? Are you here on business?"

"I'm a rugby player," Drew replied equably. "The season hasn't started yet, so I have some free time."

"Oh." Matt was obviously taken by surprise, and Kristen took up the conversation.

"What is rugby? It's a sport, right?"

"Yeh." Drew smiled. "It's a sport. A bit like your football."

"Kristen," Matt scolded. "Did you even *go* to school? Lots of countries play rugby. A whole lot more than play American football. I'll admit, though, I don't know much about it myself."

"I didn't know much either," Hannah put in, eager to turn the conversation to a more neutral topic that the men could discuss. "But there are lots of different kinds of rugby, even. League and Union, right?" she asked Drew. "And Sevens?"

"Right. Good to know you remember."

"You're a professional player, though?" Matt pressed on. "I mean, that's all you do?"

"That's all I do," he said easily. "Keeps me pretty busy, all the same."

"What team do you play for?"

"Why are you asking Drew all these questions, Matt?" Hannah broke in. "Do you not believe he's really a rugby player? Is he supposed to be a con man or something? Trust me, he's a rugby player."

"It's all right, Hannah," Drew said again. "He's checking me out, that's all. I play for the Auckland Blues," he told Matt. "You can look it up online, if you like."

Matt nodded, satisfied, as Kristen broke in impatiently. "Of course he's a rugby player, Matt. Hannah isn't stupid."

Hannah smiled at her gratefully. To her relief, the conversation slowly turned to more neutral subjects.

When she finally shut the door on her brother and sister, Hannah sank onto the couch and groaned. "I'm so sorry, Drew. I had no idea it would go that way. Well, I had some idea," she corrected herself. "Matt was kind of weird when I invited him over to meet you. He's not usually like that. He's normally a lot of fun. I didn't even know he had that streak."

"No worries. It was good," Drew assured her. "He may not have grown up with a dad, but your brother's all right. Maybe he should have thought more about taking care of his sister when he left you alone at Christmas, but I reckon he's figuring things out now."

"So that was all right with you?" she asked, surprised. "Having him grill you like that? He was almost hostile. I was so embarrassed."

He laughed. "Because you don't have a dad either. That's what dads and brothers do. It's a man thing."

"I guess I'll take your word for it. I'm glad you weren't offended. What did you think of Kristen?" she probed, looking at him anxiously.

"She's a nice girl," he answered, pulling her close to him on the couch. "Pretty, too. You don't mind if I like you better, though, do you?"

"Really?" she asked him doubtfully. "But she's so beautiful. Didn't you think so?"

"Yeh," he agreed. "She's a beautiful girl. But, and please don't be offended, you're ten times the woman she is. I'm not interested. Is that all right with you?"

Hannah let go of a breath she hadn't realized she was holding. "Kristen's great. You just don't know her well enough yet. But yes, please. Please do like me better, OK? Even though you're blind."

Drew laughed and pulled her into his arms. "Actually, I have perfect eyesight. And excellent taste."

♡

Hannah was startled to be awakened by her telephone at seven the next morning. This had better not be Felix, she thought irritably. She was entitled to this day off.

It was Matt. "Hannah," he began excitedly. "Do you know who that guy *is?*"

"Of course I know who he is, Matt. And so do you. You met him last night. Why are you calling me so early?"

"Hannah, he's the captain of the All Blacks! He's the most famous rugby player in the *world,* that's all. Why didn't you tell me? Oh man, he's probably so pissed at me for talking to him like that last night. Did you even know who he was?" he asked again.

"Matt. I can't talk about this right now." Drew was lying with his arms crossed under his head, listening, and Hannah flushed.

"Why? Is he there?" Matt realized. "Are you *sleeping* with him?"

"Of course I'm sleeping with him," she answered, exasperated. "What, do you think I'm a nun?"

She heard Drew's bark of laughter and turned to glare at him. Still laughing, he got up to disappear into the bathroom, giving her privacy for her conversation.

"Oh man, that is too much information," Matt groaned.

"Stop it. You're being ridiculous. Why are you calling me at seven o'clock in the morning to inform me of the job status of the man I'm dating? Which I *already knew.*"

"Because I was so excited, of course. Do you think he can get me tickets, if I visit? That would be so cool. Do you think he's upset that I was kind of nasty last night? "

"No. He wasn't upset. He said you did the right thing, in fact. You impressed him. And please don't ask him for tickets. *If* you go to New Zealand, you can buy your own ticket and go see a game. They're not some kind of invitation-only affairs. The public is allowed to attend."

She finally got Matt off the phone as Drew came out of the bathroom, showered and shaved. She put her head in her hands and groaned.

"Do I look like a nun? Or a virgin?" she demanded.

"Not to me. But then, you're in bed, naked, and I have a pretty good memory of what we did last night," he said reasonably. "So I may not be the best judge."

"Don't let him ask you for tickets if you see him again," she ordered. "I can't decide which is more embarrassing, having him attack you like you're some kind of stalker, or being your Biggest Fan."

Drew laughed. "The second thing I'm used to. I can deal with it. And the first—I already told you how I felt about that."

♡

"What are we going to do about this, then?" he asked as they sat over an after-breakfast coffee an hour later.

"About what?" She was confused.

"How's it been, then, since you've come back home? Is it going to work for you being this far apart?"

"I'm not sure what to say," she faltered. "Are you breaking up with me? I guess that's stupid," she corrected herself, flushing. "It's not like we're together, I mean."

He groaned and took her hand. "Hannah," he began again. "No. I'm not breaking up with you. I'm asking if you want us to be together more. How we can do that. Because I'd like to find a way. The phone and email are better than nothing, but it's not the same, is it? And practice starts next week. Super 15, then the Rugby Championship and the World Cup with the All Blacks. It'll be a long season for me this year. I'm not going to be able to come back to visit. And as we already know, you get bugger all in the way of holidays."

She felt a rush of relief, followed by more confusion. "What way is there, though? You have to be there. And I live here."

"This isn't the only place you could work, though. Would you think about moving to New Zealand for a bit, see how we go?"

"Moving?" She was stunned. "But...I never thought about it. What about my job?"

"I know it's important to you. But as a Kiwi, I have to tell you, it seems to me you work too much. How many hours a week do you spend at the office?"

"I hate to add them up," she admitted. "But probably, I don't know. Sixty? Sixty-five? Maybe more, when it's busy?"

"And you get three weeks' holiday a year. That's too much of your life working, don't you think? What are you working for, if that's all you do?"

"But that's what work is like, if you have any kind of a responsible job," she objected.

"In the States, maybe. Not in the rest of the world. Well, maybe in Japan," he conceded. "But not in New Zealand. There, you'd work all day, and then you'd go home. You might even go for lunch or a coffee. How often do you work at the weekend?"

"Most weeks," she admitted.

"See there. We don't do that either. Well, I do," he qualified. "But that's different. We spend the weekends with our families. Go to the bach. Have a barbecue with the neighbors. You can have a real job, a good job, without working yourself to death. Why not try it for a bit? You can get a work visa for a year or two, you know."

"But, Drew. What if it doesn't work? Then I'd be there, stuck in New Zealand, without a job here."

He looked at her levelly. "What if it does work? Seems to me you've jumped to the worst possible conclusion. What if this is the right thing? What will we have missed if we don't try? And maybe there's a better job out there for you, too. I know the conditions would be better, at least."

He pressed a bit more. He'd have a go, anyway. "Didn't you tell me you were thinking of moving to another job in a year or two? Would a new job be here, in this area? Seems to me you may have to move anyway to get the job you want. If this doesn't work, yeh, you'll have to move back, get another job. But you'd have international experience. Wouldn't that help you move up, if that's what you wanted to do?"

"I don't know," she said, putting her hands up to her cheeks in confusion. "I never thought about it. It's really scary. And my family. Matt and Kristen."

"I'm not too impressed by that, I have to say," he countered. "You spent Christmas alone. What kind of family life is that?"

"I know," she faltered. "But they count on me, you know. To be there if they do need me."

"And that's going to be your life. Waiting close by, just in case. Even parents cut the cord at some point. It doesn't mean you abandon them," he said, overriding her objection. "It means you get to have your own life. Get to do something that's for you, not for them. Do you notice where I am now?"

"What?" she asked, confused.

"I live in New Zealand, don't I. But here I am, sitting with you in California. And if your brother or sister needed you, if something were serious, you could be back here with them. Matt wants to come to En Zed anyway. You may have a better chance of seeing him if you live there, from what I've seen."

"What about Kristen, though?"

"What about her? You can still talk to her, can't you? She can come out for a visit too. But here's the real question. What about you? Doesn't it matter that you'll be far away from me? That we won't be together? And all right, then, what about me? I want you to be with me too."

She sat, overwhelmed. "I don't know," she finally answered helplessly. "It's so much to think about. I'm just not sure, that's all. Moving."

"I know it scares you," he went on more gently. "But I'd be there too, you know. You wouldn't be going someplace new by yourself. And you'd like living in Auckland, I'm sure of it."

"I'd love it. You know I'd love to live there. It's so beautiful. And I want to be with you. I miss you. It's just…it's putting all my eggs in one basket. Quitting my job. Leaving my friends. Can you say you'd do that, after three weeks with somebody? Wouldn't that be stupid?"

"I think it would be taking a chance," he replied seriously. "Maybe you're not ready to take a chance."

"I'll think about it, OK?" she said. "That's all I can say right now. I just need to think."

chapter seventeen

♡

"Ring me," Drew insisted as he said goodbye at the airport that afternoon. "Let me know what you decide."

"I will," she promised. "If...if I don't come, though, then what?"

He sighed. "We'll have to see. Maybe you could come out in May or June for a week or two. I'd still be playing, but at least I'd have some time. But, Hannah. Think about it. Promise me. Don't give up before you even try."

She kissed him fiercely, not wanting to let go. "I'll think about it. I'll try. I promise."

That evening, after trying unsuccessfully to calm her troubled mind, she broke down and called Susannah for advice.

"But that's great," her friend responded after Hannah had outlined Drew's suggestion. "How exciting for you. But you don't sound excited. What's the matter?"

"I can't just pick up and move to a new country like that! What about my sister and brother? What about my job?"

"What about your job? Did you sign Articles of Indenture that I'm not aware of? Why can't you get a new job? Haven't you been talking about that anyway?"

"Yes," Hannah conceded. "But in a new country? Wouldn't that be a lot harder to do?"

"I don't know. Have you checked? Did Drew seem to think that would be a big barrier?"

"Well, no. But Susannah, I'd have to move everything. Or sell my stuff. And start all over."

"I have to say, these objections aren't sounding very convincing," Susannah said slowly. "It seems to me that if you wanted to do it, going abroad for a year or two, getting a job, wouldn't be that big a deal, at this point in your life. So what's the real problem?"

"I'm not sure," Hannah admitted. "But I think it's Drew. I really like him. You know I do. But we spent a couple of weeks together, and then we've had a few days, and some phone calls and emails. And now I'm supposed to pack up my whole life and move there to be with him? What about when it ends? How am I going to feel then? I'll be stuck over there."

"So he's set a date, has he," Susannah needled. "When he's dumping you. Or are you planning to dump him?"

"You know I'm not. But I have to be realistic here."

"All right, so protect yourself. Don't move in with him. Get a job there, and figure you're trying it out for a while. What he said makes sense anyway. You do work too much. If you can go somewhere else and have the same kind of job, but with an actual life, wouldn't that be better?"

"I guess so. But I'd miss my friends."

"Like me, you mean."

"Exactly. And my brother and sister."

"And how long has it been since we've seen each other? Six months? Because, Hannah, you work all the time. You don't have that much time to see your friends. And you and I live across the state from each other. We never see each other anyway. Why couldn't we still talk on the phone? What's the time difference there?"

"Three or four hours. Well, it's more like twenty or twenty-one hours. But same thing."

"That's right. So why wouldn't we just talk on the phone like we do now? Also, you're a really nice person. You're smart, you're funny. People like you. Don't you think, if you started a new job, you'd make new friends? Maybe even have some time to spend with them? And I know you're going to talk to me about Kristen," Susannah continued. "Drew's right, you know. You don't have parents, so you don't know this. But I do. Once you're in your twenties, you can still be close. You can still call, and talk. Visit, too. But your parents aren't there, hovering, just waiting for you to make a mistake so they can scoop you up and fix it. My parents moved to Texas, you know that. I see them maybe twice a year. I still talk to them, and I love them. But they've moved on with their lives. They aren't waiting around in case I decide to stop by. It's time you did that too. You did your job. More than your job. You're not actually their mother, you know. Time to move on and live your own life now."

"You might be right," Hannah admitted. "I thought about that, over Christmas. It was hard being alone. I felt pretty stupid, all by myself in my apartment, while they went off and had fun. I don't want another Christmas like that. But still, Susannah. Just because I think I could live someplace else, doesn't make it smart to move across the world to be with a guy."

"Is he 'a guy,' though? I kind of thought he was more than that. He sure seems better than any other man you've met. He seems pretty special, in fact."

"He is. So far. But we haven't spent that much time together. And there's no guarantee this will work out. It's a huge risk. I don't know if I'm ready to take it."

"You know what this is really about," Susannah decided. "I think you truly believe he's not going to love you. That you're going to put your heart on the line and he's going to stomp on it."

Hannah couldn't say anything. Her throat constricted and she fought back tears as Susannah went on inexorably. "Your dad left you. And your mom might as well have. So you think you're on your own. That nobody's ever going to love you. You won't even give this guy a chance to show you that you're wrong. So protect yourself," she urged again. "Get your own place. Build your own life. What are you risking? If you're over there, and seeing him all the time, you'll both find out if it can last. If it doesn't, OK, you'll be alone. But you're alone now."

"I'm used to it now, though. This is my life. What if I try to change it? And it doesn't work?"

"Then you'll be strong, the same way you always are. You've got through everything that's happened to you so far, better than anyone I know. Look, I promise, if he dumps you, if you're stranded over there and you fall apart, I'll come get you. OK?"

Hannah had to laugh. "OK. I guess I can count on you to rescue me, anyway."

"You know you can," Susannah said firmly. "Now get on the computer and start doing that research. I'm not going to watch you throw away this chance. Get some guts and try, Hannah. And call me tomorrow. Tell me what you find out."

♡

She could look, at least, Hannah told herself after she hung up. That didn't mean she had to do anything. She typed "New Zealand work visa" into her search engine. Her heart began to beat harder as she clicked on "Immigration New Zealand," then moved on to "Temporary Work Visas." She found that to have the best chance to be hired by an employer, her occupation would have to be included in the "Essential Skills List." She could barely click through the lists of specialties and subspecialties that made up the list. Once she had, she sat staring at her computer. There it was. Marketing Specialist. Specifically, brand manager, product manager, category manager.

She stood up, walked around the room. Came back to her computer, and typed "Marketing Jobs New Zealand" into the search engine. There were the sites. And the jobs.

All right, she told herself. There were jobs. That didn't mean she would find one she liked, or that they'd hire her. But she could check. She pushed the down arrow and started scrolling.

She spent as many hours at the office as always, the rest of the week. But she could feel half her attention being pulled away. For the first time, she wasn't totally focused on her career at TriStyle Woman, and it unsettled her. Every evening found her on New Zealand job sites. And updating her resume.

It had been a while, she thought wryly the first time she pulled up the ancient document. She had read that resumes should be updated annually, but had never seen the point. She hadn't applied for a job since she was a senior in college. What would it be like now, more than seven years later, to interview?

It would be easier, she realized. She had plenty of experience and skills to bring to the table. This time, she would be interviewing potential employers as well, instead of just answering their questions and hoping she passed. It would have to be the right job, the right company, or she wasn't doing this. This couldn't just be about moving to New Zealand to be with Drew. It had to be about making a change for the better in her work life, too.

Susannah called on Tuesday, as promised, to check on her progress, and was delighted to find that Hannah had actually started looking into the job market. But Drew didn't call. Hannah was grateful at first, since she felt so uncertain about the whole prospect. By Thursday, though, she had begun to panic. Maybe he'd changed his mind. Her imagination leaped ahead. He was regretting what he had said. She would make the decision, and there would be an awkward pause before he told her that he had met someone new. Or that he had decided it wouldn't work.

After a restless night, she decided she had to call him and find out. If he didn't want her to come anymore, she needed to know that now, not after she had begun applying for jobs. As soon as the time was reasonable, she took a deep breath and dialed his number. A recording. She left a brief message and hung up, feeling more anxious and on edge than ever, then resolutely forced herself back to work.

When her cell phone rang at five-thirty, she grabbed for it. Seeing Drew's name on the caller ID, she quickly walked outside the offices for privacy as she answered.

"Just got your message. Sorry it took me a bit to get back to you. I had a team meeting and a practice. Just got out," he began.

"Oh, that's right, practice has started, hasn't it?" She was glad to have another topic to start the conversation. "How's it going?"

"Need to tighten up on the conditioning. Some of the boys haven't come back fit enough. Not too bad, all in all. How're you going?"

"I'm...I was wondering. Do you still...are you still interested in my coming down there to work for a while? You haven't called, and I thought maybe...maybe you were sorry you'd said it. So I wanted to ask," she finished in a rush.

"Of course I meant it. Wouldn't have said it if I hadn't meant it, would I. I should've known you'd start thinking I'd changed my mind. You were supposed to call me and tell me what you decided, remember? I didn't want to pressure you. I thought I should give you some time to think about it. Have you done that?"

"Yes," she answered warily. "And I'm checking. I'm looking at jobs and things. But will you promise, Drew? If you change your mind about it, will you please tell me? I think it's going to take a while to make all this happen. And I know you're into the season now, and you can't come here. I need you to be honest and tell me if you have second thoughts. Because I'd have to give notice at my job, and my apartment, and everything."

"Hannah. Hang on," he said, laughing. "I'm not changing my mind. I thought we'd been over this already. Yeh, I want you to come down here. You're really looking into it? That's awesome. How're you going with it?"

"There are a lot of jobs," she admitted. "I've been surprised. And there are actually quite a few that look possible. But I want to make sure I find something that really works. It seems like if I got the job, then getting a temporary work visa wouldn't be too hard."

"Shouldn't be hard at all. I'm not surprised there are jobs. The job market here isn't as good as Aussie, but not too bad, I think, if you have skills. D'you want me to have a look around for you?"

"And by that, you mean, 'Do you want me to get somebody to offer you a job?' Because I have a feeling that's what it would be. No, I'd better look for myself, thanks. I have to get a job on my own merits, to know I'm a good match and the company's a good match for me."

"If you want my help, though, just ask," he urged. "I could put in a word."

"No. No words," she insisted. "But thank you. I know you want to help."

"Nah, I just want you down here with me. The sooner the better."

"I'd better get back to work, then. So I can finish up here, and go home and look at job sites. But you never answered my question. Will you promise me that if you change your mind, you'll tell me, not feel like you've committed yourself and now you have to go through with it?"

He sighed. "If that happens, I promise, you'll be the first to know. Will that do you? Now go back to work, and get cracking on that job search."

chapter eighteen

♡

Five weeks, eight applications, and three phone interviews later, Hannah opened her email to find a job offer. And not just any job offer. The one she had wanted. Like TriStyle Woman, 2nd Hemisphere also sold fitness clothing, but with a difference. They had started by manufacturing their own activewear using merino, a specialty wool known for its softness, lightness, and warmth. Now they were branching out into casual and dressy garments made of the same material, and aiming to become a more global brand. The company had seemed interested in Hannah from the start. The United States was by far the world's largest market for fitness clothing, and she had the knowledge and experience to help them make the move they were aiming for.

She had evaluated 2nd Hemisphere, its products, and its work environment as thoroughly as she could, both online and during her videoconference interview, and was excited by what she had seen. It would be a chance not only to work with a global brand, but also to work with a company that designed and manufactured its own products, both important steps for her ultimate goals.

She had a job, as soon as she could get a work visa. And all without any help, she told herself proudly. She was happier than ever now that she had refused Drew's offer. She imagined 2nd

Hemisphere would have been even more eager to hire her if he had been involved, and shuddered at the thought.

She typed her acceptance, then hesitated over the "Send" key. It was a big step to accept this offer. Was she sure? She gave in to her hesitation and dialed Susannah's number again. It was a good thing it was Sunday. She knew she wouldn't be getting any work done today.

"That's great! Congratulations!" her friend responded enthusiastically. "Have you answered them yet?"

"No," Hannah admitted. "I've worked at TriStyle for more than seven years, Susannah. What if I don't do as well someplace else?"

"Why?" Susannah scoffed. "Because everybody who's been telling you how good you are all these years is magically mistaken? Because you've somehow been promoted above your competence level? Is that why TriStyle is doing so badly? Come on, Hannah. They're lucky to have you, and you know it. I'd love to see the look on Felix's face when you tell him," she added gleefully. "He's going to have a heart attack."

"I know," Hannah said ruefully. "I'm a little worried about that. But I realized when I came back from vacation, you know, that Beth is ready to take over my job. She's really good. Of course, Felix could hire somebody new. But I'm going to recommend that he promote her."

"You've been training her for years. I don't think you need to feel bad at all. You're giving her an opportunity. You've already thought this through, I see. So what are you waiting for? Say yes!"

"I have my visa application ready to go, too," Hannah said. "I already had the medical exam. I decided to get the two-year visa. I really had to do that to get a job," she explained self-consciously. "But if it doesn't work out—if any of it doesn't work—I can always quit and come back, right?"

"That's right. Remember, I'm coming to get you if you're in a puddle over there. Nothing to worry about, see?"

"All right. I'm hitting 'Send' now," Hannah said breathlessly. "Stay on the phone with me, OK?"

"OK," Susannah laughed. "Whatever it takes."

"Done," Hannah exhaled. "Notice I called you to check, instead of Drew. I wasn't sure what he'd do if I asked him again if he were sure."

"Smart of you," Susannah agreed. "Men don't like to be reminded over and over that you don't trust them. Better call him now, though."

Hannah said a thankful goodbye, then hung up and dialed Drew's number. *Be there,* she urged silently. To her relief, he answered almost immediately.

"I wasn't sure you'd pick up," she began. "I thought you might still be on the plane from Australia." He'd had a game on Saturday night in Sydney, she knew. "Congratulations on the win, by the way."

"Thanks. Flew back yesterday. Spending a bit of time in the spa today. It's a pretty tough side, the Waratahs. What's up?"

"I thought you'd want to know. I got a job!"

"You did! That's brilliant! What is it?" he demanded. "Did you say yes?"

"I did say yes," she answered, laughing with relief. She told him about the position and the company.

"Good on ya," he approved. "I know who they are. Even have some of their gear. Good stuff."

"Well, we'll just keep that to ourselves," she told him firmly. "I'm not using you in this job. Heaven forbid."

He laughed. "They can't use me without my consent, you know. So what's next?"

"Next I get the official letter, and I submit it with my visa application. It could take six weeks though, they say."

"Why don't you send it to me? Those applications can be a bit complicated. I'll have someone in the office give it a look, make sure there's nothing dodgy in there, then we'll hand-carry it. Should go through faster that way. When are you giving notice?"

"I thought I should wait, don't you think, until the visa goes through? If it could take that long? I can't really sit around for weeks, not working."

"I think you should do it now. They inflate those processing times. I'd bet you'll have it in a few weeks." He knew she would, in fact, as soon as he made a call or two. He'd keep that to himself, though. "And you'll have to pack up, and all. Give yourself some time. You don't want to get down here and be knackered already."

"I need to find a place to live too, once I'm down there," she said. "I thought I'd stay in a hotel while I'm looking. I have money saved. Where would you recommend?"

"Why would you do that?" he asked, surprised and not pleased. "Why wouldn't you stay with me, at least until you find a place of your own?"

"Drew. I can't move all the way to New Zealand, uproot my whole life, for a guy. I have to be moving there for work, for the experience of living someplace else. That has to be the focus. You're the…the bonus."

"The…bonus," he returned, stunned. "I'm the bonus."

"Oh dear," she faltered. "That makes you sound like some kind of boy toy." At his outraged snort, she continued quickly, "I need to move out there independently. I can't put pressure on you. And I can't put myself in that kind of dependent position. That would be starting out all wrong. Can you understand that?"

"I can understand that it matters to you," he answered resignedly. "As the…bonus, am I allowed to help you find a place to live before you get here, save you staying in a hotel? That'll be easier for me than for you. I'm here, and I know more people. And you can stay with me for a week or two while you get the place ready. I know you can do that."

"I'd love to have your help finding a place to live. And I'd love to spend a few days with you first, if I already have a place. But nothing too expensive. It has to be something I can afford."

"Am I allowed to find you a flat close to me, or do I have to keep my distance, too? Is there a perimeter we're meant to maintain here?"

"No perimeter. Please. It'd be great to live close to you. But on the other hand, have you thought about what happens if it doesn't work out? You might not want to see me on the street all the time."

"Good to know you're prepared for the worst," he answered grimly.

"Just trying to be realistic," she countered. "Just in case."

He exhaled. "Reckon I'll just be glad you're coming. The rest of it, we'll work on."

♡

The next month was one of the most intense of Hannah's life. Giving notice at her apartment hadn't been so hard. But sliding the piece of paper with her resignation on it across the table to Felix had been tough.

He'd been shocked, angry, cajoling by turns. Had offered her more money to stay, a new title, even three more vacation days. She shook her head, remembering. She'd had no idea that she'd had so much power to change the conditions of her job. Now, too late, she realized that she could have made her life easier. She would have to remember that in the future.

Felix had asked for four weeks' notice, but she'd held firm at two. She had so much to do, and once she had actually given notice, it was hard to even work out the two weeks. She had done her utmost to create a smooth transition. Luckily, Felix had gone along with her suggestion that he promote Beth to fill her position. Although Beth had been upset at the thought of Hannah's leaving, she couldn't hide her pleasure at the new opportunity.

All in all, it had been surprisingly easy to leave, once she had made the decision. Her entire adult life had revolved around TriStyle Woman. She had lived and breathed her job, and it had formed a huge part of her identity. But Emery was right. It was a job. She was proud of what she had done, and she would miss the people she worked with. But once she had left, she found to her surprise that a lot of that identification simply fell away. Or maybe, she thought, it was just that she had so much to do, and was so excited and nervous about the change.

The simple logistics were overwhelming in themselves. She thought back gratefully to Drew's suggestion that she give notice right away. She had certainly needed the extra weeks of time to get ready. Her visa had come through in an amazing two weeks, but that had still only given her three weeks before her travel date. The hardest question had been what to do about her possessions. After a lot of thought, she had decided to sell or give away most of what she had. Shipping it turned out not to be an option.

"Thank goodness I only have a tiny one-bedroom," she told Susannah on the phone one night, surrounded by boxes and bags. "But how did I fit so much into this little space?"

"How much is there that you really want to hang onto?" Susannah asked. "You could store a few boxes at my house."

"Thanks," Hannah said with relief. "I might have to do that. One box, anyway. This is where it gets hard not to have parents, you know? No childhood bedroom."

"I'm sure it's hard to figure out what to do with everything," Susannah sympathized. "But it's exciting, too, isn't it? You're really starting over. How's Kristen taking it?"

"Well, she was pretty upset at the beginning, as you know. But I think she's adjusting now. We can still talk a lot. And it's not forever. Matt's fine, of course. He's already planning his trip down there for next year. I think he's mostly worried I'll break up with Drew before he has the chance to score tickets."

Susannah laughed. "Trust Matt. But I think it'll be good for Kristen, too. It's not like you're abandoning her. Thank goodness for the Internet."

♡

One giant garage sale and donation drop-off later, Hannah sat on a duffel bag in her empty apartment, looking at the dust motes dancing in a beam of watery late March sunlight that shone down onto the hardwood floors she had loved, and waiting for Kristen to pick her up. She had even sold her little car. On the plus side, she had some extra money in her bank account—which she would need, she reflected, when she had to furnish a new apartment, no matter how small.

She jumped as the doorbell rang, and buzzed Kristen up.

"Wow," her sister said, sobered, looking around at the bare floors, the vacant rooms. "It looks so empty. Kind of sad." She teared up and hugged Hannah. "I'm so sad too, Hannah. What am I going to do without you?"

"You're going to call me, when you want to talk to me. And I'll call you too," Hannah promised. "And you're going to come visit next Christmas, remember? Christmas at the beach. You'll love that. We'll be together again soon. And I'll always be there for you. You know I will."

She held her sister close and fought back her own tears. "Now get me out of here," she said with a watery smile. "It's ridiculous to stand here crying. I haven't even left yet."

chapter nineteen

♡

Even though she had once again been upgraded to Business Premier—she hadn't even been surprised this time, she realized guiltily—Hannah found it hard to sleep on the flight to Auckland. She hadn't seen Drew for over two months now. She hadn't even talked to him much over the past two weeks, while the team had been playing in South Africa. She hoped she had made the right decision.

She was fairly sure about the job, she reminded herself. It was a wonderful opportunity. Without Drew's prodding, she wouldn't have taken it. She would focus on that, whatever happened in her personal life. At least the team had a bye during the coming weekend, and the two of them could start out by spending some time together.

When she stepped out of the automatic doors into the arrivals area and saw him, her doubts receded a bit. Standing big and solid, his arms folded across his broad chest, waiting for her. No matter that it wasn't even six A.M.

"You'll be seeing my house for the first time, I realized," he said as they made their way through the sparse early-morning traffic into the city. "Had to tidy it up a bit for you. I can show you your flat too, later. Picked up the keys yesterday."

When they pulled into the driveway of his modern house, all cantilevered levels on a hillside overlooking St. Heliers Bay, Hannah suspected there hadn't been too much tidying required.

"It's beautiful, Drew," she exclaimed as she stepped into the living room—the lounge, she corrected herself—and looked out past leather sofas through a wall of windows to Waitemata Harbour, with Rangitoto, the city's iconic volcanic island, in the distance. "And what an amazing view."

"Another sea view from my bedroom on the next level," he smiled at her. "I'll show you that next."

She laughed happily. "I want to see that," she assured him. "Just show me the shower first, OK?"

Snuggling with him later after a leisurely bout of lovemaking, she said sleepily, "I'm supposed to stay awake all day to get over my jet lag."

He tucked her more closely against him. "You've had your exercise. Take a nap. Then we'll walk down and have a look at your flat. We can have a swim later, too. I made sure you had a safe swimming beach. And I promise to help relax you tonight so you can sleep."

The flat, just a few blocks back from the quiet beach, took up the lower floor of a small villa. Built in the early 1900s, it had the old-fashioned touches she enjoyed, with a modern kitchen and bathroom. There was even a tiny flagstone patio in the back, surrounded by greenery. It looked as pretty as the pictures the realtor had emailed her, and she knew she would be happy there.

"You can take the bus straight into the city," Drew offered. "Less than half an hour. Thought you'd like that."

"I do need to get a car, though," she said as they walked back up the hill to Drew's house. "Besides furniture and everything. I was hoping you could give me some advice."

"Actually, I found you something," he said in a deceptively casual voice that made her antennae quiver. "A mate had an extra car he wasn't driving. This one," he pointed out as they entered his driveway.

"I thought that looked pretty small for something you'd drive. It's perfect for me, though," she said slowly, looking at the tiny Toyota Yaris.

"Thought it might suit you. Not flash, but it should be easy to maneuver in the city traffic, easy to park. Good fuel economy, too, and you're going to find that's a bit more expensive than in the States. I thought when we went somewhere together, we could take my car."

"I'd say that's a pretty safe assumption, since I don't see you sitting in the passenger seat while I drive you. Especially in this car," she said with a smile. "But Drew," she went on more seriously, "I can't take this. Not as a gift."

"Here it is, though," he pointed out reasonably. "I'm not going to drive it. Too small. And you need a car."

"Wait a minute." She turned and looked at him. "Your friend didn't give you this car. You bought it. From whom? And for how much? You need to tell me."

"I did get it from a mate," he objected. "His wife was driving it, and he bought her a new one."

"All right. Then tell me how much you paid for it, because I don't believe he gave it to you. And I'll pay you back. I'm grateful that you found me something," she said, softening her tone as she saw him stiffen. "But you must see, I can't let you buy me a car."

"Can't you just say I'm loaning it to you, then? I can afford it, Hannah," he said reasonably. "And you have so much to buy. Furniture and all. I'd like to do this for you."

"I know you would," she sighed. "And I know you can afford it way better than I can. But I have the money saved. I was planning to buy a car anyway. I can't be dependent on you. I need us to be on an equal footing. Obviously, you have more money than I do. But I can support myself."

"Right, then," he agreed reluctantly. "You can pay me, I'll put the money aside, and we'll use it for a holiday later, when we have some time. And that's as far as I'm going," he added when she would have objected, "so drop it, please."

♡

As she slowly furnished her little flat over the next few days, Hannah was in fact appalled at the amount of money she was spending. She hadn't realized how much there would be to buy, starting entirely from scratch. Even though she tried to keep her purchases as modest as possible, she ended each day with buyer's remorse, worrying about how much everything cost.

Never mind, she told herself. She would be starting her new job in another week or so, and earning money again. She had been making a good salary for several years, but had always saved a lot of it, planning towards the day she could buy a house. Still, she would be more comfortable when this spending spree was over.

"How're you going, with the furniture and all?" Drew asked her on Wednesday morning.

"Almost ready to move in. I'm getting the last big pieces delivered today, and I need to do some more kitchen shopping. Then I should be all set. I'd like you to come over and see it when I'm done. Maybe you could stop by after practice today."

When she heard the doorbell that afternoon, though, she jumped, then pulled the loose tendrils of hair behind her ears and wiped her face on her shirt in sweaty exasperation. Climbing over the coffee table that blocked the small entryway, she opened the door to Drew at last.

"Sorry," she explained as she bent to push the pesky table out of the way. "I thought I'd be done by now, but I've been trying to figure out how to set everything up. I lost track of time."

"So you've been shifting all this lot about by yourself," he said slowly, looking around the small lounge.

"I'm not that good at interior decoration, I'm afraid," she sighed. "I have to look at it in every position to see how I like it best."

"Why didn't you wait for me? I would've shifted it for you."

"I didn't think of that," she admitted. "It's not that heavy anyway. I just have to push and pull a little. This is how I've always moved. And I wanted to show it to you, not wait around and have to ask you to help me."

"That's the point of dating a rugby player, though. You don't have to pick up heavy things anymore. I'm here now, anyway. Tell me where you want it, and I'll do it."

With him to do the moving, she soon had the room arranged to her satisfaction. "Thanks. I appreciate you loaning me your muscles," she told him gratefully.

"Next time, ring me first, before you start lifting and carrying. I'll be much happier doing it for you."

"If it seems too hard, I'll try to remember. But what do you think?" she asked, turning around to look. Nothing was going to make her simple furnishings elegant, but the little room felt warm and welcoming.

"Bit small, isn't it?" he said dubiously, trying to stretch out on her little couch.

"All right, it's not long enough for you. It works for me, though. And this is a small place. Big furniture wouldn't fit anyway."

But when he saw her bedroom furniture, Drew put his foot down.

"No. This bed goes back, Hannah. The couch is one thing. But I plan to be here too. A fair bit. And this isn't going to work."

"It's a queen," she objected. "What's wrong with it?"

"It's flimsy, that's what. I'm not having that headboard banging against the wall every night."

She felt the traitorous color rising into her throat, up her cheeks, at his words. "Furniture is really expensive here. I bought the best I could afford. I guess we'll just have to stay at your house, if you really don't like this."

"No," he said again. "I went along with the car thing. And I reckon I don't have to be comfortable on your couch. But I'm buying you a better bed. I plan to be sharing it," he insisted. "That's fair."

There was no budging him, she found. "All right. I see your point," she conceded at last. "But I'm not shopping for it with you. They're going to know who you are. That would be too embarrassing, with you testing how solid it was. Everyone would know why." She turned red again at the thought.

"Do you trust me to buy it on my own, then? I don't trust you to do it. You won't want to spend enough to get something that will stand up to a good workout."

"Drew!" she laughed. "Stop. All right, you win. Buy the bed you want. But please, don't be here when they deliver it. That would kill me. The delivery guys..." She covered her face with her hands. "Oh, man," she breathed. "You embarrass me so much."

He smiled and pulled her hands away so he could kiss her. "Reckon I'm going bed shopping tomorrow, then. Because now I need to see just how much more I can embarrass you. A challenge, eh," he teased. "Give me the receipt for the other one," he added practically. "I'll see it's picked up and you get your money back."

Hannah wasn't entirely surprised when the furniture store— one she would never have shopped at, she admitted—called the next day to arrange delivery for the following afternoon, a much faster turnaround than she'd been able to arrange herself.

"Remember, I'm doing this by myself," she told Drew firmly. "I'll lurk in the shrubbery, shall I?"

She laughed. "I'll call you when you're allowed to come over."

At last, the huge bed—with, she found, a massive leather headboard and big, solid legs—was delivered and set up. She had wondered whether she should tip the deliverymen, and had asked Drew what the rules were.

"No," he had immediately answered. "No tip."

"Are you sure?" she asked doubtfully. "I'd give them at least a twenty, back home. They'll be carrying in that heavy furniture. Shouldn't I offer them something?"

"You'd offend them, if you did. They aren't servants. They're doing a job, and they're paid for it. You've heard the saying, Jack's as good as his master?"

"I've read it."

"Well, that's how Kiwis feel. We aren't Poms—English. Those fellas earn their wage same as I do. They'd tell you they're as good a man as I am, or as any other New Zealander. And they'd be right. Except in a flash restaurant, maybe, we don't tip."

So as hard as it was to do, she gave the men only a smile and her thanks. Drew had been right about the egalitarian attitude, she realized. They asked her cheerfully where she was from, and chatted about the U.S. and New Zealand, even offering their recommendations of places she should see while in the country, then departed with a final wave to hop back into their truck and continue on.

Hannah waved back, then called Drew. "The coast is clear," she informed him solemnly.

"I'm at the gym with the boys. Be there in an hour. You can start without me. Get naked, at least. I'll be there as soon as I can. Or sooner."

"If they can hear you say that," she retorted, "you can think again."

He laughed. "Walked away, didn't I. No worries. That was just for you."

♡

"You're not naked," he pointed out as she opened the door to him forty-five minutes later.

"You didn't give me time," she smiled. "You're early."

176

"I may have cut my workout short a bit," he admitted. "Had an urgent appointment." He kissed her, pulling her up onto her toes. "A job to do, eh. Bit of furniture testing. Let's see how I did," he suggested, taking her hand and walking into the bedroom.

"It's big enough, anyway," she offered. "Solid, too. I don't think we're moving that."

"Bad idea to challenge me," he murmured, pulling her down with him onto the thick duvet so she landed in his lap. "Thought I told you that." He pulled her hair free of its restraints, then put up a hand to cup her face and concentrated on kissing her.

There were advantages, she thought dazedly, to being with a man with that kind of single-minded determination. When her hands moved down and under his shirt, he pulled them back to his shoulders. He kept his own hands on her back, her neck, her head, as he focused on kissing her senseless. She could feel how aroused he was, but his mouth and tongue continued their slow, patient assault, until her mouth was swollen and she was breathing hard with excitement.

"You need to let me touch you," she exclaimed at last in frustration, as he pulled her hands away from him again.

"Mmmm, I don't think so," he smiled. "Not yet. See if I can tease you a bit more first."

He settled her astride him then, pulling her pelvis into contact with him so she could feel him through the thin layer of her panties, where her skirt rode up around her thighs. She squirmed against him, trying to get closer, her hands clutching at his shoulders. He continued to kiss her, his lips moving from her mouth to her throat, holding her head in place while he licked, kissed, and bit at her there. One hand around her lower back pulled her more closely against him as she moaned and pressed her body to his. Was it possible to have an orgasm from kissing? She didn't know, but she felt like she was about to find out.

This time, when she pulled at his shirt, he didn't resist, letting her draw it over his head at last, to touch his skin. She drew herself away so she could run her hands over his chest and around his back. Her fingers found his flat nipples, and he pulled her lower body in even more tightly in response. She felt him jerk against her center in response to her touches, and smiled. So she wasn't the only one being driven crazy here. She would experiment some more, she decided. If he wouldn't take her clothes off, she would start with him this time.

He allowed her to push him back on the bed. She knelt over him, her hands working at his belt and shorts, pulling everything down over his hips and tossing them to the floor. She nudged him until he swung both legs onto the bed, then lay over him.

"Your turn," she told him. "Because I don't think I can take any more. Going to do it to you for awhile."

Oh, yes, he decided. He'd let her take over for a bit. Her hands caressed, moved down his chest with the firm pressure he loved. Down to his thighs, then up to hold him, stroke him, as she kissed his chest, moving her tongue over his nipples.

When he would have turned with her, she held him down. "My turn, remember? You get to lie there and take it," she commanded.

He smiled, then groaned and gave in as she continued to torment him. She moved down his body, kissing and caressing. Then her mouth was on him as her hands continued to stroke. He reached down, held her head in his hands, felt her hair falling over his body, and surrendered to the pleasure she was giving him.

He stood it until he knew he was too close, then gently pulled her back up to him.

"I wasn't done yet," she protested.

He kissed her, felt the salty taste of himself in her mouth, almost lost it again. "Not finishing this way. Not this time. I have a few more things to do to you first."

"I don't mind taking care of you," she insisted. "I want to."

He groaned. "Stop, Hannah. You're killing me."

She was still wearing all her clothes, he realized, while he was naked. Suddenly, he was done going slowly. He slid his hands under her blouse as she lay on top of him, pulled it over her head, heard a button or two pop off along the way.

"Hey," she protested. "My blouse."

"Buy you a new one," he said impatiently. His hands went to her skirt, popped a button there too, unzipped and pulled it off. Flipped her over onto her back, and pulled back to look at her.

She lay beneath him in a bra and bikini set he hadn't seen before. He'd have remembered this one, he knew. Sheer lace embroidered with tiny flowers, in a soft peach that was somehow sexier than any black underwear he'd ever seen. He'd leave those on her for a while, he decided. He moved down to kiss her through the lacy cups of the bra. Her nipples pebbled at his touch, allowing him to pull one into his mouth as he fondled the other.

His hand went down to feel her. "You're wet," he told her. "So wet already."

She gasped. "Am I too wet? I can't help it."

"No such thing as too wet," he assured her, touching her and feeling the moisture increase. "Just want to make you suffer a little more first. Not ready to let you come yet."

"Then stop saying that," she groaned. "Or I will."

He felt the evidence against his hand, decided he'd had enough of the lacy bra, opened the clasp to reveal her breasts. Took one into his mouth again, bit down just to hear her gasp, between pain and pleasure. She bucked against his hand, hips urging him.

"Drew," she moaned. "Please. Don't stop."

He kept his hand outside the little panties, loving the feeling of her through the lace. Traveled down her body to kiss her there. Moved his lips and teeth against her, through the fabric. She bucked again, and her hands fluttered against the duvet as she lay under his mouth. He slowed down as she strained towards him, then kissed her again. Licked. Moved his teeth over her.

It was too much. With a cry that was almost a scream, she exploded against him. He didn't stop, wringing out every bit of passion that had built so slowly, so agonizingly.

When her spasms had slowed, he pulled off the panties at last, and reached up to pull the bra from around her so she was as naked as he was.

"Time to test this bed," he told her, moving back up to kiss her as his fingers ripped open the condom packet.

"Thought we did," she gasped. "I'm not sure how much more testing I can take."

"Oh, we're just getting started," he assured her. "I'm a very thorough tester. Turn over."

She obediently turned, and he pulled her up to her hands and knees. "I need to do this," he told her. "Need to see this, and feel it." He pulled her back by the hips, and slid inside.

The pace quickened. He had been telling the truth, she realized. He needed this. She could feel the urgency as he rode her hard, shoving her towards the head of the bed. She put her arms out in desperation, felt for the headboard, put her head down and held on as he thrust.

He reached around her, holding himself up with one arm, while the other hand pressed and stroked, pressed and stroked where she was still swollen. She felt her own excitement rising, caught from behind and in front, moaned, stretched her knees wider, and finally gave in to the spasms once more.

He wasn't done yet, though. As soon as she had finished gasping and jerking against him, he pulled out of her and flipped her to her back again. Then entered her again, holding himself up on both hands so he could look down into her face, watch her response.

She pulled her knees up high, wrapped her legs around his back, forced him back down on his elbows.

"More," she urged him. "Please. Harder."

The last of his self-control left him. He pumped into her, faster and harder, as she arched her hips towards him in response. Took her hands in his, pulled them up above her head. Holding her like that, the way he knew she loved, watching her respond to him, took him almost past the point of reason. When she started to cry out again, he felt himself being dragged over the edge with her, freefalling into a shuddering, gasping climax that took him to the limit of sensation, into a pleasure that was almost pain.

He collapsed onto her, quickly rolled so he wouldn't crush her, held her against him as they both fought for breath.

"Wow," she said shakily at last, still trembling as she lay against his chest. "I've never felt anything like that before. That was incredible."

"Mmm," he agreed, stroking her smooth skin, soothing her. "That was. Are you all right?"

"I think so," she said tentatively. "Was that what you had in mind, then?"

He laughed, feeling not completely steady himself. "Something like that. Wasn't quite expecting all that, though. I bought the right bed, admit it. It worked."

"I admit it," she agreed, relaxing against him. "I'd say this bed has proven it's up to your weight. You win the bed-buying trophy."

"Got the girl in the bed, anyway. Reckon that's what matters."

chapter twenty

♡

"Now that you're settled, with a good bed and all," Drew suggested the next morning over breakfast at her new kitchen table, "want to come to a barbecue at my mate Hemi's place? He and Reka decided to take advantage of the bye, get some of the boys and their partners together."

"Sure," she said slowly. "I have to admit, though, I'm a little nervous about meeting people. Reka's the one who helped you pick out my Christmas present, right?"

"That's the one. And no choice, I'm afraid. She'll never forgive me if I don't bring you along so she can have a look. Badgered me, didn't she."

"How reassuring," she answered wryly. "But I'd like to meet your friends. So yes, please."

When she walked up the shallow stone steps with Drew to Hemi and Reka's big house near Takapuna Beach, Hannah was surprised to find the door opened to them not by a rugby player, but by a short person. A *very* short person. An adorable four-year-old with dark ringlets called out, "Uncle Drew's here!"

She held up her arms to be picked up, and Drew obliged. "This is Ariana. Ariana, this lady is Hannah."

Ariana stared at her. "Are you a fairy?" she asked, eyes wide.

"No," Hannah smiled. "Sorry about that. Do you like fairies?"

"I *love* them. They're my very favorite. But you have fairy hair," the little girl insisted, reaching out to touch the long spirals. "Just like in my book. I have a fairy bedroom," she offered. "And fairy dolls too. Do you want to see?"

"I do," Hannah told her. "Will you show me?"

Ariana wriggled to get down, then put her hand in Hannah's and pulled her into the house. Drew followed, smiling and giving Reka a kiss as she hurried up.

"Sorry, Drew. I was in the kitchen. Where's Hannah?" she asked, looking around. "Couldn't she come after all, then?"

"Been dragged off to see Ariana's bedroom. Apparently she looks like a fairy."

"That would do it," Reka agreed. "I hope she doesn't mind. But come in and have a beer. I'll rescue her in a minute."

Ariana did indeed have a fairy bedroom. Her small bed was swathed in white and covered by a canopy. A fairy wallpaper border ran around the white walls, with several framed pictures of woodland fairies hanging below. A group of tiny fairies hung from the ceiling by fishing line in one corner above a small painted table with three chairs. A big, comfortable armchair sat in another corner, and Hannah could guess that this was Ariana and her mother's special spot.

Hannah didn't have to feign her delight. "It's beautiful," she told Ariana as the little girl darted around the room pointing out all her favorite possessions.

Ariana ran forward at last to pull a large picture book from a basket. "This is my fairy book. Will you read me a story?"

Reka came into the room, followed by a two-year-old boy with the same dark curls. "The lady's here to see the grown-ups, love. She can't read you a book tonight."

"Maybe I could read a story later, at bedtime," Hannah offered. "How would that be?"

"That'll do you, Ariana," her mother ordered. "Come on now, let Miss Hannah get back to the party. She'll read to you later, if you're a good girl and get ready for bed with no fuss."

"Read me too," the little boy demanded.

"We'll see," Reka temporized. "Come on.

'Sorry about that," Reka offered as she showed Hannah out to the back garden, where a large wooden deck spread under sheltering awnings, amid plantings of native cabbage trees, ferns, and flowering plants. "Those monkeys. My boy's Jamie. And I'm Reka, by the way. I'm their mum, for my sins."

Hannah laughed. "They're great," she assured Reka. "No need to apologize. Besides, I owe you something, don't I? For helping Drew pick out my Christmas present? The combs are perfect. I'm wearing them, see? I wanted to show you." She touched one delicate ornament proudly.

"They're gorgeous. He picked them out, you know. I just helped with the size."

"Well, now that I've seen your hair, I can see you knew what to buy," Hannah said admiringly. Reka's hair was pulled back into a large knot, but Hannah could tell it was as long and thick as her own, its glossy black a contrast to her own light curls. The other woman's luminescent brown skin, large almond eyes, and rich figure were a beautiful testament to her Maori origin.

"Maori hair," Reka agreed. "We know something about holding up thick hair, don't we. I've heard so much about you," she went on. "I've been dying to meet you. Let me introduce you to people now, though."

To her relief, Hannah realized she knew several of the men already, from her brief introduction in the gym.

"Good to see you again," redheaded Kevin greeted her. "Didn't know you were back in the country."

"I'm working here now," she explained a bit self-consciously. "I have a new job that starts on Monday. I'm just getting settled in now."

She found herself being included easily in the relaxed conversation. She had worried that the women would be so glamorous that they would look down on her. The only examples she had been able to come up with of football players' wives were supermodels and celebrities. If the women were glamour queens, she had thought, she'd be sunk. She would have no idea how to converse with a group of trophy wives.

But, she found, there wasn't too much to worry about. The women were certainly attractive, but everyone was fairly casually dressed, and seemed to know each other well and be comfortable. Some of the men even entered into discussions about children, to her surprise, rather than separating solely along gender lines. She found herself relaxing and enjoying herself as Hemi manned the barbecue and Reka offered drinks and what she called "nibbles."

They sat down to eat at last, spreading out among several comfortable small tables around the deck area.

"Your teammates can certainly put away an amazing amount of protein," Hannah marveled to Drew, watching the men dig into the huge steaks, quartered chickens, and sausages. "Not to mention everything else. What's this, though?" she asked, indicating the vegetable she was eating. "It looks like a sweet potato, but it's purple."

"That's kumara." Drew seemed amused. "Didn't we feed you kumara when you were here? Maori sweet potato. The original staple food. And still a staple for all Kiwis. Red, orange, purple. Wait till winter. You may wish you'd never seen a kumara. Or a pumpkin."

"Too right," Kevin agreed. "Reckon our meat's the secret of our success, though." He grinned at Hannah. "Beef, lamb, pork, venison. Best in the world. Builds rugby players, eh."

"Wow," Hannah marveled. "So successful…and so modest, too."

Drew laughed. "Reckon she's got you there, Kevvie."

"I have a rugby question, too," Hannah went on. "I keep meaning to ask you, Drew. Why do the All Blacks have that white feather on their uniforms? What does it stand for?"

She couldn't have said anything more amusing, she saw with dismay. Everyone at the table laughed, looking at each other and continuing to chuckle as Drew reached an arm around her, pulling her against him with a smile.

"That's not a feather, sweetheart," he told her. "That's the silver fern. The national emblem of New Zealand."

"Oh." Hannah felt herself turning red, but had to laugh at herself in her turn. "You have to admit, though, it looks like a feather. I thought it was some kind of bird or something. A kiwi, maybe. And I've never seen a silver fern, have I?"

"It's the underside," put in Jonah, a teammate who was clearly partially Maori. "Of the ponga—one of our fern trees. If you turn the leaves over, you'll see they're silver. Warriors used to put them upside-down in the bush when they went out hunting, or to war. When they returned by moonlight, the fronds would shine in the moonlight like beacons. Like arrows. The silver fern will always point the way home. That's the idea, eh."

"Thanks," she said gratefully. "You should see how little I know about rugby, if you think that's bad. I'm hopeless."

"Never mind," Drew said comfortingly. "It's part of your charm."

"What, ignorance? I'm not so sure about that," she answered ruefully.

"So much to teach you, isn't there." He grinned at her.

She kicked him under the table as he continued to smile, then turned with relief at a tug on her sleeve.

"Miss Hannah?" It was Ariana, ready for bed in her pink nightgown, with her little brother by her side in Bob the Builder pajamas. "Will you read me the fairy book now?"

"Read me too," Jamie demanded.

"I've been summoned," Hannah excused herself. "Back soon."

She returned at last from Ariana's room and met Reka in the hallway, coming to check on her.

"Both in bed," she assured the young mother. "We compromised—we read a fairy story and *then* a truck book. Twice."

"I'll just give them a few minutes to settle, then." Reka moved with Hannah to the corner of the lounge, where Drew was talking football with Hemi. "Come sit on the couch and talk to me. I'm ready to sit down. Did Drew tell you I'm expecting another baby? I'm flaked out."

"That's wonderful," Hannah exclaimed. "Not that you're tired," she added quickly. "You do have lovely children, though. They're so sweet."

Reka laughed. "Trying to impress you, that's all. They're not so lovely, some days. But I reckon I'll keep them. This one's about three months along. I should begin feeling better any time, and none too soon. You must have nieces and nephews yourself, though. To be so good with kids."

"No, but I helped raise my brother and sister. I used to read a lot to them when they were younger. It's nice to have the chance again."

"You'll want kids of your own, then, someday," Reka guessed.

Hannah smiled. "I don't know. I certainly enjoy them. Thanks for letting me borrow yours for a while."

"Don't you miss your family, being here now?"

"I do," Hannah sighed. "It was a tough decision to make. But it's only for a year or two."

Reka raised her eyebrows at that. "But you moved down here to be with Drew, didn't you?" He had been half-listening, and turned now, moving towards them on hearing his name.

"Sounds like it's serious," Reka went on.

"I'm not sure," Hannah answered, just as Drew said, "Yes."

Hannah flushed, confused. "I mean, I just got here."

Hemi laughed. "You don't have to answer her, you know, Hannah. Doesn't know when to stop, does she."

Drew came to sit with Hannah, taking her hand and squeezing it for reassurance.

"You're mistaken, Reka. Hannah moved down here for her job. I was just the bonus," he said solemnly. "I've already been put right on that one."

"The bonus?" Hemi shared a look with Reka and laughed. "Don't think you've ever been called that before, mate."

"So you just happened to get a job in New Zealand, after you'd met our boy here?" Reka teased.

"Could we move on to another subject, please?" Hannah asked, smiling but embarrassed. She nudged Drew in the ribs with her elbow to let him know what she thought of his sharing, but he just chuckled.

"Here's an easy one, then," Reka continued, unperturbed. "How did you two meet? You were here on holiday, right?"

"That's almost more embarrassing," Hannah admitted. "He rescued me." She told the story, laughing at herself, but Hemi frowned with concern.

"Nothing to take lightly, those rips. You need to be careful in the sea. Heaps of drownings every year. Not just tourists, either. Fishermen, kids. Good job Drew was there, I'd say."

"I know," Hannah answered, sobered. "It was my lucky day. I do know that."

"Sounds to me like it was Drew's lucky day, eh," Hemi answered.

Hannah was happy to be rescued from the conversation by the arrival of some of the other guests. She liked Reka and Hemi, but she wasn't sure she wanted to share the details of her relationship with Drew. Not when she was so unsure of it herself.

The evening wasn't a late one. Several of the other players and their wives had young children as well, and a general exodus to relieve babysitters emptied the house by eleven.

Hemi and Reka moved around slowly, picking up glasses and straightening furniture as they chatted about the evening.

"Drew's fair gone, I'd say," Hemi commented. "Not sure about her."

"She's a lovely girl," Reka answered. "I do wonder why she's holding back. She's not playing games, I don't think. Just careful, maybe. Probably why he fancies her so much. Bit of a change for him, isn't it."

"Well, don't ask her about it," her husband advised with a smile. "You embarrassed the poor girl something chronic tonight. Reckon she'll think twice before she has a chat with you again."

chapter twenty-one

♡

Hemi was wrong, though. Hannah found herself beside Reka in Auckland's rugby stadium two weeks later for a game against the Otago Highlanders, New Zealand's southernmost team.

"Welcome to the WAG section," Reka smiled at her. "Football Wives and Girlfriends," she explained as Hannah looked at her questioningly. "Don't they say that in the States?"

"If they do, I've never heard it. But this is my first game to watch in person," Hannah confessed. "I have no idea what I'm about to see. I hope you won't mind educating me a bit. I saw the game they played in Wellington last week on TV, and the announcers helped a little, but I'm still pretty confused."

"Course I'll help. How was your first fortnight at work, then?" Reka asked as they waited for the stadium to fill and the game to begin.

"Good, I think. I think I'll like it. It's different. I'm not used to that open-plan office space, for one thing. No cubicles, even. It's a little distracting, I find."

"We don't like private offices much. We like people to be on an equal footing. And to chat, maybe," Reka conceded. "But I can imagine it would take some getting used to."

"Otherwise, though," Hannah went on, "it's good. I like the people. Everyone's been really friendly. And I'm figuring out how

I can help, where I can make a difference. One thing that's better, I sure could get used to leaving by five-thirty every day. Sometimes I even leave at five," she announced proudly. "Like tonight."

"Didn't you do that before, then?" Reka asked.

Hannah laughed. "Not even close. More like eight. I still get in pretty early in the morning. But it's nice to have the whole evening."

"Reckon Drew wouldn't be too happy if you were at work late every night," Reka agreed. "The boys need their sleep during the season. How're you coping with being left on your own when he's gone? I realize it's only been a couple weeks, but it takes some getting used to. Can get a bit lonely."

"For me, this is a lot of companionship as it is," Hannah explained. "But my work colleagues have been really welcoming also. One of them took me over to Devonport for the day last weekend, and we had a great swim at one of the beaches there. I've had quite a few invitations to go out, too."

"Really," Reka replied, eyebrows lifted.

"Don't worry," Hannah said hastily. "I've declined those, the ones you mean. I meant invitations to go out for a drink with the group after work. Things like that."

"I was wondering for a moment there. But you and Drew are exclusive, eh. Not in some kind of open relationship."

"Yes—at least, I think so," Hannah answered with a frown. "We've never actually discussed it. I guess we should."

"Always good to know. Not a bad idea to make sure."

"Oh, look," Hannah pointed out, grateful for the diversion. "They're starting."

♡

"So what exactly are Drew and Hemi doing?" she asked, as play got underway. "I know Hemi's a back and Drew's a forward. But what does that mean?"

"Drew's on the front lines there, doing the grunt work, going after the ball. Hemi's more about offense—the flash bits," Reka explained. "Drew's a flanker, Hemi's a first five-eighths. Although both forwards and backs play both offense and defense. Not like American football, where you have separate teams for each. More like hockey, I reckon. Hemi's kicking now, see?" she pointed out. "Moving the ball forward. They can only carry the ball, pass it backwards, or kick it, to move it forward. You'll see them kicking it a fair bit, just to get it onto the other side of the field, even though the other team may recover. Kick and chase football. Especially if they're stuck back near their own try line. There's the breakdown, when play stops and starts again, when the player goes to ground with the ball, once he's tackled. And where they're piled up, that's the ruck," Reka went on.

"Look now," she instructed, as Drew stopped the Highlander carrying the ball in his tracks with a bruising tackle, then jumped up fast to allow the other player to pass the ball back and play to resume. "That's what makes him the best. He'll do that all game long, you watch. Got stamina to burn, has Drew."

"Hemi's an All Black too, right?" Hannah ventured.

"For the past five years," Reka nodded. "They're selected every season, though. No guarantees. A player may start one year, or even one series, then be in reserves the next—or not on the squad at all. With five New Zealand Super 15 teams to select from, there's heaps of talent, and only fifteen starters."

They stopped talking for a while, watching as the Blues got the ball back, then passed it expertly in a choreographed series of moves that steadily advanced them toward the other team's goal. Finally, Hemi flicked the ball in a deceptively simple motion to a player who came up quickly, reversed directions, and neatly outmaneuvered the charging tacklers to dive across the try line at the corner marker, sliding in on his stomach, the ball stretched in front of him.

The crowd rose and cheered the try, Hannah and Reka with them. Reka held her breath as Hemi lined up for a kick from the outside corner of the field. Hannah watched, amazed, as he proceeded to slot the ball neatly through the goalposts from the impossible angle, and another two points were added to the five already on the board.

"And that's why he's an All Black," Reka explained proudly. "The offload—the pass. And the kick. That precision, that's what New Zealand rugby's known for. Precision and toughness."

"I still don't understand the scrum, though," Hannah commented after the Blues had cruised to a seemingly easy victory.

Reka laughed. "Neither do I, entirely," she confessed. "Some things are just mysteries. You'll have to ask Drew. But wait now. They're doing the captains' speeches. You'll want to see this."

Hannah looked to the big screen, and saw Drew, standing with his hands on his hips, looking battered, and her heart leaped.

"Yeh, it was a good effort by the boys," he was saying. "We'll keep working on winning the lineouts. We held well when we had to, didn't turn the ball over." He continued for a few more sentences, then nodded to the commentator and turned away with a smile and a handshake for the captain of the losing team, coming up for his own interview.

"Do they always do that? The captain talks, not the coach?" Hannah wondered.

"Yeh," Reka answered, smiling. "You'll get used to hearing his standard speech. 'The boys did well, showed a lot of ticker. Still have some work to do,'" she mocked gently.

"Don't you worry about it, though?" Hannah asked her as they made their way toward the exits. "It's so rough."

"I never like seeing Hemi heading into the blood bin," Reka confessed. "To get stapled up on the sideline. But that's the game."

"They get stapled on the sideline?" Hannah asked, startled. "And then keep playing?"

Reka looked at her curiously. "Course they do. Can't play if they have blood flowing. Get stapled to stop the blood, and they're back on again. The trainer takes the staples out after the game, stitches them up more neatly. Didn't you notice?"

"I didn't notice the stapling," Hannah answered faintly.

"Haven't you seen Drew's scars, then? He's got a fair few."

"Yes," Hannah admitted. She had been shocked the first time she realized what all the marks on his back and chest were, not to mention his face, she remembered. "But that just seems so...brutal."

"It can be a brutal game," Reka conceded. "They say soccer players spend all their time pretending they're hurt. Rolling on the ground and that, whingeing," she said contemptuously. "And rugby players spend all their time pretending they're not."

♡

Hannah had arranged to spend a quiet Saturday with Drew as he rested after the game. Waking with a sore throat and headache, she reluctantly called him to cancel.

"Sorry you're feeling crook," he sympathized. "Rest today, then. I'll come by later, check on you."

"No," she insisted. "I'm not going to risk you getting this too. It's probably just a cold, but you don't need that. Because I can go to work if I'm not feeling well. You can't."

By the afternoon, she was glad she had kept him away, as her temperature began to rise and she felt the telltale ache in her joints that signaled the flu. She gave up the attempt to clean her apartment, turned off her phone, and climbed into her nightgown and the comfort of her bed, where she lay, shivering and miserable, the rest of the afternoon.

She woke from a doze to the sound of the doorbell. She tried to ignore it, but the buzzing persisted. At last, she pulled a blanket around herself and made her way through the fading light to the front door. She wasn't entirely surprised to find Drew there.

"I texted you, but you didn't answer," he frowned at her. "Decided I'd better check on you."

"I have the flu, I think. Don't come in," she warned, taking another step back so as not to infect him. "I just need to rest, that's all."

"What do you need?" he insisted. "Do you have Panadol?"

She squinted at him, feeling muzzy and stupid. "What?"

"Panadol. Paracetamol. Painkiller," he explained impatiently. "Do you have any?"

She shook her head, then winced at the pain. "I'm OK," she insisted wearily. "Just go away and take care of yourself. I need to go to bed, that's all."

"I'll be back in a few minutes. Lie on the couch so you can get the door again. Hannah," he said firmly when she protested. "I won't come in, if you don't want me to. But I can pop round to the chemist for you."

True to his word, he was back within thirty minutes, handing her a bag of supplies. "Flu medicine, Panadol, hottie—hot water bottle. And some chicken soup. I'll text you tomorrow. Text me back, this time. And go back to bed now."

She had to admit that the medicine helped. Waking up still feverish on Monday, though, she reluctantly called Kathryn, the Marketing Director, and made her excuses.

"I've heard it's going around," Kathryn said sympathetically. "I hope you feel better soon."

"If I'm still home tomorrow, maybe I can do some work from here," Hannah offered. "I hate to be out sick so soon after I started. I almost never get sick. I'll do as much as I can."

"No," Kathryn told her. "Stay home and rest till you're better. I've seen how hard you work. Your sickness benefit doesn't officially begin until you've been here six months, but we can extend it to you in advance, in this case. No worries. Get some rest now."

Hannah gratefully took her advice. Just making the call had exhausted her. As she drifted back into an uneasy sleep, she wondered what Felix would have done if she had been sick for several days during her first month. She'd never have had a second month.

"No," she told Drew again on Tuesday when he called. "You can't come over. You leave tomorrow," she insisted, before breaking off for a bout of coughing. "I'm not giving this to you right before that long flight to Perth. Besides, I'm better. It's just the cough now. I barely have a fever anymore."

"You may want to see a doctor for that cough, though. I'll send you a number and address. Will you promise to go, if you're not better tomorrow? Wish I weren't leaving. If you're still this ill tomorrow night, I'll ring the doctor myself, make him come round and see you."

"Bacterial bronchitis," the doctor pronounced the next day, when Hannah reluctantly dragged herself to his office after another sleepless night. The antibiotics he prescribed made the difference, and she was able to return to work for a short day on Friday. She was relieved, though, to be back home again in the evening, tucked up in a blanket and watching the Blues on TV. Seeing Drew put forth his usual intense effort, she was grateful she'd kept him from getting sick too.

"You're looking more fit than last time I saw you," he commented when she opened the door to him the next day. "I didn't ring. Didn't want to hear you tell me to stay away. Too thin, though," he frowned, stepping inside and giving her a gentle hug.

"Still a little tired," she admitted. "But I'm much better. It must be those Southern Hemisphere germs. I don't usually get sick. Come in and tell me about the game."

"Maybe I should take you to my house this weekend instead," he decided. "That way I can feed you."

"I don't have much in my fridge," she agreed. "I'm not sure I have anything to fix us for lunch, even. So if your entertainment standards aren't too high today, then yes, please."

♡

"I think you'd better take me home at the break," she sighed that evening, resting in Drew's arms as they lay on the couch and watched another rugby game on TV. "I'm falling asleep."

"No worries. I'll carry you up to bed if you do."

"I'm not sure I'm up for much tonight," she told him hesitatingly. "I should probably just go home and sleep."

He shifted position so he could look at her. "Do you think I only want you around if we can have sex?" he asked bluntly.

She dropped her gaze, not sure how to answer. "Yes" seemed a little too honest, even for her.

"I want you here because I enjoy being with you," he told her, as gently as he could manage. "It was pretty hard going, this week. Just want to relax, now I'm home again. You help me do that. Besides," he added with a grin, "If I take good care of you, maybe you'll be feeling better tomorrow."

♡

"You're looking a bit more flash today," he told her approvingly when she arrived in the kitchen the next morning as he was finishing his breakfast.

"A lot more rested." Still in her nightgown, she stepped across to the electric jug to make herself a cup of tea. "I can't believe I slept till eight-thirty."

"It's good for you. We'll have a quiet day, let you finish getting well."

"I meant to ask you about that—well, sort of about that. Last week, before I got sick," she said cautiously, sitting down next to him. "Reka said I should talk to you."

"About what?"

"About whether we're exclusive. Or if we have—what she called an open relationship." Hannah frowned into her mug of tea. "It's important to me. And I realized we'd never discussed it."

"No," he said immediately. "No open relationship. Definitely closed. I know Reka's curious," he went on, not pleased. "Surprised she'd say something like that, though. How did this come up?"

"Not out of the blue. She wasn't really being nosy. I'd mentioned that some of my coworkers had invited me to do things. We were talking about how I've been settling in here. And then she asked, I guess if we were dating other people, and I realized that we should have that conversation."

"Because fellas at work are asking you out," he said flatly.

"I should have guessed that's the one part of what I just said that you'd hear. No big deal. A couple guys asked. I'm new there. And I'm young and single," she said dismissively.

"Sounds like I should come by tomorrow, pick you up after work," he decided.

"No," she told him firmly. "No, you aren't going to do that. Because, first," she said when he would have argued, "I can take care of myself. I know how to say no. I should be more worried about whether you do. I've had years of practice, remember? I don't think you have."

He took her hand, threaded his fingers through hers. "I know how to say no. And I am," he promised. "Still, I'd be happier if I could show my face around there."

"And terrify all those poor guys with your Laser Eyes?" She shook her head. "No, thanks. For the same reason I didn't want you to 'put in a word' for me when I was looking for a job. I'm just establishing myself. Building some credibility. Having you turn up would be a distraction. It would keep people from evaluating me on what I can do, on my own performance."

"Right, then," he agreed grudgingly. "But if anyone bothers you, you need to tell me, and I *will* turn up."

"Don't worry." She moved closer, stroking his cheek. "If anyone is so overcome by my great beauty that I can't get rid of him, I'll send in my big, strong, fierce rugby player to sort him out." She punctuated her words with delicate kisses, enjoying the texture of his skin under her lips. She'd missed him so much this past week. It was wonderful to be able to hold him, touch him again.

He pulled her into his lap, his hands moving over her in her nightgown. "Seems to me, since you're obviously feeling better, that I'd better take you back to bed, work on making sure our relationship stays closed."

Lying with her later, holding her against him, he frowned, remembering. "What was that bit about my Laser Eyes back there?"

"You know," she answered, relaxed and a little sleepy again now. "When you stare somebody down like you do. Coming out onto the field, especially. Or during the game. That fierce thing you do. You look really scary."

"Wonder why you never do what I say, then," he grumbled.

She laughed, snuggled closer, and kissed his cheek. "Because it wouldn't be good for you. And because you don't use the Laser Eyes on me," she added honestly.

"Good to know I don't scare you, anyway," he said, stroking his hand down her side, and then sliding it back up to a breast.

"You thrill me a little, though," she sighed, her breath catching as his hand explored. "That's better, don't you think?"

"Definitely," he agreed.

chapter twenty-two

♡

"It hasn't been much fun for you since you got down here," Drew commented the next Sunday. He had a leg propped on his coffee table, with an icepack on his thigh, badly bruised during the previous night's game. "Hardly taken you out at all, have I."

"I went to the game last night," she pointed out. "Watching you play is about all the excitement I can handle. When you limped off there, I was plenty stirred up. Besides, I told you, I'm not used to going out much. Having dinner at home with you works fine for me."

"Still," he persisted. "Some of the younger boys are going clubbing Tuesday night, before we leave for Jo-burg. Somebody needs to be there anyway, make sure it's not too much of a piss-up. I thought you might enjoy it."

"Chaperoning, huh? That sounds about my speed," she conceded. "I might have to work late, though. We're finishing a project. Can I meet you there?"

"If you wear something pretty. You're not *my* chaperone."

She did take some extra time getting dressed that Tuesday. Mindful of Emery's frequent strictures, she chose a flirty pale blue dress that landed above the knee, shorter than she would normally have worn to work. Tiny shell buttons ran from the V-neck to the hem, while the nipped-in waist and softly draping material showed off her curvy figure. She would keep her hair up until after work, she decided, and would wear a jacket over the dress during the day. Still, the extra looks she garnered from a few of the men at work made her uncomfortable. Back to the Wicked Queen tomorrow, she vowed.

She stepped into the noisy club with its pulsing music at eight that evening, feeling a bit frazzled and not sure this was still a good idea. When she looked around without seeing Drew or anyone else she recognized, she thought for a craven moment about turning around and leaving again.

"Hannah!" She turned at the call and saw Kevin hurrying towards her.

"Good to see you," he beamed cheerfully. "Drew's held up for a few minutes, asked me to look out for you. We're over here." He motioned her to a corner table where four or five of his young teammates sat with several women, one of whom she recognized from Reka's party. Kevin quickly introduced her to those she didn't know.

"Good to meet you," said a striking young man, his Maori ancestry showing in the bronzed skin and strong, chiseled body, whom Kevin introduced as Koti James. "Can I get you a drink?"

"Beer sounds good tonight," she smiled at him. "Whatever's on tap. Thank you."

Koti came back with two glasses and slid in beside her. "So how do you know our boy Kevvie? You aren't together, are you?" he asked, watching Kevin chat up a pretty blonde at the table.

"I've met him a few times. And I've seen him play. I've seen you too, I think, haven't I?"

Koti flashed a dazzling smile, white in his handsome face. "Reckon so, if you've been going to the games. Glad you noticed me. You're from the States, eh. Just visiting, or do you live here?"

Too late, Hannah realized he was flirting with her. She had to get better at this, she thought in despair. "I'm living here now," she smiled cautiously, unsure how to explain. Out of the corner of her eye, she saw Ben nudge Kevin and nod in her direction.

"I've been enjoying learning more about rugby since I've been here," she went on, trying to keep the conversation neutral. "The games are exciting, though I'm afraid I don't understand the rules very well yet."

"I could explain them to you," Koti said confidently. "I'd look forward to it." Then turned at a tap on his shoulder from Kevin.

"Uh, mate," the other man muttered. "Need a word."

"Sorry," Koti smiled charmingly at Hannah. "Back in a minute."

"She said she wasn't with you," Koti pointed out in annoyance as he stepped away from the table to join Kevin. "If you think she is, you'd better tell her."

Kevin motioned with his head toward the table. Koti turned, surprised, to see Drew approaching. The captain bent and gave Hannah a quick kiss, sliding into the place Koti had vacated.

"The Skip's girl, eh," Kevin explained economically.

"Oh. Shit," Koti said blankly. "Thanks, mate. Reckon it's better he didn't see me trying it on."

"You ain't wrong," Kevin agreed with a sigh of relief.

♡

"How's your thigh feeling?" Hannah asked, concerned, when Drew had settled himself.

"Still a bit niggly," he admitted. "Didn't practice on it much today. May take it easy tomorrow too. Be fit for Saturday, though. She'll be right."

"I know you'll play on it no matter what. I've already figured that much out."

He smiled at her in answer, took a pull on his beer.

"Since you can't dance much tonight, Drew," Kevin suggested as he joined them again, "maybe I should take Hannah out on the floor for a bit."

"I'm not a great dancer," Hannah told him. "But I'd like to try."

She needn't have worried, she realized. Kevin made it easy. He was so cheerful and encouraging, she found herself laughing even as he caught and twirled her to the music, her skirt swinging and making her feel light and more graceful than she knew she actually was.

"That was fun," she said, dropping back down on the bench next to Drew at last and taking a sip of her beer. "I'm a bit worn out, though."

"That's what you get for dancing with a wing instead of a real man," Drew grinned. "Always poncing about, eh. Now go find your own girl, Kevvie," he commanded.

Hannah shook her head as the other man turned to leave. "Must be nice to have everybody obey you like that."

"Everybody but you," Drew pointed out.

Another uptempo number began, and Koti came up to ask Hannah to dance.

"Sorry about that," he apologized as he led her out on the floor. "Didn't know you were Drew's girlfriend."

"I gathered that," she smiled. "Never mind."

Koti was an even better dancer than Kevin, she soon discovered, and she found she was enjoying herself. It was obvious that she wasn't the only one who noticed, either. The young player's handsome face and powerful physique were attracting more than their fair share of female attention as one song followed another.

The music shifted at last, beginning the intro to a slow song, and Hannah found Drew stepping up and taking her from Koti.

"My dance," he said, pulling her into his arms. As they began to move together, Hannah recognized Sam Cooke's "You Send Me," one of her favorites.

You sure do, she thought to herself. She was still breathing a bit heavily from the exertion of the previous dances, but now she sighed, moved closer, and relaxed into Drew. It felt so good. She felt his heartbeat beneath her cheek and was as soothed by it, and by his warm body against hers, as a puppy snuggled into a basket with a hot water bottle. The image made her smile. She wouldn't share that, she decided.

As he held her and she melted into him, the solid breadth of his muscular back under her hands and his powerful thighs against hers, the warmth kindled into something hotter. She pressed herself more tightly against him and stroked her hand over his back just to enjoy the feeling of his muscles moving as he slowly turned her in time to the music. That valley where his spine ran, the ridge of muscle rising strongly on either side. That was her special place. She ran her fingers slowly down it as they continued to dance.

Drew's arms tightened around her as he spun her in a slow circle around the dance floor. He held her close to his chest as the ballad continued, the top of her head tucked under his chin. She felt so right to him there, soft and warm and so sweet. But even as she held him so closely, she kept him at a distance, too. He knew she wanted him, and she gave herself to him physically with a wholehearted joy that thrilled him. But when he would have helped her, protected her, part of her always seemed to stand back. So close and no closer.

Never mind. Someday she had to realize that she could count on somebody else besides herself. That she could count on him.

When the song finally ended, he kissed her gently on the top of her head, then pulled her into a slow, sweet kiss.

"Time to go," he told her, pulling back but keeping his arm around her. He took her back to the table where, she was amused to see, he swiftly broke up the evening with just a few words.

"That was a nice time," she told him when they were in his car, headed back to St. Heliers. "Thank you for taking me."

"My pleasure. Entirely. My place all right, or do you have an early morning?'

"Mmmm, no, that's fine," she responded dreamily.

After that, they didn't talk as he steered the car expertly through the busy downtown streets, full of pedestrians even on this Tuesday night. Drew put his left hand on her thigh and kept it there as he drove, stroking slowly under the hem of her skirt, his hand warm and hard on her leg, his fingers moving back and forth, back and forth against the smooth skin of her inner thigh.

Hannah sat in a haze of arousal, wondering just how his touch could excite her so much, whether he even knew the effect he was having on her. Was the leg an erogenous zone? she thought confusedly. She'd have to look it up.

The drive home seemed to last forever. But as he finally shoved the front door closed behind them, Drew dropped his keys on the hall table and reached to pull her close. He cupped her face in his hands and threaded his fingers through the mass of hair, pulling her in for a long, slow kiss. Keeping his mouth on hers, he leaned back against the door and pulled her bottom tightly against him.

"I've been looking at this all night," he murmured as he reached his hands under her skirt and ran them over her. "And so has every other fella in the club. Glad I'm the one who gets to hold it."

He lifted her off her feet to mold her body to his, holding her in place with one strong arm while the other stroked over each rounded globe, and down to the sensitive places at the tops of her thighs.

"I don't think so," she said shakily. "I think that's just you. But oh," she sighed, "that feels good." She squirmed closer, pressing herself against his erection and seeking out his mouth again for another deep kiss. And felt the shivery thrill of the contact go through her, all the way down to her toes.

He lowered her, moving both hands now, stroking, squeezing. As she lay against his chest, he pulled her up against him with one big hand, reaching the other under the hem of her panties from behind, touching her, rubbing, feeling where she was already wet. His fingers moved inside her, and she gasped and moved against him again, trying to get closer. He bent his head to kiss the side of her neck, moving his lips over the tender flesh, then taking a nip that brought another gasp and a moan.

She was breathing hard now, held against him tightly as his wicked hands and mouth continued to tease and torment her. She lost track of time, felt herself melting against him as he kept up the slow, steady assault. Every part of her seemed to be reaching out to him, wanting to hold all of him against her, inside her. He seemed to have the same thought, because the next thing she knew, he had picked her up and was carrying her.

"Wait," she protested. "No. I'm heavy. Your leg," she reminded him.

He laughed and pulled her more tightly against him, bending to kiss her again as she lay in his arms. "You're the sweetest armful I've ever held. But if you think you're heavy, maybe I should give you a chance to feel how heavy I am. When I'm on top of you, you can tell me."

His words sent another jolt of desire straight through her. In answer, she wrapped her arm around him and pulled him down for a kiss. Somehow he managed to get them upstairs and into his bedroom that way, slapping the light on with one swift movement and rolling with her onto the big bed. Coordination, she thought hazily.

Then she stopped thinking as he drew back, pulled off her shoes, and began to unfasten her dress, taking his own slow time with each tiny button, and kissing each inch as he uncovered it.

"Have I mentioned," he asked as he flicked open yet another little shell, "how much I like it when you wear these things with all the buttons? It's like unwrapping a present. A present just for me," he finished, parting the last button and lifting her as he pulled the dress from underneath her.

She lay in her dark purple bra and panties, her cloud of hair, the color of moonlight, spilling around her, and held up her arms to him.

"I'll be your present," she promised. "Come and be mine."

In answer, he unclipped the lace demibra, letting it fall open, and reached for her. She looked down, and the sight of his large brown hands covering her white breasts sent an erotic thrill through her as strong as an electric shock. She gasped as his thumbs reached her sensitive nipples and he bent his head to take one into his mouth. She arched against him, so aroused by now that just that contact took her close to the edge. When he shifted his mouth to the other breast and bit gently, she cried out, loudly enough that he smiled against her.

"Mine," he said as he pulled back to look at her again. Then, slowly, he was reaching inside her panties again, rubbing his fingers over her. "Mine."

She was so close, just the touch and his words were enough. She felt herself convulsing against him, her hips arching off the bed, crying out her release.

He couldn't figure out, afterwards, how he had got rid of his own clothes that fast. He only knew that he had to be inside her, now, as she lay back, still shuddering and gasping, her hips rising and falling.

"I need you...please," she whimpered as he came to her.

But as he eased inside her sweet slickness, he slowed down, reached for her hands, and threaded his fingers through hers. They made love like that, slowly and intensely, looking into each other's eyes as she gasped and moaned under him, her hands held tightly beneath his. He kept the pace maddeningly slow, even as she shuddered, begging him, her hips rising urgently to meet his, to hurry his pace.

He watched her as he kept on, slow and sweet, watched her moving beneath him, saw her arch her neck and, finally, lift into her orgasm, felt her muscles clench around him as her cries filled his ears. And then, at last, he found his own release, every muscle going rigid as he poured into her in hot, sweet spasms that left him shaking.

Afterwards, she lay with him, her hand on his chest as he stroked her hair back from her face. She drifted off to sleep without another word, entwined with him, secure in his arms.

chapter twenty-three

Hannah woke to find Drew handing her a cup of tea.

"Six-thirty," he told her. "Unless you want to go to work in yesterday's clothes, I'd better be dropping you home."

"Oh," she moaned. "It feels so early." But she sat up and took the heavy mug, grateful for the warmth and the caffeine. Normally, she bounced out of bed and moved briskly into her morning routine. But today, she felt languorous, like a spoiled cat. She just wanted to stretch out on her cushion and doze the morning away.

He smiled at the picture she made, dressed only in her hair, in the middle of his bed with the sheets rumpled around her. "Feels like a good day to spend in bed," he agreed. "Reckon I wouldn't mind. But I'll resist temptation and take you home instead."

Her feeling of blissful contentment lasted all the way back to her flat. All the way through his lingering goodbye kiss and promise to call her that night from the hotel in South Africa. All the way through her shower, getting dressed, and preparing her breakfast. Right up until she sat at her kitchen table, a spoonful of oatmeal in her hand, looking at a teaser just below the newspaper's masthead. A picture of Drew, with the caption, "Is he taken?" directing her to page B15.

Hardly knowing what to think, she turned to the photo gallery at the back of the sports section. And stared with shock at a picture of…herself. Herself and Drew, more accurately. It was from the night before, she realized, when he had kissed her following their dance.

Cell phone, she thought. Somebody had sent it into the paper, and they had already shoehorned it in. She quickly scanned the few lines, finding with relief that she wasn't named.

"Drew Callahan gets up close and personal with a blonde beauty at a City nightspot," she read. "Sources say she's a Yank. Why not give the Kiwi girls a go, Skipper?"

"Oh no," she groaned. She wished it weren't a Wednesday morning, that she didn't have to go in to work. But maybe nobody had seen it. Many people never read the paper, she reminded herself, certainly not in the early morning. She wasn't named, and it was just one picture in the midst of many. So maybe nobody would notice. Or nobody would recognize her, she thought hopefully.

As soon as she stepped into the office, though, she saw with a sinking heart that her hope was misplaced. Several people stood in a group, talking over a copy of the offending newspaper. They turned as they saw her, falling silent and moving away a bit guiltily.

She put on a bright, nonchalant smile, and called out, "Morning, everyone."

"Morning," she heard, as the others stepped back to their desks and began to look busy. She sighed with relief. But there was Lisa, from the sales staff and frankly, not her favorite person, approaching with an avid smile. No such luck.

"Morning, Lisa," she said briskly. "How are you?"

"Hannah," Lisa gushed, with a warmth she had certainly never showed Hannah before, "why didn't you *tell* us you were dating Drew Callahan? What's he like? How long have you two been going out? How did you meet him?"

"He's a friend. People put all sorts of things in the paper, you know. You can't believe all the rumors you hear. Nothing exciting to tell, I'm afraid."

Lisa wasn't to be discouraged so easily, however. "Come on, then," she urged. "We can all see how he was kissing you. You can't tell me that's nothing."

"I'm afraid that's all there is," Hannah replied firmly. "The newspapers can make a whole story out of one picture, you know. Sorry, but I really need to get to work now."

"Maybe next time you know where the team is going to be, you could take me along." Lisa wasn't ready to give up yet. "I'd love to meet them."

"They don't necessarily all hang out together, Lisa," Hannah answered, as patiently as she could. "They're individual people, you know. And I've only met a few of them. It's not like I'm invited to team functions. I'm afraid I'm not in a position to introduce you to anybody. But it's not a very big place, Auckland. You're probably just as likely to run into one of them as you are any other guy. And you're a beautiful woman. I'm sure you don't have any problem attracting men without my help."

Lisa preened herself a little. "Well, I do think I've got something to offer." Her quick glance at Hannah's less-spectacular chestline confirmed just what it was that Lisa thought she had that Hannah didn't.

Hannah could almost feel the question, "Why did he pick *you?*" Your guess is as good as mine, girlfriend, she admitted to herself. But she was glad for Drew's sake that he *was* dating her, instead of someone like Lisa.

Mollified at last, Lisa moved off, and Hannah was thankfully able to lose herself in work. Others, she saw from the speculative glances and occasional comment she received throughout the morning, were curious as well, but nobody else possessed the effrontery or the sheer bad manners to make as bald an approach as Lisa had. Or perhaps Lisa had told them there was nothing in it, after all. They'd probably believe that, too. She was nobody's idea of WAG material, she knew.

The ordeal of her day wasn't over, though, she found. While going over the new U.S. campaign with Kathryn, she found herself being invited to lunch by the Marketing Director—an event unusual enough to raise her antennae. Sure enough, when they were seated in the café with salads before them, Kathryn wasted no time in starting in.

"Hannah," she began warmly. "I didn't realize you had already begun to get so well acquainted with important people in the country. Well, hiring you was certainly a good decision. I wanted to be sure to mention that we're always happy to provide free merchandise to any of our celebrities, especially our sportsmen. As a marketing professional, you will have realized how important our rugby teams are to us here. I'll tell Henry to make sure you have access to stock for that purpose."

Oh dear, Hannah thought. She paused for a few breaths, choosing her words carefully.

"I think you may be jumping to a conclusion," she finally answered. "I'm not really in a position to offer merchandise to the team. And I'm afraid it would be inappropriate for me to use any...personal connection to further my professional goals."

She trembled a little, waiting for the response, but determined not to get herself into a position to be pressured.

Kathryn was clearly disappointed, but she smoothly changed tactics. "Of course, I understand that," she said soothingly. "I'd never ask you to do something that felt wrong to you. But you know, in your case, we could make an exception to our normal employee clothing discount. If you're going to get your picture into the paper, maybe next time it could be in some 2nd Hemisphere clothes, hmmm? We have that new raspberry wrap dress, you know," she mused. "I think that would look wonderful on you, with your coloring. That's a perfect dress to wear on an evening out. Why don't you stop by and get one in your size today? Go through the jerseys, too, and take anything you like. Wearing our clothes wouldn't compromise your principles, surely."

Hannah smiled at her. "Of course, I'd love to have more 2nd Hemisphere items in my wardrobe, Kathryn. You know I love the products. That's why I work here, after all. And if I should get my picture taken in them, that will be a bonus. I'll take care not to abuse the privilege."

She was grateful that Kathryn had backed off so graciously, and even more grateful that she had held firm. She shuddered at the thought of shilling her products to Drew's teammates. Ugh. She'd never make a saleswoman, that was for sure.

Kathryn wasn't quite done, however. "And of course, dear," she assured Hannah, "any time you want to bring a…guest to one of our events, you're more than welcome. Like the new shop launch in Hamilton next week," she suggested slyly. "You'll be there, of course, and I could arrange things so you could slip away partway through, if you wanted to make a day of it. I understand Drew comes from that area. Perhaps he'd like the chance to show you around?"

"Again, I think you may be overestimating my…importance to the team, or to any members of it," Hannah returned. "Of course, I'm planning to be at the launch. It's a big event and I'm excited about it. But I'm afraid it will just be me."

Kathryn recovered once again. "Well, any time, dear," she smiled. "You just let us know. We can always make a bit of a splash."

Hannah could just imagine the "splash" they would make, of her dragging Drew into an unpaid, unagreed-to endorsement. *Over my dead body,* she thought.

"Thank you, Kathryn," she answered coolly. "I don't envision that coming up, but I appreciate the thought."

♡

By the time Drew called her late that evening, Hannah was fed up with the whole thing.

"How do you do this?" she exclaimed in frustration as she told him about her day. "How do you handle people asking you about your private business all the time? They called me a WAG," she confided, outraged.

"Reckon you are a WAG, though," he pointed out reasonably. "What, were you thinking we were pen pals?"

"It just sounds so much like...an appendage," she complained.

"Never mind," he said soothingly. "I still respect you. But I handle it the same way you did today. They can ask, but I don't have to answer. Men aren't that interested anyway. They just care about the footy."

"Then why did you make sure everyone went home on time last night?" she asked shrewdly. "I don't think any of the women in the bar would have minded if the boys had stayed around a bit longer."

"Maybe that's why," he admitted. "Don't want the team to get a bad name. The young boys—it's all new to them. They can make mistakes. And they have to be thinking about getting right for Saturday. Can't do that if you're out getting pissed. Can't keep them on too tight a leash either, though, all season long. Better to be there, keep an eye on them."

"Well," she conceded. "I had a good time being a chaperone, so I won't complain."

"Noticed you having a good time, didn't I," he agreed. "Heard you, too."

"Don't you have some game strategy to plan, or something?" she asked crossly. "Instead of embarrassing me?"

He laughed. "You have to let me have some fun, when I'm this far away. Give me something to think about, get me through to Sunday."

chapter twenty-four

♡

"There's a gala dinner in aid of the Australasian Childhood Cancer Foundation coming up next month," Drew mentioned one evening in June, as they ate a relaxed dinner at her apartment. "After the end of the season. Some of the boys and I will be there. Would you come with me?"

Hannah looked at him speculatively. "Just how gala? What does it involve?"

He shrugged. "Dress up a bit, get your photo snapped, chat up the major donors, eat dinner, listen to some speeches. Not too bad."

"Well, I'll admit it'd be fun to see you dressed up. Not that I have any objection to looking at you in your uniform. Just like every other woman in Auckland," she teased, laughing as he grimaced in disgust.

"I told you, I'm not the pretty boy. Nobody's paying me to get naked on the billboards. I'm not the one they're looking at."

"Yeah, yeah," she mocked. "Tell it to the Marines. But when you say get your photo snapped, you mean for the newspaper, right?"

"Yeh. And they may even call you a WAG again. Think you can stick it? I'd like you to come. Keep me company."

"I'll admit I'm a little nervous about the publicity part," she said. "I'm not as used to it as you are, you know. But how fancy is it? What kind of dress would I need?"

"Well, it's quite posh," he shrugged. "The men wear dark suits, or dinner jackets. The women wear long dresses, mostly. Some short, though."

"Well, that's extremely helpful," she sighed. "I can see I'm going to have to get my information elsewhere."

When she went online later to check out the prior year's function, Hannah found that the event was even dressier than she had supposed. Red-carpet photos showed women in a variety of formal gowns, many beaded, embellished, and low-cut. It looked like the Oscars, she thought in dismay. She knew she had nothing remotely suitable in her wardrobe. Gala dinners and photos on the red carpet had never been part of her normal routine. She would have to go shopping.

But after a fruitless Saturday spent trying on and taking off a succession of ill-fitting, slightly trashy, or simply unattractive dresses in two department stores and several boutiques, she called Emery in despair.

He was thrilled. "Girl, we are going to make you smoking *hot,*" he enthused. "You just leave it to me."

"But Emery," she objected. "How can you help? I know you'd go shopping with me if you were here. Can you help me find something online, maybe? And I don't know about shoes, or what to do with my hair, or anything. You know I'm no good at this stuff."

"Honey, you don't buy a dress like this online," Emery told her firmly. "But haven't you ever heard of the Queer Fashion Mafia? We'll get you beautiful. Trust me."

"Well, nobody knows more about fashion than you, and I certainly haven't been very successful on my own looking for a dress. So I'll have to leave myself in your hands, I guess. Too bad Drew isn't taking *you,*" she teased. "You'd know exactly what to wear."

"You are so right. *However,* as you unfortunately keep pointing out, I'm not his type. But I'd love to see *that* picture in the paper."

Hannah laughed and hung up, feeling comforted. Emery wouldn't let her down, she knew. Somehow, he'd help her find an outfit that worked.

Sure enough, two days later, she got a call at work from a man named Edward, who introduced himself as a personal shopper at one of the city's most exclusive designer boutiques. Hannah had never even considered checking his store, as she knew it was out of her price range.

She hesitantly mentioned her concern to Edward, but he overrode her smoothly. "Just come in," he told her. "We'll get you sorted, I promise. Best set aside three hours," he said briskly, after she had made an appointment to meet him that Saturday.

She asked him doubtfully, "Will it take that long, just to find a dress in your store?"

"The *right* dress," he corrected her sternly. "Shoes, bag...Yes, we definitely need three hours."

Well, she thought, she could at least give this a try. After all, she didn't have to buy anything if it didn't work out.

She duly presented herself at the appointed hour, resigned to yet another day of trying things on. She quailed a bit, though, on entering the elegant store in Auckland's most prestigious retail space. The clothes were so exquisite, and the assistants so beautifully groomed, she wondered if they'd even let her in. Suddenly, everything she was wearing felt just a little scruffy.

But here was Edward—it could only be Edward, slim and faultless in a black suit—coming towards her with a welcoming smile. He took her into a large fitting room, complete with curtained-off changing area and padded benches, and urged her to sit. Over coffee brought by yet another assistant, he took her measurements.

"I brought out a few things already." He showed her a rack of short and floor-length dresses. "But after seeing you, we definitely need to go with floor-length. Classic, Emery said, and he's right, of course. But we want a bit of flash to bring out that hair and skin."

Hannah found herself dressing and undressing for yet another Saturday. She had to admit, the choices were a lot better than those she would have made for herself—*had* made, she reminded herself. The colors were clearer, the fabrics more luxurious, the cuts more refined and closer to her body, without being overly revealing.

And still Edward kept bringing them out, satisfied with none.

After an hour, Hannah was flagging. "Maybe I should just choose one of these," she suggested. "They all look nice. Maybe this purple one. It's pretty."

Edward looked at her severely. "We aren't after *nice*," he informed her. We're after *stunning*. And we'll know it when we see it. The difference between pretty and beautiful is just attention to detail." He relented, though, and let her take a break.

Attention to detail, she thought. Whatever. This was the second Saturday she had wasted, and it began to seem a little ridiculous to spend this much time choosing a single outfit, for an event she felt dubious about anyway. But Edward wasn't allowing her to quit. On and on she went, pulling each dress over her body, watching him shake his head, and taking it off again.

And then, midway through the second hour, when she was having visions of herself eating lunch on the floor of the fitting room, they found it. As soon as she pulled the gorgeous silk jersey over her shoulders and the dress settled around her, she knew this was The Dress.

"But it's red," she told him doubtfully. "I never wear red. It's so...bright."

"That's not just red," Edward assured her. "That's *Valentino* Red. And it's you."

Somehow, the blood-red hue made her cheeks look pinker, while the pale skin of her bare arms glowed in the reflected color. The cut, too, was beautiful. Tiny cap sleeves embraced just the tops of her shoulders, gathering at her collarbones and flaring into the neckline in a flattering, feminine bow shape. The twisted bodice, with its wide V-neckline, was glamorous, but didn't show too much cleavage, while the diagonally shirred bodice made the most of her curves and trimmed her waistline. The shirring stopped at the hip, the gathered folds dropping from one side to the floor in a graceful, slim bell with a slight train.

She turned to see her rear view. The V back wasn't too low, she saw thankfully, and the shirring was certainly flattering back there, too. The cap sleeves gave the dress an elegant silhouette both front and back that the sleeveless gowns she'd tried on couldn't match.

She looked at Edward, her fatigue forgotten. "I think this is it. Isn't it?"

He smiled back. "This is the one," he agreed. "Congratulations."

She sighed in satisfaction, and took a look for the first time at the price. She had peeked at tags throughout the morning, of course, and had been shocked but, finally, resigned at the parade of fifteen-hundred-dollar-plus dresses she had tried on. This was a special occasion dress, she had told herself firmly. She had never had a real evening gown, and this was an investment piece she could wear whenever she was invited somewhere very special. If she bought something classic, it could last for years.

But now she gasped and dropped the tag. "Two thousand five hundred dollars? I'm sorry. I love this dress, but I can't afford it."

Edward smiled at her. "Did I mention we're having a sale? Today, that dress is eighteen hundred dollars."

She looked at him in surprise. "I didn't see a sale sign in the store. Oh," she realized. "Did Emery say...who I was going with? He shouldn't have done that. I wouldn't want to accept a discount under false pretenses. I'm not in a position to be all that helpful to your store, I'm afraid."

He just looked at her, amused. "Emery told me you were in marketing. Don't you have a promotional budget? Trust me, we're in this business to make money too. You'll have to believe me that when your photo turns up in the paper and online, people will want to know where you bought your dress. It's in my best interests to have you out there, looking glamorous and reflecting well on the shop—and, if I may say so, on me. And of course, I'm hoping for your repeat business, though you're under no obligation."

She blushed. "I can't promise anything," she warned. "I don't know that there will be any…repeat business."

He answered smoothly, "Well, whether or not that's the case, this is your dress. You want it, and I want to sell it to you for eighteen hundred dollars. Now let's get you some lunch, and then try on those shoes."

When Hannah left the store that afternoon, she felt a little sick at the hit her credit card had taken, but for once she felt confident about how she was going to look. Edward had not only helped her pick out strappy black heeled sandals and a small black clutch that were, he assured her, perfect with the gown. He had also advised her on jewelry, hair, and makeup. Who knew there was so much to getting really dressed up? She had always thought she was doing well if she fixed her hair nicely and actually wore mascara. But she apparently *absolutely* needed her hair, makeup, and nails professionally done before the gala.

Well, at least she didn't have to lug any packages. Everything was being delivered to her once the dress was hemmed to her measurements. That was what thousands of dollars bought you, she supposed. Delivery service.

Grateful to be home, she took a long, hot shower. She hadn't realized trying on clothes would be so exhausting. She felt as if she'd run a marathon. In her robe at last, with a comforting cup of tea, she called Emery and told him how the day had gone.

"But Emery," she wailed. "I spent—I hate to tell you what I spent. $1,800, just on the *dress!* And shoes, and a bag, and…and

I'm still supposed to buy chandelier earrings, whatever those are. How can I spend that kind of money?"

Emery was unimpressed. "You know you have it, you little tightwad. So you aren't adding to the House Fund this month. But first, didn't you tell me you were wearing a lot of those 2nd Hemisphere pieces now? So how much have you spent on clothes since you got there? Nothing, I'll bet. *Maybe* underwear. And I'm just going to throw out a wild guess here, and assume that your travel and entertainment budget is a whole lot less these days. And maybe your grocery bill, too?" he asked slyly.

She had to laugh and agree. "It's true, Drew isn't exactly a twenty-first-century guy when it comes to sharing the expenses. And you just keep your nasty mind off my underwear. But still... isn't it a little wrong to spend that much on clothes?"

"Yes, if you're a shopaholic. But nobody, in their wildest *dreams,* would ever call you that, girlfriend. Live a little. Take a walk on the wild side. The red dress side," Emery teased.

"How do you know what color my dress is?" she asked suspiciously.

"Hmmm...Edward *may* have sent me a picture," Emery admitted. "Perfect choice, sweetie. And he's right. Chandelier earrings, no necklace. Very simple. Nice updo on your hair."

"OK, but what *kind* of an updo?" she asked, worried. "And I don't care what you say, I can't afford to make a big jewelry purchase, especially now."

"Take yourself to one of those replica stores. Tell them chandelier earrings, silver, not gold. Dangly, you know. They'll help you. Then just pick something you think is pretty. I'll say this for you, you might be too conservative, but you do have good taste. Zip me pictures of yourself in some of them, if you want, and I'll help you choose. As for the hair," he went on, "you go to your stylist, tell her about the event, show her a picture of the dress. Which I will e-mail to you. And make an appointment for her to come to your apartment before the gala and make you beautiful. Hair, makeup, brows, lashes, fingernails, toenails."

"Come here?" she faltered. "How does that work? Don't I need to go in there, that afternoon?"

"Trust me. And before you ask, yes, you'll pay for it. And it'll be worth it. Just do it, this one time. Trust Auntie Em. You know I'm right."

Hannah laughed. "Well, you haven't steered me wrong yet. I guess I'll have to take your advice. It'd better be worth it, though. Otherwise, I'm wearing jeans and T-shirts every day from now on. I'll have to anyway, once I've spent my entire annual clothing budget on this one night."

♡

The weekend before the gala, Drew took her back to the bach on the Coromandel for a three-day break from the city. The Super 15 season had ended with the Blues losing in the final to the Stormers, a South African team. It had been a closely fought game, and she knew Drew and his teammates had been bitterly disappointed not to have brought the trophy home to New Zealand.

When she asked him about it, though, he shrugged. "Losing's part of the game. Win or lose, you can't take it too seriously. Life goes on. When you lose, you pull up your socks and get on with it. Think ahead to the next game. The next season."

She knew he needed a break in any case. The toll the game took on the players' bodies was appalling. Injuries were a constant problem. Drew had told her that the rules were stricter these days about playing injured, particularly with concussions. She wondered, though, just how bad it had been before. She had seen his battered body after the games, with its huge bruises, scrapes, and wrenched joints, and wondered that he could ever recover quickly enough to play the following week. Some of the players, she knew, limped onto the field with injuries that would have had the normal person bedridden, let alone throwing themselves into combat with a group of 225-pound men bent on destroying them, wearing not so much as a helmet.

Now he would have a couple of weeks to rest before the All Blacks season began. Training would continue, but at least his body could take a break from the fearful beating it received, week in and week out. And he would get an occasional respite from the pressures of the captaincy during this brief period. As captain of both teams, he was involved in much more than just game strategy, she was beginning to understand, and she knew the responsibility weighed on him heavily.

Today, though, none of those pressures intruded. Drew had spent the morning fishing, while she had taken herself out for a solitary winter hike on one of the longer coastal tracks. It had rained, but she was prepared by now, and had merely hauled out her rain jacket and pants and pulled them on, continuing her walk and enjoying being outside and looking at the ocean. She had been glad to have the time alone to let her mind wander after a somewhat contentious week at work. And although Drew had invited her to join him, she thought he had needed some quiet time too, and had been just as glad to go out by himself.

It certainly seemed to have done him good, she thought now. They had had a quiet dinner together, and now relaxed by the fireplace in the cozy lounge, each lying at one end of the long leather sofa, their legs and feet entwined, reading and chatting. She sipped a glass of wine and snuggled more comfortably into the cushion behind her, rubbing her stockinged foot against Drew's thigh and enjoying the feel of his powerful legs next to hers.

He smiled across at her. "Good to know you're comfortable," he joked. "Meant to ask you. Did you get yourself sorted for that do next weekend? A dress, and all," he explained when she looked at him in confusion.

"Yes, I'm fine," she answered, thinking wryly about the time and effort it had taken her to 'get sorted.' Easy for you to say, she thought.

"Because I was having a chat with Reka the other day," he went on. "And she says I was thick, asking you to that kind of thing without thinking about your dress. She says you won't have had anything like that, and it will've cost you. I didn't think about that. I can help, if you're strapped for cash."

"No," she replied firmly. "No, I bought a dress, and it's fine. No need to worry about me."

"Sure?" he pressed. "You know I'll see you right."

"I wouldn't have accepted if I hadn't been able to buy myself a dress, Drew," she answered, a little stiffly. "And I wouldn't buy anything I couldn't afford." Barely, she thought, but he didn't need to know that. "I don't want your money. We've had this conversation already. You pay for so much as it is. You never let me do anything to pay my own way."

"And we've had *this* conversation too," he responded grimly. "I don't want you to 'pay your own way.' If I take you out, I'll take care of you."

"And if I go out with you, I'll at least get myself ready, by myself. You can't buy my clothes. It would make me feel like a... like some kind of gold-digger," she finished defiantly. "Like I'm looking for a sugar daddy. That's not me."

"No worries," he grumbled. "I'm in no doubt of that." But he dropped the subject, to her relief.

chapter twenty-five

♡

Despite the shock to her system as she had paid her VISA bill that month, Hannah thought on the evening of the gala that it just might have been worth it after all.

She was standing in front of the full-length mirror of the wardrobe in her bedroom, checking her appearance. The stylist and her assistant had come and gone. Hannah's fingernails and toenails now shone with a nude polish ("We'll keep it subtle," Amy had said firmly. "That dress gives you all the flash you need"), her brows were perfectly shaped and tinted, and her makeup elegant but not overstated, to her immense relief. Her eyes looked greener, her skin flawless, and the bow of her top lip was accented. She looked like herself, only better, she thought happily.

Amy had done her hair last. Hannah had never had her hair specially styled for an event before. She had worried about being left with a turban of hair, or a teased, curled construction that looked like it belonged on a B-list actress falling out of a hot pink dress. Instead, her hair was pulled softly back into a simple, somewhat messy knot, which somehow managed to look much better than when she did the same thing herself. A few tendrils around her face softened the effect, while not detracting from the gown's beautiful neckline.

She looked, in fact, better than she ever had in her life. If she were stepping onto the red carpet, at least she was going in style. She wouldn't disgrace Drew, and unless she fell over in the unfamiliarly high heels, she wouldn't disgrace herself, either.

When the doorbell rang, she took a deep breath, checked herself in the mirror one last time, and opened the door. That was one seriously attractive man, she thought, eyeing Drew with enjoyment. The suit—black, of course—suited his dark looks, and the perfectly tailored garments emphasized his athletic physique.

"You look wonderful," she told him. "Very distinguished. I didn't know you cleaned up quite so well. Everyone's going to envy me, that's for sure."

He wasn't paying much attention, she realized. Instead, he stood still, just looking at her. She stood back and smiled.

"What do you think?" she asked. "Good?"

"I'm a bit stunned, that's all. Didn't expect it to be red. It's beautiful," he hastened to add, seeing her crestfallen look. "I'm making a hash of it. Let me try again. You look gorgeous. I'm not sure I want to take you out for all my mates to have a look, is all."

"You'd better," she laughed with relief. "You have no idea how much effort all this took. I'm awfully glad you like it, though."

"There's only one thing I don't like about it." She looked up at him, startled, as he continued. "It's the earrings."

Her hands flew to her ears. "Oh, no. I sent Emery a picture before I bought them, and he said they were just right. I'd better find some others to wear, if these don't look good."

"I may have some here," he told her, pulling a slim velvet box from his inner pocket.

She opened it and gasped. Delicate bell-shaped panels in white gold set with diamonds hung from graceful hooks, while graduated chains of more tiny diamonds set in white gold dangled below. The effect was dazzling, yet feminine and ethereal.

She held the opened box in her hand and looked up at him. "These are too much," she said slowly. "They're so beautiful. Are you sure?"

"Oh, I'm sure," he answered firmly. "I lost the receipt and I can't return them, and they look shocking on me. So I'm afraid you'll have to wear them."

"But how did you know?" she wondered. "What kind to buy, I mean? They're just what I would have chosen if I could have had anything at all."

"How do you think?" he answered, a little proudly. "You're not the only one who can call Emery, you know."

She glowed with pleasure at the gift and his thoughtfulness, but still felt compelled to protest. "You didn't have to do this, though."

"Oh no," he groaned. "Are we going to have this again? Sweetheart, I wanted to get you a present. And now that I've seen you in that dress, I can see I bought you the right thing, so I'm happy. At least I will be if you'll put the damn things in so we can get on to this bun fight."

She laughed, distracted. "I've clearly lost my manners. Sorry, you just took me by surprise. Thank you. I love them. They're perfect."

She quickly unfastened the old earrings and replaced them with the new ones. "I have to look in the mirror now, though. You can't give me something this beautiful and not give me a minute to look."

The earrings were even lovelier in her ears than they had seemed in her hand, she decided as she stepped across to the mirror. The diamonds sparkled as the tiny chains swayed and caught the light, and the effect with the dress was indeed perfect.

She came back to Drew, put her arms around him, and pulled him down for a kiss. "Thank you," she said again. "You are a wonderful man. And now, take me out to dinner, please, and tell me what in the world a bun fight is. I hope your car isn't too far away," she added as he held the front door for her. "Because I'm not too good at walking in these shoes."

He smiled down at her. "Good thing you won't be walking far, then. Here it is." He pointed to a large town car waiting at the curb.

"Do you know," she told him as the driver stepped out to hold the door for her, "other than a car service to take me to the airport, this is the first time I've been driven like this. How exciting."

Drew laughed. "Best not hold back," he teased. "Better to be open."

"Well," she answered cheerfully, "I'm sure I'd give myself away pretty quickly if I started pretending to be high-maintenance now. Might as well be honest. It would take me a while to become blasé about these things, though. It's pretty luxurious, admit it, to be picked up and dropped off anytime you like."

"It is," he agreed. "Especially when you're walking in your new shoes. And don't forget that photo op. Can't have you all sweaty and windblown."

She groaned. In the excitement of preparation, she had almost forgotten about that. Almost. She reminded herself that she was now as polished as any of the women whose red-carpet pictures she had studied online, and that her gown was beautiful. That was the main thing people—women—looked at anyway, she decided. The dress, and the man. In both of those, she was confident.

So, when they stepped out of the car (onto an actual red carpet, she was amused to see), and were directed into a backdrop area featuring the society's logo to have their picture taken, she gave the camera her best smile and directed her thoughts toward the man at her side, his arm firmly around her waist. If he had to do this, so could she. It was only posing and looking happy for a minute or two, after all, and that was easy enough to do right now.

Drew steered her away at last. "There's the worst bit done," he assured her. "Easy as pie from here."

In spite of his reassurance, she was more than pleased to see Hemi and Reka in the group of players, wives, and girlfriends they were approaching.

Hemi smiled a welcome and bent to kiss her cheek. "How ya goin', Hannah. You look beautiful."

Hannah greeted him in turn, then turned to give Reka a hug. "I'm so glad to see you," she told the other woman. "And look at you. That baby must be cooperating, because you're looking wonderful."

Reka was indeed glowing, in a gown of ivory silk that wrapped around her baby bump and set off her luminescent Polynesian skin and long, curling hair.

"Don't ask me how long it took to get this way," she sighed. "Luckily the nanny was able to stay straight into the evening, so I had some peace to get myself ready. But thank goodness I don't have to get gorgeous every day."

Hannah laughed and privately agreed.

"But you look lovely too," Reka went on. "Your earrings are stunning."

"Aren't they beautiful? Drew just gave them to me," Hannah announced, looking over at him with a smile. "Wasn't that nice of him?"

"Yeh, he's charitable like that, eh. Always willing to do a good turn," Hemi responded solemnly, and the other men grinned into their drinks as Drew shot them a fierce scowl.

"Hey," Hannah chided. "You're not supposed to use the Laser Eyes on your own teammates."

"Reckon they need it most of all," Drew growled. "Cheeky buggers." But he smiled and pulled her gently towards him, handing her a glass of champagne from a tray held by a passing waiter.

Reka leaned forward and gave her a conspiratorial wink. "Never mind. Sometimes I think they don't like it when we look too beautiful, that's all. Makes them go all territorial."

Hannah laughed. It was good to know Reka would be there to chat with during the evening. They were soon interrupted, however, by the first in a string of major donors and other guests who approached Drew, either already acquainted or being introduced for the first time. Drew was gracious and friendly, focusing on each person in turn and exchanging polite chat about the evening and, of course, the season. He listened to the men's would-be knowledgeable comments about strategy and tactics with what Hannah knew must be assumed patience, and she found herself admiring his self-control. Surely none of these men really knew what he was talking about. Drew never let on, though, just listened, smiled, and looked thoughtful.

He insisted on including Hannah in every introduction, making her feel less like a fifth wheel as she stood by his side. At her request, he kept her supplied with water after her single pre-dinner glass of champagne. The last thing she wanted was to get tipsy, and she knew it would be a long night.

"I know what a lightweight you are," he agreed. "Not up to Kiwi standard."

She was just thinking that the evening was going more smoothly than she had feared when she saw the handsome figure of Koti James approaching, leaving a stir of interest in his wake as usual. This time, he was accompanied by a tall, stunning redhead, her slim but luxuriant figure draped in a gown every bit as red as Hannah's, but more figure-hugging, cut low, and sparkling with thousands of tiny bugle beads.

The effect of red on red was electric. Hannah wasn't surprised to see the male heads swiveling to watch her progress, though she had to admit that Koti was attracting almost as much attention from the women.

"He's brought the talent, eh," she heard Hemi mutter to his wife. "Show's about to start."

As Koti neared the group, offering Hannah a smile and a quick wave, Hemi called out, "Hiya, pretty boy. We were just missing your gorgeous self." The others laughed, and Hannah listened, amused, as they joined in the banter.

"Tall poppy," Drew whispered in her ear.

"What?" She wasn't sure she had heard him correctly.

"Tall poppy. Cutting him down a bit," he explained. "Gets a wee bit above himself, does Koti. Need to give him stick, time to time, keep him humble like the rest of us," he grinned.

Hannah smiled. She knew that the players' dislike of arrogance was reinforced by Drew's own example, and she admired him for it. If anyone had the right to be arrogant, surely it was him, yet she had never seen that quality in him. Which must take a serious effort, she knew. And some good parenting, to keep his feet on the ground and his head unswollen in the early years of his success.

Gradually, she became aware that Koti's beautiful date was working her way through the group toward them, her gaze constantly flicking to Drew. As she approached and leaned into him, her eyelids lowered, and she breathed, "Hello, Drew."

Drew kissed her briefly on the cheek. "Hello, Dena. Good to see you," he said politely, then turned to introduce Hannah. Dena responded curtly, and gave Hannah a sweeping look that seemed to assess and dismiss her as no competition.

Hannah felt her hackles rise, and briefly considered some Laser Eyes of her own. But her best weapons had never been offensive, so she decided to kill the other woman with kindness instead. Who knew, she thought. Maybe Dena was insecure, and was hiding it this way.

"Hello, Dena," she responded warmly, and held out her hand. "It's nice to meet you. What a beautiful dress. It looks so good with your hair."

Dena took her hand briefly, but almost instantly turned back to Drew. Oh…kay. So, maybe not insecure. Hannah didn't allow herself to be upset by the other woman's predatory act, as Drew gave her no encouragement, and very soon was engrossed in yet another introduction.

At dinner, Hannah wasn't overly surprised to find that Dena had maneuvered so that she sat between Koti and Drew. Hannah wondered why, having ensnared one successful rugby player, not to mention the most handsome of them all, Dena should have her sights set on Drew as well. She couldn't know much about him. It seemed obvious to her that Drew would never pursue a teammate's girlfriend—or whatever she was. But Dena's gifts didn't appear to be primarily mental. She was seeking out the lead dog in the pack, and she seemed confident she could get him.

She was certainly giving it her best effort. While taking care to laugh and flirt with Koti, Dena turned often to Drew as well, taking advantage of being screened from the other man's view. She leaned into Drew, inviting glimpses into her impressive cleavage, even placing her elbows on the table at one point to offer him the best possible display. She touched his hand, stroked her own hair, and generally, Hannah thought with some heat, did everything short of lying down in the middle of the large round table and offering herself to him.

If Drew noticed, he gave no sign. He responded courteously to her questions and comments, but kept most of his attention for Hannah and the other guests at the table. As people finished their meal and others shifted seats and moved to talk to people at other tables, he first checked that Hannah was well situated, then moved away to make his own rounds.

Dena looked disappointed, and Hannah couldn't help smiling a little. The beautiful redhead recovered, though, seeming intent on cementing the relationship she did have.

You work on that, Hannah thought. Rule number one, don't lose one till you've landed the next.

She found Reka easing into the seat beside her with a sigh as it was vacated by Hemi, who had kept Hannah well entertained during the meal with his cheerful chat.

"I see Dena's lost out again," Reka grinned. "Hemi and I always enjoy the show she puts on, though. I tell him to go ahead and look, that's as close as I'm ever letting him get. But that one is out for your man, you know that. She'd love to steal him from you."

"He's not mine to steal," Hannah answered firmly. "And if he's fool enough to choose somebody like that, he doesn't deserve me anyway."

"Too right," approved Reka, though she looked a little surprised. "No worries, anyway. Drew's been looking after himself too long now to be caught like that. I'm glad to see you don't have your knickers in a twist, though. Most women would, watching her try it on."

"I figured that one out a while back," Hannah answered wryly. "If I'm going to get upset every time a woman throws herself at Drew, I'm going to have permanent heartburn. I try not to, anyway. What about you? Surely you've faced this, over the years. It had to be especially hard when you were first pregnant."

"I'm Maori," grinned Reka. "We've always had weapons, and we know how to use them. Hemi knows I'd cut it off. Besides," she continued more seriously, "he doesn't get the kind of pursuit Drew does. He was never New Zealand's Most Eligible Bachelor, eh. They all have their chances, though. Can't answer for all of them, but Hemi's happy at home."

"That's obvious to anyone," Hannah assured her. "I can't imagine anyone lucky enough to be married to you wanting to jeopardize that."

Reka beamed and gave her a hug and Hannah laughed, grateful for the other woman's easy friendship. She asked Reka about the children, and they were soon chatting happily about

Ariana's preschool and Reka's troubles with potty-training her stubborn son.

Then it was time for the after-dinner speeches, and Hannah soon discovered what Drew had meant by "a few words after dinner," as one speaker succeeded another for a full thirty minutes. She wasn't entirely surprised to find Drew getting an award for his service to the charity, or that he hadn't mentioned it to her. Of course, he had to go up to the podium and give another speech in response, which he accomplished with his usual grace. Hannah could tell he didn't relish his moment in the spotlight, though, and that he was glad to return to his seat. She squeezed his hand and smiled at him in support, and he grinned back at her ruefully.

♡

"How'd you go, then? Rather schedule a root canal instead, next time?" he asked when they were in the car again at last.

She laughed and admitted, "Not nearly as painful as I'd feared. It was wonderful to have Reka and Hemi there. I like them so much. Reka invited me to Ariana's fifth birthday party next weekend," she added with enthusiasm. "Wasn't that nice?'

He sighed. "Here I take you to this glam do, and you're more excited by a four-year-old's birthday party. What am I going to do with you?"

"I think you're missing the point," she told him severely. "It's a *five*-year-old's birthday party. But you must admit, the dress code is easier. Phew, I never knew how much effort it was to get this fabulous. I can't wait to get out of these clothes."

"Funny," he smiled, "I was just having the same thought."

"You'll have to help unwrap me, I'm afraid," she told him. "This dress requires a remarkable amount of underpinning. Look, double-stick tape." She showed him the bodice. "Just to make sure nobody gets a bonus peek. And I don't want to tell you about the foundation garments. Apparently only those skinny models are allowed to wear these things without support. I always knew there was a reason I avoided the whole glamour thing. Now I can see how smart I've been all this time."

"I'll be happy to unwrap you," he said with a wicked gleam. "I'm a trained professional, remember? But I know what you mean. I always feel like this tie is choking me."

"Poor you," she comforted him solemnly. "Having to wear a whole...*tie*. What a nightmare. But never mind, I'll unwrap you if you unwrap me." She smiled at him and, mindful of the driver in the front seat, contented herself with holding his hand and giving him a kiss. "Thank you for taking me," she went on more seriously. "I actually had a good time. I like your teammates. They make me laugh. Although some of their girlfriends leave a bit to be desired."

He laughed. "She's a picture, eh. Reckon she'll get the message one of these days."

"It's too bad for Koti, though, don't you think?" she asked. "Being with someone who doesn't care more about him."

"Don't waste your sympathy. They're not exactly, what's that word you like? Oh yeh. Exclusive. Just some arm candy, that's all. On both sides," he concluded firmly, cutting off her protests.

They were sharing an early breakfast before Hannah headed in to work on Monday morning when the telephone rang, and she heard Emery's voice on the other end.

"I saw the pictures online," he crowed. "*What* did I tell you? Am I good, or what?"

She reached for the paper and thumbed through. Sure enough, there was a blurb about Saturday's gala, and color photos of several of the celebrity guests, with herself and Drew prominently featured.

"Well, I guess that's the secret," she told Emery resignedly. "Thousands of dollars on clothes, a private army of people to fix me up, and I can get a decent picture of myself. Drew looks great, though, doesn't he?"

"Testosterone on the hoof," Emery confirmed. "Just like always, only even yummier than usual. It's an unfair world, isn't it? All he has to do is show up, whereas you and every other woman in the world have to go through what I *know* you're going to tell me was a nightmare of preparation to look that good. Some women actually enjoy it, you know. Maybe you're just not used to it. We'll have to get you out there more."

"Heaven forbid," she sighed. "I think I'm ready to go back to my down-to-earth self for now, thank you very much. But yes, Emery. You were right, you did great, and I owe you."

"Oh, I'm paid back. It's all worth it," he assured her. "Just seeing your beautiful face on my screen. I can't wait to post the link."

She groaned. "There goes my privacy, lost to the Internet Age. Oh well, if it has to be out there, thank goodness it was flattering."

"How did the earrings work out?" Emery asked eagerly. "I can't really see them in this picture. Send me a close-up of you wearing them, sweetie. I want to admire them. I do such good work."

"So modest, too," she said admiringly. "Wait, Drew wants to talk."

"Emery," Drew began, once she handed him the phone. "Thanks, mate, for the shopping help. And for getting my girl togged up." He grinned across the table at her. "She looked awesome."

He listened a moment, then smiled again. "More," he said succinctly, then, "Here's Hannah back. Cheers."

"What did you ask him?" Hannah questioned Emery suspiciously.

"I asked him if you looked as smoking hot in person as in that picture. He thinks you did."

just this once

Hanging up, Hannah looked across at Drew. "That was nice of you, thanking Emery like that. Not to mention the 'smoking hot' thing. That's not something I've heard a lot, I have to say."

"I thought I made that dead clear the other night," he protested. "Maybe I need to remind you again."

"Maybe so," she said happily. "But if you remind me now, I won't get to work this morning. I'm sure nobody wants to lose the chance to comment on my being in the paper again. Better go get it over with, I guess."

And she would just head Lisa right off at the pass, she told herself firmly. The last thing any of those boys needed was another predatory female hunting them down.

♡

"I couldn't believe it, when I saw the pictures," Kristen exclaimed over the phone the next weekend. "I've never seen you so dressed up. How exciting."

Hannah laughed. "You'd better enjoy looking at it while you have the chance. Because that's not happening very often. There's a reason you're the glamour girl in the family. Too much work for me."

"It's hard to believe you've only been gone, what, four months?" Kristen said wonderingly. "It seems like your life has changed so much."

"It has," Hannah admitted. "I still work a lot. But that's about the only thing that's the same."

"Yeah, I noticed. I just wish I knew how you did it. How you found somebody so great. Do I have to come to New Zealand to find a guy like that?"

"I don't know," Hannah answered honestly. "I'd say I had to kiss a lot of frogs. Or maybe I'd say I *didn't* kiss a lot of frogs. I've always been so picky. You know that. I really don't have the answer," she admitted, giving up. "Just luck, is all I can say. So far so good, anyway. How's it going for you? You haven't said much lately."

"I've been trying not to kiss frogs too, now that you put it that way. That therapist I've been talking to has helped me see that I've been looking for a guy to fill something that's missing in me. Which is why it never works. And I know," Kristen hurried on, "that that's what you've been telling me all along. But somehow it's easier to hear it from her. So I'm taking a break. That was her suggestion. I'm not dating at all for six months."

"Wow. Six months. That sounds like a big change. How's it going?"

"It's weird. A little lonesome and boring so far. It's only been a month, though. I didn't want to tell you about it at first. I guess I didn't want to admit you were right."

"I'm really pleased. That doesn't sound easy. I'm proud of you for trying it."

"I think a lot of it, the man thing, is not having had a dad, don't you?" Kristen asked. "I mean, you were closer to Daddy. And you were older. But for Matt and me...I don't even remember him that well," she said sadly.

"I know, honey," Hannah sympathized. "You're right, I have more to remember. But I miss him too. All the time. It was Mom too, though. She didn't exactly give you a lot of validation for anything except being pretty. So it's no wonder if you've looked to get that from outside, from a guy."

"That's another thing Barbara and I have been talking about," Kristen confirmed. "But you know, I've been lucky too, that I've had you. You've always cared about me. And I know I've disappointed you."

"No," Hannah said firmly. "You've never disappointed me. You've had a tough time. I've been sad when you were unhappy. But I'm really proud of you now. I want you to know that."

"I'm proud of you too," Kristen answered, a catch in her voice. "Having you gone, I've realized how much I count on you. I miss you. And I know I sometimes say nasty things. I'm sorry about that. It just seems like your life is so easy, sometimes. Like you always know exactly what to do, and then you go ahead and do it."

"I don't always know the right thing to do, though," Hannah protested. "Lots of times I just do the safe thing. There's a difference. I'm as confused as you are, a lot of the time."

"Really?" Kristen said doubtfully. "You always seem so sure. So confident."

Hannah laughed ruefully. "Not exactly. Some of that's an act. You know, fake it till you make it? It works pretty well. But it isn't always how I'm feeling inside."

"I never knew that. That actually makes me feel better," Kristen said more cheerfully. "I mean, if you aren't as perfect as I always thought, maybe there's more room for me to catch up."

"Plenty of room. I'm glad you have that straight now, anyway. I hope it helps."

chapter twenty-six

♡

"What would you think about crossing the Ditch, seeing the last All Blacks game against the Wallabies Saturday night?" Drew asked her a few weeks later. "I've hardly seen you these past couple weeks. I won't be able to spend time with you till Sunday, but I'd like you to be there all the same."

"It's in Brisbane, right?"

"Yeh. Think you'd like Brissy. You could have a bit of a wander round, anyway. It'd be a nice holiday for you. Warmer, too."

"I'm not sure I'll enjoy myself that much at the game," she said. "Unless you blow them away from the beginning. Since whoever wins this one wins the Rugby Championship, now that the Springboks and the Pumas are out of it. I'll be really nervous for you."

"It'll be a pretty physical encounter," he warned her. "Can't promise a blowout. We're ready to get stuck into business, though. My mum and dad will be there too," he added casually. "They're flying out as well. Give you a chance to meet them."

"You won't want me there, then," she protested. "Not if your parents are coming. They've hardly seen a game all season. They'll want to focus on you. And they don't even know me."

"This would be the chance, then, wouldn't it? I've met your family, remember?"

"That was just my brother and sister, though," she tried to explain. "This is your parents. I don't think I'm ready to meet them."

"They're not so bad. They don't bite. And you don't have to spend the weekend with them. May sit next to them at the game, that's all. Watch me run around the paddock. Admire my form," he joked, trying to reduce her tension.

"You know I do that," she told him sincerely. "But it won't bother them, not having you to themselves?"

"Grown up now, aren't I? They haven't had me to themselves for a fair bit now. I'll get you sorted with your plane and hotel, then, let you know."

She hesitated. "I'd like to come. I love to watch you play, even though it does make me anxious. But I can get myself there."

"Hannah." He expelled his breath in frustration. "I'm inviting you. I promise, you don't have to sleep with me in return," he went on over her protests. "This isn't prostitution. But I don't want to worry about where you're staying, how you're getting there."

"You know that's not what I meant. But other people go to games. They travel to Australia, too. I can afford the trip."

"And what about the World Cup?" he retorted. "I'd like you to come to as many of the pool games as you can manage, and the knockout rounds, too. All three of them, I hope. That'll be a lot of trips to Aussie, and I know you can't afford that. I think you're going to have to resign yourself. Think of it as a date."

"Some date. Like those millionaires who take women out to dinner in Paris. It's a lot for you to do."

"Nah," he countered. "It's me being selfish. I'll be in Aussie for two months running. If we want to see each other at all, I'll have to get you there."

♡

Drew had been right, Hannah thought the next Saturday as she explored Brisbane. The capital of Queensland, Australia's northeastern state, was a beautiful city built around a river that wound through the town. Even in winter, the subtropical climate was pleasant, the gardens lush with foliage and noisy with exotic birds. She set aside her nervousness about meeting Drew's parents and tried to enjoy her day.

She normally got to the stadium early for a game, enjoying watching the seats fill and anticipating the evening ahead. Tonight, though, she found herself delaying in setting out.

When she finally arrived, she thought she would have recognized the man in the seat next to hers as Drew's father even if she hadn't known he would be there. Sam Callahan had the same strongly-marked features as his son, his body equally tall and sturdy, if a bit thickened by age.

"Hello," she ventured shyly as she finished edging her way through the packed row of spectators to find her seat. *Brilliant opening,* she thought disgustedly, and felt the heat rising to her cheeks.

Sam stood, offering his hand. "You must be Hannah. Sam Callahan. And this is my wife Helen, Drew's mum."

"We were so pleased when Drew told us we'd meet you tonight," Helen said, a smile lighting her pleasant face. "Have you had a good day, then, in Brisbane?"

Hannah found herself relaxing a bit as they chatted easily about the city. Drew's mother was an attractive, trim brunette with a ready smile and a warm manner that soon put Hannah at ease.

"I'm sure Drew's happy you made the trip too," Hannah offered. "You must be very proud, watching him."

"He'll do his bit," agreed Sam gruffly.

Despite his parents' understated expectations, however, Hannah noticed that they were as keyed up about the game as she was herself. Nobody shouted louder than Sam when the All Blacks scored a try. And when the referee finally signaled the end of the long eighty minutes, with the All Blacks clinging to a 17-10 winning margin over Australia, both parents jumped and cheered, waving their flags with the rest of the fans. They might not want to proclaim their pride too openly, but it was clear to Hannah in every intense gaze they directed at their son as he championed his troops to victory in the close game, leading the charge against the opposing team.

"Don't you get so nervous?" she asked Helen, sitting down again at last as the crowd began to disperse. "I didn't realize how anxious I was until after it was all over. In fact, I'm still shaking."

"I've watched a fair few games now," the older woman smiled, her blue eyes warm as she squeezed Hannah's arm in sympathy. "But I'll admit, it still makes me hold my breath, watching Drew go in boots and all like that. He only has one speed, flat to the boards. I'm always worried he'll be hurt. Must be a mum thing. I don't tell him, but I care more that he's safe than whether they win. It's the last thing he thinks about, I know."

"You're right," Hannah agreed. "It seems like the adrenaline takes over, and he'll do anything. I don't think he even notices all the bruises and scrapes until the next day." She stopped, embarrassed. Helen didn't seem fazed by the thought of Hannah seeing Drew's various bruises and scrapes, just smiled at her again.

"We can go onto the field," Helen offered, once Drew had made his winning captain's speech. "Watch them get the trophy from down there."

"Oh, no," Hannah faltered. "You go ahead."

"Are you sure?" Helen asked, eyebrows lifted. "I'm sure he'd like you to be there too."

"No," Hannah insisted. "You've come all this way to see him win. Go have your family celebration."

"Where's Hannah?" Drew looked around after kissing his mother and shaking hands with his father following the awarding of the trophy. "She came to the game, didn't she?"

"She did," Helen assured him. "Not sure how much she enjoyed it. She was pretty nervous for you. She wouldn't come down with us, though. She thought we'd want some family time."

Drew exhaled. "I'm glad you could make it, anyway. Got to go back to the sheds now. Are you still staying on till Monday?"

"We'll be here. If you have a few minutes before you fly home tomorrow, ring us and we'll have a coffee."

"Thanks, Mum." Drew gave her a quick hug and trotted off to the locker room.

"Why didn't you come down after the game?" he asked Hannah brusquely, reaching her by phone an hour later.

"I thought you'd want some time with your family," she answered, surprised. "You all didn't need me in the middle of it."

"I wanted to see you. I was glad to have my mum and dad there. But I wanted to see you too. Wanted to share it with you. I'll be with the boys tonight, till late. But I'll come by and take you to breakfast."

"Aren't you going to eat with the team?" she asked, surprised.

"You're pushing me," he warned her. "I'll be there to collect you at nine."

♡

"I was thinking of bringing Hannah down for a visit next weekend," Drew told his parents later the next morning. "I'd like to show her the place, have her get to know you better, before everything gets mad with the Cup. Will that work for you?"

"That would be lovely," Helen agreed immediately. "Please do bring her, Drew. We can have a barbecue," she began to plan.

Drew held up his hand. "Mum. No rellies. No neighbors," he insisted.

"But darling, everyone will want to see you," his mother protested. "Auntie Mary will be so hurt if she isn't invited."

"The two of you will be more than enough for Hannah to be going on with," Drew told her. "I don't want to scare her off." He looked to his father for support.

"Sounds like Drew knows what he wants," Sam put in. "We'll have a family dinner," he promised his son. "We'll keep it quiet."

♡

Hannah had her own doubts when Drew proposed the trip the next day. "Don't they want their own time with you, though? To have you to themselves for a weekend?"

He laughed. "If I know Mum, we'd have had a house full if I were going down there by myself. She likes a do. Not likely to be hanging over me, weeping happy tears."

"They're not going to have a party while I'm there, are they?" she asked in alarm. "I'm not going to have to meet everybody?"

"No worries," he reassured her. "Saw that one coming and headed it off. It'll just be us."

"I'm not so good at family things," she said slowly. "I hope they like me."

"What do you mean?" He pulled her down to sit beside him. "I've seen you with your family, remember. Seems to me you know all about family."

"But when I'm with...with other people's families," she explained haltingly, "I never feel normal. I'm like a...a visitor, you know? People with parents, I mean," she said, her eyes falling. "So I'm worried that they'll be able to tell."

"What?" he asked gently, one arm going around her. "That you have lizard skin? What are they going to find out about you?"

♡

When they were actually sitting at the table over a late Saturday lunch with his parents the next weekend, though, Drew began to get a glimmer of what she had feared.

"So, Hannah," Helen asked, passing her the platter of lamb chops. "Where do your own parents live? They must be missing you, so far away."

"They've both passed away, I'm afraid, years ago. But I have a younger brother and sister," she added quickly. "They both live in the San Francisco Bay area, in California. We grew up in a more rural area, though. More like this. Not quite as beautiful, though."

"Were you raised by grandparents, then?" Helen asked, eyebrows lifting.

"No. My mother didn't die until my brother was eighteen. We pretty much stayed together, though, even after that."

"That must have been hard to manage," Helen commented.

"No, it worked out well. I went to school—to University," Hannah corrected herself, "near San Francisco, and they ended up joining me there. My brother and I went to the same University, to Berkeley. I was working there by that time, and we were able to share an apartment his first couple of years. My sister lived with us for a while as well. She wasn't in school, but she was working. We saved money that way, too. We were lucky to be able to help each other."

Drew looked at her in surprise. He hadn't realized that. But of course Hannah wouldn't have left Matt by himself, not at eighteen, or Kristen, either. He knew already that she had gone home every summer while she had been at University, working and helping out. It made sense that after her mother had died, she would have pulled her little family together, made sure she was watching over them.

"What did they think about your coming to En Zed, your brother and sister?" Helen asked. "It must have been hard to leave them alone, after all that."

Hannah looked at Drew, eyes stricken. He reached for her hand, held it reassuringly. "Mum, you're undoing all my good work here. You don't know what a job I had to convince her it was all right to leave them for a bit. They're twenty-three and twenty-five now. Matt thinks he's won the Lotto, doesn't he. A sister in En Zed and the chance of free footy tickets."

"My brother's a dedicated traveler," Hannah explained, grateful for Drew's interjection. "With a newfound passion for rugby, I'm afraid. And he's not allowed to ask you for anything," she scowled at Drew. "I told you that, remember? You haven't promised him tickets for next season, have you?"

He held up his hands, laughing. "I may have done," he confessed. "You can take it up with me later. Anyway," Drew turned back to his mother. "That's Matt sorted. And the way Hannah talks to Kristen on the phone, she may as well have never left. They're both coming down for Christmas, actually, so Hannah will have her family around her then. The way it should be," he said with a meaningful look Hannah chose to ignore.

"Sounds like you did well," Drew's quieter father put in. "Can't have been easy for you. Drew tells me you have an interesting job here now," he said, turning the conversation.

Hannah gladly entered into a discussion of her work, grateful for his tact. "The best part is the wardrobe," she confessed. "The products really are wonderful. I'm wearing them now. And so is Drew," she smiled.

"That's right," he agreed proudly. "Merino tee, eh, Dad."

"I'm glad to see that kind of success story coming out of New Zealand," Sam said. "We don't have a wide variety of exports, but one thing we do have is sheep. I've read about 2nd Hemisphere. Good on them for making a go of it."

"Dad's a vet," Drew told Hannah. "So you could say he knows sheep. Large animal as well as pets. Country vets have to do it all."

"Just like James Herriot," Hannah observed with delight.

"Not as good a writer. Or as rich," Sam pointed out. "But the life's not so different, for all that."

After lunch, Hannah stood to help clear the table, but Helen shooed her away when she would have helped with the dishes. "Sam's my washing-up partner. Always has been. You two go on. Take Hannah for a walk, Drew. Show her about. It's not raining, for once."

Drew laughed and obeyed. "You can see my mum has her opinions," he told Hannah once they were walking on a path by the stream that ran beside the road into town. "My dad's quieter, but when he does talk, you listen."

"I noticed that," she said. "They're both wonderful. Thank you for rescuing me, though. I was so worried that they would think I was a terrible person, leaving my brother and sister like that." She shook her head, still upset by the conversation.

"Hannah." He turned her to face him. "You didn't abandon them. You recognized that they have their own lives now, that's all, and that you could try something new yourself."

"Your dad reminds me a bit of mine," she ventured as they began to walk again. "He was quiet, too. My mom was lively. Beautiful, like Kristen. A little unstable, maybe. Wrapped up in Dad. But he was different. He always called me his pal," she said after a minute. "He'd say, 'My pal and I are going to do some fishing today.' Or, 'Come help me fix the sink drain, pal.'" She swallowed. "Maybe that seems strange. But his son was little, still. And my dad and I...we were close, always. Right up until he died."

"You always say, 'when he died,' when you talk about him. Was it sudden, then? He wasn't sick?" Drew probed cautiously.

"No," she answered soberly. "He died in a car accident. Well, no. It wasn't exactly that. It was a hit-and-run. He liked to bicycle home from work for lunch. He was a teacher at the high school. We always wondered if it was a student. Somebody young, who just ran away, especially when he saw who he'd hit. But we never found out. He was just...gone."

"How did you hear about it?"

"The police came. To school. They went and told my mom first, of course. It was bad, though. They asked her who else should they tell. Who else could help. She told them to come to school and get me. She didn't have a lot of close friends. Just some people at the bank where she worked part-time."

He frowned. "So they came and got you to help your mother?"

"Not exactly. First we had to get my brother and sister. They were little," she reminded him. "Seven and nine. The police were so nice, though. They took me to the elementary school. Waited with me while I told them. Took us all home, to my mom."

"You told your brother and sister that your father was dead," he said slowly. "How can that be? Wasn't there someone else?"

"If there was, they didn't show up. That's not fair, though," she amended. "The neighbors were kind. They brought food, as soon as they heard. Women are amazing. They didn't just bring cakes, things like that. They brought casseroles. Dishes already wrapped up, ready to be frozen, with cooking instructions. Some of them kept on bringing them, too. That was a lifesaver during those first few weeks. I could pull something out of the freezer every night. My teachers were helpful too. Some of them were wonderful, in fact. They'd take me aside. Talk to me. And after a while," she said bracingly, "it got better. My mom got better. And I started to know what to do. How to help. Things settled down."

Drew was overwhelmed. He'd known it had been bad, but he hadn't imagined it could have been like this. "Don't they have social services, then, in the States?" he asked slowly. "Someone to help people in your situation?"

"What do you mean? There's foster care. But we had a mother. And we weren't neglected. I don't mean it to sound like that. We ate, and we went to school. We had enough money to live on. It might not have been that much fun, but we still had a family. And it got better," she insisted again. "Especially once I got older. By the time I was sixteen, I had a job, and a plan. Everything was better once I had a plan. I knew what I was doing, then. I just kept following the plan. Until you came along," she said, smiling and trying to lighten the mood. "You pretty much wrecked my plan. And could we please talk about something else now? This is too sad, and I don't want to be sad. Tell me what I'm looking at. Tell me about growing up here, with your parents, and your brother. Did you always live in that house?"

He wished she would let him comfort her, but he was glad she had shared so much. He would back off now, he decided. Let her change the subject.

"Yeh. My parents moved in soon after they were married, when my dad qualified as a vet and came to the practice here. They never left. They like being a bit out of town, a bit of quiet. That's how I come by it, I suppose."

"You know," she said, "every young football player in the NFL talks about buying his mother a house with his earnings. I'm guessing it wouldn't be too easy for you to offer something like that to your dad, though."

He laughed. "Like to see his face if I did. Suggesting that he couldn't support his family. He'd have something to say about that. My parents are like me, though. A good holiday for them is a trip to the Coromandel, some fishing. I've shouted them some trips overseas when I've been playing somewhere like Ireland or France. They'll let me send them the tickets, maybe a hotel room. Have to tread lightly, though, with my dad. Still my dad, isn't he."

She nodded. "I can see that. So when did you start playing rugby?"

"When didn't I play rugby? Started when I was just a wee fella, kicking the ball, throwing it with my dad, like every other Kiwi boy. Started playing in a league when I was six or so. Right here in the Domain." He pointed to the large grassy park they were passing, which indeed was outfitted with several sets of rugby crossbars.

"That must have been touch rugby, then. They don't have little boys tackling, do they?"

"Touch rugby's mostly just for fun. What you play at the beach, or during the offseason. And girls play touch rugby."

"Didn't you get injured?" she asked, shocked.

"Knocked about a bit, that's all," he said dismissively. "I loved it. We all did. Well, maybe I loved it more than most. By the time I was a teenager, it was my focus. I did all the usual things too. Had friends, fished, went to school. But I knew I wanted to play. So I stayed fit. Worked on my skills. Got picked up by a club when I was nineteen, and been playing profession-ally ever since."

"What will you do after you finish playing, do you think?" she asked. "I'm not saying that's soon," she hurried on. "But I'm sure you've thought about it."

"No worries. I've thought about it, yeh. Your body gets bashed up all these years, can't help but have an effect. Reckon I'll coach, in the end. Do a bit of that already, as captain. It seems like a logical extension."

"Will you go somewhere else to do that? I've noticed how many of the overseas players and coaches are from New Zealand."

"No," he said positively. "I've been asked. I could make twice as much money even now, playing in England or France. Not interested. Even in going to Aussie. Good thing. Be a traitor then, wouldn't I. But, nah, I'm doing all right. And I wouldn't be happy living somewhere else. I've seen the world. Nice to visit, when you live someplace this small. But I'm a Kiwi. Reckon I'm lucky, spending my life in paradise. There's a reason we call it Godzone, eh."

"I don't blame you," she agreed. "This is the most beauti-ful place I've ever been. And it seems...cohesive, I guess is the word. Everyone here seems so proud of being from New Zealand. Which makes me wonder why people do leave."

"Wages aren't as good here," he explained. "It can be hard to raise a family. You can earn more in Aussie or the UK, doing most things. Including playing football. And some people miss the opportunities you get with a bigger country, the variety. Miss the culture, want to be someplace where they can go to the opera. Not too much for that myself. I'm a pretty simple bloke. I just want to get into the bush, go fishing, camping. Auckland's too big for me. Too busy. I'm always glad to get away from it, first chance I get."

"I'm beginning to understand why you don't have much in the way of opera or art," she said. "I'm guessing that if you ask the average New Zealand man, would you like to go to the ballet tonight? Or to a rugby game?, it's not going to be much of a contest."

He laughed. "You're right about that. Know which one I'd choose. It's all about sport here, and being outdoors. Fishing, hunting, camping, being on the water. That's the Maori influence on us, partly. Only Maori call themselves Tangata Whenua—people of the land. But there's a bit of that in all of us. The land, and family. That's what matters to New Zealanders."

They were in sight of the house again, and Hannah hesitated, then stopped.

"Drew," she said. "Could you please not share what I told you, earlier, with your parents? I suspect they're curious about me. I don't want them to think badly of me, that I didn't have a normal family, and there's something wrong with me. Even if there is," she finished a bit forlornly, "don't talk to them about it, OK?"

Drew pulled her close, wrapped his arms around her, tucked her head under his chin, and stood holding her for a minute.

"There's nothing wrong with you," he said at last. "You've done an awesome job. You're an amazing woman. But I won't share anything you don't want me to. Even though my parents would think nothing but well of you, if they knew what I do."

She stood in his embrace, feeling the vibration of his voice as it rumbled in his chest, and something in her unwound just a bit.

"OK," she said shakily. "Thanks. I'm ready to go back inside now."

chapter twenty-seven

♡

She wouldn't have been reassured to know that Drew's parents had indeed been discussing her.

"Did you know that Drew convinced Hannah to move here?" Helen asked, handing Sam a plate to dry.

"Nah." He took the plate, wiped it with a tea towel. "Doesn't confide much, does he."

"He's quite protective of her, isn't he?" she frowned.

He chuckled. "That's a good thing, sweetheart. There'd be something wrong with him if he didn't try to protect her. Even from you."

"Me? I'm not scary," she protested.

Sam smiled. "I'm not so sure. Don't know how comfortable she was."

"I just wish we knew her a little better. That we knew her family. That she had a family," Helen went on slowly.

"If I'm guessing right, we may meet her family soon enough," he said. "Her brother and sister are coming for Christmas, eh. We'll be lucky if Drew brings them all here, Christmas Day. We may want to make a point of inviting them."

"You think they're that involved, then?"

"We'll have to watch and see what happens, won't we?"

♡

"Do you really have to go back today, Hannah?" Helen objected as they sat over lunch the next day. "Couldn't you wait until tomorrow and go back with Drew? You're more than welcome, you know."

"I have a meeting tomorrow morning," Hannah explained. "And I'm sure you want some time alone with your son. I've really appreciated having the chance to visit. It's been a treat to meet you, and see where Drew grew up. Get the full tour," she smiled.

"That didn't take long," Drew pointed out. "All of a few minutes. But I could drive you up early tomorrow, take you straight in to work."

Hannah shook her head. "You don't have that much time to relax. This way you can stay as long as you like. I'm sure you have people you'd like to visit. Besides, I've been wanting to take the train. It'll be fun, and it'll put me down at Britomart this evening, right next to the bus stop."

"No," Drew said firmly. "Take a taxi home. It'll be dark by then. Hannah," he continued, exasperated, as she prepared to argue. "If you don't promise to take a taxi, I'll leave now and take you back myself."

"All right." She threw up her hands. "I promise. Man, you're bossy. Has he always been this way?" she asked Helen.

His mother laughed. "That's Drew. Doesn't talk much, but he's used to being in charge. You'd have to be a saint. Or stubborn yourself."

"No worries, Mum," Drew said wryly. "Hannah doesn't give in too easily. I've lost more battles than I've won. You'll notice she's still leaving today."

"Women have a way of doing that," Sam agreed. "You think you've won, and then you turn around and find you're doing what they want, aren't you."

His wife just laughed. "We've been married thirty-two years," she explained to Hannah. "He thinks he can get away with that."

"That's wonderful," Hannah answered. "You're very fortunate. And now," she said, getting to her feet, "I really do need to get ready to leave, or I'll miss my train."

♡

"You can just drop me at the station," she suggested as Drew drove her the short distance to the center of town. "I have my ticket already, so I'm all set."

"Why would I do that?" he objected. "Why wouldn't I take you for a coffee while you wait for your train, see you onto it?"

"Because I saw the sign at the entrance to town," she pointed out. "The one that says 'Welcome to Te Kuiti—Birthplace of Drew Callahan.' Not to mention the giant Number 6 jersey that, you will notice, is right...over...there," she motioned, "hanging up next to the railway station, where we happen to be going. Why not say goodbye to me here, go back to your parents' house and enjoy yourself, instead of getting involved in all that?"

"This is my life," he said. "This is my home. People here have given me a fair bit of support over the years. You're an All Black 24/7. And part of the responsibility that comes with that is to this town. If that means signing a few autographs, having my photo snapped with a few kids, it's a small price to pay."

"I'm not so sure," she said slowly as he pulled her suitcase from the boot. "I think it would be a fairly high price, having to watch everything you do, having everyone watch you, for so long. It's a lot of scrutiny."

"Good job I'm not too exciting, then," he said cheerfully. "Not that hard for me to stay out of the news. Only thing I do is kiss a blonde now and then."

♡

Pulling back into the driveway again after seeing Hannah off, Drew found his father heading towards him.

"Going out to replace that shed door," Sam told him. "Come give me a hand, why don't you, mate."

Drew settled in to the comfortable routine of working with his father, wrestling off the heavy door and preparing the new one to put in its place.

"Got Hannah safely off, eh," Sam observed at last. At Drew's grunt of acknowledgment, he went on, not looking up from his task. "That's a fine young woman. Don't break her heart."

"More likely to break mine, isn't she," Drew returned glumly.

Sam looked up, eyes sharp under the strong brows.

"Not sure I can do it," Drew admitted. "Get her to trust me. She's been alone so long. Having to shift for herself. To take care of her brother and sister, too. Seems like she just can't believe I'm willing to get stuck in. I don't know how to convince her."

He stopped, shaking his head. "She's always like that, like what you saw," he said slowly, struggling to express himself. "Kind. Giving. Loving even, you could say. Never seen her rude or angry. Never seen her pack a sad. Wish I had, really. Every time she gets close, she just…closes up. Back to being cheerful again. And getting her to take anything from me—even a lift to the station—that's a struggle. Every time."

"And you want to give her more," Sam offered slowly.

"I think I want to marry her, Dad. But I don't know if she'll have me. Scares me rigid," Drew confessed.

"Seems to me you haven't done too badly, so far," his father said. "Got her over here, you said. That must have taken some doing."

Drew smiled reluctantly. "It did. Didn't think it would work. I had a job just getting her to stay with me after we met, come to that," he remembered. "Seems like she's ready to give up before she even tries. She's so sure it won't work."

"Good thing you've got enough determination for two, then. Never known you to pike out yet, have I. And it seems to me she trusts you more than you think," Sam said. "Came to meet us, eh. That took some courage. And yesterday. Did you know that, about her family?"

"Nah," Drew admitted. "She said more yesterday—to me, too—than I've heard before. I think it was being with the two of you. She misses her dad something chronic, I know that."

"Then she knows how to love someone. How to trust them," his father pointed out. "She's just scared to try again, I reckon. Anyway, you're a good judge. If you're sure she's right for you, that's enough for me."

"Cheers for that, Dad," Drew said gruffly. "I'm sure."

♡

They finished the job without talking more, before Drew changed and set off on a long trail run into the hills around town.

"He left in a hurry," Helen commented as Sam washed up from the dirty job. "Everything all right?"

"Yeh," Sam answered. "Got a lot on his mind just now, though."

"Problems with Hannah?" Helen wondered. "They're serious, then?"

"When was the last time he brought a woman here to meet us? He's serious. Reckon we'll find out if she is, soon enough."

"She's a lovely girl," Helen said slowly. "Doesn't she care for him, then? That wasn't my impression."

"Skittish, I'm gathering. Like a good dog that's been mistreated," Sam mused. "Have to go slowly with a dog like that. They can be the best in the end, though, if you're patient."

Helen laughed. "Sam Callahan. Better not let Drew hear you compare her to a dog. I'd hate to see him hurt, though," she went on after a minute. "I hope it works out."

"My money's on Drew," Sam said. "When's the last time that boy set his mind to something and didn't achieve it? He's relentless, when he has a goal. I've never seen anybody to equal him that way."

"The Steadfast Tin Soldier, I used to call him, remember?" Helen asked. "After the story."

Sam smiled. "He's in the same boat as the rest of us now, isn't he. All that money, all those women he never told you about. Now he's just like every other poor bloke. Trying to find a way to convince some unfortunate girl against her better judgment that he's the man for her."

chapter twenty-eight

♡

At work again on a rainy Monday, Hannah was pleased to get a call from Reka.

"I've missed you," the other woman told her. "Haven't seen you for a month, I was realizing. I'm not allowed to fly. Too soon before the baby. I need some company, though. Would you and Drew like to come for dinner next Saturday? I thought we could have a quiet one, just the four of us. Last chance before the boys head to Aussie for the World Cup next week."

"I'd love it," Hannah said. "Let me check with Drew, and I'll get back to you."

She was touched to be greeted as an old friend by Ariana and Jamie when she and Drew hustled in out of the rain the following Saturday.

"I'm in my nightie, see?" Ariana told her proudly. "Mummy said if I was ready for bed when you came, I could ask for a story. We don't get to stay up with you," she added with disappointment. "We had fish fingers and chips for tea, though."

Jamie nodded enthusiastically. "With tomato sauce," he announced. "I like to dip them."

"Choice as, eh," Drew agreed solemnly.

"Do we have time?" Hannah looked at Reka.

"Of course, if you don't mind," Reka apologized. "She thinks you've come over just to visit her, I'm afraid. You shouldn't have given her those fairy wings for her birthday. She's even more certain you're a fairy yourself, now."

Hannah laughed. "I don't mind. All right, miss, let's go," she ordered the little girl.

"Me too," Jamie called out.

"Reckon she'll be reading the train book, too," Hemi grinned. "Come have a beer, mate. This could take a while."

Hannah felt the familiar constriction at her heart as she settled into the big armchair with Ariana and Jamie. The warmth of their little bodies pressed against her own brought back vivid memories of her own brother and sister. Of lying together on Matt's narrow bed, reading *The Hobbit* aloud to them when they had been scared and sad, in the weeks after their father's death.

She had loved them. But she had resented them at times, too. She thought of her irritation when she would be trying to study, and Kristen would come in, snuggling too close, wanting to talk, invading her space and her life with her demands. When she hadn't been able to take a summer job as a babysitter at fourteen, because Matt was still only nine and she needed to be at home with them.

These children, raised in the warm, stable family Hemi and Reka had created, wouldn't grow up wondering if they were acceptable, not sure they were lovable, she thought with a pang, even as she read the poems from *Complete Book of the Flower Fairies* to an enraptured Ariana and stoical Jamie. When Jamie climbed into her lap to have his train book read, she pulled him close, kissing the top of his curly head and smelling his clean little-boy scent, and wished she had the chance to go back and start over.

When Reka came in to help put her children to bed, Hannah pulled herself together. She was dangerously close to crying, she realized, and that was ridiculous.

"We're just finished," she smiled.

"I want Miss Hannah to tuck me in," Ariana insisted.

"Don't let her keep you," Reka warned.

"Don't worry, I know how to do this," Hannah assured her.

She helped Ariana get comfortable, pulled up the covers. "Sweet dreams," she smiled, leaning down to give the little girl a kiss.

"Stay with me," Ariana pleaded. "I'm not sleepy. I think I need another story."

"Hmmm. How about if you just rest your eyes for a while. I'll turn out the light and it'll be like the forest, when the fairies curl up under the flowers and go sleep."

"Leave the door open, please," Ariana begged. "I don't like it too dark."

"She didn't keep you chatting, then," Reka said with a smile when Hannah joined her in the hallway, carefully leaving Ariana's door open a crack.

"No," Hannah agreed. "I'm up on those delaying tactics."

♡

"How much longer till your due date?" she asked, once they were all settled at the dinner table and tucking into Reka's usual substantial fare.

"Four weeks," Reka sighed. "They say third babies are more likely to come early, though. Two weeks would be fine with me."

"Just glad the World Cup's being held in Aussie, not farther away this time," Hemi said. "At least I can be here a day or two every week."

"You have to stay over there the whole time, then, otherwise?" Hannah asked. "You said something like that, I remember," she said to Drew. "The training must be pretty intense."

"It's a major, the World Cup. Only happens once every four years. It'll be hard yakka. Two practices a day. The pool games are one thing," Drew explained. "But once you're into the knockout rounds, you have to keep improving, three games in a row, if you want to win. Everyone has to be fit, mentally and physically. Takes a fair bit of training and focus."

"Not to mention keeping the boys in the hotel, making sure none of them is slipping out, getting on the sauce," Hemi put in. "The joys of being the skipper, eh. It's a lot of pressure on the young boys. And the media's always watching as well."

"You have so much support from the public, though," Hannah said. "I've never experienced anything like it. All the flags on houses and cars. And it hasn't even started yet. It isn't just men, either. I've been surprised. I went to the doctor last week, and the staff at the clinic had decorated the front desk with black and white balloons and an All Blacks flag. Even the kindergarten up the road has a huge banner out front made by all the kids. Have you seen that, Drew? 'Go the Mighty All Blacks.' By four-year-olds. I'd think that would mean they'd be forgiving, if something did go wrong."

Drew and Hemi looked at each other and laughed ruefully. "Watch a lot of sport, do you?" Hemi asked with a grin. "As long as it's all ka pai, eh. As long as we're winning, and nothing's gone wrong. But as soon as there's an injury that knocks out a key player, or as soon as one of the boys does go on the piss, or, God forbid, we lose a pool match—which has never happened yet, by the way— you'll see the panic start. That's the coaches' job—and Drew's. Keep things on an even keel, keep the boys focused on getting themselves right for Saturday. Keep them from looking past the next game."

"Not just mine, mate," Drew objected. "There's a good bunch of leaders on this team."

"Reckon you're the one they're scared of disappointing," Hemi said.

"All that support," Reka explained to Hannah. "It's lovely. But it's also that much more pressure. When you're an All Black, you're carrying the whole country on your shoulders. And they can't play for you, can they."

"Do they really care that much?" Hannah wondered. "The whole country?"

Reka smiled. "Wait and see."

When Reka got up to clear the table at the end of the meal, Hemi forestalled her. "You're tired. Go sit down for a bit. Take Hannah with you, keep you company. Drew and I can wash up. Can't go a whole night without talking about footy anyway. Give us a chance to do it without boring you."

Drew rose to help, and Reka laughed. "Get a photo of that, Hannah. You can sell it to the papers. Thanks, though," she told her husband gratefully. "I wouldn't mind a bit of a rest."

"So," Hemi grinned as he joined his wife on the couch again some time later, pulling her up against him. "Have you got Hannah's life sorted yet?"

"I keep trying," Reka admitted. "But she's too cagey for me. Keeps asking about my kids instead. It's not fair. Bound to distract me, isn't she."

"She's good at that," Drew agreed, sitting with Hannah. "Likes to keep the conversation off herself."

"Never mind," Hemi consoled his wife. "You can still push the kids and me about. That'll have to do you. It'll be good to have another name on my wristband, these next weeks," he told Drew, resting his hand briefly on his wife's swollen belly. "Sweet as, eh."

"Do you mean where you wrap your wrists?" Hannah wondered. "Do you write things on there, then?"

"Most of the boys do. Especially the ones with families," Hemi explained. "Got the names of their partners, their kids on there. Reminds them who they're playing for."

"You play for your kids and your wife?" Hannah asked. "What does that mean, exactly?"

"Hannah's dad died when she was young," Drew told Hemi. "These sorts of things are a bit of a mystery to her."

"My wife and my kids give me the incentive to go out and play well. They're my inspiration," Hemi said, taking Reka's hand. "Not sure it works that way with women."

"I've been working for a long time," Hannah mused. "But even though I had some responsibility for my brother and sister," she said, ignoring Drew's snort at her description, "I never thought of myself as working for them. It was separate. If anything, I have to admit, it felt more like a conflict. Almost a burden, trying to think about them and also about everything else I had to do. Trying to juggle everything. It doesn't feel that way for you? Like a…an extra weight? The responsibility?"

Hemi shook his head firmly. "Maybe men need something beyond themselves to remind us that it's not all about us. Reckon we're more selfish. We need somebody to work for. In my case, somebody to play for. When we're busting a gut, trying to grind out a win, and I'm feeling ready to chuck it in, I look down at my kids' names, at Reka's name. And it reminds me, this is why I'm doing this. Gives me strength."

"Wow," Hannah said quietly. "I never knew that."

"I knew it," Reka put in. "But I love to hear it." She smiled mistily at her husband.

"On that note," Drew said, pulling Hannah to her feet, "we'll leave the two of you to get some rest, and I'll take Hannah home. Monday'll be here soon enough."

♡

"I hope it's all right, my taking these days off," Hannah told Kathryn the next week at work. "I know it's a lot, almost every Monday for the next couple of months. Please let me know if any of these days won't work out."

"No worries," Kathryn assured her with a smile. "The World Cup only comes along every four years. We understand you want to be there. I was wondering, though," she added in a casual tone that immediately put Hannah on guard. "Would you be willing to go over to Sydney a few days before the final, and put in a few hours in the VIP area of the Fanzone each day? Of course, that's assuming the All Blacks make it to the end."

As Hannah mentally winced at the thought of the heavy expectations on the team, Kathryn continued. "We want to give away some products, raise the company's profile with the international VIPs. I'll be there myself, and I thought you might be able to lend a hand as well. You can schedule the time when it's most convenient for you, of course."

Hannah agreed. What else could she do, after all, when Kathryn had been so accommodating of her request for time off so that she could be with Drew after most of the games?

When Susannah called her for their weekly chat that evening, though, she couldn't help complaining to her friend.

"I know the only reason she wants me there is so she can 'mention' to people that I'm Drew's girlfriend. It's so uncomfortable. Like I'm some kind of a secondhand celebrity. When really, so what? What do I have to do with anything? I'm certainly not going to introduce anyone to him," she shuddered.

"How's that been going, at work?" Susannah asked her curiously. "You haven't said anything for a long time."

"It's not that much of an issue at this point," Hannah admitted. "After the gala, when that big picture showed up in the paper, I couldn't very well keep saying there was nothing in it. I suppose people here have got used to it, though. I don't share any details, just focus on work. And there's plenty of that to do. It's so busy. Really exciting too, getting ready for the expansion to the U.S. market."

"So taking the job was the right choice," Susannah prompted.

"It was. I work just as hard while I'm there, but I've been able to have a life outside the office, too. I didn't realize how much I was missing out on. Now I actually go out for lunch and coffee with people sometimes. To discuss work, of course. But I also don't have to choose between eating my lunch and working out. I'm not trying to cram everything, including dinner, into a couple of hours each evening. I even have a social life. I think the company Christmas party might be a bit more fun than the TriStyle one, too."

"I'm guessing you get fewer guys hitting on you at work," Susannah suggested. "That there won't be anyone at the party listing their dimensions."

"You're right about that. It's a bit odd, actually. It's like I have some kind of 'taken' sign on me now. Very different from the way it was when I first got here. They must have had some interesting ideas about American women. Now, the guys are so respectful, it's as if I've aged twenty years."

"I haven't had the chance to meet Drew yet," Susannah pointed out. "But from what I've seen online, I can see why. He looks like he could take somebody's head off. And eat it."

"He's not like that, though," Hannah protested. "He's actually pretty quiet off the field. He doesn't throw his weight around at all."

"Does he have to?" Susannah countered. "And I'll bet he'd be in someone's face pretty quickly if he thought he needed to be, from what you've said."

"Probably true," Hannah admitted. "It's a bit like a dog pack, isn't it? And no question," she sighed, "he's an alpha dog."

♡

"I just called to check on you," Hannah told Reka two weeks later. "Hemi said the baby was still hanging in there, when I saw him in Melbourne the other day. Not much further to go, anyway."

"I hope you're right," Reka sighed. "Wish I could've been there, the past couple weeks. You went to both games, didn't you?"

"Yes, and they were so exciting," Hannah said. "Of course, it helped that they won both of them. But I can see how the World Cup is different. The intensity level of the games, right from the beginning, from the haka—I wasn't expecting that. I'd seen them doing it before, during the Championship. But wow, are they intense now. The way Hemi prowls around when he's leading it, it's like he really *is* sending them into war."

"Your boy's dead fierce too," Reka laughed.

"I know. It gave me a chill, the first time I saw it. I'd seen his Laser Eyes before, the way he stares somebody down, but in the haka, it's pretty scary."

"That's how they get themselves right for the game," Reka explained. "And if it intimidates the other team, all the better. Wish I could've been there with you," she said again. "Hemi said you weren't going to be there this week, eh."

"I can't make it. I have a meeting in Wellington on Monday morning."

"How about coming over, then, watching with me?" Reka asked. "Assuming the baby doesn't come before then. I could use the company. Getting to that uncomfortable point now."

"Of course I will," Hannah said immediately. "It would be so much better for me too."

♡

"I have a hard time watching alone," she admitted to Reka that Sunday night during the halftime break. "I get so anxious. I know everyone assumes they'll win these pool games, and they're favored tonight again, though Samoa is playing well, aren't they?"

"They are," Reka agreed. "They're a good side. A lot of these boys play during the regular season for overseas teams. They'll put up a good fight."

"Really, though, the thought of their losing isn't even what scares me so much," Hannah mused. "It's more that somebody will get hurt."

"Somebody?" Reka smiled at her. "Or somebody special?"

Hannah flushed. "All right, I worry more about Drew, I'll admit it. I know he's tough, but I still hate to see him throw himself in there the way he does. He's always at the bottom of the pile. And I can tell it's rough in there. He takes such a beating."

Reka laughed. "Yeh, he's likely to be at the bottom of the ruck. That's because he gets there first. That's his position, to do that. And he has to charge in there. Has to lead from the front."

"I wanted to ask you about that, that leadership thing," Hannah ventured. "I know we were talking about this when Drew and I were here for dinner. But it's become even crazier since then, the way the whole country's focused on the All Blacks and the World Cup. I had no idea it would be like this. I counted fourteen pictures of Drew in the paper one day. And of course, a lot of the other players too," she added quickly, hoping Reka wouldn't think she was boasting on Drew's behalf. "But it's like he isn't even a person. Maybe even more so than the others. Like he's some kind of symbol. Or public property. It makes me feel really strange."

"He's been out in front of the ABs for a fair few years now," Reka explained. "And it's his mana."

"His what?"

"You haven't heard that? The power of his spirit. Mana's a sort of natural authority. Prestige, I suppose you'd call it. Hard to describe mana, but it's important to us. To Maori, but to the rest of New Zealand as well. And Drew has huge mana. What it means in his case is that the boys want to walk out there behind him. Want to do their best, live up to his example. It's his team, isn't it. Not so much because of what he says. It's more about what he does. He'll be the first one with his boots on, warming up. Trains the hardest too. That's why he's so...so beloved. And the fact that he says so little about himself, that he's a humble bloke, that just adds to his mana. It's not something you can claim. It's obvious to everyone, or you don't have it."

269

The game started again, but Hannah watched the second half without much concentration. She said her goodbyes as soon as the final whistle sounded on another All Blacks victory, and made her thoughtful way home. She moved into her bedroom, pulling off her shirt mechanically, then sank half-dressed onto the bed, her hands tucked under her thighs, staring at the rug.

She was in love with Drew. She wasn't just having a good time, enjoying his company. She'd been in love with him, she told herself honestly, since before she had left home. That was why she had moved. Sure, she had told herself she was moving for the job, and seeing how their relationship developed. But who was she kidding? This was the reason for her reluctance to take anything from him. She had tried to protect herself from being hurt, because deep down inside, she had known she *would* be hurt. Because what she had responded to in him, right from the start, had been his strength, that quality that Reka had described in him. She wanted to lean on him, to use him to prop her up when she wasn't feeling strong herself.

What would happen to her when he moved on? She needed to stop herself from taking his caring attention for granted. Needed to guard her heart. That treacherous heart that gave a lurch at the thought of pulling back, of not seeing him anymore.

She couldn't do anything about it anyway, not during the World Cup, she thought desperately. She couldn't distract him, not at this critical stage in the campaign. And, she confessed to herself, she wanted more time with him. If this were going to end, she wanted this time to remember.

She'd make the most of the time they had now, as much as she had of it, she decided. Would watch him play with her heart in her throat. Would spend a quiet day with him afterwards, help him recover and wind down after each brutal contest. Would be there for him now, when he needed her. And worry about the rest later.

chapter twenty-nine

"Did you hear, Reka had the baby?" Drew asked on Wednesday, calling from the team hotel. "Had him Monday night. Good timing, eh. Hemi was with her by then. He'll be back here tomorrow. Got a couple days there, anyway."

"That's wonderful. How's she doing? And the baby?" Hannah asked eagerly. "It was a boy? I'm surprised they didn't know the sex beforehand. I wondered about that."

"Everyone's fine," he assured her. "And that was Reka. She said she had one of each, so she wanted to be surprised this time. Wouldn't let Hemi look either, on the scan."

"She gets what she wants, that's for sure," Hannah laughed. "But I'm so pleased for them. I'll give her a call tomorrow, see if she'd like some company once Hemi goes back."

"Yeh, you should ring her. Her mum's there, helping with the kids. But I'm sure she'd like to see you. Hemi's not happy about leaving her, I know. He'd be glad to hear you popped by."

♡

"I'm not going to stay long and tire you out," Hannah assured a happy Reka early the next evening. "I just couldn't resist getting a look at him."

"Hold him, if you like," Reka offered, as Hannah bent over the little bundle in the bassinet. "Take advantage of the quiet time, while Mum has the kids at McDonald's."

"I don't want to wake him up."

"He's just had a feed," Reka assured her. "He's good for a bit now. And they're easiest like that, when they're asleep."

"He's so adorable," Hannah sighed, picking up the swaddled bundle with her hand supporting the tiny head. She settled herself on a chair next to the couch where Reka rested, carefully adjusting her hold so the baby was secure in her arms.

"They have to be like that, don't they. Otherwise their mums would never go to all the trouble," Reka smiled.

Despite her words, Hannah could see Reka's flush of pride at her beautiful new son. "Hemi must be thrilled," she offered, stroking the soft cheek under the warm knit cap.

"Over the moon. Said we need a matched set now, though."

Hannah laughed. "He could at least let you recover from childbirth before he starts talking about Number Four."

"Easy for him to say," Reka agreed. "He only has to do the fun bit."

"Have you decided on the name yet?" was Hannah's next question. "I know you'd narrowed it down, but I never heard the final decision."

"Lucas. Luke for short."

"I like that. Very manly and strong."

"Well, not so manly yet. But he'll be there soon enough. You'll be wanting one of your own, one day soon," Reka said, watching Hannah's tender delight in the newborn.

"I wondered how long it would take you to get around to that." Hannah cuddled the little body closer to her. "I love kids. I guess that's no secret. But I don't know. I wasn't so good with my brother and sister, a lot of the time. You're so loving with your kids. You and Hemi both. That's the way it ought to be, I know."

"What makes you think you won't be just as loving?" Reka objected. "Seems to me you already are."

"Because I know how I was," Hannah tried to explain. "How often I was impatient. How often I resented them."

She sighed, looking down at Luke's sweet baby skin, his dark lashes lying spikily against his puffy cheeks. "I remember once," she went on slowly, "my brother lost his homework on the way to school, came back crying. I went with him to look for it, but I was so annoyed, because all I could think was how I was going to be late to school myself. I didn't comfort him or anything. What kind of parenting would that be?"

"How old were you?" Reka asked her.

"Fourteen, fifteen, in there."

"How would you know how, at that age? Who was showing you how to do it?"

Hannah stopped, stared at Reka. "I never thought of it like that," she faltered. "I've felt so guilty, always. About my sister, especially. I've wished so often that I could go back, do it differently. Do it better."

"Do your brother and sister blame you, then?"

"No. At least I don't think so. We're very close. We always have been. I'm lucky."

"They were lucky too, I reckon. Lucky that they had someone who loved them so much, who tried so hard. There's a reason girls aren't supposed to be mothers in their teens, Hannah. Because they aren't ready for it. And now you're grown, aren't you. Ready to do it right, this time. Especially if you weren't doing it alone. It helps to have a good man to be the dad, you know."

Hannah flushed. "I'm really not ready to think about that. And I need to let you get some rest now." She reluctantly surrendered little Luke to his bassinet again, watching his sweet lips purse as he settled into sleep. "But thank you, Reka. Thank you for being so kind." She leaned down, gave the other woman a hug and kiss. "You're a good friend. And you have a beautiful son. I'm so happy for you."

"Can't wait until I can say the same thing to you," Reka told her seriously. "You deserve it. I hope you realize that. But come back and visit me again soon. And give Drew my love when you see him this weekend."

♡

Hannah tried to push the thought of the future out of her head during the next few weeks. She was really too busy to think about it anyway. Working during the week, trying to focus in an atmosphere of World Cup fever that seemed to have the whole country in its spell. The excitement was contagious, the newspapers full of the team and the games, the conversation everywhere centered around the contest and the All Blacks' chances of victory.

And then, every weekend, traveling to Australia to watch Drew play. Spending time in Melbourne one week, Brisbane the next, and finally in Sydney, exploring the beautiful Australian cities as she tried not to worry about the game ahead. A quiet day with Drew afterwards as he nursed his injuries, his body more battered after each brutal contest.

The final pool game had been as anticlimactic as expected, the All Blacks notching up 68 points against a woefully out-manned Namibian team. But with the beginning of the quarter-finals, all that had changed. First had come a tough win over a strong Irish team. Then, a week later, an easier victory over a surprisingly ineffective English squad, which seemed to have chosen this moment to implode, to the New Zealand public's delighted relief. Any success against the Poms was savored, the onetime colony always thrilled to dominate their erstwhile masters. This semifinal victory was especially sweet, though, in its thoroughness and as the means of launching the All Blacks into the final.

And now, in just a few days, the matchup would arrive that everyone in New Zealand had simultaneously hoped for and dreaded throughout the two months of the tournament. The Wallabies, Australia's national team, had long been one of the All Blacks' toughest competitors. Both teams had won the World Cup twice, and were well matched in skill and tactics. Both were coached by New Zealanders and knew each others' strengths and weaknesses. It would be a true World Cup matchup, and the tension in both countries proved it.

Hannah had been surprised by the intensity of the rivalry. Like many in the outside world, she had thought of the two countries almost synonymously, if she had considered them at all. She found, though, that the transtasman contests were the hardest fought of any, in an atmosphere of almost sibling rivalry. Losing the World Cup would be hard in any case. Losing to Australia would be a crushing blow.

Now all the preliminaries were over, and the final game was upon them. Hannah had arrived in Sydney on Wednesday, well in advance of Sunday's event. After Thursday and Friday morning stints in the VIP tent, enduring speculative glances and curious questions, sparked, she knew, by Kathryn's behind-the-scenes explanations and hints, she was more than glad to leave. For once, the players had been spared an afternoon practice, given one last chance to relax before preparations for the game resumed, and she and Drew had arranged to spend a quiet Friday afternoon together.

"Will you be all right sitting outside?" she wondered, when they stopped at a harborside café for a late lunch. "It's busy here. Would you rather be inside?"

"Nah," Drew shrugged. "We may as well enjoy the sunshine." He leaned back, sighing, watching the boats on the water, and relapsed into silence.

"Hi," The moment of quiet was broken by a group of young women approaching their table. "You're Drew Callahan, aren't you?"

"I am," he answered evenly.

"That's so awesome," one of the women breathed. "Will you autograph my shoulder for me?" She turned her back, exposing her tanned, toned shoulder and back in a skinny tank top, pulling her blonde hair flirtatiously to the side with one long arm and cocking her hip.

"Sorry," he told her. "I don't autograph body parts. My girlfriend doesn't like it."

The blonde pouted in disappointment as she pivoted back, flashing a length of tanned leg and tossing her mane of streaked hair.

"Good luck on Sunday," another of the women put in. "We'll be watching you." She smiled at him, lascivious eyes and curving mouth telegraphing an unmistakable message.

To Hannah's relief, their food arrived, and Drew was able to turn away with a nod. She saw how the women's avid gazes remained on him even as they moved away, and cringed a little.

"They look at you like they want to devour you," she muttered as she picked up her fork. "They weren't even from New Zealand. Can't they find somebody from the Australian team to bother?"

He smiled. "Just a little starstruck, that's all."

He had barely started on his own sandwich when two older couples approached the table.

"Don't want to interrupt your lunch," one of the men said politely. *Then why did you,* Hannah thought. "But we want to wish you luck. We'll be backing Black on Sunday."

"Thanks for your support," Drew answered. "We'll do our best."

♡

"Maybe we should have had room service instead," he smiled ruefully after yet another interruption, this time by young boys, for whom he did sign autographs. "My disguise doesn't seem to be working. Finish your salad, and we'll head back to your hotel. I'd like to get you back there anyway," he teased, seeing that she had been upset by the interruptions.

"You're quiet today," he observed after they had reached the sanctuary of her hotel room again. "You've been that way these past weeks, now I think about it. I know it's hard, all this. Just a couple more days to go. There'll be a few more obligations after that. Then we can take a trip to the Coromandel, have a chance to relax. It's been a long season. I'm ready to have a beer without having to think about next week's game. And to spend some time with you."

Hannah smiled cautiously. "I'm not sure," she temporized. "I've taken a lot of time off to come to these games. Plus all that time when I was sick, earlier this year. I'll have to see. Let's just wait till after the final. I know that's all you can really think about right now."

He looked at her more sharply. "Thought we'd talked about it," he said slowly. "Are there problems at work, then?"

"No. Nothing's wrong at work. It's going well. I just think we shouldn't look too far ahead, that's all."

"Why not?" he asked bluntly. "Why don't you want to make plans? What's happened during these past weeks, anyway? I know I haven't paid much attention to you. Is that it?"

"No. I understand that," she assured him. "It's just...this whole fame thing. Seeing you in the paper every day. Being with you here, seeing all that attention. Those girls. It's made me realize that I'm not equipped to deal with all of it. I didn't mean to say this. Not now. But it's been there."

"So let me understand this," he said slowly. "You don't want to go away with me because my photo's in the paper too much, and people recognize me."

"I just can't handle this legend thing," she struggled to explain. "It's getting worse and worse. When I flew over here, I had to walk past a life-size picture of you, staring at me on the jetway. My coffee cup on the flight had your picture on it, for heaven's sake. It's all too strange for me. You need somebody more glamorous, who can fit into this celebrity lifestyle. Who can deal with you being that kind of symbol for the country."

"Do you see me that way? As some kind of bloody symbol?" he demanded.

"No. Not at all. But that's my point. When I met you, I didn't know who you were. What you meant to everyone in New Zealand. How big a deal it all was. And now I do, that's all," she admitted wretchedly.

Drew stared at her, his gray eyes burning into hers. "I'm not any kind of legend," he said at last. "I haven't saved any lives. I'm no hero. I'm just a bloke who plays football. I've been lucky enough to play on the best squad in the world. And to play in the professional era, so I get paid well for it. Twenty years ago, I'd have had a regular job, be lacing up my boots in the afternoon to play footy. That's all that's changed. And don't you see, it's because they make such a fuss about it all. That's why I need somebody who knows me better. Who knows I'm a pretty simple fella, and who wants to do those simple things with me. Somebody I can relax with, the way I can with you. Be myself with. I know I get shirty when you won't let me buy you things. But at least I know you're not with me because of what I can do for you. I want a simple life," he went on. "A life like my parents have had. And I've been thinking that I'd like to have it with you. I wasn't going to say *that* now, either. I know you're not ready to hear it. Reckon I'd better, though."

Hannah drew back, startled, then focused on the part of his speech she could deal with right now. "But you don't have a simple life," she pointed out. "You can't say that."

"Why not?" he challenged her. "So I travel, some weeks. When I come back, though, how is my life not simple? I train, maybe do some publicity. Afterwards, I want to have dinner with you. Sit on the couch and watch sport on the telly. Go fishing, once the season's over. Have a beer with my mates. It's a job, that's all. And I won't always be an All Black, you know. Someone else will be wearing the Number 6 jersey in a few years. I won't be forgotten, maybe. But my photo won't be in the paper every day, either. Kiwis need their sportsmen to look up to. Somebody for the kids to admire. I've tried my best to be that person. But it won't last forever."

"And what about after that? When you're coaching, or whatever? Whatever you say, you're always going to be an important person, Drew. And that's wonderful. But it's what makes me wrong for you. You're always going to be larger than life. And I'm not."

"I'm getting pretty bloody tired of you telling me what I need," he told her, his anger rising. "Seems to me I know my own mind. But that's not what this is all about, anyway. It's not about my being famous. So I'm well known just now. So I make a dollar or two from it. Likely that'll continue, though I'm no David Beckham. But that's not what's bothering you."

"What do you mean?" she faltered. "It's exactly what's bothering me."

"No, it isn't. It's that I want you to count on me. That if you stay with me, if you marry me," he said, overriding her shocked protest, "you'll have to say, 'Yes, Drew. I rely on you. I depend on you. I trust you to take care of me.' And you can't stand the thought of depending on anyone. Because if you do, if you let down your guard, you're sure I'm going to let you down. That I'm going to leave. With one of those stupid girls, maybe," he threw out in frustration.

He paced the room, came back to confront her. "Hasn't it occurred to you that *I* may bloody well need *you?* That I may need someone to count on too? You've said often enough that you understand the pressure this job puts on me. Don't you understand that I need someone who cares about me for myself, who doesn't care whether we win or lose the game?"

"I do understand that," she faltered. "And you must know how much I care about you. But it isn't good for me to rely on you. You're so strong, it makes me want to lean on you. And I can't do that."

"Damn it," he exploded, "relying on someone else doesn't mean you're not strong! Even I can't be strong all the time. I need to be able to show you all of me, weakness and all. I need you to know the pressure sometimes gets to me, even if I don't say it. And I don't want to see just the pretty pieces of you either. I don't want to know that you don't trust me enough to let me see when you hurt, when you're weak. That you don't think I can take care of you."

"But I don't want someone to take care of me! I know only I can take care of myself. I've always taken care of myself, and I can do it. I can't rely on anyone else to save me. We're all alone, in the end. I have to know that. That has to be OK with me, or I can't survive. And it is. I don't need to be rescued!"

Drew pulled his hands through his hair. "Everyone needs to be rescued sometimes. Including me. And we're not alone, in the end or any other time. Not if we're lucky, we're not. We're in it together. That's the whole point, don't you see? But you won't let me in. You won't let yourself need me. You have to be so perfect, there isn't room for anything less in your world. Not everyone leaves, Hannah. Not everyone is going to let you down. You don't let people down. Why do you expect less from everyone else? Why do you expect less from me? What have I ever done, that you can't trust me?"

"Nothing," she answered, trembling. "You've done nothing wrong. You're wonderful. But don't you see, I can't. I can't. I can't make that kind of promise to you."

"Then that's no kind of strength," he told her, his anger replaced by sadness. "Not being able to take a risk. To keep yourself trapped like you do. Not having the courage to show all of yourself, even to me. Even to the man who loves you. You never even cry, do you know that? Women cry, Hannah. I've seen my mother cry, and she's a strong woman. But you won't even let me see you cry. And you won't let me love you."

"I'm sorry." She was twisting her fingers together now in her distress. "I care about you so much. But I'm scared. I can't be all those things you need. I can't be more than this. I can't trust someone else to take care of me. It would be stupid, don't you see? It just isn't safe. And I can't do it."

"If you can't need me, though," he told her in frustration, "that means you can't let me love you, don't you see? I can't love you," he repeated slowly.

He started to say something else, stopped. Shrugged once in defeat, then turned and left the hotel room, closing the door behind him.

chapter thirty

♡

Hannah sank down on the bed and hugged her arms around herself, trying to warm her chilled body. What had just happened? Why couldn't she be normal? Why did she have to wreck this?

If only they could have gone more slowly, she thought miserably. She needed more time. She wasn't ready. Not yet.

She shook her head in confused distress, her thoughts in a jumble. She couldn't even figure herself out. She didn't even understand what she wanted. And she didn't know how to be what Drew needed.

In agitation, unable to sit still, she paced the room, her arms wrapped around herself to hold in the pain, to hold herself together, trying to walk off her confusion and the turmoil of her thoughts. But nothing worked. His words kept echoing in her head, and her mind kept replaying the sight of him walking out. Walking away.

She stopped at last, exhausted from emotion and her pacing, and sat down again in the side chair. Moving woodenly, she opened the minibar and poured a glass from the bottle of red wine there. The first time she had ever used a minibar. She had always resisted the overpriced items, and had wondered why anyone would incur such an unnecessary expense.

Alcohol wouldn't solve her problems, she told herself. But when the glass was gone, she poured out another one and drank that, and followed up with the scotch. It might not solve her problems, but it numbed the pain.

She thought vaguely at some point that she should brush her teeth and change for bed. But the effort seemed monumental, far beyond her. Instead, she sank to the floor with her back against the bed and stared in front of her.

Now she was drunk, she thought fuzzily. Four...five big drinks. That was just stupid. And she still felt terrible.

At some point during the long night, she lay down on the floor, pulled a pillow to her and fell asleep, hugging it to her. She woke in the morning with a headache, an upset stomach, and a memory of confused, troubling dreams. Scratch alcohol off the anesthetic list, she thought. It had only made her feel worse. She suddenly realized she was due to spend a morning shift in the VIP tent. She couldn't do it. It was too much.

And so, for the first time in her stellar career, Hannah Montgomery called in sick when she wasn't. Instead, she took a hot shower and dressed, drank some coffee and several glasses of water, and bought a box of Panadol from the hotel shop for her headache.

Feeling a bit better, physically at least, she knew she had to get out of her hotel room. Anything was better than that. She didn't feel up to changing into workout gear and using the hotel gym. So she just walked, all the way to Pitt Street Mall, Sydney's fashion center, looking dully into store windows at the fabulous clothes and shoes. Partway along the street, she was drawn to the Victorian ornateness of the Strand Arcade, and found herself looking at even more shoes.

So many shoes. They didn't even have prices showing. That had to be a bad sign. They were beautiful, though. She began to pay attention, to distract herself from the pain and confusion in her head.

She didn't need new shoes, she reminded herself. But they were certainly pretty. She stopped, looking at a pair of beautifully shaped pumps in a black and brown zebra print. Funky and sexy, they seemed to call to her.

Ten minutes later, she walked out of the shop carrying a brand-new pair of Marc Jacobs Italian-made shoes in a shopping bag. Six hundred dollars, she told herself dazedly. Australian. That was even more than U.S. dollars, she knew. She would have to take money from savings to pay her credit card bill. But her feet had carried her, and her hands had reached for her wallet and pulled out that card. She hadn't seemed to have any control.

Suddenly she stopped, right in the middle of the walkway. Someone bumped into her, muttered an apology. She found a bench in the middle of the crowded arcade and lowered herself into it, holding the bag with her new shoes in her lap and twisting its string anxiously, over and over, between her fingers.

Out of control, she repeated to herself. She was out of control.

She remembered Kristen's questions. Didn't she ever get tired of being so responsible all the time? Hadn't she ever wanted to buy a pair of shoes she couldn't afford, to drink too much, to sleep with Mr. Right Now, to call in sick to work?

She had laughed, she remembered. None of those things had seemed even possible, then. But she had done all those things now. Every one of them.

Well, didn't that prove that love wasn't for her? She wasn't good at it. She couldn't be enough. And other people wanted too much. That's why she had always held back. Because she knew, deep down, that when they found out what she was really like, all the pieces she never showed anyone, they wouldn't want her. And that would hurt too much. She needed to keep her own space around her, her own boundaries. Otherwise she wouldn't be able to master herself. Wouldn't be able to cope.

She could do it, she told herself. She could be strong. She'd always done it. She just needed to get over this, and she could be strong again.

But she didn't feel strong. She just felt confused, and unhappy, and so alone.

The rest of that day, and the following one, she spent trying to pull herself together. She made herself do a workout at the hotel gym, read a book to take her mind off her tumbling thoughts, eat in the hotel restaurant. She knew she should go back to Auckland, not stay for the game. It would be too hard to watch Drew and know she couldn't have him. But she couldn't bring herself to leave. She had to watch him play, had to will him to be all right.

Perhaps nobody went to that World Cup final with a heavier heart. The excited supporters of both teams turned up prepared to celebrate and, likely as not, wrapped in their team's flag. Hannah saw the groups sporting their black clothing, their black flags with the silver fern, amidst all the Australian flags, the fans dressed in yellow and green, and her heart lifted for a minute to see the support for the All Blacks. Faces were painted and team gear was everywhere. Bands played at street corners, and the crowds spilled through the streets. Those who didn't have tickets were finding spots at the outdoor Fanzones, or crowding into pubs to watch the game.

Hannah walked soberly through the crowd, handed her ticket in, and found her seat. At least Reka wasn't with her, she thought gratefully. Her sharp eyes would have seen too much. Instead, Hannah exchanged pleasantries with the women she knew, envying them their wholehearted devotion to their partners, then relapsed into a silence that went unnoticed in the tense preoccupation gripping those around her.

If Drew had been distracted by what had happened between them, she admitted as the team came onto the field, it certainly didn't show. He led the team out with even more than his usual intensity, radiating determination. In the close-ups on the big screen of the haka, his features were contorted with what looked like genuine rage, his performance of the stylized movements of the challenge ferocious and intimidating.

But from the moment of the opening kick, it became clear that this game wouldn't be easy. The Wallabies, on their own turf and in a stadium mostly full of their raucous, hugely supportive fans, had come for a fight.

The rugby was exciting, Hannah could see that. At least, it would have been if she hadn't cared so much, both sides putting on a blazing display of kicking, passing, and tackling skills. Penalties were few, both teams determined not to lose this game through a lack of discipline. At the break, the score stood at 14 to 10, with Australia in the lead.

When the second half began, the All Blacks seemed to raise the bar a notch. Drew was everywhere on the field, exploding into the opposition with fierce tackles, barking out orders, forcing a turnover. The score remained stubbornly unchanged, however, as the minutes ticked down.

With twenty minutes to go, Hemi reversed during a run, stumbled, and went down. Hannah's breath caught as she saw him struggle vainly to rise, saw Drew standing over him and signaling the medical team. A replay showed the hyperextension of his knee that had brought him down, and she winced, imagining Reka's distress as she watched from home.

Hemi was helped off the field, and his replacement ran on. Still the score remained unchanged, as both teams' defenses held firm, neither side able to gain an advantage.

Finally, with nine minutes left on the clock, the All Blacks scored a try in a brilliantly choreographed series of moves that broke the stiff Australian defense, and the supporters in black breathed a huge sigh of relief at the reprieve. The kick following, however, went wide, and the Australian fans cheered wildly as the score sat at 15 to 14 in favor of the All Blacks.

It was too close, Hannah thought in despair. All the Wallabies needed was a three-point penalty kick and they would pull ahead again. They hadn't scored during the entire half, but she could see the All Black defense tiring at the constant assault by the talented Australian backs.

With just six minutes left to play, the Australians had moved within 20 meters of the New Zealand try line. As Drew tackled the Wallaby player and began to pull back again from the ruck, he seemed to shudder, then fell to the ground, lying motionless.

Hannah strained, trying to see. The blood drained from her head, and she felt sick as she searched the big screen overhead for some clue to what was happening. The camera zoomed in on Drew as he slowly pulled his knees under him, leaning on his hands for support, head down. And stayed there as the medical team began to come out onto the field.

Time froze as she watched him, still down. The stadium grew quieter as he stayed there, unable to rise, on hands and knees.

"Kneed in the head," the man next to her explained to his companion. "Got a good knock there. Reckon it may be lights out."

"Bad news, eh," the other man answered. "Don't know if they can hold, without him."

Still on the turf, Drew shook his head as the medical team approached, pushed off with his hands, and slowly got to his feet to a roar from the crowd, moved back into position and crouched, hands on knees, ready for play to resume.

Hannah sat, her hands over her mouth, her heart thudding, trying to process the fact that he was all right. Seeing him lying on the ground, all his strength gone, something had shifted, changed inside her. She felt as if she were seeing things in focus for the first time.

She didn't care, she realized, what happened in this game. And it didn't matter what happened in the future. It didn't matter if she got hurt. Because nothing could hurt more than losing Drew right now.

All her anguish of the past two days began to make sense. She couldn't lose him. She couldn't throw away what they had. He mattered too much to her. She loved him, and she needed him. She needed him to be safe, and she needed to be with him, be there for him. Nothing else mattered, not any more.

The entire stadium was a riot of sound and motion, as the Australian fans shouted, pumped their fists, and chanted "Aussie! Aussie! Aussie!," their flags waving around them. The outnumbered All Black fans stood too, but silently, as the minutes ticked down. Gone was any sense of festivity. Their faces strained and their hands gripped as they tried to will their team, their country, to victory.

Hannah didn't care. She wanted, needed to get to Drew. Now. Win or lose, she needed to hold him and know he was all right. Her heart was with him, and she needed to be there, too. She began to fight her way through the roaring, surging crowd, desperate to get to the exit and down to the edge of the field.

She was in the corridor now, and she began to run, down the ramps to the lowest level, cursing the huge stadium, afraid she would be too late. That she would miss her chance. That she wouldn't be able to get to Drew.

She made her way through another door, down to the lowest level, just above the field. She saw that the All Blacks had regained possession, and were grimly hanging on. Over and over, they set up in the breakdown, passed, and passed again, holding onto the ball at all costs, determined not to give the Wallabies another chance with it.

Up this close, Hannah could see the effort in faces and straining bodies as they held on. The crowd was wild, shouting, cheering, chanting, as the team carried the ball forward, passed it, unyielding in their determination, focused only on holding the ball.

Now the noise level rose even higher, swollen by thousands of Kiwi voices as the clock ticked down. Ten...nine...eight. They were going to do it. Five...four...three...two...one.

The clock showed 80:00 in its large red numbers. An All Black gave the ball a final kick out of touch, the referee blew the whistle, and the game was over. New Zealand had held. Had won the Rugby World Cup.

All around her, the Australian fans cheered their team's effort, while the Kiwi chant swelled through the stadium. "All... Blacks. All...Blacks." Fans in black cried, jumped, cheered, and held each other in exultant triumph, all the strain of the past ninety-five minutes now released in wild jubilation.

Hannah noticed none of it. She saw the members of the team embracing and the bench emptying as the players there burst onto the field to cheer, pump their fists, and share the moment with their teammates.

But Drew just stood, looking down, hands on hips, breathing hard. And Hannah knew that he had somehow given more than his all. He had reached down deep and found what it took to lead the team, and his country, to this victory. She saw what it had taken out of him. The effort had taken all his famous reserves of stamina and courage, and then he had found some more. But it was too much.

She was still too far away. She needed to be with him. She pushed back to the corridor and ran to another door. Still not close enough. Another door, and another. Finally, she was as close as she could get to the part of the field where the team gathered, still celebrating, hugging each other and roaring their triumph.

Hannah pushed and pulled her way to the front of the crowd, not caring how she got there, not knowing what she would do when she reached him, what she would say. She only knew she had to be there, had to see him and hold him.

Finally, she reached the edge of the barrier, with a security guard in front of her. She ran to him, tried to explain. "Please," she gasped. "I have to see him. I have to see Drew Callahan."

He put an arm out to stop her. "Have to stay back. You can see the team. But you can't go out there. Stay back," he warned again.

She tried to argue, but she knew there was no way he was going to let her get to Drew. She was trapped, irrationally desperate now. Could she climb over? She began to lean across the barrier, the guard, alarmed, coming forward to grab her, stop her from moving forward.

As she searched for a way over the barrier and tried incoherently to explain to the security guard, now with his hand on her arm, Drew looked up from the crowd of teammates, coaches, and support staff, his eyes meeting hers. Then he was running to her, crossing the expanse of the turf. She reached out her arms to him blindly, and he hauled her bodily across the barrier, the guard stepping back in surprise as Drew pulled her onto the field.

She threw her arms around him and just stood, trembling, holding him tightly, then pulled back, the words tumbling out in an urgent babble that was beyond her power to control. "Are you all right? Are you...are you hurt? Are you OK?"

He shook his head at her, beginning to smile. Hannah knew it wasn't true, could see the exhaustion and pain in his face, the scratches, bruises, and patches of raw skin. She ran her hands up over his face, down his arms, needing to check for herself that he was whole, that he was safe.

"I'm so sorry," she said, her voice catching. "I'm so sorry for what I said. For what I did. I couldn't stand it. I can't stand it if you're hurt," she burst out as she started to cry. "I need you to be here with me. Please don't leave me. I love you. I love you and I need you to be with me."

She was sobbing in earnest now, shoulders shaking and chest heaving, her nose running as the tears poured out. She threw her arms around him again and held him to her, willing him to stay with her, to love her and need her as she needed him.

She hadn't put it right, she thought in despair. She didn't know how to explain it to him, and she was out of control, and she had done this all wrong.

Drew lifted her away from him, reached out to hold her face in his hands. "Haven't you heard, I don't know when to quit? Take more than that to get rid of me." He laughed suddenly, exultant with joy and relief, and hugged her hard to him again. "I love you," he said, fierce in his triumph. "I will always love you."

He stood back from her then, put his big hands on her shoulders, and looked at her with level intensity. "I can't promise never to die, Hannah," he said soberly. "I can't promise to be perfect. And neither can you. But I can promise that I'll always take care of you. I'll give you everything I have to give. And whatever you face, I'll be there to face it with you."

She stood still, taking in his words, and slowly nodded. "I can do that," she told him. "I can be there for you, too. I promise. I'll give you all of me." She laughed shakily then, through her tears. "I've sure shown you I can cry, anyway. You know you have the weak parts now."

An assistant was with them then, motioning to Drew that it was time for him to head to the microphone to give the winning captain's speech.

He nodded briefly, then turned to Hannah again and laughed at her. "You're a mess. Here, wipe your face on my jersey. It's buggered anyway."

She smiled and wiped her face as best she could across his chest, the skintight fabric already wet with sweat and blood. "I'm making it even worse, though."

"That's why they're black, eh," he grinned at her. "Don't go anywhere. I'm coming back to you."

As he strode off and the assistant directed her to a side exit to wait for him, Hannah knew it was true. He would come back to her. Always. There was no quit in Drew. He was hers.

All the relief and joy she felt swirled inside, leaving her light and giddy. I'm out of control, she told herself happily. I'm a mess.

But it didn't matter. She could relax now. There was no need to hold back anymore. No need to guard her heart. She had given it to Drew, she realized at last. He held it. And it was safe with him. Now and forever.

epilogue

♡

Hannah turned from the oven, where she was warming up the dinner left by the housekeeper, when she heard Drew's key in the door. He dropped his kit in the entryway, and came to meet her with a hug and a kiss.

"You're early," she smiled up at him. "What a nice surprise. How was practice?"

"Tell you later. I'm ready to be home and work on being weak for a while. Want to be weak with me?"

"I can do that," she assured him. "A bit tired today, actually. Working with two of us in here is tougher, even with that nap you force me to take."

He put a hand over her barely visible belly. "How's my son today, besides tiring out his mother?"

"Hungry," she sighed. "He must be growing into a rugby player."

They had found out the sex together a week earlier, when they had seen their baby boy for the first time on the sonogram. Drew was thrilled to be having a son, she knew, although he teased her that he hoped being pregnant got better, because he needed a daughter to spoil, and soon.

He pulled her into his arms and held her in the way he loved, his chin resting on the top of her head, her cheek pressed against his heart. They stood like that for a minute, drawing strength and comfort from each other's presence.

She thought suddenly of how close she had come to throwing all this away, how grateful she was to him for sticking with her, rescuing her from her lonely self-sufficiency. And to herself for finally dropping her defenses to let him in. He was her rock, steadfast and solid. Overwhelmed with love for him, she whispered, just loud enough for him to hear, "You have my heart."

He pulled back, his familiar intense gaze hard on her face. Slowly, he smiled. "Changed my mind. I'm going to have to be strong a bit longer tonight." With that, he lifted her gently into his arms, his lightest and most precious burden.

As he made his way toward the stairs, Hannah smiled up at him. Nothing in the world, she thought happily, was better than being picked up by her wonderful, perfect husband.

And Drew smiled back, and thought that of all the men he had lifted off their feet, all the trophies he had held in his arms in his long career, nothing in the world was better than picking up his beautiful, imperfect wife.

Who was just perfect for him.

The End

Sign up for my New Release mailing list at www.rosalindjames.com/mail-list to be notified of special pricing on new books, sales, and more.

Turn the page for a Kiwi glossary and a preview of the next book in the series.

a kiwi glossary

A few notes about Maori pronunciation:
- The accent is normally on the first syllable.
- All vowels are pronounced separately.
- All vowels except u have a short vowel sound.
- "wh" is pronounced "f."
- "ng" is pronounced as in "singer," not as in "anger."

ABs: All Blacks

across the Ditch: in Australia (across the Tasman Sea). Or, if you're in Australia, in New Zealand!

advert: commercial

agro: aggravation

air con: air conditioning

All Blacks: National rugby team. Members are selected for every series from amongst the five NZ Super 15 teams. The All Blacks play similarly selected teams from other nations.

ambo: paramedic

Aotearoa: New Zealand (the other official name, meaning "The Land of the Long White Cloud" in Maori)

arvo, this arvo: afternoon

Aussie, Oz: Australia. (An Australian is also an Aussie. Pronounced "Ozzie.")

bach: holiday home (pronounced like "bachelor")

backs: rugby players who aren't in the scrum and do more running, kicking, and ball-carrying—though all players do all jobs and play both offense and defense. Backs tend to be faster and leaner than forwards.

bangers and mash: sausages and potatoes

barrack for: cheer for

bench: counter (kitchen bench)

berko: berserk

Big Smoke: the big city (usually Auckland)

bikkies: cookies

billy-o, like billy-o: like crazy. "I paddled like billy-o and just barely made it through that rapid."

bin, rubbish bin: trash can

bit of a dag: a comedian, a funny guy

bits and bobs: stuff ("be sure you get all your bits and bobs")

blood bin: players leaving field for injury

Blues: Auckland's Super 15 team

bollocks: rubbish, nonsense

boofhead: fool, jerk

booking: reservation

boots and all: full tilt, no holding back

bot, the bot: flu, a bug

Boxing Day: December 26—a holiday

brekkie: breakfast

brilliant: fantastic

bub: baby, small child

buggered: messed up, exhausted

bull's roar: close. "They never came within a bull's roar of winning."

bunk off: duck out, skip (bunk off school)

bust a gut: do your utmost, make a supreme effort

Cake Tin: Wellington's rugby stadium (not the official name, but it looks exactly like a springform pan)

caravan: travel trailer

cardie: a cardigan sweater

chat up: flirt with

chilly bin: ice chest

chips: French fries. (potato chips are "crisps")

chocolate bits: chocolate chips

chocolate fish: pink or white marshmallow coated with milk chocolate, in the shape of a fish. A common treat/reward for kids (and for adults. You often get a chocolate fish on the saucer when you order a mochaccino—a mocha).

choice: fantastic

chokka: full

chooks: chickens

Chrissy: Christmas

chuck out: throw away

chuffed: pleased

collywobbles: nervous tummy, upset stomach

come a greaser: take a bad fall

costume, cossie: swimsuit (female only)

cot: crib (for a baby)

crook: ill

cuddle: hug (give a cuddle)

cuppa: a cup of tea (the universal remedy)

CV: resumé

cyclone: hurricane (Southern Hemisphere)

dairy: corner shop (not just for milk!)

dead: very; e.g., "dead sexy."

dill: fool

do your block: lose your temper

dob in: turn in; report to authorities. Frowned upon.

doco: documentary

doddle: easy. "That'll be a doddle."

dodgy: suspect, low-quality

dogbox: The doghouse—in trouble

dole: unemployment.

dole bludger: somebody who doesn't try to get work and lives off unemployment (which doesn't have a time limit in NZ)

Domain: a good-sized park; often the "official" park of the town.

dressing gown: bathrobe

drongo: fool (Australian, but used sometimes in NZ as well)

drop your gear: take off your clothes

duvet: comforter

earbashing: talking-to, one-sided chat

electric jug: electric teakettle to heat water. Every Kiwi kitchen has one.

En Zed: Pronunciation of NZ. ("Z" is pronounced "Zed.")

ensuite: master bath (a bath in the bedroom).

eye fillet: premium steak (filet mignon)

fair go: a fair chance. Kiwi ideology: everyone deserves a fair go.

fair wound me up: Got me very upset

fantail: small, friendly native bird

farewelled, he'll be farewelled: funeral; he'll have his funeral.

feed, have a feed: meal

first five, first five-eighth: rugby back—does most of the big kicking jobs and is the main director of the backs. Also called the No. 10.

fixtures: playing schedule

fizz, fizzie: soft drink

fizzing: fired up

flaked out: tired

flash: fancy

flat to the boards: at top speed

flat white: most popular NZ coffee. An espresso with milk but no foam.

flattie: roommate

flicks: movies

flying fox: zipline

footpath: sidewalk

footy, football: rugby

forwards: rugby players who make up the scrum and do the most physical battling for position. Tend to be bigger and more heavily muscled than backs.

fossick about: hunt around for something

front up: face the music, show your mettle

garden: yard

get on the piss: get drunk

get stuck in: commit to something

give way: yield

giving him stick, give him some stick about it: teasing, needling

glowworms: larvae of a fly found only in NZ. They shine a light to attract insects. Found in caves or other dark, moist places.

go crook, be crook: go wrong, be ill

go on the turps: get drunk

gobsmacked: astounded

good hiding: beating ("They gave us a good hiding in Dunedin.")

grotty: grungy, badly done up

ground floor: what we call the first floor. The "first floor" is one floor up.

gumboots, gummies: knee-high rubber boots. It rains a lot in New Zealand.

gutted: thoroughly upset

Haast's Eagle: (extinct). Huge native NZ eagle. Ate moa.

haere mai: Maori greeting

haka: ceremonial Maori challenge—done before every All Blacks game

hang on a tick: wait a minute

hard man: the tough guy, the enforcer

hard yakka: hard work (from Australian)

harden up: toughen up. Standard NZ (male) response to (male) complaints: "Harden the f*** up!"

have a bit on: I have placed a bet on [whatever]. Sports gambling and prostitution are both legal in New Zealand.

have a go: try

Have a nosy for...: look around for

head: principal (headmaster)

head down: or head down, bum up. Put your head down. Work hard.

heaps: lots. "Give it heaps."

hei toki: pendant (Maori)

holiday: vacation

honesty box: a small stand put up just off the road with bags of fruit and vegetables and a cash box. Very common in New Zealand.

hooker: rugby position (forward)

hooning around: driving fast, wannabe tough-guy behavior (typically young men)

hoovering: vacuuming (after the brand of vacuum cleaner)

ice block: popsicle

I'll see you right: I'll help you out

in form: performing well (athletically)

it's not on: It's not all right

iwi: tribe (Maori)

jabs: immunizations, shots

jandals: flip-flops. (This word is only used in New Zealand. Jandals and gumboots are the iconic Kiwi footwear.)

jersey: a rugby shirt, or a pullover sweater

joker: a guy. "A good Kiwi joker": a regular guy; a good guy.

journo: journalist

jumper: a heavy pullover sweater

ka pai: going smoothly (Maori).

kapa haka: school singing group (Maori songs/performances. Any student can join, not just Maori.)

karanga: Maori song of welcome (done by a woman)

keeping his/your head down: working hard

kia ora: welcome (Maori, but used commonly)

kilojoules: like calories—measure of food energy

kindy: kindergarten (this is 3- and 4-year-olds)

kit, get your kit off: clothes, take off your clothes

Kiwi: New Zealander OR the bird. If the person, it's capitalized. Not the fruit.

kiwifruit: the fruit. (Never called simply a "kiwi.")

knackered: exhausted

knockout rounds: playoff rounds (quarterfinals, semifinals, final)

koru: ubiquitous spiral Maori symbol of new beginnings, hope

kumara: Maori sweet potato.

ladder: standings (rugby)

littlies: young kids

lock: rugby position (forward)

lollies: candy

lolly: candy or money

lounge: living room

mad as a meat axe: crazy

maintenance: child support

major: "a major." A big deal, a big event

mana: prestige, earned respect, spiritual power

Maori: native people of NZ—though even they arrived relatively recently from elsewhere in Polynesia

marae: Maori meeting house

Marmite: Savory Kiwi yeast-based spread for toast. An acquired taste. (Kiwis swear it tastes different from Vegemite, the Aussie version.)

mate: friend. And yes, fathers call their sons "mate."

metal road: gravel road

Milo: cocoa substitute; hot drink mix

mind: take care of, babysit

moa: (extinct) Any of several species of huge flightless NZ birds. All eaten by the Maori before Europeans arrived.

moko: Maori tattoo

mokopuna: grandchildren

motorway: freeway

mozzie: mosquito; OR a Maori Australian (Maori + Aussie = Mozzie)

muesli: like granola, but unbaked

munted: broken

naff: stupid, unsuitable. "Did you get any naff Chrissy pressies this year?"

nappy: diaper

narked, narky: annoyed

netball: Down-Under version of basketball for women. Played like basketball, but the hoop is a bit narrower, the players wear skirts, and they don't dribble and can't contact each other. It can look fairly tame to an American eye. There are professional netball teams, and it's televised and taken quite seriously.

new caps: new All Blacks—those named to the side for the first time

New World: One of the two major NZ supermarket chains

nibbles: snacks

nick, in good nick: doing well

niggle, niggly: small injury, ache or soreness

no worries: no problem. The Kiwi mantra.

No. 8: rugby position. A forward

not very flash: not feeling well

Nurofen: brand of ibuprofen

nutted out: worked out

OE: Overseas Experience—young people taking a year or two overseas, before or after University.

offload: pass (rugby)

oldies: older people. (or for the elderly, "wrinklies!")

on the front foot: Having the advantage. Vs. on the back foot—
at a disadvantage. From rugby.

Op Shop: charity shop, secondhand shop

out on the razzle: out drinking too much, getting crazy

paddock: field (often used for rugby—"out on the paddock")

Pakeha: European-ancestry people (as opposed to Polynesians)

Panadol: over-the-counter painkiller

partner: romantic partner, married or not

patu: Maori club

paua, paua shell: NZ abalone

pavlova (pav): Classic Kiwi Christmas (summer) dessert.
Meringue, fresh fruit (often kiwifruit and strawberries) and
whipped cream.

pavement: sidewalk (generally on wider city streets)

pear-shaped, going pear-shaped: messed up, when it all goes
to Hell

penny dropped: light dawned (figured it out)

people mover: minivan

perve: stare sexually

phone's engaged: phone's busy

piece of piss: easy

pike out: give up, wimp out

piss awful: very bad

piss up: drinking (noun) a piss-up

pissed: drunk

pissed as a fart: very drunk. And yes, this is an actual expression.

play up: act up

playing out of his skin: playing very well

plunger: French Press coffeemaker

PMT: PMS

pohutukawa: native tree; called the "New Zealand Christmas Tree"
for its beautiful red blossoms at Christmastime (high summer)

poi: balls of flax on strings that are swung around the head, often to the accompaniment of singing and/or dancing by women. They make rhythmic patterns in the air, and it's very beautiful.

Pom, Pommie: English person

pop: pop over, pop back, pop into the oven, pop out, pop in

possie: position (rugby)

postie: mail carrier

pot plants: potted plants (not what you thought, huh?)

poumanu: greenstone (jade)

prang: accident (with the car)

pressie: present

puckaroo: broken (from Maori)

pudding: dessert

pull your head in: calm down, quit being rowdy

Pumas: Argentina's national rugby team

pushchair: baby stroller

put your hand up: volunteer

put your head down: work hard

rapt: thrilled

rattle your dags: hurry up. From the sound that dried excrement on a sheep's backside makes, when the sheep is running!

red card: penalty for highly dangerous play. The player is sent off for the rest of the game, and the team plays with 14 men.

rellies: relatives

riding the pine: sitting on the bench (as a substitute in a match)

rimu: a New Zealand tree. The wood used to be used for building and flooring, but like all native NZ trees, it was over-logged. Older houses, though, often have rimu floors, and they're beautiful.

Rippa: junior rugby

root: have sex (you DON'T root for a team!)

ropeable: very angry

ropey: off, damaged ("a bit ropey")

rort: ripoff

rough as guts: uncouth

rubbish bin: garbage can

rugby boots: rugby shoes with spikes (sprigs)

Rugby Championship: Contest played each year in the Southern Hemisphere by the national teams of NZ, Australia, South Africa, and Argentina

Rugby World Cup, RWC: World championship, played every four years amongst the top 20 teams in the world

rugged up: dressed warmly

ruru: native owl

Safa: South Africa. Abbreviation only used in NZ.

sammie: sandwich

scoff, scoffing: eating, like "snarfing"

second-five, second five-eighth: rugby back (No. 9). With the first-five, directs the game. Also feeds the scrum and generally collects the ball from the ball carrier at the breakdown and distributes it.

selectors: team of 3 (the head coach is one) who choose players for the All Blacks squad, for every series

serviette: napkin

shag: have sex with. A little rude, but not too bad.

shattered: exhausted

sheds: locker room (rugby)

she'll be right: See "no worries." Everything will work out. The other Kiwi mantra.

shift house: move (house)

shonky: shady (person). "a bit shonky"

shout, your shout, my shout, shout somebody a coffee: buy a round, treat somebody

sickie, throw a sickie: call in sick

sin bin: players sitting out 10-minute penalty in rugby (or, in the case of a red card, the rest of the game)

sink the boot in: kick you when you're down

skint: broke (poor)

skipper: (team) captain. Also called "the Skip."

slag off: speak disparagingly of; disrespect

smack: spank. Smacking kids is illegal in NZ.

smoko: coffee break

snog: kiss; make out with

sorted: taken care of

spa, spa pool: hot tub

sparrow fart: the crack of dawn

speedo: Not the swimsuit! Speedometer. (the swimsuit is called a budgie smuggler—a budgie is a parakeet, LOL.)

spew: vomit

spit the dummy: have a tantrum. (A dummy is a pacifier)

sportsman: athlete

sporty: liking sports

spot on: absolutely correct. "That's spot on. You're spot on."

Springboks, Boks: South African national rugby team

squiz: look. "I was just having a squiz round." "Giz a squiz": Give me a look at that.

stickybeak: nosy person, busybody

stonkered: drunk—a bit stonkered—or exhausted

stoush: bar fight, fight

straight away: right away

strength of it: the truth, the facts. "What's the strength of that?" = "What's the true story on that?"

stroppy: prickly, taking offense easily

stuffed up: messed up

Super 15: Top rugby competition: five teams each from NZ, Australia, South Africa. The New Zealand Super 15 teams are, from north to south: Blues (Auckland), Chiefs (Waikato/

Hamilton), Hurricanes (Wellington), Crusaders (Canterbury/ Christchurch), Highlanders (Otago/Dunedin).

supporter: fan (Do NOT say "root for." "To root" is to have (rude) sex!)

suss out: figure out

sweet: dessert

sweet as: great. (also: choice as, angry as, lame as…Meaning "very" whatever. "Mum was angry as that we ate up all the pudding before tea with Nana.")

takahe: ground-dwelling native bird. Like a giant parrot.

takeaway: takeout (food)

tall poppy: arrogant person who puts himself forward or sets himself above others. It is every Kiwi's duty to cut down tall poppies, a job they undertake enthusiastically.

Tangata Whenua: Maori (people of the land)

tapu: sacred (Maori)

Te Papa: the National Museum, in Wellington

tea: dinner (casual meal at home)

tea towel: dishtowel

test match: international rugby match (e.g., an All Blacks game)

throw a wobbly: have a tantrum

tick off: cross off (tick off a list)

ticker: heart. "The boys showed a lot of ticker out there today."

togs: swimsuit (male or female)

torch: flashlight

touch wood: knock on wood (for luck)

track: trail

trainers: athletic shoes

tramping: hiking

transtasman: Australia/New Zealand (the Bledisloe Cup is a transtasman rivalry)

trolley: shopping cart

tucker: food

tui: Native bird

turn to custard: go south, deteriorate

turps, go on the turps: get drunk

Uni: University—or school uniform

up the duff: pregnant. A bit vulgar (like "knocked up")

ute: pickup or SUV

vet: check out

waiata: Maori song

wairua: spirit, soul (Maori). Very important concept.

waka: canoe (Maori)

Wallabies: Australian national rugby team

Warrant of Fitness: certificate of a car's fitness to drive

wedding tackle: the family jewels; a man's genitals

Weet-Bix: ubiquitous breakfast cereal

whaddarya?: I am dubious about your masculinity (meaning "Whaddarya...pussy?")

whakapapa: genealogy (Maori). A critical concept.

whanau: family (Maori). Big whanau: extended family. Small whanau: nuclear family.

wheelie bin: rubbish bin (garbage can) with wheels.

whinge: whine. Contemptuous! Kiwis dislike whingeing. Harden up!

White Ribbon: campaign against domestic violence

wind up: upset (perhaps purposefully). "Their comments were bound to wind him up."

wing: rugby position (back)

Yank: American. Not pejorative.

yellow card: A penalty for dangerous play that sends a player off for 10 minutes to the sin bin. The team plays with 14 men during that time—or even 13, if two are sinbinned.

yonks: ages. "It's been going on for yonks."

Find out what's new at the **ROSALIND JAMES WEBSITE.**
http://www.rosalindjames.com/

"Like" my <u>Facebook</u> page at facebook.com/rosalindjamesbooks
or follow me on <u>Twitter</u> at twitter.com/RosalindJames5
to learn about giveaways, events, and more.
Want to tell me what you liked, or what I got wrong? I'd love
to hear! You can email me at **Rosalind@rosalindjames.com**

by rosalind james

Cover design by Robin Ludwig Design Inc.,
http://www.gobookcoverdesign.com/

Read on for an excerpt from
Just Good Friends
Available now

just good friends—prologue

♡

Please, please, don't let him get in. Don't make me have to do this. Please, somebody help me.

Kate Lamonica crouched under her kitchen table, the worn yellow linoleum cold under her bare feet, and prayed. She shifted her weight, lurched a bit to one side as her knee caught in the fabric of her fleece robe. That wasn't going to work. She had to be able to move. Forcing herself to move deliberately, not to panic, she set the big knife down carefully on the seat of the chair beside her. Pulled her right arm out of the robe. Shifted her silent cell phone to her right hand with a quick movement, held it to her ear again. Shrugged her left arm out and shoved the bulky robe aside. The brightly printed red poppies on the fabric gleamed at the edge of her vision, incongruously cheerful in the dim light. She transferred the phone back to her left hand, picked up her knife again with the right, feeling better once it was back in her hand. Ready to use.

She was shivering a little now, her pajamas no match for the chill of the early February morning. Still no sound from outside, or from the phone in her hand. She lifted it from her ear to check the display. Her call was still connected. And she was still on hold. How could 911 put somebody on hold?

Pick up, she prayed. But the phone remained silent. No competent voice offering protection. No help at all. Instead, the sounds she'd been dreading. The rattle of the kitchen door handle, and Paul's voice calling to her.

"I know you're in there, Kate. Don't make me have to come get you. That's only going to make it worse for you."

She visualized again what she would do if he broke in. She'd wait until he was close. Then burst out from under the table in one movement, launch herself at him, and strike. Nothing tentative. No hesitation. Because if he made it in here, she was in real trouble. She had to take her chance. If the police didn't come, she was going to have to save herself.

"I never wanted to hurt you, you know that. I loved you. But you've let me down so many times. You haven't given me any choice."

She knew how he'd look to the arriving officers. If they ever came. His pressed slacks and button-down shirt, every blond hair in place. His easy smile, his plausible explanations. His insistence that she was the one with the problem, the vendetta against him.

Silence, then a *clunk* as something heavy dropped on the concrete slab. She could feel her heart knocking against her chest wall as she heard a scrape, then the sound of metal on metal against the door frame. She stared out from under the table as if she could see around the corner, through the door. Her hand tightened around the knife as her mind went over and over the scenario. Leap. Rush. Slash.

"911. What is your emergency?" The phone in her hand came to life at last. She started at the sudden noise in her ear, banging her head painfully against the bottom of the table. Juggled the phone for desperate moments. Forced herself to answer calmly as her eyes stayed trained on a kitchen door she couldn't see.

"I need the police. 2111 Fifth Street. Apartment B. I have an intruder. He's threatened me, and he's trying to break in now."

"Is he on the property now?" the dispatcher asked, maddeningly calm.

"*Yes.* I just told you. Her voice sounded unnaturally high in her ears. "He's trying to break in, through my kitchen door. It's the ground floor. Around the side."

Her breath was coming in gasps now. She fought to control it, but the fear was rising into panic now. "Are you sending them? Are they coming?"

"Don't worry, ma'am," the calm voice reassured. "I've dispatched a unit. Stay on the line with me. Don't hang up."

Finally, the blessed sound of a siren in the distance. And Paul's voice through the door again.

"You shouldn't have called them. You've only made it harder for yourself. Because I'll be coming back for you. You can try to run, but you know that I'll find you in the end. There's nowhere you can hide that I won't find you."

She remained in her painful crouch, kept her grip on her knife and her phone, unable to trust that he'd really left. She had to be ready. Just in case. When she finally heard the knock, a deep voice reassuringly unlike Paul's identifying himself, it was a struggle to pull herself out from under the table. Her limbs were so stiff with tension and fright that she could barely uncoil them, and she was shaking with the aftereffects of adrenaline.

By the time the sympathetic officers had walked her to her car, checked the back seat, and watched her lock her doors, she was shaking again, but with fury as well as fear now. She followed their car to the station, then parked in front of the building and tried to decide what to do. She couldn't afford the luxury of denial anymore. Paul would be back. He might even be at her apartment again by now, waiting for her. She'd been lucky this time. But he only had to get lucky once. And meanwhile, she'd be living every day in fear. Moving from friend to friend, sleeping on couches, looking over her shoulder.

Screw this, she thought fiercely. She was done. Whatever it took, however much it cost her, she was getting out of this. Running somewhere he couldn't find her. To some distant place where she could live her life normally again. In peace.

chapter one

♡

The line for Passport Control snaked and twisted, tired passengers waiting obediently, shuffling forward one slow foot at a time. Kate felt disoriented and dizzy with fatigue. Maybe it was the overnight flight, or the speed of the decisions she'd made over the past week, but her mind seemed to be lagging several steps behind reality right now. It kept drifting off, forcing her to bring it back again. To remind herself where she was, what she was doing.

"You're going *where?*" her father had demanded a few days earlier, arriving home to find her packing.

"New Zealand," she repeated patiently. "I've bought my ticket, and I leave the day after tomorrow."

"Surely this can't be necessary," her mother objected. "Couldn't you find a new job and a new place to live, maybe in a different city? Or even stay here with us for a while. You know how happy we'd be to have you, to know you were safe."

"That's just it, though," Kate tried to explain. "I don't think I would be safe, or that you would be either. It's only a matter of time before Paul turns up here looking for me. I hate knowing I'm putting you at risk, even being here a few days. I wouldn't have come at all if I'd known where else to go."

"I hope he does turn up," her father said grimly. "I'd know how to deal with him."

"You can't sit on the porch with a shotgun on your lap twenty-four hours a day, Dad," Kate sighed. "I know you want to protect me, but it isn't possible. Not for more than a couple days. Which is all that I'm staying."

"Besides," she said, sitting down wearily on the familiar, narrow bed of her childhood and hugging an embroidered cushion to her for comfort, "I can't live like this anymore. Maybe you're right. Maybe I could move to a new state, or even someplace else in California, and this would be over. Maybe he wouldn't find me. Who knows, maybe he'd even give up. But I don't think so. Stalkers are obsessive. It's what they do. Everything he's said, everything I've learned tells me I'm in danger. And I can't live like this anymore," she said again, tears filling her eyes. "I just can't. It's too much."

Her mother sat down next to her and put an arm around her shoulders. "You need to do whatever it is that's going to keep you safe. And make you feel safe, too. You know we want what's best for you. And if that means moving to New Zealand, well, that's the way it is. We'll help any way we can."

"Thanks, Mom." Kate blinked the tears away and gave her mother a fierce hug. "You guys are the best. Love you so much."

"Who is this Hannah, though, in New Zealand?" her father persisted. "Is she somebody who can help you once you're there? She doesn't sound like she's been in the country all that long herself."

"Only a couple years," Kate agreed. "She was a work friend. Before she moved to New Zealand, of course. Even though it's been a while, she offered to help right away when I called. She seems pretty confident that she and her husband can help me find a job. He's a big deal over there, apparently. A rugby player."

"How's a rugby player going to help you find a job as an accountant?" her father objected.

"I'm not quite sure myself, to tell you the truth," Kate admitted. "But Hannah was positive. It seemed like my best bet, and I'm going to take it."

"And they'll put you up for a few days when you arrive?" her mother asked. "I don't like to think of you getting to a strange country and being on your own."

"They do speak English, you know, Mom," Kate reminded her. "I'll be fine. Better off than I am here, that's for sure. Who knows, it might even be fun."

The brave words seemed foolish now, in the echoing, alien territory of the arrivals hall. Her international travel experience was limited to a single trip to Canada. What was she doing here? Reaching the front of the line at last, she handed her passport with its two lonely stamps to an immigration officer.

"Working holiday visa," he commented. "What are you planning to do whilst you're here?"

"Accounting, I hope," she told him.

He raised his eyebrows. "That's one I don't hear every day, have to say. Beats kiwifruit picking, I'm sure." He stamped her passport firmly and handed it back to her. "Best of luck to you. And welcome to New Zealand."

By the time she had collected the two suitcases that contained all she had brought with her from her old life and made her way through various stops to the arrivals area, Kate was overwhelmed. The huge space, the crowds, the instructions given in a clipped accent barely intelligible in her exhausted state had all taken their toll. When she pushed her luggage cart through the automatic doors and saw Hannah waiting, she couldn't help the tears that spilled over as her friend folded her into welcoming arms.

"Oh, sweetie. What a tough time you've had. I'm so glad you're here." Hannah pulled a Kleenex out of her purse and handed it to Kate as she continued to cry. "Come on," she urged. "We'll get you a coffee, and then we'll take you home. You're going to feel so much better after a shower, I promise."

Kate wiped her eyes. "Sorry. I'm better now. What a first impression." She reached out to shake hands with the big man standing beside her friend. "Hi. You must be Drew. It's so good of you to agree to help me like this. You don't even know me, and here I am intruding on your life. I can't tell you how much I appreciate it."

"No worries." He smiled down at her easily. "We invited you, didn't we. Tell you the truth, you're doing me a favor as well. I'm off to Safa tomorrow for a couple weeks. I'm glad you'll be here with Hannah. I wasn't happy about leaving her alone that long."

"South Africa," Hannah translated. "Road trip. Two games in a row. And don't worry, you'll figure out what they're saying eventually."

"I hope it won't be too much for you, having me," Kate said, eyeing Hannah with concern.

"I'm pregnant, not sick," Hannah countered. "And perfectly healthy, despite how fragile Drew appears to think I am." She looked at her husband with affection as he took Kate's trolley over her objections. "Let him push it," she counseled Kate. "We both know you could do it. But it'll make him much happier."

Once they were on their way into the city, Hannah turned in her seat to smile at Kate again. "I can't wait to go look at flats with you. I've already started setting up visits for Saturday. There are so many great neighborhoods here. I'm sure we'll be able to find you something that suits you. You're going to love it."

"They say converts make the best missionaries," Drew put in. "Reckon Hannah's proof of that. Best cheerleader En Zed could have."

"I'm glad to hear it's a good place to live, though," Kate said. "Because I'm not sure how long I'll be here. I just hope I can get a job fairly quickly."

"I've already got the word out," Drew assured her. "She'll be right."

"And believe me, he's connected," Hannah said. "Between the two of us, we'll have you employed before you know it. You'll probably wish you had a longer break."

"I guess this would be all right." Kate eyed the dark little flat dubiously.

"No way," Hannah told her firmly. "Too gloomy. We can do better than this."

"This is a good neighborhood, Mt. Eden," she told Kate as they settled back into the car. "But that was the wrong flat. And you'd have quite a bus ride—or drive, of course—to the beach. Which isn't ideal."

"I've always just hoped to live someplace that didn't actually have drive-bys," Kate said. "I don't think I'm in any position to turn something down because it isn't on the beach."

"Sure you are," Hannah countered. "Maybe you won't be able to walk there. But we can get you closer than this."

"That would be a big plus. Are all the beaches as nice as where we swam this morning?"

"Oh yeah. They each have their own character. Just wait. Soon you'll think your own beach is the best, and you won't want to come swim at mine."

By the end of the day, though, Kate was discouraged. "Maybe I should take that first place after all," she told Hannah over dinner. "It was the cheapest one we saw. I didn't realize a decent furnished apartment, even a small one, would cost so much. And I still need to buy a car."

"No, you don't," Hannah said. "Because I'm going to loan you the Yaris while you're here. I have a new car, and I don't need it. I've meant to sell it, just haven't got around to it yet. You'll be doing me a favor, getting it out of the way."

"Won't Drew mind, though?"

"Not at all. It's mine, anyway. You'll have to pay for the Warrant of Fitness and get insurance, so it won't be entirely free. But that should help a lot. I did this myself, remember. I know how expensive moving here can be."

"I'd really appreciate that. Driving on the wrong side, though," Kate said worriedly.

"We'll go out early tomorrow and practice," Hannah promised. "Then you'll be able to check out other places on your own during the week. And you're supposed to say "left" side, you know. Right and left. Not right and wrong."

"Still going to feel wrong to me," Kate told her. "But I'll try."

"This is it, don't you think?" Kate asked Hannah on Friday evening.

"I think so," Hannah said, looking out a window at the tree-top view. "Even though it's tiny."

"Just a granny flat," the realtor escorting them agreed. "Well done up, though, not like some of these dodgy places you see."

"Plus it's not on the ground floor, which makes me feel more secure," Kate said.

"Takapuna's quite safe," the realtor told her. "You won't need to worry much about that."

"That's good to know. I'm extra cautious, that's all." Kate's mind went back to the night she had sat at her kitchen table and, feeling the hair rise at the back of her neck, turned slowly around. The galvanizing shock of seeing Paul's face, pale against the window. Smiling at her through the glass. She shivered now, remembering. No ground-floor apartments. This one seemed secure enough, though. The single door opened onto a tiny landing, and all the windows locked. She had checked.

"One down. Now all I need is a job," she told Hannah resolutely once they were in the car on the way back to St. Heliers. "But I'm afraid that's going to be tougher."

"That reminds me. I have some news about that too. I completely forgot. Drew called me today and told me the Blues office has an opening for an accountant, can you believe it? And he's already talked to them about you. Email your CV—your resume—to them tomorrow and you should get an interview, at least."

"The Blues? You mean the team?" Kate asked in surprise.

"Sure. It's a business, you know. A little different from apparel, but money's money, right? I figured it wouldn't matter for an accountant."

"I'm not sure I want to work around a bunch of rugby players, though," Kate said dubiously.

"They're pretty nice," Hannah argued. "You've met one of them already, after all. Drew didn't seem scary, did he?"

"Well, a bit. Sorry. I know he's a good guy. But big guys make me nervous. And he's so...I don't know. Commanding."

Hannah laughed. "Granted. On to my second point, then. You'd be working in the back office. The boys might come in from time to time, but you wouldn't be dealing with them much, I wouldn't think. Most of the people working there are women."

"I'll check it out," Kate said. "I can talk to them, anyway. If they do offer me the job, I'll decide then. I can't afford to turn anything down without looking into it."

Stocking her new kitchen cupboards the next week after a ruinous first trip to the grocery store for supplies, Kate was revising her grocery budget in her head and worrying about her rapidly shrinking savings when her phone rang.

"It's Bethany Edmonds, here at the Blues," she heard. "I'd like to offer you the position, if you're interested." She named a salary that had Kate doing some more rapid calculations. She wouldn't have much left over at the end of each month, but she'd be able to live. She'd liked Bethany, as well as the cheerful, professional atmosphere she'd sensed in the Blues office. Hannah had been right that most of the employees were women. And Bethany had told her that she'd have limited contact with the players. As if she'd be disappointed by that. Little did she know.

It might be interesting to work for a sports team. Something different, anyway, she told herself bracingly. And she needed a job. If it didn't work out, she'd look for something else.

"I'm happy to accept," she told the other woman. "I do want to say one thing, though. I know that Drew had a lot to do with my getting this job. But I'll do my very best to make sure you don't regret offering it to me."

"He had a fair bit to do with my looking at your CV," Bethany corrected her. "But after that, it was down to you. As highly as we think of our captain around here, I wouldn't have offered you the post if I didn't believe you were the best candidate. Start on Monday, and we'll see how we go."

chapter two

♡

"I was meeting Drew for dinner anyway, so I decided to come over and check on you," Hannah said. "The first week is always tough, I know. How're you settling in?"

"Good, so far." Kate got up from her brand-new desk to give Hannah a hug. "Getting to know what's what. Everyone's pretty easygoing, which helps."

"Always," Hannah agreed. "But you're a hard worker, and you pick things up fast. I know you'll be up to speed soon."

A sudden hush in the big room, followed by a buzz of conversation, had both of them turning to see what the fuss was about. A tall, absurdly handsome young man in track pants and gray hoodie was sauntering across the open office with a loping grace, casting out a grin and a word to the clearly enthusiastic staff members he passed.

He brought the dazzle to a stop in front of Hannah. "I heard you were in, thought I'd pop by and say hello." He smiled, white teeth flashing and dimples creasing in his bronzed face, and gave her a quick kiss on the cheek. "You're looking as gorgeous as ever. Want to run away with me?"

Hannah laughed. "Flatterer." She turned to Kate. "I'd better introduce you. This is Koti James, centre and first-class flirt. So watch yourself. And Koti, this is my friend Kate Lamonica. She's just joined the staff here as an accountant, but we used to work together, back in California."

"What an intro," Koti complained. "Good thing you aren't in the matchmaking business, Hannah. You'd be sacked straight away."

"How ya goin', Kate." He turned his brilliant smile on her. Pretty, he thought, even though she looked a bit small. Nice hair, beautiful skin. She had a good figure, too, what he could see of it. He reached across the desk to shake hands—and get a closer look—as Kate murmured a response.

"Welcome to the Blues. What brought you all the way down here, besides Hannah?" He might as well take the opportunity to chat her up before she met the rest of the boys. "Had you been before, on holiday? Or did you just hear that the scenery was beautiful and the men were good-looking?"

"No, I'd never visited, but I needed a change," Kate answered, dropping his hand quickly. "And Hannah and Drew were good enough to help me find a spot here."

"Because Kate's the best," Hannah assured Koti. "The team's lucky to have her."

"And we're always happy to have another pretty girl around the place, eh," Koti confirmed with another dazzling smile. He was surprised to see Kate draw herself up stiffly and take a step back.

"I think—" Hannah started to say.

"Sorry I'm late." Drew came up from behind them, slid an arm around Hannah, and bent down to kiss her cheek. "Been in a meeting that's dragging on a bit. I need to get back to it for a few minutes more, I'm afraid. But I wanted to come out to let you know."

"Good to see you, Kate," he told her. "Settling in all right?"

"Yes, fine. Thanks for all your help."

"No worries. That was mostly Hannah."

"And why are you here?" the captain asked Koti with a frown. "Need something?"

Koti put up a protesting hand. "Just saying hello. Can I help it if you married my dream girl?"

"Your dream girl's six months pregnant, is she?" Hannah asked. "You have interesting tastes."

"You're pushing it," Drew warned Koti. "And if you ever do find your own dream girl, you won't be holding onto her long if you don't pay more attention to what she needs. You'll have to take better care of her than this. Can't you see Hannah needs to sit down?"

He reached over to lift a chair across from an empty desk and set it down next to his wife. "You've got your hand on your lower back again," he told her. "You haven't been resting enough, I can tell. Sit."

"Woof," Hannah laughed as she sank into the chair. "You're right, though. That is better."

"Are you all right for another twenty minutes or so?" Drew asked her. "I'll wrap up as fast as I can."

"I'm fine," Hannah assured him. "Go on back and do what you need to do. It'll give me a chance to catch up with Kate."

Drew nodded and left, throwing one last warning look at Koti as he went.

Kate watched him go, then turned back to Hannah with a frown. "Doesn't it bother you when he tells you what to do?"

"What, that he tries to take care of her?" Koti asked before Hannah could answer. "What could possibly be wrong with that?"

"Sorry, by the way," he apologized to Hannah. "Should have seen that myself, got you a chair."

"Surely Hannah knows if she needs to sit down or not," Kate countered. "She doesn't need you to tell her. Or anyone else, for that matter."

"So a man can't even look after his wife, the way you see it," Koti retorted. "Pretty extreme. Is that the way it is in the States now? Glad I don't live there."

"I didn't say that." Kate flushed. "Just that it can be another form of domination, if you're not careful. A woman isn't a child who needs to be looked after."

"Reckon we should be more like women," Koti shot back. "Sit around and share our feelings instead. God forbid we try to protect the women we love. It'd probably be better if we got rid of all that shocking testosterone entirely. Because first it's fetching a chair and holding a door, eh. Next thing you know, she's in a burqa."

"Whoa." Hannah held up her hands. "Time out. Drew doesn't push me around, Kate. Far from it. And Koti, where's all that famous charm? If the two of you want to argue about this, how about doing it when I'm not around? Come to think of it, how about not discussing my marriage in front of me, too? Have a heart. Do it behind my back, like everybody else."

"Sorry." Koti looked shamefaced. "Out of line."

"That was so rude of me," Kate said, chagrined. "After everything you've both done, too. Sorry, Hannah. I got carried away."

Hannah nodded in acknowledgment. "Thanks for coming by to say hello, Koti," she told him. "It's always good to see you."

"Dismissed." Koti smiled ruefully. "No worries."

"Kind of a jerk, isn't he?" Kate asked after Koti had left the room, accompanied by longing looks from the female staff. "He sure thinks a lot of himself."

"He's just a flirt, that's all," Hannah said. "And he gets a lot of reinforcement for it. Believe me, most women flirt back. But underneath it all, he's really a sweetheart."

"If you say so. I can't say I got that. Just because he's nice to you, you like him."

"Well, of course I do. How else am I going to judge somebody, except by how I see them behave?"

"Everyone's nice to you, though. Even me. Because everyone knows you're an angel on earth, and you like everybody," Kate complained. "That's a lousy test. How about if you judge him by the way he behaved towards me? Which would make him, let's see now, a jerk."

"I'm not sure that was your most shining moment either, though," Hannah told her with a wry smile.

"You're right," Kate said penitently. "And I apologize again. But Hannah. You've always been my role model. You know that. You've always been so strong, so independent."

"Don't get me wrong," she hurried on. "I can see how much Drew cares about you. It's really all right with you, though, having him talk about looking after you?"

"It's really all right. I take care of him too. It works both ways. And you're wrong, you know," Hannah told her gently. "I understand why you said what you did, after the experience you've had. Being protective is part of a man's makeup, true. But it's not the same thing as being domineering or abusive."

"Who's abusive?" Drew came up behind her.

"Not you," Hannah assured him.

"I hope not," he said, startled. "Ready to go?"

"Sure. See you later, Kate. Thanks for entertaining me for a few minutes. You're still going to the game with me Friday, right?"

"I'm counting on it. Have a nice dinner, guys."

Kate sighed as she watched them leave. She wished she could think somebody would ever look at her like that. True, she could take care of herself. But it would be nice to have somebody care that much.

"Be careful there."

Kate turned at the words. "Sorry?"

Her neighbor Corinne, a pleasant woman in her early 30s, nodded at her. "Dead easy on the eyes, Koti. But he's a player. Always has an eye out for the new girls in the office. If you want a bit of a fling, he's your boy. It may only be for a night or two, though."

"It sounds like he's cut quite a swath around here," Kate said with surprise. "For you to know that much about him."

"There've been a fair few girls through here who could give you a review of his performance, let's just say. Always someone ready to put her hand up where he's concerned. And some hearts broken too. That's why there was a vacancy for your position, you know."

"What? How?"

"Bridget. Lovely to look at, and a kind girl as well. Too soft, though. She fancied him for ages. When he started taking her out, she was over the moon, hearing wedding bells. Course it didn't last more than a month or so. It never does, with him. He moved on to someone else, and that was the end of Bridget. The same old sad, short story."

"He cheated on her?"

"Not cheated, exactly," Corinne admitted. "Gave her the push all the same, though. She stuck it out here for a bit after that. But it got to be too much for her, seeing him around the place, and she gave notice. So, from what I hear, if you want a bit of fun, you'll have it. But be warned, that's all it'll be. He's not a keeper."

"Thanks for the warning," Kate told her. "But I think I can safely promise you that I'll never be interested in dating Koti James."

72759854R00203

Made in the
USA
Middletown, DE